MONICA LA PORTA

PRINCE AT WAR

BOOK THREE OF THE GINECEAN CHRONICLES

To my husband, Roberto. Always.

TABLE OF CONTENTS

CHAPTER 1

Prince was staring at the river of people slowly flowing through the dunes. The sun had finally set below the horizon, and he had given the order to move. Pax was by his side. His constant shadow.

"I don't want to decide for them." He looked at her. *What do I know about the desert and leading people around? I have you to think about.*

"Someone has to do it." Pax leaned against him and he felt immediate solace.

Slightly more than two weeks had passed since they had been reunited back at the City of Men, and he couldn't go five minutes without touching her. The need to feel she was real was an urge as demanding as breathing. "Can you walk?" He laid his arm around her waist, bringing her closer to him.

She nodded.

"Are you going to tell me when you can't anymore?" he asked, already knowing the answer. She never complained and never asked for special treatment. Instead, she worked hard every day.

"Yes, don't worry." She tilted her head to the side and looked up at him, attempting a smile.

Her eyes were too sad to convey the reassurance she had meant, but Prince appreciated the effort and gave her a small peck at the corner of her mouth. Her lips were chapped and her skin was dry. He slowly caressed her face and she moved against his hand. Her gesture reminded him of a calico cat some of the men had adopted at Sundial. She looked tired. He was tired; resting during the day wasn't easy. Fortunately for all of them, the exodus wasn't taking place during the hottest days of summer. It was fall and the temperatures were mild in comparison to the scorching heat he'd experienced at the beginning of his stay in the City of Men. *It could be worse,* he thought.

"Please, tell me if you need to stop." He had already slowed his pace to accommodate hers.

"I'll tell you." She didn't let go of him and they walked united at the hips, exchanging a few words now and then.

They took several breaks, waiting for the column to regroup. Prince was grateful for those forced pauses. The muscles in his legs were aching from the effort of walking on the unforgiving surface, and he knew she must have been in pain. He was concerned about the baby, but didn't say anything. He noticed every time she caressed her stomach her eyes clouded, and he didn't want to add to her burden.

"I hope Lucas comes back soon," he murmured and looked around to see if anyone was close enough to hear their conversation.

"The desert is big." Pax bent to stretch her legs.

"Let me." He kneeled and took her right calf in his hand.

"I should probably keep walking." She looked ahead, her eyes lost and unfocused for a second. Then she came back and smiled at him. It was the pale echo of a smile, but, once again, the intention was there.

Prince was proud of her. Pax was trying hard not to let him down, but he knew she was grieving for her mothers—Claudine, who had died, and Maurice, who had left her without looking back.

"We're moving to the back of the column with the kids," he proposed, massaging her contracted muscles.

"And leave the front to a bunch of family men who've never left the Caves before?" Pax stopped his fingers and stood with a groan.

He didn't even bother replying. She was right. But he didn't feel any more entitled to lead these people than the family men. At least they had been free all of their lives. He hadn't had time to wrap his head around the mere concept of freedom. And fatherhood.

"Be patient. Lucas had to choose a leader, and you're the only one he trusted."

"He could've asked Randal. He's his son, after all." He let his fingers trail on the sand. He wanted to punch something, but didn't want to scare Pax. His anger toward Lucas made him feel uncomfortable and added to the constant pressure he felt at the top of his stomach. He had taken the habit of pressing his hand right under his sternum to alleviate the feeling.

"Would you entrust Randal with everybody's life?" Pax arched her brows and looked around to encompass the human army painstakingly crossing the desert.

Again, he didn't have to answer. He had met Randal briefly, but it had been clear he wasn't mature enough to handle such responsibility. "He could've left some of the able men behind with us, or at least Cordelia could've stayed to help you." Prince wasn't in the mood to excuse Lucas for his absence, yet. He was too worried for Pax and felt inadequate to make decisions for the group.

"We've already managed three days by ourselves. You're doing a great job, and I don't need Cordelia to babysit me." Pax lowered her voice when two women went to sit nearby. "Give us five more minutes, and then we go again."

"Okay." Prince smiled up at her. That was the closest she would come to asking for a reprieve. He knew she needed to be in constant motion when awake. She refused to talk about her mothers, but he saw her silently crying when she thought he wasn't looking. The memories of one morning, many years before, when a guard had commented to another woman about his father's death, rushed back to him. He could hear the woman's cold voice saying the words that had made him an orphan. *"We can use the extra space in this cell. Tomorrow, the new load of slaves arrives,"* she had added, giving him a brief look as if he were a fixture on the floor, nothing more. He was only eleven years old. He couldn't know what was passing through Pax's head, but it was painful, and it would take years to lessen. He pulled her closer and put his head on her stomach. All the suppressed anger of the last few minutes melted away.

A moment later, Prince regretfully unhooked himself from her, stood up, brushed his pants of all the sand stuck to his knees, and called the end to the break. A slow wave of rising people obeyed the word-of-mouth order. A heavy blanket of clouds obscured the moon, and they had several hours of walking ahead of them before the sun would rise on another bright day.

He should have asked for a horse when Lucas had left scouting for an oasis, but at the time, he hadn't thought it necessary. When they had gone back to the City of Men to look for bodies to bury and provisions, Lucas managed to round up a few horses that hadn't died during the fires. In the midst of burnt rubble, he had also found Randal alive. And Rosie Layan. And a small number of men, who, along with Randall, were lost during the desperate rescue that took place at the city's outskirt and thought dead.

"They're stopping. Why are they stopping?"

Prince's head was engaged in so many thoughts at once he didn't hear Pax the first time she asked.

"What's happening?"

He regretted, again, not having asked for the horse. Whatever was happening at the end of the column wasn't close to where he was standing, and at night it wasn't easy to assess how high a dune was.

"Stay here," Prince asked Pax, hoping she would listen.

He couldn't see well. The clouds, their allies under normal circumstances, were hiding the moon and creating a serious problem. The dim light and the dark shadows cast by the uneven terrain didn't help. He heard someone scream and started running. His legs weren't up to the task. Walking at a regular pace was possible; anything else was not.

While climbing the steep wall of a treacherous dune, Prince's right calf had enough. He rolled in pain and, for a moment, forgot anything else that wasn't his aching leg. Then the screaming resonated closer and closer, and the fog in his head cleared.

"Help! My wife needs help!"

Prince dragged his legs until he saw the silhouette of a man standing over a heap of clothes lying on the sand. Something small detached from the man's shadow and cried. A child, no more than a toddler attempted a few steps and then fell.

"I'm here!" Prince called, walking toward them.

"My wife's giving birth. She needs Marie. Please, go get her," the man said without turning to look at him. "And take her with you. I can't mind her now."

Prince scooped the crying toddler in his arms and left. The column was still moving, and he couldn't recognize any faces, so he started calling Marie's name.

"What's that?" Pax answered instead, leaving the column and walking toward him.

"A child." Despite asking her not to follow him, Prince was relieved to see her. The man's anguished cries for help had unsettled him.

"Where are her parents?" Pax instinctively opened her arms to receive the girl.

Prince thanked her and delivered the squirming child in her arms; the girl had done her best to free herself from his hold from the moment he had taken her away from her parents. "Her mother is giving birth and the father is trying to help, but there's something wrong with her. I need to find Marie."

"Why are you limping?" Pax cradled the small body, cooing soothing words.

"A knotted muscle." Prince heard people approaching and walked toward them.

"Are you looking for Marie?" someone asked.

"Yes, a woman needs her."

Voices buzzed from one end of the column to the other, and a few minutes later, Marie came forth, followed by the rest of her family.

"Follow me. A woman needs your help." Prince reiterated the need for a fast approach by starting moving and briefly told Marie what he knew.

"Was she crying?" Marie asked after he had summarized the situation.

"No, the child was crying. The man was frantic…"

"But she wasn't complaining, moaning, or expressing her distress in any way?"

"The child was being loud. Maybe I didn't hear her. Why?"

"Well, there're women who stay silent during labor," Marie said, but it sounded as if she wanted to reassure herself.

Hearing her tone, he didn't ask anything else. He didn't know anything about giving birth, other than the few facts the women had let men know over the years. Only recently had he discovered Ginecea was built on top of centuries of lies.

"Where are they?" Marie was briskly walking along beside him and her breathing was labored.

"Behind that dune." He strained his ears to catch any sound from the woman, but he could barely hear the man's cries for help.

Prince led Marie up the dune, then ran when the man's voice became shrill.

"Don't leave me," the man repeated over and over. He didn't seem to notice when Prince tried to move him, and Marie reached for the unconscious woman.

A silver sliver of light escaped from the clouds, illuminating the scene. Prince looked, paralyzed, with his hands firmly holding the man down, while the midwife touched, probed, and sighed. "Is she going to be okay?" he finally asked.

Marie didn't answer but raised the woman's skirt. Prince turned away, and the man scampered back to his wife.

"Tell me she's going to survive," the man implored.

Marie remained silent. Prince thought the man had the right to know what was going on.

"How long has she been in labor?" she asked.

"She said she was in pain at the beginning of the day, but it was just a few cramps. After we rested, she was feeling better. When we started moving again, she said it was fine to walk, that it would help with the process. You remember; the first baby was so easy... I couldn't imagine anything could go wrong so soon," the man said, holding his wife's limp hand.

Prince looked at them, but didn't want to.

"Give me your jacket," Marie asked the man, and when he gave it to her, she put it between the woman's legs, under the tent made out of her skirt.

Prince averted his eyes a second time, but a muffled cry followed by an even softer yelp made him turn.

"Congratulations, you have another daughter," Marie whispered, holding a small bundle high for the man to see.

"Rina?" The man didn't look at the baby, his whole body tensing when Marie tried to release his daughter to him.

Prince saw the baby's head peeking out of the jacket she had been tucked in and was humbled by how small she was and how much she needed to be protected. One look at the still figure lying on the ground and at the man stroking his wife's hands made him feel a sadness he hadn't felt in a long time. *I'm so sorry, little one. You don't deserve this...*

Marie tried once more to persuade the father to hold his baby, then sighed and cradled the bundle against her chest. "You must be strong for them—"

"No!" The man shooed her away. "Rina!" he shouted to the night and collapsed on the woman, shaking with sobs. He called to his wife until his words became unintelligible.

Hours later, when they camped to rest the day away, Prince was still speechless. He didn't want to talk to Pax about what he had witnessed, and they still had the small girl to think of. A few women, who had kept Pax company while he was away, had offered to help, but Pax decided she could take care of the toddler, and the father was too shocked to have an opinion on the matter.

"Does she have a name?" Pax asked, stroking the girl's hair.

"I'm sure she does..." His thoughts kept going back to the child's father, and sadness engulfed him. They had left him grieving over the woman's body; he hadn't even asked once for the girl, for either of his girls. Marie, who was still nursing her boy, had silently accepted the task to keep the newborn well fed.

"I can't—" Prince looked at Pax singing a lullaby to the girl, who now had a sister, and didn't finish the sentence. He thought of all the times he had stirred trouble back at the farm and how men had followed him. Every time the women caught him and punished him, he never complained. He knew the price to pay for rebellion, but he was the only one paying it. Here, in this unforgiving desert, everything was different. He didn't want to lead these people to their death. He could handle physical pain, but not the sight of a dying human being because he hadn't been fast enough to get help. "I should've checked on them," he murmured.

"Marie told me there were complications. The baby was too big, and the mom was a small woman." Pax sat down before him and took his hand in hers.

"What's going to happen to this one?" Prince reached out his hand to caress the girl's head. She had finally fallen asleep, safely sheltered in Pax's embrace.

"Her dad will love her," Pax said, and she looked at him. "Tonight, we'll take the girls to him, but now he needs to be alone."

Prince helped people settle for the day. Only after he saw everybody had found shelter against the looming height of the dunes did he proceed to throw sand on the makeshift tents. The sun was shining bright in the sky, when he went back to Pax. He fell asleep curled around her, framing her small body with his—the only way he could let his mind relax, and woke drenched in sweat, feeling he hadn't slept at all. Heart beating against his chest, he thought he heard a whooshing sound.

"Don't go out," Pax said, her eyes pointing at the blanket that made their tent's ceiling.

He heard the noise more clearly.

"It's flying over us," she explained. "The helicopter..."

Prince carefully opened the tent by moving with a finger one of the three shirts hanging from the pole stuck in the sand wall.

"This is the second time around," she added.

Ginecea hadn't forgotten. The women were looking for them. He shouldn't have expected anything less, but it still wasn't fair. He was hoping for more time. Then, while drowning in desperation, it hit him. "The man's still outside," he said and, without thinking, made to get out.

"Wait! Where are you going?" Pax pulled him back inside.

"They will see him from the helicopter. He didn't want to leave his wife, and I didn't force him to take shelter."

The helicopter shot the first round, breaking the silence of the desert.

"Nobody moves! Stay under the canopies!" Prince screamed as soon as the firing stopped. He hoped the order would travel from tent to tent. He repeated the words between one firing spree and the next and stopped counting after ten. He could hear crying, praying, and uttered curses nearby, but he couldn't go out to check on the people.

The helicopter hovered over the plain for the longest time, and Prince knew that until the pilots believed them all dead, it wasn't going away. The girl, peeking from Pax's arms, looked at him with her big eyes and wailed. He couldn't do anything but cover them with his body, praying to the Heavens that he was enough to shield them.

The harsh sound of bullets hitting the sand became a blessing to Prince's ears. He dreaded when the sound was richer and people screamed in pain, fear, or sorrow. It lasted longer than any sane person could bear. He covered Pax's ears with his hands; he didn't want her to hear the sound of death coming to claim them. The blanket was thrown away from the pole, and he felt a gush of warm air slapping his neck. He pushed Pax against the sand wall, and the action resulted in a mini avalanche, burying their bodies. Darkness and cold stunned him. For a few seconds his perception of reality was out of focus. Only fear remained a lucid constant. A sense of déjà vu possessed his mind. It seemed only a few moments ago he had been buried under the crushing weight of the sand. The Priest had been with him. Past and present mixed, he blindly reached out, looking for Pax; somehow he had lost contact with her. The moment stretched and panic made him thrash around. Sand shifted all around him and he was terrified to have worsened the situation. Then his fingers finally touched her arm, but she didn't react to his touch. He screamed only to be silenced by sand filling his mouth. Almost choking and on the verge of fainting, he grabbed her arm and pulled her body outside. Sand covered her from head to toe. He saw her from behind half-closed eyes, a still figure holding the girl to her chest, and desperation set in. He called her name, cried, and shook her. "Please, please, please…" He rocked her body back and forth and cleaned the sand from her face. Then, Pax coughed, the baby cried, and he started breathing again.

"It's gone," she croaked, sputtering sand and trying to open her eyes.

The world came back to focus and he heard it—the sound of the helicopter flying away.

"It's gone," he repeated, barely believing the words. His body wasn't collaborating and the drumming of his heart was pounding against his ears. Uncontrollably shaking, he locked her mouth with his. "You're here."

"Not leaving you." She shivered against him. The girl demanded their attention and they hastily checked that nothing had happened to her.

"She's just scared, but she's fine. You're fine." Prince finally crashed down and they silently hugged until he wasn't shaking anymore. Then he opened his eyes to take in the devastation.

"Heavens, no!" Pax was looking ahead, her mouth frozen on the "o," her face stricken by tears that mixed with the dusty sand on her skin.

"Oh, no… no," he could only say at the sight.

The dunes, golden yellow only a few moments before, now were dotted with red blossoms. The silence left by the helicopter's departure had been filled with cries, and Prince felt his stomach heave in horror once again. "It's my fault," he said, kneeling on the sand.

"You couldn't have known a helicopter was coming." Pax slowly lowered her body, and he saw she couldn't stop her hands from shaking.

"I should've known five days without a single accident wasn't normal. Of course the women were still looking for us. What was I thinking, leaving a man unprotected in full view?" Prince looked around and felt even worse when he realized he was wasting time recriminating. "You take a look here for survivors. I'll walk farther south," he said and left. He stopped once or twice to raise a piece of cloth, only to find lifeless eyes staring back at him. He closed those eyes, put the cloth back down, and proceeded to the next heap of unmoving fabric.

"Help my boy here," a voice called from a trembling mound of sand.

Prince dug out a woman and a child, and when he saw they were scared but unharmed, he walked away toward other cries for help. Soon, a few men and women who had escaped the massacre joined him. It took several hours to count the losses, round up the survivors, and tend to the wounded. It was late afternoon when he saw Pax again. She was with the orphaned kids, trying to keep them under her wings. He ran to her, forgetting the pain in his leg and how tired he was. Her expression changed when she saw him, and for a moment, his eyes lit with joy. He leaned to tightly hug her, but was careful not to hurt the girl she still held in her arms. He wondered if the child had ever touched ground since he had left them. "How are you doing?" The crying kids forced him to break contact and he finally looked at them.

"These two have already escaped three times to go back to their moms," she said, pointing at two boys who were sitting with their backs to the others.

Prince saw in her defiant stance how tired she was. "We are going to bury the dead tonight. We'll have to move right after." *Before they come back to finish us.* He took the girl from her, and she sighed in relief.

"How many?" she asked, stretching her arms and moving her neck in slow circles.

"Forty-four—and at least eleven are seriously wounded. Marie and her husband have been working nonstop to save some of them, but I don't think they will survive the night."

"I'd hoped it wasn't so bad."

"When the attack started, the majority of them panicked." Prince sat with the child on his lap.

Pax sat by him and rested her head on his shoulder, her hand reaching over to caress the girl's fine hair. "What about her father?"

"I found him by his wife's pyre." The image of the couple, united in death by the melting power of the fire, would haunt him for the rest of his life.

* * *

Prince dug with a shovel made out of wood that once, only a few hours earlier, had been someone's tent support. When the tool broke, he cried at the realization they weren't going to make it.

His mind clouded with a string of dark thoughts full of shouldn't and wouldn't. *I should've checked on that couple… It's all my fault. I should've never left the man alone. He wouldn't have lit the pyre. The helicopter would've never spotted us…*

When a few brave volunteers arrived with the first bodies, Prince had to leave. By the time they buried the dead, another five were added to the shallow graves. He sagged behind a dune and sat there until Pax found him. He hadn't gone back to her. He had wanted nothing more than to bury his pain in her mouth and caress her until nothing else existed, but realized she didn't need to see him in that state. "My love." He looked at her, unable to conceal the horror still showing on his face, but managed to calm his voice.

"We're ready." She offered her hand to haul him up.

He let her help him, slowly straightening his body until he was flush with her. "All those people—" He felt lightheaded and faltered. Pax immediately circled his back with her arms to sustain him from falling. "I couldn't watch," he said, his head resting on her shoulders, her hands stroking his back.

"I know." She softly kissed his forehead.

He didn't want to break contact with her, but knew his people were waiting for him. "I must talk to them."

Pax nodded and released him from her embrace. "They need you." She took his hand.

He followed her to face a silent group of people waiting for his words. He didn't have any and could barely talk, but forced the eulogy out of his mouth to commemorate the lives of women, men, and children who had followed him blindly. A sense of hollowness engulfed him and tears cleaned two trails on his dusted face; the feeling he would never forgive himself etched itself deep in his heart. Some of the bodies resting under the thin layer of sand had belonged to people he had come to know, who had confided to him their small secrets and desires. And he had done the same.

"We'll never forget you." He finished his broken speech. *I'm sorry it's not enough. I'm sorry I wasn't good enough.* After a long moment of silence to give everybody time to salute their friends, he gave the command to leave with barely a whisper. Avoiding eye contact, he took Pax's hand in his and started walking away from there. He put one foot in front of the other, ignoring the pain searing through his leg. He led the mourning exodus through the night, resting only once, keeping a slow but consistent pace. Nobody complained, and if anybody did, it never reached his ears. He wouldn't have listened anyway. The more he tried to erase the images of the small lifeless bodies being carried to their final bed, the more details he remembered. One of the youngest kids had died holding a toy, a doll made out of discarded rags.

"It's dawn already," Pax whispered to him several hours later.

"We can still cover some ground before the day starts." He had barely noticed the sky changing color. The girl was sleeping inside a blanket he had secured to his shoulders like a backpack. He wouldn't let Pax carry the child's weight, and his gait had lulled her into a peaceful slumber.

"The adults are getting too tired to carry the children and the wounded. We better stop now, while we still have some energy to prepare the camp. We need to hide better." She pulled him aside and reached for his face.

He automatically closed his eyes, focusing on her touch. "It's not safe here."

"I can't walk anymore." Pax forced him to look at her.

Prince's eyes immediately shot down to see if she was bleeding.

"They're just mild contractions, but I must rest now." She sat on the ground and patted the space beside her. "You need to rest too."

The image of the dying woman flashed before his eyes. "I'm going to call Marie to take a look at you."

"There's no need to call her; I'm telling you, I only need to stop walking." Her voice was calm and she didn't look distressed, no more than she already was, but Prince was too worried to listen. She had bled before, not so long ago, and the recent memory of the tragic childbirth wouldn't go away. "Something could happen—"

Pax grabbed his hand and pulled him down. "You can't even think straight." She kissed his lips softly.

The warmth of her body seemed to wake him from his foggy state. "You're alive." He finally said what he had wanted to say from the beginning.

"Yes, and I'm with you. Everything's going to be fine." She reached around him to unburden him from the girl and took her in her arms.

Prince had to smile at that declaration. She even sounded sure of her words. *Nothing will be fine, ever again,* he thought. "Yes, everything is going to be fine." He wished for the hundredth time that they were somewhere else. Anywhere else, alone.

A small crowd had gathered before them; some of the families had stopped and were looking at Prince for guidance. He thought he had to give them something to hope for.

"Let's camp here. I need someone to go scouting with me to see what's beyond that ridge."

Three men came forward, and Prince was surprised to see Randal among them. He had seen him at the grave, crying for his boyfriend who hadn't made it.

"Randal, come with me, and, you two, help the others to settle."

Prince hadn't even noticed the ridge until Pax had stopped him. But now, here it was, looming before his eyes, a dark wall that could mean salvation. He had requested company should anything happen to him during the hike. The dunes were treacherous, and his eyesight was playing tricks on him. He saw the wall coming into focus and then receding to the distance.

"Drink some water," Randal said, offering him his bottle.

"Thanks—" Prince took a sip from it and then gave it back. "I'm sorry for your loss." One look at Randal and he knew the man was in shock.

"He pushed me aside at the last second." Randal's eyes were focused on some distant point, his voice preternaturally calm.

Prince realized for the first time they were probably the same age. He had always thought of Lucas's son as a young man, freshly out of his teenage years. Now he saw the lines under his eyes and around his mouth and how defeated he looked. Prince's heart went to him.

"I didn't know I meant so much to him." Randal's eyes were bloodshot, but he held his head straight.

Prince wanted to say something to comfort Randal, but the man's loss was devastating and words failed him. They walked in silence until the crest of a massive dune cut the view of the ridge. Prince braced for more pain and slowly started climbing, followed by Randal, who easily surpassed him in a matter of minutes. He was still working his way up when the man called him from the top.

"I think we found something."

Prince clenched his teeth hard and suppressed the tears caused by the pain in his calf. He labored through the last part of the climbing and sat on the crest with a loud sigh. *It's only physical*. He thought of Randal's pain and felt blessed.

"What do you think of this?" Randal asked, looking down at what lay on the other side of the ridge.

Prince didn't answer at first. He took his time to form an opinion. Then, he slowly went down, and when he touched the hard floor, he called Randal. "We might've found a system of caves."

"That's what I thought."

Prince limped toward a dark shadow in the ground. "I can't see anything," he said, carefully testing with his toes to see if there was a natural ledge.

"I'll go down," Randal proposed.

"It could go straight down to the bottom. I won't let you go unless I see it's safe." The darkness seemed to suck him in and he automatically stepped away from it. Claustrophobic memories assaulted him, but he didn't have time to dwell on them.

One foot already trespassing into the void, Randal said, "I don't care one way or the other."

Prince grabbed Randal's arm and pulled him to his side. "I do, and your father would be devastated." Prince kept a tight hold on him, his fingers leaving bruises on Randal's skin. Without softening his grip, Prince looked straight into his eyes. "I won't let you do anything foolish."

Randal flinched, opened his mouth to say something, then sat at the edge of the black hole, staring at it.

"Tomorrow we'll have time to be in shock, but now, we must fight to keep the others alive," Prince said, even though he wanted to sit with Randal and hug him and let him cry on his shoulder. He shifted his weight from one leg to the other.

"What do we do now?" Randal asked after a long silence.

Prince mentally thanked the Heavens he had taken the right approach in dealing with Randal's pain. "We wait until there is enough light to show us the way, and then we hope it's worth the wait." Prince felt restless despite what he had just proposed. "I hate to ask, but I could use some help reaching a better spot," he said, wincing when he tried to put the foot down and the pain shooting through his calf reminded him it wasn't a good idea.

15

Randal took Prince's arm under his shoulder and hoisted him up. They hopped to the closest wall of rock and sand and ducked under a rock platform protruding from it. "If nothing else, the geology of this place will help us," Randal said, sampling small debris that had fallen from the sheet of rock.

Relieved the mood of the conversation had shifted, Prince took a better look at the ground. "Do you know anything about it?" He took a handful of sand and let it pass through his fingers. It was still cold and gave him a jolt similar to when he tested the waters of the frigid showers back at Sundial. He shivered at the memory and cleaned his hand on his pants to remove all the particles of sand from his skin.

"Oh, yeah, the Priest drilled us on the subject every day at school. I have never cared for geology, but he was adamant we studied our land. The most boring class, if you ask me, but I have a great memory, so I never got in trouble." Randal seemed lost in thoughts too.

Prince thought he would have loved being in a school, having classmates, and studying boring subjects. As every other man enslaved by the women, he knew how to read and write thanks to his loving father. Men had been teaching their sons in secrecy since the dawn of times—in their language, so their knowledge was kept hidden from the women. "What did you mean about this place's geology?"

"See the veins in this piece of pebble?" Randal showed him a small rock with light-blue speckles.

Prince nodded, reached for the pebble, and weighed it in his hands. He could see it was of the perfect shape and size for the target game his father had taught him when he was little. He had kept exercising his aim when growing up. Free time was a semental's privilege and rocks abounded at Sundial.

"When they were building the new well at the City, we were asked to look for this kind of rock. They are normally close to a stream of water." Randal pointed at the similar pebbles on the ground; they were disseminated everywhere.

"Are you sure this is the one?" Prince was looking at the insignificant piece of rock with renewed interest.

"As I said, the Priest was thorough in his teaching. We had to spend hours cataloguing rocks. I could tell them apart by smell, if requested." Randal's lips imperceptibly curved up before he realized it, but didn't last long enough to change the expression on his face.

"Really?" Prince brought the pebble to his nose and arched his brows.

"Dead serious," Randal said.

Prince shivered at how literal the man's words were. He saw the somber expression on Randal's face, and felt his heart sympathetically shrink for him. Not knowing what to say and in need of a physical outlet, he carefully aimed at a pile of rocks a few yards from them. He steadied his breath, threw the pebble, and squarely hit the pile of rocks.

Randal looked at him in surprise. "Did you do that on purpose?"

Prince nodded. "It calms my nerves."

"It's a useful hobby to have." Randal tried to hit the rocks now scattered on the ground and failed. "Doesn't calm my nerves, though."

Meanwhile, the sun had taken its place in the sky, and the shadows had moved. "Time to take a better look." Prince pointed at the hole now illuminated by the sunrays.

Randal helped him walk back, and they both stared at the entry of what they hoped it was a subterranean cave. "Okay, I guess I'll have the honor." He didn't wait for Prince's permission and went down.

"At least be careful." Prince's eyes followed Randal as he was swallowed by the shadows. He watched the man carefully choosing where to put his feet and hands, becoming smaller, and finally disappearing. A muffled yelp traveled up soon after. He squinted at the darkness, already worrying for Randal. He called him and thought he heard noises answering back, but he couldn't be sure. "Are you okay?" he asked again when it was clear that Randal hadn't said anything for a while.

"Randal?" Silence answered back. Even the noises had stopped. Prince took a big breath and tried to convince himself that he should wait a few more minutes before thinking the worst had happened.

"Randal?" He knew that going down wasn't a possibility for him, but he couldn't leave Randal down there. He started contemplating the idea of dragging his legs back to the camp and asking for help, hating that he wasn't in perfect physical condition and dreading that he was, indeed, wasting precious time.

"Hey, Prince?" Randal's voice came from somewhere behind Prince's back.

He almost jumped into the hole. His heart pounding in his throat, he turned around to face a dirt-covered Randal making his exit from a dune. A streak of blood stained his left leg.

"My fingers missed the hold at the very end. Nothing to worry about," Randal said, cleaning his hands on his pants. "Well, it is a system of caves and going down is going to be easier than we thought. At the bottom of this vertical well there are several lava tunnels. One of them was brighter than the other, and I followed the light up here. I didn't want to leave you here unprotected, so I didn't go scouting for chambers, but there is enough room for everybody to hide."

"Blessed be the Heavens above. We can relocate somewhere safer." Prince skipped toward Randal, and he saw he hadn't come out of a dune, but from a rocky structure covered in sand. "Go bring them here. You'll be faster alone. I'll look for other entrances." Heart lighter than a moment before, he walked toward what he hoped would be their temporary haven.

CHAPTER 2

"At least we can finally sleep at night." Pax smiled, her eyes encompassing with a brief glance the whole place.

"It's not much, but it's ours." Prince rearranged his legs to make room for her and the girl in the narrow space. While scouting the caves that morning, he had found several small chambers branching from the tunnels and claimed one for them. He assigned the bigger rooms to the larger families and told them they could move in right away. By the time everybody had settled, it was late afternoon.

"It's more than I could've dreamed of only a few hours ago." Pax opened her backpack, one of the few remnants of her former life—the now worn and sun-faded bag had followed her from Ginecea—pulled out several items of clothes, and prepared a thin mattress out of the rags formerly used to make their tent. They sat on it and nested the girl between the two of them.

"It's more than I could've dreamed of... ever." Prince would have preferred some privacy with Pax, but to be with her was already a gift. "Randal thinks there's water nearby." He propped his body at an angle to better look at her in the semidarkness surrounding them. He should have been tired, but myriads of thoughts kept him awake.

Pax raised her eyebrows at the news.

"Yeah, I know. It seems too much luck all together, doesn't it?" Prince still found it hard to believe.

"We deserve it." She leaned to give him a kiss and the girl stirred and complained at being disturbed, stealing a chuckle from Pax. "Can you imagine our baby?"

Prince wasn't sure when Pax had truly laughed last, but he knew he loved the sound of it. He caressed the girl's head and she went back to sleep. "Yes, our baby's beautiful and she'll look like you."

"It's a boy." Pax grinned. "I know."

"He'll still look like you." He lowered his eyes to hide from her his true thoughts. *Heavens above, let it be a girl. I don't want a child of mine to suffer like I did.* The momentary joy he had felt was ruined by the consideration.

* * *

The next morning, after taking charge of the empty chambers to recreate the same organization he had seen back at the Caves, Prince gave each space a denomination and then organized everyone into groups, assigning them all a task. From looking for the vein of water to keeping the younger kids occupied with something to searching for any form of sustenance, no activity was left unassigned. Idle minds got in trouble. He knew it all too well.

Several hours into the strenuous undertaking of keeping everybody busy, Prince was pleasantly interrupted by the familiar sound of Pax's steps. He knew it was her several seconds before she appeared. He liked the idea he could recognize her by the way she walked. He came out of the nook in the rock wall that was now his office and took her in his arms. "Couldn't wait to be with you again." He spun her around until he almost lost balance and had to lower her to the ground.

"How's your leg?" Pax's concerned expression worried him and he hugged her close.

"I'll walk again." He thought he was hiding it from her, but anytime he attempted a step, the calf cramped and she must have seen through his façade. "Any luck calming the kids?"

Pax had asked to be assigned to babysitting duty; she was taking care of the girl already and the orphaned kids had grown attached to her in the brief time they had been together. "They're asking for their parents. It's heartbreaking." Pax rested her head on his chest and he knew her thoughts were darkening and her eyes were wet. "Fortunately for the newborn girl, Marie was still breastfeeding her little one or our girl would be without a sister…"

Prince noticed how the girl had become *our* girl in a matter of hours. "How are you?" She looked exhausted, not that she didn't have reasons to be, but there was something else he couldn't quite catch. Tilting her chin up with his fingers, he looked at her and when she turned sideways, he repeated the question.

"I already saw Marie," Pax answered, still avoiding his eyes.

"Is there anything…?" His own thoughts revisited his usual nightmare about Pax losing the baby, and he gently turned her body until she was forced to face him.

"No, I felt a little bit of pain last night, but it was nothing." She buried her face in his chest, her arms around his back to hug him tight.

"Why didn't you tell me?" Prince caressed her head.

"I didn't want you to worry—"

Again, he placed a finger under her chin and made her look at him. "Of course I worry." He gave her a thorough look before kissing her softly. "Please, don't hide things from me."

"I was only tired. A night of sleep was all I needed." Pax melted in his embrace once more. "I'm okay now."

"You promise?" He looked for her lips and made her say it twice. He forgot they weren't at their place. Pax had the power to transport him far away from their daily struggle. It had been that way from the very first time he had met her. Caren and Lauren had been punishing him and he couldn't remember why. Celeste, who was holding his chain, had gasped and started blathering before a girl who demanded his torturers to stop hitting him. Beaten, humiliated, and on the verge of fainting, he had seen her, a pure breed woman, and her presence, against all odds, had conjured a sense of calmness in the midst of mindless brutality. His hands traveled from her shoulders to her abdomen and he smiled through the heat of a kiss that was leaving both of them breathless.

"What's so funny?" she asked, but she had taken charge of his lips again and he couldn't answer that her stomach felt slightly rounded under his hand.

Someone coughed out loud. They both startled and separated like teenagers caught red handed. Prince cursed under his breath and Pax laughed at his outburst and squeezed his arm to silently tell him to be nice. He kissed her head and counted to three. "Yes, Randal." He raised his eyes to look at the man and let him know how much he had appreciated the interruption.

"I found the water." Randal didn't excuse himself. He didn't even try to look contrite and his seriousness furthermore dumped Prince's mood.

"Good!" Pax turned to face the newcomer.

Prince studied Randal's lack of reaction to her comment. "But?"

"I was outside, and I saw a cloud of dust rising at the horizon. A compact column of dust."

"Tanks." Prince sighed, the beautiful moment he had just shared with Pax already lost in the past. *At least*, he thought, *we had a good night sleep.* He knew he couldn't ask for more. They had defied Ginecea, and the women were striking back with all their might once more. The helicopter had only been scouting for them. The killing spree had been an added bonus for the women.

"How fast are they?" Pax asked.

"They're slow," Randal answered, sitting on the floor.

Pax followed him, but Prince straightened his back against the wall. "But they can go on night and day until they find us," he said. "We must cover all our tracks and hide." Prince had thought to use the subterranean tunnels as a temporary shelter, but now he looked at the rock walls with a different eye. Not even a week outside of the City of Men, and it already seemed years. "From now on we stay inside. Nobody goes out without my permission and a good reason."

"What about my father?" Randal asked, his hands nervously playing with his pants' frayed hem.

Prince had to remind himself somebody had to lead these people and that leading meant making unpopular decisions, but he would rather give Randal a different answer. "I wish Lucas was here too, but I can't send anybody looking for him and leave behind traces for the women to find us."

"I'll be careful. I'll go out at night and look for anything out of place."

Randal's eyes were on him and Prince felt even worse for having to add, "I'm sorry, but I need you to scout the caves. We aren't going to stay here, close to the surface, longer than necessary."

"He's my father! I can't simply bury my head in the sand and forget he's somewhere out there. You can't ask me that!" Randal stood up to confront Prince.

For a moment, he thought Randal wanted to take a good swing at him, but a few second of tense silence passed and the man finally stepped back. "I know you've been through enough already, but I have no choice." Prince kept his voice even.

"I hope you know what you're doing." Randal stormed out before Prince could say anything back.

"You and I both," he answered to the walls.

Pax, who had kept quiet and still the whole time, went to hug him. "He found the water we need to survive," she said, leaning to softly bump his forehead with hers.

He could tell Randal's confrontation had scared her by the slight shaking in her hands. She had lived all her life safe and surrounded by love until she had met him. He wished he could give her at least peace. "That he did." He nudged her nose.

Later, he called a meeting to explain their situation. Tired from the daily chores, a somewhat nervous crowd filled the biggest chamber with the highest ceiling to its limits. "We need to go into hiding from the women." He summarized his plan after announcing what Randal had told him.

"You're asking us to go underground, permanently. Is that right?" a man standing at the far end of the chamber asked, his tone of voice showing how much he liked the idea and echoing what most of the people thought as well.

"No, not permanently, but probably for a long time." Prince hated to play with words, but he didn't have all the answers and needed them to understand they didn't have a choice.

"What about Lucas? Are we going to forget about him?" a second man, standing close to the first, asked.

Prince had no doubts from whom those words had originated. He steeled himself from the barrage of comments and veiled accusations that were going to follow and decided to strike first. "Nobody is forgetting anybody, but do you think Lucas wants you to die for him? He's risking his life outside in the open to give everybody a chance to make it." Randal silently stood in a corner, not far from the two men who had just spoken. Prince looked at Randal, and the man averted his eyes.

"Do you want to disregard Lucas's sacrifice and risk your kids' lives as well?"

Nobody answered that question; a few heads turned toward Randal, but he lowered his eyes and everybody scattered when Prince declared the session concluded. He watched with relief at the dispersing crowd, eager to finally lie down with Pax and sleep in her arms. He led her, and the omnipresent child clutched to her by a scarf draped on her chest, to their hole in the rock. "Honey, we're home," he bitterly joked. In his mind it had sounded funnier.

"It's been a long day. You won't believe me, but I missed our nest," Pax said with a smile.

She was right. He didn't believe her. He didn't know what her house looked like, but once he had seen pictures of Ginecean houses in a magazine other workers had stolen, and he knew she was used to having anything money could buy. The irony of it all was that he couldn't know what money bought. He had never possessed anything. Even the clothes he was wearing weren't technically his. Until the age of eighteen, he had never worn shoes. Then he became a semental, a glorified slave, a forced semen donor, and the guards started paying attention to what he was eating and wearing.

"Come here. I missed you." She patted the makeshift cot, beckoning him to join her.

He noticed the girl was drinking something milky white from a bottle. "And this? Where does it come from?"

"Marie made some rice milk for the younger kids. That woman never stops surprising me." Pax angled the bottle to facilitate the child's suction. A moment later the distinct sound of dry suckling was followed by desperate crying. Pax removed the bottle and rocked the girl close to her chest, whispering a few words meant to soothe her.

Prince slowly lowered his battered legs on the thin mattress and cringed at the stab of pain that shot through his muscles. He didn't complain. "I hate confined places," he said instead. "I hate the darkness, the dampness, and oppressive air of the caves." Memories came back to him and, unable to drive them away, he gave voice to his thoughts. It was the first time he shared this fear of his with anybody. It was also the first time he had a quiet moment with her after leaving the carnage that followed the demise of the City of Men. He was sure there was an explanation for that, but he hated ruining the present when he didn't know what tomorrow would bring.

Pax freed one of her hands and rearranged the girl's weight to caress his jaw while still rocking the soft bundle.

Her sympathetic reaction prompted him to elaborate despite the fact he didn't want to add another word about the topic. "I prefer corporeal punishment to being incarcerated in the underground cells. I imagined things in the long hours spent down there alone." The weight of the dark images pressed on his chest as if he were back there.

"I'm with you now. Everything's different," Pax murmured and leaned in to brush his lips.

"I felt I was suffocating, and I screamed the first time the guards put me in the isolation chamber." He lowered his head and closed his eyes. The lingering softness of her kiss anchored him to the present and he focused on that.

"They put you in an isolation chamber…" She made him look at her by applying some pressure to her caress.

Prince nodded and shivered. He never had anybody to confide his pains and sorrows to, and talking to her about one of the darkest moments of his life was both comforting and terrifying. The compulsion to share with her was stronger than a moment ago, as if he hoped she had the power to clean the shame and the mental suffering those memories still caused him.

"How old were you when it happened?"

His pain was as unbearable now as it had been when it had happened. Another light kiss gave him the strength to keep going. "Eleven."

Pax gasped, shocked at his confession. "You were only a boy." Cradling him to her, she murmured several times, "I'm so sorry," and covered him in small kisses and caresses.

"I wanted to see my dad… He was everything to me. I couldn't believe he was dead. I needed to see him one last time. I asked the guards and they beat me. But I didn't care. I kept screaming for hours—I wanted to be taken where my dad was. They laughed at me and beat me some more. Eventually, when it was clear I wasn't going to stop screaming, they got tired of beating me and threw me in the isolation chamber."

Pax's chest was rocked by sobs. "How long were you there?"

Prince's first visit to the dark chamber was etched in his mind, but by saying the words, a veil lifted from his heart. "I don't know. Days? Weeks? I was too young to keep track of time, but I thought I would never see the light again."

Pax said something to him, her voice a whisper muffled by the sobbing. He wiped her face with his fingers.

"Don't cry for me. It was a long time ago." For the first time, he felt that part of his life was in the past. "Thank you." It was his turn to comfort her.

"For what?" Pax looked at him from under a river of tears.

"For everything." He went for her lips, but the girl decided it was the right moment to call for her mom. He saw how exhausted Pax was and took the girl from her embrace to give her some respite, but the girl was too young to listen to reason, so he cradled her tight and sang.

"What song is that?" Pax asked, embracing him from behind, her head resting between his neck and shoulder, her breathing ragged from crying.

The girl had gone to sleep again and Prince carefully deposited the bundle on the cot. "It's a love song. Something the older workers used to sing at the farm." Prince took one of her hands and kissed it, gently pulling her on his lap, tilting her head until she was looking at him and kissing the tip of her nose until she smiled. He softly sang the rest of the song for Pax, keeping his eyes on hers. He never had enough of seeing her blush under his stare.

"I have never heard this language before."

"I doubt other women have. It's the men's language. My father taught me the words when I was little and told me to never speak them before a guard." He smiled at the thought.

"So, this is how it sounds. Would you teach it to me?" Her eyes held a mischievous light.

"Yes, if you want."

Pax's happiness at his answer was evident and made him feel as if he was gifting her with something precious, and he liked that immensely. "It seems only fitting, given that your name comes from it." The first time he had heard of a Pax Layan coming to volunteer at the farm, he had wondered about that. "Ego te amo," he said in the men's language.

"What did you say?" Pax's eyes shone bright while she kissed him.

Prince forgot her question lost in her warmth and the way her body reacted to his caresses.

"What does it mean?" she asked him again long after.

"I love you."

* * *

Two days and one helicopter's nocturnal raid later, everybody was finally convinced hiding was their best option. The tanks were far away, but closing in. Even Randal had been mollified by the end of the second sleepless night.

"We need to get deeper inside to be safe. I'm not sure we were able to cover all our tracks, but I'm counting on the desert to do the rest," he told Randal the first time they exchanged paths. Prince had left his office looking for him and found him just outside the meeting room, the big chamber that had been unanimously named such after that first speech. He knew Randal had been avoiding him and understood why, but he didn't like they weren't on talking terms.

"Give me three men, and I'll follow the main tunnel to its end." Randal didn't linger to make conversation, but his whole demeanor was more amenable than last time they had exchanged words. Prince decided it was a small victory; deep inside, he was relieved Randal had accepted the job without complaining and went back to his office to coordinate the daily tasks. People came to visit him, bringing to his notice the myriads of problems in need of immediate resolution and leaving him no time to think about the women and their plans regarding them—for which he was grateful. He would have missed his lunch break if Pax hadn't come to remind him.

"Walk with me and the kids." She was accompanied by the orphaned kids, but she wasn't carrying the girl; Marie had taken her to visit her baby sister. "They need to breathe some fresh air," she explained when she directed everybody toward the end of the long corridor that opened to the outside desert.

Prince looked at her and didn't have the heart to tell her it was too dangerous to walk so close to the entrance. She looked tired already and the dark circles under her eyes attested to the nightmares that kept her awake at night.

"We have limited supplies," he concluded after explaining to her the reason he had sent Randal to explore the caves. They were closer to the exit; he could already feel the quality of the air changing. It was cleaner and warmer. Even the short walk was taxing on his injured calf and he stopped to take a breather while stretching his muscles, but couldn't repress fast enough a moan of pain. He shushed Pax's worried question before she could voice it by resuming his talk. "Only a few torches are left. Food is becoming scarce."

The kids came, distracting Pax by demanding her attention. "Fortunately we have clean water," she finally said as an afterthought, spinning around one of the troublemaker boys who squealed with joy.

Randall, without saying anything to Prince, had personally tested the quality of the water before announcing he had found the spring.

"You could've died." Prince was so angry with him he could barely speak after Randal explained how he had waited for several hours alone to be sure the water was safe to drink. Randal had shrugged in response and mumbled some nonsense about his life being over anyway. Conversely, Prince felt terrible for having yelled at him.

Pax squeezed his arm, a gesture she had been repeating frequently when he was lost in his thoughts. "We can ask the girls to gather more herbs. They're doing a great job with the wild berries," she continued, explaining in great detail what Tai, Sonia, and Cara had found in their brief forays outside.

When it was clear they weren't ready to go into semi-permanent hiding yet, Prince had to allow people to get their five minutes of air. He didn't budge about being cautious, and every time someone was out, there was at least one person checking the sky for helicopters. The only rule nobody could infringe on was about setting a fire. Too many people had died because of that.

"Yes, ask them." Prince was feeling lightheaded, and his eyes were twitching. "I'll go drink something; go back inside," he said to her before the kids could run to play outside where the sun shone bright.

"But..." Pax looked at him with pleading eyes.

"Please, there's nobody else outside now, and I'm not in great shape. I can't be of much help at the moment if—" Prince waved his hand in the air when a pair of curious eyes appeared by Pax's side. "You're the most precious thing this community has, you know that?" he asked the small girl, who nodded happily, bouncing her head full of curls.

"Ego te amo," Pax whispered with a kiss. The older kids made choking sounds, followed by giggles.

He watched as she put the kids in line, some of them loudly complaining they hadn't been outside at all. He had his eyes on her until she disappeared behind the cave's entrance between the rocks. He walked toward the other side of the rock wall where the subterranean stream surfaced and peered at the sky with renewed fear. The helicopter hadn't shown for several hours, almost a day, and it didn't seem natural.

He briefly washed his tired body, taking advantage of being the only one using the Baths, as Tai had called the little splash of water that became nothing more than steam when the sun was high in the sky. Finally, he put his worn clothes back on and drank, cupping his hands and pouring the warm water in his mouth. His head cleared again, and even the ache in his leg seemed to lessen.

"Stay where you are and raise your hands in the air," a voice from behind him commanded. "Don't turn around and don't try anything funny." The sound of a shot being fired exploded a few feet from the Baths.

Prince's first thought went to Pax and decided it was better to comply.

"Good job, now slowly step aside from there and kneel down."

Prince's second thought was the voice was muffled. It could have been a woman or a young man.

"What do you want from me?" he asked when it was clear the person talking to him had no intentions to kill him right away.

"I want to know what you, and the rest of your sorry folk, think you're doing trespassing on my land."

Prince, surprised by the last words, turned his head to take a look at the voice's owner. The next shot landed closer to his legs and convinced him to stay put. "We're looking for shelter." The sound of a helicopter getting closer hastened Prince's words. "We can't stay outside," he said and, without waiting for permission, ran toward the cave's entrance. He wasn't shot in the process.

"What is it?" a small person, covered from head to toe in sand-colored rags, asked him. He, or she, had decided to follow Prince inside, gun aimed at his head.

"Ginecea. The women are looking for us," he answered, staring down at whomever had talked and hoping to show he wasn't intimidated by the loaded weapon. He was angry at himself for having invited danger in what should have been a safe haven for Pax, the kids, and the rest of the refugees.

"What the...? I can't believe it—" The person's head tilted, as if trying to get a better look at him.

Prince noticed how she—he decided his captor was a woman by the way she moved—had slightly lowered the gun that was now aiming at his knees.

"Is it you?" Uncertainty sounded in the woman's voice and he steadied himself to take advantage of any mistake she would make. "Prince?" she asked, surprising him.

He looked at the pile of rags talking to him. "Who are you?"

"It is you!" She put down the gun, and Prince attacked. He placed his arm against her throat, while pushing the small body against the wall.

"It's okay," she croaked and made to lower the piece of cloth covering the face. "Please—I'm not a threat to you."

Prince looked straight into the eyes peering out through the rags and thought they were familiar. He softened his hold. She coughed, rubbed a now red throat, and finally removed the cloth. Prince leaned on the wall to steady himself. It took a few seconds to get used to the sight, but finally he started breathing again. "For being dead, you look well." Once the shock subsided, he couldn't help but smile at the last person he had expected to see there, or anywhere else. "I guess you have quite a story to tell, Celeste."

"I'm dead?" Celeste asked, puzzled.

"I killed you."

"That explains a lot," she whispered after a long pause.

Prince started asking what she meant, but the helicopter was circling right above the cave's entry, closer and closer, and its noise was drowning their voices. "Follow me," he yelled to her. He briskly navigated the tunnel, clenching his teeth at the pain renewed by the recent sprint to get out of danger's way. He went directly to Pax; she would have wanted to know right away that Celeste was alive. Prince found her in one of the innermost chambers. It had been chosen as the nursery because, having some light streaming down from fissures on the ceiling, it wasn't completely dark. There was also enough recirculating air to safely cook for the kids without choking on the fumes.

"The helicopter's back," Pax said in despair. She was sitting on the floor among crying children. She stood up as soon as she saw him, one kid clinging to her pants. She outstretched her arms toward him, her eyes moved to the walking rag doll, and she froze.

"Mistress! What are you doing here?" Celeste walked past Prince, but then stopped at a respectful distance from Pax.

After a few seconds, Pax's voice came out as a choked whisper. "Celeste?"

"Yes, Mistress, it's me."

"But you're dead..." Pax distractedly caressed the kid's head. The boy seemed frightened at Celeste's appearance.

Prince was still recovering from the shock of seeing the girl alive, but one look at Pax and he saw the turmoil of feelings her eyes were expressing. He went to her side and stroked her arm in reassurance. He couldn't know what she was thinking, but she still looked like a statue.

"No, Mistress, I'm fine."

Celeste stood still for a good while. Finally, Pax walked the final steps and took the girl in her arms, dragging with her the boy, who was now looking at the adults with bewildered eyes. "Celeste!"

"Mistress…" Celeste shot a surprised look at Prince.

"Pax missed you," he explained, confusing the girl even more. And it was then Prince realized how far they had come. A pure breed hugging a fathered woman as if they were sisters was a sight only a few months ago he would have never thought possible. He could understand Celeste's perplexity at Pax's effusions.

"They told us you were dead," Pax repeated.

"I ran away. I'm sorry I left you, but Lauren was coming after me, and I knew she wasn't going to let me live." Celeste stepped outside Pax's embrace.

Prince saw the hesitation in the girl's movements, and he gently took Pax by the side, brushing her temple with a peck. "Why?"

"Because I threatened to talk to the Layans about what was going on at the farm and about what Lauren did to the Mistress," Celeste said all at once, without breathing. "I'm sorry I left you. I'm sorry I couldn't stop Lauren from beating you."

"You're alive! You don't have anything to apologize for. It wasn't your job to protect me," Pax rushed to say.

"I think we have a lot to talk about." Prince stirred the two inside the nursery, where the kids were now crying for supper.

"Do you have enough food?" Celeste asked, looking around. One of the older girls shyly pulled at her rags.

"What we have left is going to last for a day or two. We're working on it," Prince answered, helping Pax prepare the bottles with the rice milk. He sniffed the pot where the rice was slowly cooking. "It's fermenting."

"I know, but there isn't anything else I can give the younger ones." Pax went to stir the content in the crude terracotta pot.

"How long have you been hiding here?" Celeste took in the makeshift nursery.

"Just a few days, but we're planning to hide deeper inside the cave, where the women can't find us," Pax answered.

Prince looked at her and couldn't help but notice the way she had used the term *women*. He saw Celeste looking at her in the same way.

Pax continued, "I have so much to tell you. I don't even know where to start. But, first, tell us about you. How did you survive alone in the desert?"

"Well, I wasn't alone." Celeste looked uncertain for a moment and then made a decision and resumed talking. "I had help. Someone from the farm was headed to the City of Men, and he took me with him at the very last second. We never reached the city—"

"So, it's true that men were breaking out of Sundial." Prince had always wondered about that. There was lots of talk among the workers, but the guards had a way to silence mouths before the rumors could spread.

"It has been a steady stream for the last ten or fifteen years, from what I gathered," Celeste commented, biting her lips at the last word.

"It's okay. We aren't going to betray you, or anybody else," Pax said, and Prince could hear the bitterness in her tone.

"We're in this together," he said, taking Pax's hand to make his point clear.

"No, I didn't mean to offend you, Mistress," Celeste said, and with an evident effort, reached out for Pax.

"There's no Mistress." Pax's lips turned up, but it was a sad smile. "I'm not even a Layan anymore. I'm just Pax."

"There's a colony of men and women just two miles south from here. The man who was with me greatly exaggerated his sense of directions, and we ended up stranded in the middle of nowhere with no food or water. We were half-starved and dying when they took pity on us," Celeste blurted out.

Prince was surprised by her abruptness, but the helicopter's muffled noise from outside reminded him they didn't have time to waste. "How do *they* survive outside in the desert?"

"The colony is underground. It's like a more organized version of what you have here. They've been living there for a while now—"

"Where do they find food?" Pax asked, filling bottles and passing them around to the kids, who had formed a silent line.

"The men and women of the colony have proved to be quite resourceful. They have dug a well and planted a small orchard and a vegetable garden that produces enough food for the whole community."

"But what about meat and proteins?" Prince was looking at the kids drinking sour rice milk without complaining.

"The men smuggle meat and other items from the farm," Celeste said, biting her lips again.

"From Sundial? How?" Prince asked.

"You don't know anything about that?" Pax asked him.

"There were rumors, and someone got punished for mysterious reasons, but we all thought it was just the women being crazy. Anyway, how do they manage to get anything out of the farm?"

"With the help of fathered women, like me."

"You smuggled food for the men?" Pax asked, dropping the ladle in the pot.

"Yes, I knew someone outside, and I couldn't let him or anybody else starve," Celeste answered, her voice colder than a moment before.

"I was only surprised. I wasn't judging." Pax raised her hands in peace. "But now everything makes sense."

"Yes, by the way, thank you for not ratting me out, back at the farm." Prince interrupted the two women.

"I saw you doing a lot for the workers, and once you helped a… friend of mine. He's alive because you took responsibility for something he did. I tended to your wounds afterward. You wouldn't remember; you were unconscious the whole time." Celeste lowered her eyes.

Prince racked his mind trying to figure it out whom she was talking about, but he had taken so many beatings over the years that images and situations were a blur. And, at the moment, he didn't have time to reminisce. "How did you find us?"

"We heard noises—" Celeste was reluctant to talk again.

"You heard noises from where?" Pax asked what Prince had immediately thought.

"From the caves," Celeste answered, her mouth a thin line.

"This cave and the colony are connected?" Hope surged in his heart.

Steps and loud voices echoed inside the nursery, and Prince walked into the corridor to check what the commotion was about. "Randal? What are you doing?" he asked the man, who was accompanied by people he had never seen before.

"I brought some company home; hope you don't mind," Randal stated as a greeting.

CHAPTER 3

Prince saw Randal's hands tied behind his back. "Your friends?" he asked Celeste, who lowered her head in response.

"He's okay," she whispered to the newcomers.

The men, five of them, looked at Celeste without saying anything. Prince found the whole situation unnerving and shot a furtive glance back at the nursery, satisfied he couldn't see Pax. She was hiding around the corner, keeping the kids safely out of sight.

"This is Prince," Celeste announced, her voice now steadier, even confident, as if she knew her statement would make a difference in the outcome of the introductions. "Carlos, he's *that* Prince." She directed her words to a slim, fair-haired man, the oldest of the lot. Some sort of understanding passed through the man's eyes and he turned to stare at Prince.

"So, you're Prince," the man, Carlos, said after a moment that stretched for several heartbeats. At his acknowledgment, other men murmured comments Prince didn't catch.

"Do I know you?" He was scared and tried to mask it with some bravado. The fact they seemed to know who he was didn't worry him as much as the thought of them discovering Pax and the kids hiding behind the rock wall. *Think of something. Fast, for Pater's sake.* If only could he convince them to go somewhere else, anywhere far away from her.

"No need to be uncivilized," Carlos said with a smile, his stance relaxed while Prince was feeling more nervous by the minute. "As you just heard, name's Carlos—"

Prince didn't have time for pleasantries; he wanted the men out. Desperation made him bolder and he decided to cut to the chase. "You have my man with his hands tied—" At that moment, one of the kids escaped Pax's hold and ran outside, interrupting him and making his fear a reality. Prince grabbed him by the collar of his shirt without daring to look back to where Pax was, but another kid followed the first, while a bunch of them started crying. He moved to block the nursery's entry, but Carlos took advantage of the small commotion created by the kids pushing at Prince's back. One of the younger kids managed to breach Prince's hold by sneaking between his legs and he turned to stop him. That was all it took for Carlos to walk past him.

"You have kids." Carlos stood at the entry, seemingly taken aback by what he saw in the nursery, and Prince ran toward Pax.

"Don't harm them!" She was holding several kids at once.

"We're not here to harm children," Carlos said. "Who do you think we are?"

"Exactly who are you and *why* are you here?" Prince helped Pax regain some control over the kids.

"We saw the army of tanks and the helicopter flying back and forth. Then we heard noises coming from the northern part of the caves." Carlos walked inside the nursery. Prince automatically stepped forward, but relaxed when the man kneeled down to tussle a child's hair. "We thought the women had finally discovered our colony."

"How do you know me?" Feeling that Pax wasn't in imminent danger anymore, Prince focused on getting some answers.

"I know *of* you. You saved my son's life three years ago." The man stood up and went to shake hands with Prince, who was even more confused than before. "I'd hoped to meet you one day."

He reluctantly accepted Carlos's hand, but looked at Celeste, silently asking for an explanation.

"Carlos is Remy's father, my companion," she said, which only added to the riddle.

Prince's eyes shot toward the men to see if this Remy was one of them, but none of the faces looked familiar.

"He's not here," Celeste explained, understanding his silent question.

"I'm sure he'd love to see you." Carlos put his arm over Celeste's shoulders in a paternal gesture.

At least you aren't a woman hater, Prince thought with relief.

"Absolutely." Celeste's happiness reflected in her eyes and she patted Carlos's hand. "We should go now."

"I don't think—" Prince started to object.

"She's right. You should come and take a look at our colony," Carlos said, mirroring the girl's enthusiasm.

In a moment, the atmosphere had changed from tense to joyous for everybody but Prince. "We can't leave our people here." He made sure to stress the *we*. He didn't like the turn things were taking. *Nothing is free*, he thought.

"No need to. We can accommodate a few more refugees, if they want to contribute to the colony with some labor." Carlos smiled.

"I'll have to talk to my people and see if they're interested in your proposal. I can't decide for them." Prince didn't smile back. "I would free Randal, here, to start proving your good intentions." If Carlos or the other men, who had said nothing so far, were piqued by his tone, they didn't show it. But he had seen the furtive glances the men were exchanging behind Carlos's back. They were looking at him and Pax together.

"My apologies, just a precautionary measure. I must think of my own." Carlos nodded at one of his men, and Randal's hands were untied.

"Are you okay?" Prince asked Randal as he stepped aside.

"I'm fine." Randal massaged his wrists.

"And the others?" He had just remembered Randal had asked for three men to accompany him and was worried they were kept somewhere else.

The man shrugged. "I wanted to be alone."

Prince sighed in relief and patted his arm. Helped by Randal, he managed to gather his flock inside the meeting room and briefly explained their new option for survival. As he had expected, everybody was in favor of moving to the Colony. There wasn't any need to put the decision to vote. The tanks were advancing, and the helicopter had a good idea of their position.

A line made by recalcitrant kids and hopeful women and men formed in less than an hour. Prince looked at them as they walked past, tired and battered, but with a different spring in their step. And he silently wept, a mix of relief and sadness weighing on his heart.

Relief because one of his fears of leading all of them to their death hadn't proven true. Sadness because he felt he had let them down somehow.

"I can't save them by myself," he said to Pax. The last refugee had entered the darkest part of the tunnel, and the two of them closed the column. Carlos had come prepared with enough torches to illuminate the place to a safe gloom. The kids were still scared, but the adults were chatting almost amiably. "Since we left the Caves, this is the first time I've heard them talking. Not whispering in fear or screaming in terror and pain, just talking."

"You brought them here. Don't forget that." Pax squeezed his hand. "When they needed you, you rolled up your sleeves and got to work."

Prince planted a kiss on her head, her words affecting him deeply. He had experienced camaraderie with the workers at the farm. And even though they were men like him, only after years of fighting the women's abuses had they accepted him. To see the admiration in her eyes was something that dumbfounded him.

"I think we should name the girl," she said as a non sequitur, but Prince had the feeling she had been thinking of little else since Marie had relieved her once again from babysitting duty when they had started the march toward their new home. She had noticed Pax's pallor and decided she needed a longer break.

"Baby's nice." Prince didn't like to remember the girl already had a name, although nobody knew it. Her family had kept to themselves and she couldn't talk yet. He often thought about her future, and even if they hadn't had much time to discuss it, it only seemed right she stayed with them. He saw how Pax was becoming attached to her and he was worried about her, too. She was small, and he couldn't help drawing comparisons with their unborn baby and all the what-if scenarios that kept playing in his mind.

"She can't be *Baby*, forever." Pax slowly rolled a strand of hair around her fingers.

Prince brought her closer to him; he had come to learn her little tale-tell signs. Pax caressed her stomach when she was worried, became hyperactive when she was sad, and just recently had started playing with her hair when she was anxious.

"She isn't going to be *Baby*, forever." The words sounded bitter in his mouth. Their kids, if they were lucky enough to have both parents alive, weren't going to be kids for long. But he didn't want to dwell on those thoughts and most of all didn't want Pax to think about it.

She seemed to read his mind. "With you by our side, everything will be fine," she said and gave him a smile.

And with those simple words, Pax had managed to make him feel better one more time. To be the recipient of such trust was still shocking to him. He wondered if he could ever get used to being loved by her. He had spent his whole life shielding himself from feelings. Boys, handsome ones, had approached him, but he had never let them close. And now, here she was, a woman. Not a fathered woman forced to accept being a vessel for other fathered women. But the purest of the pure breeds looking at him as if he, a man, really mattered. He had never felt compelled to remain alive until he had found her.

They walked for a while, and when the column stopped, Prince deduced they were several miles south of the caves.

"Welcome to the Colony," Carlos greeted them at the end of the tunnel.

Prince helped Pax navigate the rocky floor and was surprised when he raised his nose and saw a giant chamber. The rest of his people were staring at the view with the same expression he knew showed on his face.

"You've been busy," Prince quietly commented to Carlos. He couldn't believe his eyes; he had expected a more or less organized copy of the Caves, but wasn't prepared to see a well-established underground world. The Colony was a sight to behold. A placid lake took most of the space. Bordering the lake were rows of small houses connected by roads. Hundreds of lights shone bright against the mirrored surface, and in the middle of the lake, a pale moon glowed.

"Fifteen years are enough to build a community." The man looked ahead of him with pride.

"You've been living here for fifteen years?" Pax asked, her head shaking in disbelief. "This is amazing. And the luminosity of this place. Unbelievable."

At Pax's statement, Prince raised his eyes toward the ceiling and saw where the light came from. Several dozens of feet up was a big opening in the rock ceiling. It was shaped as if a giant had slashed it with a knife.

"The Eye of the Cyclops is what allows us to go in hiding for long periods of time without having to go out. The light coming from this natural gash is what makes the plants grow and the fruits and vegetables ripe."

"Amazing, absolutely amazing," Pax kept repeating, her eyes pausing over a detail and then roaming again. "Look at those houses." She indicated a square bordered by several cottages, each sporting hanging flower baskets from their small porches. Behind the curtained windows, people were busy with their lives. "Prince..."

Prince took her under his embrace, her unfinished sentence echoing his same hope. "This is perfect."

"You understand why we're wary of uninvited guests." Carlos's voice intruded Prince's daydreaming of a place where he could live with Pax without worrying about the outside world.

"Is there any place where we can sleep for the night?" he asked, giving the small but comfortable-looking houses a longing gaze.

"Tonight, you'll be our guests. Tomorrow, you'll start building your own homes." Carlos indicated that Pax and Prince should follow him, while their people were already being helped by the colonists.

Prince relaxed when he saw *his* kids being treated with small gifts. Dolls made of rags and crude wooden toys, but more than they could have ever dreamed of. "Thanks," he murmured to Carlos, who smiled back. They reached a courtyard bordered by several cottages, which at closer proximity looked sturdier than Prince had imagined. The variety of materials gave the buildings a quaint touch—reddish and yellow bricks for the walls, wooden doors, windows bays, and thatched roofs. "The smuggling was more extensive than I thought." *We could live here...*

"Well, we learned how to use the resources at our disposal." Carlos smiled again.

Prince saw several men were working outside the cottages, mending the roofs from the look of it.

"It gets humid and cold at night, and the thatch we use rots easily. We've got to replenish the grass several times a year."

"We'll help with that," Prince offered, his eyes following Pax's to a deserted spot nested on a small bay created by the recess of the lake into the rocky ground. He could read her thoughts loud and clear and reached for her hand to give it a soft squeeze. "Yes," he whispered to her, "I'd like it too." She lit up at his words and he forced himself to focus back on Carlos, who was giving him a list of the things that needed to be taken care first. It wasn't easy with Pax caressing the inside of his wrist and making him shiver, but Carlos raised his voice and she stilled her fingers. The images of the two of them lying intertwined on the mossy shore didn't go away though, and he had to redouble his effort to listen to the man.

"What kind of skills do your people have?" Carlos raised one eyebrow, betraying his real question.

"As far as I know, I'm the only semental, but I'm a fast learner. Don't worry." Men regarded Prince's kind as worthless freeloaders. Sementals had privileges the workers didn't have; one of the privileges—the most despised—was that they weren't used in the fields, but kept in relative good health inside the facilities, instead.

"I wasn't—"

Prince dismissed Carlos with a half-smile. "Don't worry, I'm not easily offended." He pointed at the men and women who had followed him through thick and thin and added, "Regarding them, they've been living out in the desert for quite some time now, so you won't have a problem with them either. They'll work hard to ensure the safety of their families."

"Good to hear."

"Is there anything else?" Prince saw that everybody was being housed and fed as they spoke.

"That's all for tonight."

"Do you mind if we retire, then?" Pax asked.

"Not at all. You'll sleep at my house. I'm on sentinel duty tonight." Carlos stepped to the right toward one of the houses Prince had been fantasizing about a moment earlier, when Celeste and the men who had escorted them came back.

"Before I fetch Remy, is there anything in particular you need?" Celeste asked in their general direction.

"No, thanks. Everything's been already taking care of," Pax answered.

Prince couldn't wait to disappear with her behind a closed door, but one of the men who had kept silent the whole time back at the caves approached them. "You have a familiar face," he said, looking at Pax.

Prince had known they were up to something when they were staring at the two of them, but had hoped it was just his worried imagination. "She's my companion." He raised his voice loud and clear for everybody to understand.

"I've seen you somewhere." The man drew near.

Prince felt chills running along his spine and steadied himself before doing or saying something he would regret. The safety of the cottage began to seem like a vanishing dream as the seconds passed and the crowd got too close for Prince's liking.

"Of course, her face's on every magazine lately," another man added.

"She was working with Celeste at the farm," Prince tried, already knowing it wasn't enough.

"She was at Sundial, all right," the second man said.

"You're the famous Pax Layan every woman in Ginecea is talking about, aren't you?" Carlos stepped aside to take a closer look at her, his face betraying the array of sentiments he was feeling and it was clear he didn't like the news.

Prince automatically swung Pax behind him, but it was too late.

"Is she the one you were talking about?" Carlos, his face darkening at an alarming rate, asked Celeste.

"She's a good person," she hurried to say.

"She's alive—" Carlos moved aside to counteract Prince's attempt at shielding her.

"She's a Layan." Someone snorted.

Prince turned to face who had said that, only to hear another snarky comment. The hostility was tangible and he was outnumbered with none of his people around.

"I'm sorry, but this changes everything... I don't think we'll be able to help you after all," Carlos said slowly.

"You can't let the kids die. You can't bring us here, show us a glimpse of serenity, and then destroy our hopes. We can't make it outside, and you know it. We left the City of Men looking for safety and when, by a chance, we manage to reach this place, you throw us out?" Pax yelled, stepping out of his shield.

Prince sent her a silent pleading, but she was too outraged to notice him.

"We need your help. Don't you have a conscience?" she asked.

Prince hugged her close to his chest. He could sense the angry energy in her body, but his touch didn't calm her this time.

"Pax, the kids are going to be fine. Everybody's going to be fine," Celeste answered.

"Then what are they talking about?"

"They're talking about *you*, Pax." Celeste took her hand in hers.

Prince saw the tears slowly falling down Pax's cheekbones and his heart shattered.

"Me?" Her hands went automatically to her stomach.

"Why?" Prince wasn't surprised, though. He just wanted to hear it from their mouths.

"You don't know...?" Carlos asked, seemingly taken aback by his question.

"You'll kill two innocents," Prince said.

"I don't have a choice." Carlos shifted his gaze from Pax to Prince. The anger he had shown a moment before now became sadness. Something akin to shame flickered in his eyes.

Prince pressed, hoping to open a breach in the man's heart. "She's defied her own mothers to be here. She doesn't deserve to be thrown outside to die."

"What she's done doesn't change her name." One of the men raised his voice and everybody agreed equally loud.

"You can't—" Forgetting he didn't have a chance against so many men, Prince felt his temper rising, his legs moving of their own volition toward the man who had spoken.

Carlos stepped in. "Do you know what's happening right now in Ginecea?"

"We have been stranded in the middle of nowhere for the last week, so no, I don't know anything about anything else that isn't about surviving." Prince's anger was taking a toll on his judgment, his hands aching to release the pent-up energy. Carlos's face hovering too close to his looked like a good target.

"Prince," Pax said, touching his arm with shaking fingers. He hadn't seen her approaching from behind. "What's happening in Ginecea?"

"Well, maybe you'll be interested in knowing your mother's been elected president—"

"My mom's president? Already?"

"Yes, she was elected before the votes were even cast. The first time in the history of Ginecea that something like this has happened. The Priestess declared Maurice Layan president under war laws."

"War laws?" Pax looked even frailer than usual.

"What war?" Prince stepped back and threw his arm over her shoulders to give her physical support. She leaned against him and he felt her skin was cold and shivering despite the humid heat surrounding them.

"The war men supposedly have declared on pure breeds. Per presidential edict, women have orders to kill men on sight."

"But why?" Pax's voice was strained.

"Officially, because of you. You're a martyr of the men's brutality. Your face is everywhere."

"I don't believe you. My mom would never do that."

Oh, Pax, my love... I'd put the whole world on fire had I lost you...

Prince bent to lay a kiss on her head and hugged her closer. "How do you know this?" he asked Carlos.

"We read," Carlos answered.

"We got our hands on a load of magazines and newspapers at the beginning of the week," Celeste explained.

"It's too dangerous having you at the colony," Carlos concluded.

Silence engulfed the place. Prince was now shaking, or maybe it was Pax's body. He couldn't be sure. He only knew he had to make Carlos and the other men see reason. Against all odds he had reached the system of caves he was looking for. There was no going anywhere else. There was nowhere else for them and their unborn child. "She didn't know about her mother's plans. And she can't go anywhere else."

"I'm sure she can go back to Ginecea any time she wants." Carlos dismissed Prince's words with a wave of his hands. "Her mother would rejoice at knowing she's alive."

"This—here—is the only place where she can be free." Prince felt like crying and he would have done so if that would've helped. "I'm begging you—"

"I understand you don't want to lose her, but you must listen to reason." Carlos shrugged his shoulders, but his demeanor showed he was being affected by Prince's plea.

"You're a father—" Prince started. His voice broke and for a moment he fought against the tears menacing to flood his eyes. "We're expecting a baby," he finally said in a low whisper, but everybody seemed to be listening.

He heard Celeste gasping, but his eyes were on Pax, who had turned around to look at him. "I'm not going to let you down," he murmured to her as she laid her head on his heart. For a brief moment, the whole universe disappeared. It was just the two of them.

"Mistress… Pax, is it true?" Celeste intruded in their private moment.

"Yes," Pax answered without raising her head from his chest. "The Priestess will have my baby killed. She doesn't even want to wait and see if it's a girl. She doesn't care."

And your mother will permit it, Prince thought, but kept his thoughts to himself.

"We must help her." Celeste walked by Pax and Prince and stood there, waiting for Carlos to say something.

The other men and a few of the refugees had gathered around them, and the awkward silence that followed was interrupted by low murmurs. Prince couldn't decide if sentiments were shifting in their favor. He had used the only card at his disposal, honesty, and wasn't sure it was enough. When the silence lasted longer than necessary, he started thinking it hadn't been a good idea. He felt Pax's anxiousness and it became his, or maybe it was the other way around.

"He saved Remy's life..." Celeste softly reminded Carlos, at last.

"I know!" Carlos wasn't happy with Celeste interfering. After swearing out loud, he directed his eyes on Pax and said, "You can stay."

Prince exulted at his words, but he had heard the silent *but*. He didn't think it was a good idea asking what the terms were, not with Pax listening to every word, and a sudden commotion prevented him from saying anything at all.

"Remy, I was going to look for you," Celeste greeted a young man slowly advancing toward them on a noisy wheelchair.

"You're Prince. I heard the rumor, but I couldn't believe you were here!" the young man said, staring at him.

"I—" Prince wasn't comfortable being the focus of the attention. Everybody had stopped talking, and the young man was expecting him to say something back. The look of adoration in Remy's eyes didn't help either. Prince was sure he had never seen the slim-built blond, but didn't want to be rude.

"I'm Remy. I'm honored to finally meet you."

"I told him you took the whip in his stead," Celeste promptly added.

"He wouldn't have survived another punishment," Carlos said, his voice broken while caressing his son's shoulders. Father and son looked remarkably alike, both fair-haired and with light-blue eyes.

"They were going to kill me over a damned piece of charcoaled meat." Remy's face darkened at the memory, and at his words, Prince finally remembered.

For a period of time, a few years back, the women had decided to starve the workers to improve productivity. Soon, the men resorted to petty thefts, trying to steal scraps of food from trashcans. Prince happened to be there, when two guards went after a boy whose only sin was to be hungry. The women were smashing the young man's legs, keeping him helplessly facedown while taking turns, and he had intervened, creating a diversion. Other men were present at the scene and took the young man to safety, while Prince had been forced at gunpoint to stay behind. He had confessed to be the mind behind the thefts, bore the punishment, and never knew what had happened to the guy. Imprisonments in the isolation chamber and beatings were an ordinary occurrence in his life. He had learned to forget the details. "Glad I could help."

"I only hope one day I'll be able to repay you," Remy solemnly said.

Prince wanted to say something along the lines of it not being necessary, but the look on Remy's face was too serious to be dismissed. He murmured a botched thanks, explained his leg was giving him problems and that he needed to rest. In reality, Pax was the one who needed to lie down soon, but he didn't want to attract unnecessary attention to her.

CHAPTER 4

The day after, Carlos called Prince and they discussed at length plans to increment the production for the enlarged population. The first action to take though was to secure the entry to the system of caves the refugees had come from. It was too dangerous to leave them open and accessible to the army pursuing them. Prince and Randal took care of that, helped by a few men Carlos lent them for the purpose of exploding the rock walls at the entry, effectively closing the tunnels. It took the whole day, but in the end, everybody felt safer. The day after, Prince and Carlos inspected the land at their disposal to find where it would be easier to plow new lots to help with the shortage of food that was to be expected, given the Colony had grown overnight. Prince took the lead of the field workers, and the same day they started breaking boulders and hauling away the remaining smaller pieces of rocks to make space for the new orchard.

Two weeks later, they had cleared a good portion and they were ready to plant fast-growing vegetables. The Colony had been very generous and gathered for them seedlings ready to bear fruits. Carlos came to observe the work, complimented them for their alacrity, and went on explaining all there was to know about taking care of an edible garden. Despite the rocky start they'd had, Prince couldn't help but admire the man for everything he had done with so little. In a way, Carlos reminded him of the Priest.

"In a week or two, you should have the first crop of tomatoes." Carlos gave Prince a friendly pat on his shoulder and showed him the small, green-and-red globes hiding under the leaves. "Another three weeks for the potatoes—"

"Already?" A sense of relief descended on him; he didn't like to feel in debt with the Colony, and the sooner he and his people were able to sustain themselves and give back to the community, the better it was.

Later, after having debriefed his crew about the next day's chores, he hurriedly walked toward the shelter—a Spartan, big room hastily erected to give the new colonists a place to stay while building their own houses. He massaged his shoulders and stretched his neck, counting the seconds to see Pax. The day had been longer than usual and he couldn't wait to talk to her again. He never had enough of her tales about the kids and what new mischief they came up with. Pax had kept working with the orphaned kids and Marie, and it seemed that every day something new happened.

The moment he entered the big, squatted room, he saw worried faces looking back at him and a quick scan of the place confirmed his worries. "What's going on? Where's Pax?"

Every night, she would wait for him with a big smile and her arms open to welcome him, no matter how tired she was. They were separated the whole day, but at night, they were inseparable. They were never alone, since the shelter didn't have any separation inside—everybody slept in cots arranged in rows—and they had the girl with them as well, but somehow they managed to cut some privacy for themselves.

"Where's she?" he asked again when realized Marie was missing too. Someone said the words *big hall*, and he ran to the large building that served every purpose from celebrating unions to births to tending wounds of various degrees. He found Pax there and Marie talking to her in shushed tones.

"Pax?" He saw her red eyes and the mask of pain she wasn't fast enough to hide, but she did smile and she did open her arms for him.

"Come here, my love. I missed you." She tried to move from the short, padded bench she was lying on. Marie stopped her with a gentle "no."

He was at her side in two long strides and kneeled on the cold, tiled floor. "What is it?" His eyes traveled down to her abdomen, but a blanket covered her lower body. In his nightmares, she always bled to death and he couldn't remove the image from his mind.

It showed because Pax took his hand and put it on her stomach. "Baby's fine," she hurried to say.

"But what about you? Are you fine?" He wanted to take her in his arms to be sure she was intact, but refrained for fear of hurting her.

"I fainted, nothing serious." Pax smiled at him, reached out to take his other hand in hers, and brought it to her lips. "I'm fine."

Prince didn't comment on her statement; he tended to worry about anything when she was concerned, but he knew fainting wasn't *nothing*. "Please, don't faint again," he whispered in her ear.

"I'll try my best." Pax chuckled and turned slightly to brush his cheek.

Prince moved the blanket and bent to leave a soft kiss on her slightly showing belly. Then, he raised his eyes to ask Marie for reassurance, his hand caressing the bump in slow circles.

"She's fine and the baby's fine. Just a scare, nothing more." Marie, who must have felt like the proverbial third wheel, blushed and looked down. "I'll go back to check on the kids. If you need me, just call." Her departing steps echoed in the deserted room and a few seconds later a door opened and then closed.

"You're working too much." Prince lowered his head again and took possession of her mouth. "If anything happens to you or the baby..."

"Nothing's going to happen to me or the baby." She played with his hair. "Let's stay here tonight." To illustrate her words, she moved her slim body toward the wall to make space for him on the bench. "Don't want to go back to the shelter, and Marie has already taken care of Carola."

"Carola?" He immediately knew what and whom she was talking about. "That little scrawny thing's a Carola?" Pax never forgot to finish a conversation when she started it, even if it had taken place days—or even weeks—earlier. He pretended to think about it and made a noncommittal "hmm" sound followed by, "I see."

"She looks like a Carola to me." She smiled and waited for his reaction, as if challenging him to negate that truth.

"I agree. She does look like a Carola." Prince didn't have any intention to contradict her and he did like the name. "It sounds so nice." He lay down beside her and she pillowed her head on his shoulder; his thoughts went in a different direction. "I can't wait to have a place of our own. Not being able to touch you whenever I want is driving me crazy." He inhaled the scent of her skin and sighed. During the last two weeks, whenever they had found someone to take care of the girl for an hour or two, they had escaped to their safe haven: the deserted mossy shore they had claimed as their own the very first day at the Colony. "I asked Carlos if we can build our cottage on Paradisus." They had named their spot with the men's word for heaven. Pax loved they had their own language and he taught her new words every day.

"And?" Pax hoisted herself up to better look at him, her eyes already shining at the possibility.

"And he said yes." He had waited the whole day to deliver the news and see her reaction. The scare made the moment even sweeter.

She made a sound that was pure joy and hugged him so close he worried he would hurt her. "I don't think I could be happier." She kissed him and didn't allow him to move.

"I'll start tomorrow. Randal said he'd help me dig the foundation and raise the beams. Even Remy wants to lend a hand to speed the process."

"That's nice of them." Pax cradled herself against his chest and he rearranged his body to shelter her in their preferred position to sleep. She was always cold and he was warm enough for the two of them.

"What do you want in our home?" The mere idea of being able to ask such a question to her made him happy. He had daydreamed about their love nest and all the things he wanted to build for her and the baby.

"You." Was all she said and then she told him all the things she loved about him and it took a long time.

* * *

Despite Prince's attentions and Pax's dedication to Marie's instructions to the last letter and resting most of the time, her health didn't visibly improve. Finally, Pax's frail condition prompted Marie to suggest the name of a family who could take care of Carola.

"There's this couple who has just lost a baby and—" She had come several nights later with a tentative smile and nervous hands, tying and untying the strings keeping together her old sweater.

"No." Pax raised one hand and refused to listen to the rest of the proposal. "We can take care of her." She clutched the girl to her chest, caressing her back.

"I'm worried about you. Between working at the nursery and minding her the rest of the time, you're getting slimmer and slimmer."

"I'm not the only one." Pax was getting agitated and Prince didn't want that. "There isn't enough food to go around—"

"Marie…" He tried to have a word, but Marie didn't let him finish.

"Yes, everybody's getting slimmer. But you're slimmer than most and pregnant." Marie paused for a moment.

"Is she in danger?" Prince was still shaking after the last scare and he was aware that food was scarce for everybody, but he had noticed Pax losing weight at an alarming rate.

"I'd feel better if she could rest more. We don't have anything remotely close to the facility we had back at the City of Men, and even that was obsolete. Any complications and we'd be powerless to help her and the baby." Marie looked at Pax, although she was answering Prince. "The couple I was talking about, they can't have other kids"—she looked at Pax's stomach—"and they're good people. You'd make them so happy. Please, think about it."

Marie left, but the day after, Carlos came to visit them at the shelter, accompanied by a man and a woman in their thirties. Pax tensed immediately when she saw them, and Prince had to pick up Carola who had sensed the tension and had started crying.

"*Carlos?*" Prince didn't like his getting involved one bit.

"Tula and Carter, Prince and Pax." Carlos made the presentations, ignoring Prince's stare.

Tula saluted Pax with an open smile, but her eyes wandered over Pax's pregnant belly and for the briefest moment, her eyes clouded. "How long are you?" she asked with genuine interest.

Prince was surprised by Pax's reaction, because not only did she answer Tula's question, but in a few minutes, she started having a conversation with the woman. He saw how Carter was looking at Carola and when he accosted her, he let the man take the child in his arms. Prince watched as Carter swung the girl around and how she giggled at the funny voices he was making. A few minutes later, Carola was back in his arms, but he knew why Carlos had wanted them to meet the couple and silently cursed him, because he couldn't help feeling sympathy for them. "Do you want to come visit her tomorrow?" he asked Carter.

"If you'll let us." The man couldn't contain the hope in his words.

And so, little by little, the couple's presence became a constant in their daily life. Once or twice, Pax didn't feel well, and Tula and Carter minded Carola for a few hours. Until a month later, Pax had a bigger scare than usual. Marie was called, and the child had to stay several days at the couple's place. When Marie finally declared Pax out of danger, she and Prince went to pick up Carola and they witnessed from the opened windows of the couple's cottage a domestic scene that moved them. Both Carter and Tula were playing with her. Their faces couldn't contain the happiness and Carola looked at them in adoration; the three of them seemed oblivious to the world outside the four walls of their home. Prince and Pax looked at each other and silently retreated out of the line of sight and went back to the shelter.

Once in their corner inside the big communal room, Pax spoke first, tears already wetting her face. "We can't be so selfish."

"No, we can't." He consoled her the whole night. The next morning, they both went to deliver their decision to the couple. The pain they felt at having to say good-bye to Carola was mitigated by Tula and Carter's joy at the news.

The first few days, getting used to not having the child around proved difficult. Pax didn't feel good and life at the Colony wasn't easy. Food was still scarce and everybody had to work overtime to reach the minimal quota of produced goods needed to survive. Outside, the women were still actively looking for them and the sentinels reported helicopter raids daily. Carlos had to stop the smuggling of much-needed items from Sundial when one of the fathered women who served as carrier was almost caught in the open. The precious content of the basket she was carrying, a First-Aid kit filled with antibiotics and painkillers, was buried in the sand before anybody could retrieve it. As the condition in the community worsened, resentment against pure breeds grew, and on more than one occasion, Pax was treated with disrespect. Unbeknownst to Pax, Prince managed to effectively mute the louder voices, in two instances with his own fists. It hurt, but he found it satisfying. Pax and Prince's budding friendship with several of the original Colony couples—apart from Tula and Carter, they had started frequenting also Celeste and Remy—helped as well to contain most of the comments made in front of Pax.

* * *

Meanwhile, among health scares, heart pains, and hard work, Prince had started building their own cottage by the shore. At the same time of the first tomato harvest, their love nest was completed. After a morning of checking that the structure was sound, he finally secured the last nail on the thatched roof of their home. He looked down at Remy and Randal, who were cleaning the entry to make sure everything was ready for Pax to move in later at night, and saw Celeste walking toward them with their lunch.

"She'll love it." She said once within earshot. Her and Remy's cottage wasn't far away and she had taken upon herself to prepare their daily meal.

Since the construction of their house had started, Pax normally came along too so they could eat lunch together, but Prince wanted to surprise her tonight and had made excuses for the last three days to keep her away from Paradisus. He didn't want her to know how close their cottage was to completion.

"That's really pretty." Celeste's voice came from within the cottage. "Nice touch with the flowers," she commented once outside. She looked up and winked at Prince, whose cheeks became instantaneously red.

Both Randal and Remy had already given him a hard time for the cot he had covered with wild flowers.

"You know those petals are going to wither in a few hours and you'll have to put fresh ones later, right?" she asked, all innocence. It was clear from the expression on her face she knew he didn't know. "Otherwise, it's going to smell terrible in here, and she's pregnant."

"No, really?" He jumped down on the ground and landed before Celeste.

"Yes, really." She put the basket with their food on the table Prince had built only the day before and waited for Remy to roll the wheelchair by her side.

Prince stepped inside the cottage and at the threshold could already smell a cloyed flowery aroma lingering in the air. "It's never going to be ready for tonight, is it?" He sighed, noticing a few details out of place.

"She won't care." Celeste walked closer to him and patted his arm. "Just take a shower, go pick up some fresh flowers later, and we'll finish the rest."

"She's right. You stink," Randal said with a big smile.

"Well, you could use a bath." Remy made a face.

Prince looked at Randal and Remy who both nodded at the same time and couldn't help but laugh. "Thanks a lot." He left them and headed first toward the shelter to grab a change of clothes and then to the communal baths, where he cleaned himself thoroughly and tried to calm his nerves. He was restless and hadn't felt so excited in a long time. Sitting in the steam room with other men didn't relax him. Instead, having to endure polite conversation reminded him he wanted to be somewhere else altogether. After having donned the clean clothes on his wet skin, he decided to go see Pax.

By the time he arrived at the nursery, half walking and half running, he was covered in sweat again. He saw her before she saw him, and it stopped him in his tracks. Pax was sitting with a girl on one of the benches in the garden just outside the nursery. She was smiling and gesticulating, some sort of game she was playing with the girl. Prince's heart grew several sizes at once. Before his eyes was more than he could have ever dreamed of.

"Prince?" Pax was looking at him, happiness and surprise at seeing him early showing through her eyes.

He walked to her and took her in his arms. All the words he had wanted to say stuck in his throat.

"Are you done for the day?" She gave him a peck on his lips as her eyes went to the girl for the briefest moment to let him know she couldn't be more effusive.

"It's okay. We've all the time in the world..." He put some distance between their bodies to better look at her. "I couldn't stand one more minute without seeing you."

"The kids are due inside for a nap." She sighed.

"I'll come pick you up later." He stole a kiss from her and let her go. "Pax?"

She turned at the nursery's door.

"Can't live without you." He saw her shiny eyes, but smiled and added before leaving, "See you later."

He ran to Paradisus in time to catch Randal, Remy, and Celeste before they left.

"We're done cleaning." Celeste spoke for everybody else, a broom in her hands and a big pile of dirt on the ground.

He went to the back of the lot where Randal and Remy were busy hauling the construction waste away in big-wheeled baskets they had attached to Remy's wheelchair. Prince approached them to help with the task, but they both told him it was the last load.

He walked back to the cottage where Celeste was now dusting the windowsill of one of the two windows.

"The very last touch." Celeste passed a finger on the wood Prince had taken great care to stain with a whitewash layer of color.

Pax loved to fantasize about their home and she had once said she liked whitewashed accents. When Prince saw the can of white paint lying forgotten in the storage room, where all the construction materials could be bought by bartering manual work, he immediately asked for it. He would have accepted any task to please her, but the white windowsill only cost two hours of road maintenance.

"What can I say?" From the open door, he could see everything inside looked perfect. He entered to make himself useful there.

"Go get some roses from my garden." Celeste pushed him out. "And go refresh yourself again."

"Thanks!" Prince was already on his way to Celeste and Remy's cottage. Celeste was proud of her roses and it touched him deeply that she had given him permission to pluck her flowers. He knew the girl had grown fond of Pax, and more than once, he had found the two of them talking secrets and blushing when caught. When asked, both Pax and Celeste had refused to say what they were talking about, leaving Prince and Remy curious.

He picked a bouquet of white roses, and on the run back to Paradisus, he met Randal and Remy and Celeste. Without stopping, he thanked them again, went directly to the cottage, put the flowers in a stone basin, and then headed to the small waterfall north of Paradisus to refresh himself. He barely had time to walk back home and lay the white, perfumed petals on the cot before he was out the door again.

"What happened to you?" Pax ruffled his hair after giving him his welcome kiss.

"I have a surprise for you." He reached in one of his pocket and produced a long strip of cloth.

"What is it, a blindfold?" She looked at it and laughed. "What for?"

"Told you, it's a surprise." He gestured for her to turn around so he could put the strip over her eyes. "Trust me."

"With my life." She closed her eyes and turned.

He secured the strip without tightening it too much on her skin. "Let's go for a stroll."

"Okay." She sounded amused by his behavior.

"Tell me about your day." He leisurely led her toward Paradisus, listening to her tales. For the first time all day, he enjoyed walking and didn't hurry her. When they finally reached their destination, Prince leaned to give her a kiss and then lifted her from the ground and took her in his arms. He walked to the threshold of their cottage and stopped just before the step. "Ego te amo." He removed the blindfold from her and breathlessly waited for her reaction.

Pax looked at their house and tears sprung to her eyes. "Prince—" Her voice broke.

He crossed the threshold with his heart bumping so loud against his chest, he was sure she could hear it. He had prepared a few words he wanted to say to her, but couldn't remember his speech anymore, so kissed her instead while depositing her on their bed.

"Prince," she murmured once more, her eyes as unfocused as his, her voice as breathless as his.

He looked at her, lying among white petals, her hair fanning on the dark red quilt beneath her. Emotions overwhelmed him, and Prince fell to his knees. "You are the love of my life." He leaned over her to lay a trail of soft kisses from her head to her toes, while he removed her clothes one piece at a time, until she was naked on the rose petals. His hands brushed her skin and he saw goose bumps rising on both their arms at the same time. Pax went for his shirt as he got rid of his pants, her hands moving over his body, knowing what made him catch his breath.

"I love you." Pax pulled him closer and he could feel she was shaking as he was.

He hesitated, wanting to etch the memory of that moment forever in his mind. His fingers traced the contour of her small breasts and followed the slim line of her body toward her disappearing navel, where her belly formed a pleasant arch.

"Please..." He took in her bright red lips and dark eyes. She could barely talk, but he couldn't at all. He descended on her, being careful to not crush her body with his weight.

They both gasped at the same time; the feeling of being one transported them to another plane where nothing else but them existed. "You're so beautiful," he murmured in her mouth. He moved them to the side and took his time, showing her how much he had missed her in the few hours they hadn't been apart. Tears swelled in his eyes like the first time they had been together.

Later, much later, into the night, he wrapped her with the quilt and fed her a few morsels Celeste had prepared for them.

"When did you have time for all of this?" Pax was looking at the decorations he had put together in the last three days. "Where did you find this quilt?"

"Do you like it?" He reached inside to caress her skin and was pleased by the way she reacted.

"Love it." The mischief in her voice made him smile.

"I built a garden shed for Tai, who owed someone who owed Marline—"

"The quilt lady." Pax gave a better look at the quilt she was wearing. "Did you ask for this design?"

"Yes, I wanted the intertwined hearts and I asked Marline for the deep red color—"

"It's so rich."

"I imagined you on it..." The explanation regarding the rest of the few items lying around the cottage had to wait. Several hours passed before they finally fell asleep.

Prince was awakened by Pax frantically calling his name. "What's happening?"

"Something's wrong." She was touching her stomach. "Go get Marie, hurry!"

Pax had never looked so worried and that alone would have scared him to death. In no time, he was before Marie's cottage, banging at her door and waking up the whole colony. He kept banging and asking for Marie until the door swung open.

"What...?" Grant, Marie's husband, held the door open with one hand while cradling his youngest son with the other. The child was crying and the man wasn't pleased. Marie, hastily buttoning up the front of her nightgown—she had probably been nursing Carola's sister—came to check on the ruckus, followed by their oldest kid, George. The wailing of the girl came from the far corner of the hut and George went back to calm her at his mother's request.

"Is it Pax?" Marie asked, the sleepiness in her eyes replaced by sudden focus. At Prince's nod, she told her husband she would be right back, went for her first-aid kit, and started briskly walking toward Paradisus. She fired question after question about Pax's condition, but Prince didn't have any answer and so he redoubled the pace, almost running, with Marie in tow.

He entered their cottage, fearing the worst. Pax was sitting on the bed, rocking back and forth under the quilt; her eyes lit when she saw him.

"Marie, I don't know what's happening," Pax said as soon as the woman came inside.

Marie was at her side in no time. "Lie down and let me take a look." She peeled the quilt from Pax and helped her on her back with a smile. "You sit and make yourself useful," she said to Prince, but her tone was gentle and she waited to examine Pax until he positioned himself behind Pax's shoulders to support her.

Prince saw Pax had donned one of his shirts and it looked too big on her. She tilted her head back to look at him with her big eyes and his heart shriveled. "Don't worry. Everything's fine," he whispered to her, holding her hand in one of his and caressing her hair with the other. He felt her flinch when Marie opened her knees. He pressed a kiss on her head.

"Any contractions?" Marie asked a moment later, a puzzled look on her face.

"Something different from the usual contractions." Pax kept caressing her rounded belly.

"Well, there's no bleeding and I don't see anything wrong." Marie went to touch Pax's stomach and sudden understanding hit her. "Did you just have one of those *different* contractions?" For some reason, the corner of her lips turned up and she gave them an enigmatic smile.

"Yes, it just happened! Did you feel it too?" Pax took Marie's hand and moved it. "Here, another contraction!"

"I felt it all right." Marie started laughing.

Pax turned to look at Prince and he raised his shoulders. "What is it?"

"Oh, how I wish all the emergency calls were of this nature." Marie cleaned a tear with the palm of her hands, tried to repress a giggle, but failed and started laughing again.

"I guess she's fine, right?" Prince wasn't sure about anything.

"The baby just moved," Marie explained. When nobody reacted to her announcement, she added, "Your baby's growing accordingly and is big enough now that you can feel him or her moving inside of you."

"So, Pax's fine and the baby's fine." Prince felt as if waking from a nightmare.

"Yes, everybody's more than fine. Now, if you'll excuse me, I'll go back to sleep." Marie smiled at them and went to the door.

Prince followed her. "Marie, thank you and I'm sorry for having ruined your night."

"Anytime." Marie patted his arm and exited the cottage.

Prince heard her laughs for several minutes.

"Did she just insult me?" Pax asked.

"She did say something about pure breeds and their lack of common sense." Prince joined her back on the bed and lay down, his eyes on the ceiling, his breathing uneven. "This business of having kids will be the death of me." He pressed a hand on his chest to still his galloping heart.

"Prince...?"

"What is it?" He jumped to a sitting position, ready to spring after Marie.

"He just moved." Pax sheepishly smiled, raised the hem of his shirt to uncover her stomach, and directed his hand to it. "Can you feel it?"

Prince let her guide his hand in circular motions, but other than the rigid firmness of her skin stretched over her round belly, he couldn't feel anything else. "I don't—" Suddenly, something pressed against his hand and he couldn't help but gasp as she had done a few seconds earlier. "Was it the baby?"

Pax nodded, and he tentatively caressed the spot where he had felt the movement. A small bump formed under his fingers and moved away from his touch. "Did you see that?" He looked at Pax in wonder and she smiled and nodded again. Prince lowered his head to lay a kiss on her stomach. "Baby girl—"

"It's a boy."

Prince smiled at her correction and continued, "Baby girl, Daddy loves you so much and can't wait to see you."

"You'll see I'm right." Pax took his face in her hand. "It's a boy."

"We'll see about that." Her lips called to him, and he pulled her down for a kiss. "Let me talk to her now."

Pax shook her head, but didn't say anything. She listened to him singing a lullaby for their baby. Long after she succumbed to sleep, he stood watching her, marveling at the miracle of life.

CHAPTER 5

"I went to visit Carola today. She's grown so much since we saw her last." Pax smiled.

Prince had waited for this moment to arrive. Her voice didn't break anymore when she talked about the child. Three months had passed, but there were days when Prince caught her cradling Carola's old clothes to her chest, the ones that were too small when she went to live to Tula and Carter's that Pax had wanted to keep.

"I wish I could've seen her." He, like every able man or woman, was working two or three shifts at a time to help with the shortage of food. Instead of improving, the situation at the Colony had gotten worse despite all the communal effort. They were just too many, and the impossibility to acquire goods from Sundial, as the colonists had done successfully in the past, had exacerbated an already delicate state of affairs. The crops simply didn't reach maturation fast enough. Carlos kept reassuring his flock about the impending changes when things would get back to normal, but in the meantime, spirits were low and malcontent high.

"In a month or two, she'll probably be ready to spend a few hours at the nursery with the other kids." Pax went to the stove and bent before the small opening to start a fire with a few pieces of dry firewood.

Prince automatically went to open the window to aerate the room, while she dragged the terracotta pot on the grate over the fire. The silvery light of a full moon shining through the Eye of the Cyclops, reflected by the dark waters of the placid lake, bathed the interior of the cottage in a pale blue. In the project phase, he had oriented the foundations so that two of the four windows opened on the lake. First thing in the morning, before going to work, he loved to sit on the bed, back against the headboard, Pax by his side, and look at the peaceful scenery framed by the window on the opposite wall. Born and raised in the desert, he was fascinated by the water. He and Pax had taken the habit of relaxing the day off by wading in the shallow water until their fingers pruned. They hadn't gone today and he longingly looked outside for a moment.

"What are you cooking?" He helped her position the pot to prevent another burnt finger.

"Rice porridge." She lowered a handful of dark rice inside the pot with a wooden spoon and then started stirring it. "I know you're hungry—"

He didn't want her to feel sad because they hadn't had solid food in a long while. It wasn't her fault and he admired her resolution to make the best out of everything life was throwing at them. "I'm sure it's good." Their allotted quota of food seemed never to be enough, but instead of complaining, she found new and creative ways to spice up their meager portions with aromatic herbs and a pinch of the salt she kept guarded in a small jar. The salt had been a gift from Celeste and Remy. The jar was given to them by Randal. In a few months, the new crops would finally bear enough vegetables to feed the whole Colony, but for now, she was doing an excellent job with just unrefined rice and tarragon.

"It smells good." He reached for the wooden spoon from behind her, caging her much too slim body with his frame, one arm just atop her round belly. Swaying her slowly, as if they were dancing, he whispered, "*You* smell so good," and started nibbling at her earlobe. Pax shivered against his body, but he felt something was amiss and spun her to face him. "Are you nauseous again?" Bouts of nausea had made an appearance lately. Marie had said that it wasn't uncommon for pregnant women, especially if under stress.

A sheen of sweat covered her brow and she looked pale, but she shook her head. "No, just my back. Could you work your magic?" She pointed a finger to her back.

"Tense?"

She nodded and went to sit on the bed. Prince kneeled behind her for the nightly massage. They had discovered, a few months earlier, that one of the side effects of the pregnancy was constant back pain. Having to sleep on a thin mattress didn't help either, and he was always looking for ways to make the accommodation more comfortable for her. He had bartered his labor to acquire a second quilt, blue with red accents, with a little more padding, and made her sleep on top of it to soften the bed.

"Oh, yes, like this." She moved under his fingers so he could press on the rigid knots. "Tonight, it feels like I have been kicked in the kidneys with steel boots."

Prince was concerned about her health, but she kept saying she was fine. "You really should eat more. Why don't you eat some of my food at least?" She normally filled his plate to the edge. She insisted he needed the sustenance for all the hours he worked in the fields. He was always ravenous, but would've gone without eating for days if it meant she would gain some weight.

"I'll throw it up anyway. Why waste food?" She shrugged. It was true. She didn't seem to be able to retain anything but small portions. Not that there was any danger to get overstuffed on food nowadays, but even that little seemed too much for her stomach.

"Any better?" He was touching her spine and the tight skin outlining the ridges of her bones.

"Much better, thank you." She took one of his hands and kissed it.

"Did Marie check on you?" He had expressly asked her that morning. He was on his way to the fields for another day of claiming land from the rockiest part of the Colony when he had seen Marie walking toward the nursery. She had the habit of arriving almost an hour earlier than everybody else to put everything in order so Pax would not have to.

"Yes, she did." She gave him a knowing look, but smiled. "She says that for being almost eight months pregnant, I'm in excellent condition."

Since Prince didn't have any prior knowledge about woman's physiology and how things worked when one was expecting a baby, he had to rely on Marie's expertise. In times like this, he sorely missed the City of Men. Although he had lived there for a short time, he had gotten used to the few pieces of technology the Priest had introduced. But the thing he missed the most was Mauricio's scientific library. Prince understood now why the man had studied to become an obstetrician, among other things.

It wasn't that he didn't trust Marie. Since she had to work in extreme conditions, she was probably better skilled than any midwife working in the sterile labs in Ginecea. Prince didn't like the idea of being powerless should anything go wrong, and he couldn't understand how both Pax and Marie thought she was fine when he saw her disappearing before his eyes.

Steps resonated in the quiet night, and someone paused outside their door.

"Who is it?" Pax asked, approaching the door. She opened it before seeing who their guest was.

Prince expected to see either Remy or Randal. In the last three months, they'd taken the habit to coming for late-night chats, especially when they knew Pax and Celeste were having their knitting lesson. Celeste once had showed Pax a small sweater she'd made for one of the kids in the nursery and Pax had decided she wanted to knit something for their baby. So far, nothing useful had been produced by her hands, but Pax seemed to greatly enjoy her time with Celeste, and Prince was content to see her happy. Tonight, Celeste was supposed to teach her a new stich.

Much to their surprise, neither Randal nor Remy and Celeste were outside. "Hi, Carlos—" Pax looked perplexed by the visit.

The man looked too serious for a casual visit. An unpleasant tingle ran through Prince's spine. "Hi, Carlos, what can we do for you?"

"I'm afraid I've bad news," Carlos said, a dark figure looming from the outside world.

"What is it?" Prince felt his stomach crunching in anticipation.

"You aren't safe here anymore." Carlos's words surprised him.

"What? Why?" Prince's hands started to shake.

"The women are coming for Pax—"

Prince looked at Carlos in disbelief. "They think she's dead."

Carlos shook his head. "There's no time for details, but there's a reward now for any woman who can give information about Pax's remains."

"A reward?" Pax searched for Prince's hand and held it as if she wanted to draw strength from him.

Prince pulled her closer to him.

Carlos looked first at Prince, as if asking permission to say what would come next. Then decision donned on his face and he directed his eyes to Pax. "Your mother has promised a fortune to any woman who discovers what happened to you."

"How much?" Prince asked, finally understanding why Carlos was there.

"What?" Pax looked confused.

"How much is she worth?" Prince saw her flinch and regretted his choice of words, but he had the feeling time was of the essence.

"Enough to tempt many to try to kidnap you," Carlos answered, looking directly at Pax.

"I don't understand," Pax whispered, and Prince supported her weight, worried she was going to fall any second.

"The president made a public speech, announcing she will give ten times her salary to any woman who'll bring her your remains. No questions asked."

Pax didn't move. She didn't seem to breathe at all.

Carlos silently reached in one of his pockets and offered her a folded paper.

"What is it?" She didn't accept it, her body shaking against Prince's.

"Take a look at it, please." Carlos gently pushed the piece of paper into her hand.

Pax opened it and Prince saw it was an article cut from a newspaper. "Oh, Mom..." After reading its contents, she looked for several minutes at a picture resting on the top portion of the article. It was a snapshot of her smiling between her mothers. Tears clouding her eyes, she finally passed it to Prince. "I need to sit."

He helped her down and sat by her side. "How long have you known about this?" he asked Carlos.

"Just discovered it myself. One of the servant women who works for us at the farm has a sister here. They've found a way to smuggle items in behind my back. The news is two months old already. They've been scheming for a while, and judging from the little I found, they've involved other people from the Colony..."

"But why?" Pax was breathing heavily, one hand distractedly massaging her belly.

"People are thinking with their stomachs, and I know there're several angry enough to attempt to overstep my direct orders."

Prince didn't say anything. He knew it was pointless. Carlos was right. Hungry people didn't use their brains.

"But they can't believe they can just turn me over to my mother and get the money." Pax looked from Prince to Carlos, looking for consent. "And what would they do with the money anyway? What are they thinking? It's not that they can spend it."

"No, they aren't that stupid, but giving you back to Ginecea could bring a period of peace to the Colony. Without the army looking for you, we'd be free to roam the desert and smuggle from Sundial and the other farms like we used to before you arrived." Carlos shifted his weight from one foot to the other. "That is what they're thinking."

"Of course." Pax stared ahead, a sad smile on her lips. "What now?"

"We must hide." Prince was already thinking of what to do.

Carlos nodded. "You can come to my house for the time being. Nobody would dare search my place."

Prince wasn't sure of that plan, but it was better than sitting and waiting for their doom. "Thank you—"

Steps resonated from outside and he grabbed the broom while silently asking Pax to stay behind him. Someone stopped outside and three knocks followed.

"Nobody's home?" Celeste called.

Prince almost didn't recognize her voice, his heart was beating too loud, but he went to the door and let the girl in.

"Forgot it's 'knit night?'" Celeste entered, her face hidden by the big basket she was carrying, several balls of wool bouncing on top. "Widow Lane gave me a bunch of supplies. She says her arthritis doesn't let her enjoy knitting anymore. Maybe we can make something to thank her. What do you think?" She put the basket down, then realized Carlos was there and smiled at him. "Oh, hi, Carlos…"

Carlos nodded at her. "Celeste—"

Celeste looked at the three of them, a deep frown replacing her previous smile. "What's going on? Are you okay?" She walked toward Pax and took her hands in hers.

"People from the Colony have betrayed me and we must go into hiding." Pax shook her head as if she still couldn't believe they had done this to her.

Celeste hugged her. "Is it true?" she asked Carlos.

The man nodded, weariness tugging at his shoulders. "I don't know how many are privy to this information," Carlos confessed, head low. "But I know someone is coming for Pax and they must not find her here."

"So, where are you going?" Celeste had released Pax from the embrace, but still held her hands.

"Carlos is offering his place. Hopefully, nobody will think of looking for us there." Even as he said the words, Prince could see all the things that could go wrong with that solution, but they didn't have any choice. They couldn't leave the Colony.

Sounds came from outside and everybody turned to look at the door. Carlos checked outside and sighed in relief when no one was there. "It's nobody. Grab what you need for tonight and let's go."

Pax looked around the room and then went to their bed, snatched the red quilt and hurriedly folded it. Another external sound made her jump and she ran through the doorway and into Prince's arms.

"No, wait." Celeste walked around them. "I have a better idea."

"Thank you, but we must hurry." Prince's nerves were on edge and he thought he heard running steps.

Celeste put a hand on his arm. "I know of a safer place."

"You do?" He felt Pax's fingers digging in his skin.

"Yes, it's a small cave just outside the Colony. Nobody knows it exists. Remy and I found it a few months ago and kept it a secret..." A small blush covered Celeste's cheeks when her eyes darted toward Carlos. "You can stay there and I'll come check on you and bring food and water. Things could change in a week or two. Carlos is going to take care of this and soon it'll be safe for you to come back."

Farther away, sounds echoed, and this time, there was no mistake—they were real. "Where to?" Prince asked, taking the quilt from Pax's hands and draping it over his shoulder.

"Follow me." Celeste was already outside of the door, Prince and Pax at her heels. "Aren't you coming?" she asked Carlos, who had stayed behind.

"I'll take care of them." He pointed at some far-away figures moving toward them at increasing speed. In a moment, they started hearing the voices. Carlos's eyes widened. "Move!"

Celeste broke into a run. "This way!"

Prince grabbed Pax's hand and sprinted forward, only to have to pull her up once or twice when she stumbled on the uneven terrain. His legs ached, and his lungs couldn't pump enough air to let him breathe. Terrified something would happen to Pax and the baby, he kept reassuring her everything would be fine. He followed Celeste through the less-crowded section of the Colony, looking back every few seconds to be sure nobody tailed them. They kept running for what felt like hours, following a trail north of their cottage until they reached a tunnel hidden by bushy vegetation.

Finally catching his breath and making sure Pax was still fine, Prince looked one more time right and left, but it seemed that they were alone. "I've never seen it. I've walked back and forth this route several times and never realized there was anything else behind the foliage but rock."

"Remy told me it was excavated two years ago, when they were trying to expand to other chambers, but stopped because it only opened to small caves that nobody was interested in." Celeste moved the green curtain aside. "Wait a moment." She reached behind the foliage and retrieved a small candle and a lighter. "Let's go. The cave is just at the end of it."

They had just entered the dark tunnel when two hooded figures ambushed them. Prince barely had time to react when his head was forcefully propelled against a jutting rock on the wall. The last thing he thought before passing out was that he had failed Pax.

CHAPTER 6

"Please, reconsider," Carlos was saying to Remy. His face was swollen and sported several cuts where the assailants' fists heavily landed. He nursed a limp and probably a broken rib or two. Still, he had apologized to Prince about not being able to stop the two men. "Give me time to make a plan. A better plan."

Prince barely listened to the two of them going back and forth, discussing the sanity of what he and Remy were going to do. He had tried to dissuade Remy from following him in his quest to find Pax, but had soon realized his words were wasted on his friend and let the father do the talking. He tore another strip of sand-colored fabric and carefully draped it around his hat. He had already donned a large suit made from the same crude cotton. It was rough on the skin and heavy, and he was sweating profusely. He needed the physical distraction to function. The bump on his head wasn't as swollen as when he had woken on the tunnel's floor, alone, three hours ago.

"Celeste needs my help. Who knows what they're doing to her," Remy answered again.

The discussion between father and son had soon become a repetition of words, and Prince ached to leave. His own thoughts became a graphic rendition of Remy's fear and he felt sick at only imagining what could be happening to Pax and their baby. At least they had progressed from the deep center of the Colony to one of the exit tunnels. A slow procession that had attracted unwanted attention. Prince's eyes were focused on the sliver of bright light that cut the end of the tunnel in two different spaces.

"I'm leaving." Prince turned his back on them and moved toward the sun and the world outside of the Colony.

"Don't go. You aren't strong enough." Carlos tried to reason with Remy.

Wrong thing to say. Prince inwardly sighed, anticipating more unnecessary delay.

"I'm no coward." Remy was shaking, resentment in his voice.

"No, of course not, but you're my only son!"

"What kind of man would leave the person he loves behind?" Remy stared at his father and Prince couldn't help but admire his friend's courage.

"I can't hear the helicopter, and it's too early for the tanks to be on the move. It's now or never." Prince went to salute Carlos. "Thank you for everything you've done for us. I won't forget it." He couldn't wait any longer. "Vale." *Good-bye.*

"I didn't think they were going to attempt anything so soon. I was sure there was time—" Carlos didn't look at Prince until the last moment when he whispered, "Vale," back to him and then added, "Fiat voluntas Dei." *God's will be done.* "Please watch out for my boy."

Prince acknowledged the man's well wishes with a nod. "I'll try my best to keep him safe." If he hadn't been so desperate to find Pax, he would've tried to convince Remy to stay back. The boy had proved to be strong-willed and the clock was ticking, but he understood Carlos's anguish at seeing his son leaving.

"It's all I ask." Carlos shuffled to Remy to give him his salute and blessing.

Prince gave father and son one last moment together—the sight reminding him of how much he still missed his father. Even after so long, he still longed for his father's embrace. Again, his heart shrank, imagining his baby and Pax alone in the world without him to protect them. He centered his mind on a positive outcome and then walked out into the light. He breathed the fresh air of the morning and felt dizzy. The throbbing ache in his head hadn't lessened, but he could see straight now, had stopped puking, and could put one foot in front of the other without falling sideways. He would have gone anyway, even half dead.

"Right behind you." Remy's wheelchair announced him before he spoke.

"Leaving without me?" A familiar voice resounded from the cave's entry.

72

Prince swore out loud. *Not now.* "What are you doing here?" He should have left an hour ago.

"Helping?" Randal came out into the light, and he, too, inhaled the morning air at length.

"No, you aren't," Prince answered, already on the go. *Please, Randal, go away. We're already a crowd.*

"Well, I didn't expect to be hugged and kissed, but a modest show of gratitude would be fine. You have no hope of getting out of this alive without me, and you know it." He gave Prince, then Remy, a telling look.

"We can make it," Remy pouted, fresh from his father's words.

I don't have time for this. Normally, Remy's and Randal's exchanges made for a great time, but not now. Prince saw Remy wheeling against Randal, getting stuck in the sand.

Randal laughed, Remy groaned in anger, and he had to wheel the chair out of the rut. The usual scene.

"If you want to risk your life along with us, be my guest, but don't be rude," Prince said to Randal.

"You're welcome?" Randal's mockery set Remy on fire again.

"That's enough." Prince's headache flared up. "Please, be nice."

"Back to the farm, then?" Randal asked.

"How do you know where we're going?" Remy asked before Prince could even form the words.

"About that... you should've told *me*." He glared at both of them. "I can't believe you'd leave without me. Anyway, it's a small colony, people talk, and others shout first thing in the morning." Randal looked at Remy, who had the decency to blush. "Next time you plan to do anything heroic, I would suggest keeping it quiet. You never know who's listening. And Sundial is the closest place around here where kidnappers would take two women. Only an idiot wouldn't reach the same conclusion."

"Please, Randal, could you shut up?" Prince's headache was pounding against his temples, and when he closed his eyes, images of Pax assaulted him. "I really need to move." He took Remy's wheelchair's handles and pushed ahead.

"Wait." Randal reached in his backpack to retrieve two items. "Take this." He passed him one of the two planks of wood he was holding and some rope. "Here, look, secure the skis to the wheels. It's going to be easier to push the wheelchair on the dunes this way."

When the work was done, Randal proudly looked at the improvement on the wheelchair. "Not bad, ah?"

"Actually, clever." Prince regarded Randal with respect.

"Thanks!" Remy smiled.

"Told you. You need me." Randal took the helm of the wheelchair and started walking toward the expanse of sand and sky before them.

"When did you make them?" Remy was baffled by his friend's foresight.

"It was a gift for your birthday." Randal's cheeks slightly colored, as if he had confessed some crime.

"Well, thank you. It's a cool gift." Remy leaned over the right wheel to better look at how the skis worked. "Really cool."

"To the farm," Prince reminded them.

"Ready." Remy reached for his satchel strapped to the side of the wheelchair and produced a folded paper. "Here." He opened a crude map of the desert he had sketched beforehand and Prince bent to memorize the route they would take.

When Remy had showed him the map an hour ago, explaining how food and other goods were smuggled following the trails on the paper, Prince had hardly believed him. He still could barely believe that right under the women's haughty noses a system of tunnels connected the farm to an oasis that was only a day from the Colony.

Prince looked down at Remy, hoping nothing was going to happen to him, and shook his head. He had only wanted the map Remy had painstakingly sketched, but no amount of persuasion from Prince and yelling from Carlos had convinced Remy to stay behind.

"*I won't give you the map if you don't take me with you,*" he had said and then went on about his love for Celeste, followed by the fact that he had given his word to Prince to repay his moral debt.

Prince could sympathize with Remy's reasons and eventually had yielded to his will.

* * *

"Nice day for a long walk," Randal commented several hours later.

"Time to take a break," Prince said with a sigh. He had gotten used to Randal's oblique talking, but sometimes, like now, it still was unnerving. Although, he had to admit, Randal was right. A single glance at Remy's chapped lips reminded him they needed to drink more often. They had been walking far too long under a merciless sun. Worries about how Pax was crossing the desert assaulted him once more. *They wouldn't mistreat the president's daughter, would they? They must have planned for a vehicle beforehand... They'll see she's pregnant...*

Without further discussion, he drove Remy toward a tall dune to rest for a few minutes. His arms were aching after having pushed the wheelchair up and down the dunes. By himself, he would've kept going the whole day, but he was smart enough to know that pushing beyond his limits wasn't going to help Pax. He sat, sheltered by the sand, with his back against the cool wall. Pacing to accommodate the wheelchair's rhythm had been useful in a way. His legs were sore, but not cramping, and he wasn't in pain.

"So, what's next?" Randal asked.

"We reach the oasis, enter the tunnel, reach Sundial, and finally, we take Pax and Celeste back with us."

"Is that right?" Randal looked at him with disbelief.

"Yes." He knew his plan wasn't a plan at all, but there wasn't a better
plan.

"Like that? You must be kidding." Randal laughed.

"That's my plan." Prince was tired, his worries for Pax adding to the mix of feelings. "Do you have a better idea?" He was hoping the other two would come up with something better.

Randal shook his head.

"You should've stayed behind." Prince didn't want to hurt his feelings, but he felt responsible for the two men. "Don't let anything happen to you. I already have Carlos to report to."

Randal's expression changed from one of bravado to a more subdued one at the oblique mention of Lucas.

Prince inwardly cursed himself for not being thoughtful.

"I'm still hoping to find my father." Randal's voice reflected his pain.

Prince stretched to pat Randal's shoulder. "Afterward, I'll help you."

"You know I'll help too," Remy offered.

"I know. Thanks." Randal shook his head and rubbed his eyes. "Sand's so annoying."

"Time to go." Prince's statement was received by two long stares. "Sorry." He stood up and shook his tired limbs. "We've lingered enough." He firmly grabbed the wheelchair by its handles and steered Remy away from the safety of the dune. He resisted the urge to speed up and set his legs on a slow but constant stride.

He silently walked the rest of the day, taking small sips from his water bottle and making sure Remy was doing the same. The sun was slowly descending toward the desert, and the oasis was in plain sight, when the loud noise of the helicopter broke the natural quiet.

"Help me cover him," Prince said to Randal, then reached for the backpack on the back of the wheelchair and threw a sand-colored towel across it. Randal pulled the hem until it covered the wheels.

"Fortunately, the metal parts are rusty," Remy added, reading Prince's mind about the fact the wheelchair's colors blended with the rest of the desert.

The helicopter flew over them and continued on its trajectory without pausing.

"It's directed toward the farm." Remy pointed ahead with his chin.

In a matter of seconds, the helicopter became a dot in the sky. "Time to go underground," Prince finally said when he couldn't hear the whirring noise anymore. He pushed Remy's wheelchair at full speed through the dunes, eager to reach Sundial.

The oasis was a small patch of green in the middle of a sea of golden waves. A few palms guarded a small water basin, a splash of refreshing blue Prince immediately entered to wash away the dusty sand from his skin. Randal took Remy in his arms and helped him clean in the water.

"So, where's the entry to the tunnel?" Prince asked a few minutes later.

Remy pointed at a heavy-looking boulder sitting by the edge between the green grass and the sand. "There. We just need to move that boulder. The entry is behind it."

Prince tried to estimate the weight of the rock. "Are you sure?" After having replenished his water bottle, he walked to the boulder, put his hands on it and gave a tentative push. "Oh... it's fake."

"It's basically paper ad glue," Remy explained. "It's anchored to the ground below by a rock tied to a rope."

Prince tilted the fake boulder on its axis until he found the rope jutting from its bottom. He gave it a tug and felt the heavy stone being dragged in the obscurity below. He squinted, but saw nothing beyond the rope, all being devoured by darkness, and couldn't suppress a shiver. Passing the palm of his hand over his drenched forehead, he moved the rock back to its place. "Let's take a look at your map."

Remy reached into his backpack and offered him the map.

"Thanks." He studied the map and then nodded to himself. "Okay, that's what we'll do. We'll walk the whole length of this tunnel, and we'll get out at this exit, just outside the farm," he shared his thought with the two men. "Once I'm inside, I'll bring down the wheelchair, then you'll lower Remy," he finally instructed Randal.

"You'll need these." Remy reached inside his backpack and handed Prince a torch with matches. "They're also good to scare the rodents off." He tipped his head toward the tunnel's entry.

As if on cue, soft scuffling noises reached Prince's ears from beneath the fake boulder. "Of course," he murmured, while his hair was ruffled by a gust of air. He mentally counted the matches he was holding and decided to wait until he was safely inside the tunnel to use them. He pushed the boulder out of the way and took a good look at the entrance shrouded in darkness. The breath caught in his lungs for a moment, but he thought of Pax and sat on the edge, letting his legs dangle inside.

"Okay, wait for my signal." He gave himself a mental push and lowered his body into the hole, looking for footholds. Several seconds later, he finally saw the floor. "A few more feet to reach the ground," he yelled toward the ceiling. A scurrying noise amplified by the cavernous walls distracted him and he lost his hold and fell, hitting the ground with his right foot. He yelled and swore, rocking on his side.

"What is it?" Remy asked from above.

"Nothing. I'm okay." Prince massaged the ankle and swore again. He rolled back up and gingerly put down the foot and tried to put some weight on it, and it worked. A few steps later, he was swallowed by the subterranean gloom. Prince fumbled a few seconds with the matches and lost two of them on the floor, but he was finally able to light the torch.

"Welcome home," a voice said with a cold sneer before he was embraced by the darkness once more.

* * *

Uncomfortably familiar smells welcomed Prince when he opened his eyes in a small room with a low ceiling. Dampness and sense of desperation radiated from the tuff brick walls surrounding him. A barrage of painful memories overwhelmed his mind and his chest constricted.

Not again.

He let the moment pass as he had learned to do early on when he was a boy. Once his heartbeat slowed, he focused on the here and now. He wasn't surprised to find his hands tied behind his back. He tried to sit; his back was sore from lying on the concrete floor and his nose tingled at the sharp smell of the hay scattered on it. The women were anything but practical. His eyes soon adjusted to the light, and he saw the contour of a door with a small window.

He opened his mouth to say something, but his voice wouldn't cooperate. His lips were cracked and his throat felt dry. He looked around to see if there was any water, but there was none. He tried to talk again. "Thanks for keeping the suite free for me. I appreciate the courtesy," he finally said to anybody who would listen. He knew there was someone out there.

"The slave's awake," a guard called. The pejorative *slave* instead of *worker* was said with a casualness that cut Prince deep. A few months earlier, he would have thought nothing of it, but he had lived as a free man and it stung.

He squinted and saw the silhouette of the woman through the window bars. Soon after, he heard the distinct sound of keys rattling against the door. Next, he expected the familiar lash of the whip on the floor. The guards at the farm liked to announce their intentions.

"You must be the stupidest man alive." Caren, the farm's wiry chief-in-command, sauntered inside the cell without the whip.

Where's Pax? How's my baby? Prince wanted to know, but asked instead, "Where are my companions?"

"I would've never come back here, of all places." Caren ignored his words, but she gave him a thorough look.

Prince felt like a specimen under scrutiny. Time rewound and he was ten years younger, skinnier, and waiting for the next time the door would open—not knowing if it was for food or a beating.

"You could've saved yourself." Caren kept talking to him with her haughty tone and walked the two steps separating her from Prince with barely concealed anger. "You were nothing more than a nuisance, before. But now..."

"What happened to the two men who were with me?" Prince steadied his voice and tried a second time. He didn't expect the woman to answer him, but he couldn't let her know how frightened he was.

Caren closed her eyes and pinched the bridge of her nose. "Can't believe we're still dealing with this piece of filth and that Layan bitch...," she muttered.

Her voice rose barely above a whisper, but Prince heard her and recoiled at the way she had spoken about Pax. For Caren to take such liberty, it didn't bode well for Pax. Pure breeds were a highly hierarchical race; the only time he had heard one of them showing disrespect to another had been back at the City of Men, when the Priestess's guards had talked down to Pax and Rosie. The horror of those moments came back to him and he shivered.

"Yes, be afraid. Your presence here infuriates me." Caren misunderstood his reaction.

"How did you know I was there?" He didn't want her to think he was scared, because she would have greatly enjoyed that.

Caren stared at him for a moment. "Take him to the recreational facility," she ordered the guard outside and left the door open when she left.

Prince wished he could wipe the cold sweat from his forehead, worried the women could smell his fear, and sagged on the floor.

"Move," the guard ordered from the archway.

He didn't look at the woman and tried to stand without humiliating himself. Not an easy task with his hands still tied behind his back. He angled his body sideways and slowly pushed his legs up.

"Are you done? I told you to move." The guard's voice was grating.

Prince straightened his back, raised his chin in defiance, and followed her outside. He walked the whole time without limping. He wasn't going to reveal he was already injured. It would have been a rooky mistake to give the guard any amount of power over him. Instead, he plastered a neutral expression on his face and swallowed hard anytime he wanted to scream in pain. It wasn't just the ankle; his head was still sporting the good-sized lump from the previous night, and the skin on his back was raw from the more recent fall. The rough cotton chafed the fresh wounds. Still, not a single moan escaped his mouth. He stared straight ahead and put one foot in front of the other.

The guard never looked back to check if he still was behind and kept walking at a brisk pace until they reached the recreational facility. She opened the door and barely waited for him to get inside the cavernous room. "There." The guard indicated a corner, where she secured his tied hands to a ring on the wall. "Don't make any noise." She went to sit by the corner, facing him.

Prince made an effort not to look at the woman, and his eyes drifted to the swimming pool dominating the room. The blue water was still, and the brightness emanated by the lights at the bottom recreated a sense of calm he'd once experienced. His lips curved at the memory of Pax emerging from the water. He'd been looking for her, unable to resist the urge to talk to the girl who had stirred his imagination. Heedless of the consequences, he had followed Pax through Sundial just to have a glimpse of her. Once he found her at the pool, he had stood there watching as she dove into the water and sunk to the bottom where she simply sat. He remembered being worried about her not reemerging, and when he approached to see if she needed help, she'd broken the surface and turned to stare at him, as if she knew he was there. She saw him looking at her and hadn't screamed or called for help. Instead, she had locked gazes with him.

"He looks comfortable, and we don't want that. Do we?" Lauren, Caren's right hand, or the *butcher*, as she was known by the men suffering under her command, asked the guard.

Prince, focused on Pax's memories, hadn't noticed Lauren coming. He kept looking at the blue water, hoping that her presence meant something else other than to fulfill her quota of beatings for the day. *Tell me what I want to know. Bring me news of her*, he mentally asked.

"No, we don't want that," the guard answered with a laugh.

A plumper Lauren than he remembered made a show of parading a brown satchel in front of him. She opened it, letting him see the surgical instruments neatly aligned inside. "No, those are my toys," she said to the guard, when the woman went for the satchel. She reached for a wooden stick hanging from her belt and gave her that instead.

Both women found it amusing that he fell to his knees as soon as the wooden stick hit him in the groin. They kept laughing when his eyes filled with tears he couldn't hold back. Shock replaced fear as soon as the pain allowed him to breathe again. Then, he realized the truth behind the women's action. They didn't consider him a semental anymore. Prince lowered his head to hide his face. He didn't want them to see him crying, but his arms were stretched behind his back, keeping his neck at an awkward angle. He closed his eyes. Even if they could still see his face, at least he didn't have to see theirs.

"Oh no, you'll watch what happens next. I'll keep your eyes wide open if I have to," Lauren whispered too close to Prince's ears, and when the wooden stick probed him, he obeyed.

The door opened and several women entered. Prince couldn't see their faces from his position, but the guard kneeled, and Lauren bowed low.

"Come, child, and see what your foolishness is going to cost you." The Priestess's booming voice resonated in the room.

Prince's hair stood on end. Anticipation and dread grew strong inside him. He tried to move, but Lauren thought better of it. "Stay. Put," she said.

He heard the steps and then the gasp and he knew.

"Prince!" Pax screamed.

He strained his neck to look at her. Shock hit him at her sight and rage blinded his rational thoughts. Pax's ankles were bleeding from the metal shackles she wore and her wrists were tied with a crude rope held by one of the Priestess's soldiers. Then he looked at her face. Her split lips and bruised cheeks painted the rest of the picture for him. Prince forgot Lauren was beside him and managed to curse the Priestess and every pure breed in Ginecea before the stick connected with his head.

"No, please! I'm begging you, stop hitting him!" Pax cried.

"You should answer my questions, or your pet is going to get the proper beating I can't give you," the Priestess said to Pax and gave her a hard push.

Prince saw red and tried to kick Lauren, missing the target, and was hit in retaliation.

"Please, don't touch him again. I'll ask my mother to give you whatever you want." Pax flung herself on Lauren's legs.

The woman didn't listen to Pax. Lauren got a nod from the Priestess and smiled at Prince.

Memories of every time Lauren had bestowed her cruel smile upon him crowded his mind. He knew she was skilled in the art of torture, but this time, Lauren had the Priestess suggesting new tricks. He was never allowed to lose consciousness. Prince resented more than anything that he couldn't help but listen to Pax's anguished sobs, hoping she would faint and not be forced to see what they had in mind for him. But she didn't.

He tried not to scream when Lauren became creative with the instruments she'd brought, but near the end, the pain was more than he had experienced in his whole life. "Forgive me," he whispered under his breath, looking at Pax who was staring at him, eyes wide open, a silent scream frozen in her mouth. She had crumbled on the floor soon after Lauren had started working on him, and she hadn't said anything since.

"Don't worry. I don't want him killed today. I'm having too much fun. Besides, after everything he's done to me, death would be a reward I'm not willing to concede," the Priestess cheerfully said to Pax.

Prince saw hope coloring Pax's expression, and he hated the Priestess even more for that. "You're making a big mistake. You should kill me," he said, collecting all the strength he had left in his voice.

The Priestess didn't appear as if she had heard, but one of the women said, "The ant is sneezing!"

"I'll tear down Ginecea before I even start with you." Prince ignored the roar in his ears.

The Priestess laughed at someone else's comment and yanked Pax up by the rope.

"Anything you do to her, I'll do to you ten times over, and then I'll start again," Prince said, putting every effort on keeping his voice steady. Anger, pain, and fear for Pax had taken control of his brain.

His last words granted him the final blow, and he went down with Pax's image memorized in his retinas. She had hit the Priestess, and the woman had struck her back, full force. Prince closed his eyes as Pax fell, blood oozing out of her mouth.

CHAPTER 7

Two days passed. The Priestess, helped by an eager Lauren, took her time having fun with him. She had promised so, and she wasn't a woman to break a promise. Prince's body wasn't reacting anymore by the end of the first day, and the Priestess didn't seem happy about that.

"Tomorrow we'll find something more stimulating," she said, and she did.

The next day, Prince lost consciousness more times than he could count. He didn't care. He kept opening his eyes, waiting for the next round, hoping and fearing to see Pax. But she wasn't there, and he didn't dare ask. That last, bloodied image of her played constantly in his mind, until he wasn't sure of what was real and what wasn't.

The third day, or maybe it was the fifth or the tenth—Prince had no way of knowing how long he had been there—he woke to a different scenario. He felt the presence of other human beings before opening his eyes. The familiar smells and low murmurs told him he was in a communal cell with other men. He was in so much pain he passed out from the sheer effort of trying to talk to them. Some time later, he felt a wet cloth touching his lips and croaked, "Thanks," to the person helping him.

"How are you?"

Prince recognized the voice, but he couldn't focus on it. "Where's Pax?" he asked.

"She's fine," the voice reassured him.

"Where is she?"

"Her mother came to pick her up," someone else answered.

Prince accepted more water, this time from a flask, and kept it down with some effort. Slowly the cell and its occupants came to focus. "Remy, Randal," he acknowledged the two men.

"The women did a number on you," Remy said.

"We weren't sure you were going to wake up," Randal added.

Prince tried to sit and failed.

"One step at the time." Randal put a hand on Prince's chest and gently pushed him down. "What did they want from you?" he asked after a prolonged silence.

"I don't know," Prince answered.

"What did you tell them?" Remy lowered his voice and gave a sideways glance at the rest of the cell.

"Nothing." Prince slowly raised his head over his shoulders.

"You must've said something." Randal helped Prince adjust his back against the wall.

"Nothing... I swear." And then it hit Prince that the women hadn't asked him anything.

"He's still alive, after all," Remy reasoned.

"What happened to you?" Prince tried to keep his eyes on both Randal and Remy, but it wasn't easy, and he lost focus for a second.

"Easy, don't tire yourself. Randal and I were brought here immediately. We were roughed up a bit, the guards took my chair, but other than that, we were left alone. I don't know why we got different treatment than you, but we weren't asked anything." Remy gently straightened Prince's wobbling head.

"I don't understand. The Priestess wanted something from Pax..." Prince forgot what he was saying mid-sentence. "You told me she's fine. How do you know?" he asked Remy.

"I don't know for sure," Remy amended.

"What do you know?" Prince's eyes were playing tricks, and he was looking at two Remys and two Randals. He still maintained his mind fully focused on the topic.

"I heard some of the workers whispering about having heard guards talking..." Remy lowered his head.

"About what?" Prince's voice got louder, and he regretted it immediately.

"It seems the president flew here first thing yesterday morning and whisked her daughter away against the Priestess's will," Randal finished for Remy.

"That's what I heard a worker saying," Remy explained with a shrug of his shoulders.

Prince thought about the news, trying to decide if it was good or not. Rationally, he preferred that Pax was safely in her mother's arms, but his heart couldn't stand the idea he was going to die without having talked to her one last time. There was no doubt, this time, he would never leave the farm. *I hope it's a baby girl.*

"Why's it so cold?" Prince asked when he realized he was shaking.

"We gave you all our blankets already." Remy tucked him tighter.

Prince raised his head to take a look at the rest of the workers sharing the cell with him. The men had kept silent the whole time he had talked with Remy and Randal, and he had forgotten about them. He knew two or three of them, but the others were young, probably new additions to the farm. "Thanks," he said to them, his teeth chattering.

Steps from reinforced boots echoed in the hallway, and everybody stopped talking at once. A guard opened the cell, and two women, wearing the Priestess's gold-and-black insignia, went to grab Prince.

"He just woke. Give him a break!" Remy's words had the effect to divert the women's attention for the time it took them to order the guard to silence him.

They lifted Prince, while Remy was reminded of the stupidity of his words. Nobody else dared intervene. "Throw the slave into confinement and let him starve for a few days," one of the Priestess's soldiers suggested, looking at Remy.

"Right away," the guard said, bowing to the woman.

Prince tried to walk along with the soldiers, but his body wouldn't obey, and soon, he fell between them. The two women dragged him by his arms. He couldn't say how long they walked up and down through the various level of the farm. He was too focused on not passing out again, but he did notice they didn't exchange a single word the whole time. Finally, when they turned a corner and entered a wing he knew, one of the soldiers knocked on the closed door of the infirmary he had visited so many times, and he sighed in relief.

"Special delivery from the Priestess," the soldier said with a flat tone as she opened the door.

The place looked exactly like the last time he had been there. Unsettling white lights inundated the room from white ceilings to equally white floors, leaving nothing in the dark. *Easier to spot bloodstain,* he'd been told once. The rows of narrow beds covered in immaculate white linens completed the picture.

"I've been waiting for you. Everything's ready," Doctor Linda answered from the other end of the infirmary. "Help them strap the worker in place," she told the nurse.

Prince was forcibly put on a bed, his arms and legs secured to it by leather belts.

"Thank you. You may go now. Tell the Priestess I have everything under control," Linda said, her words gentle, her voice calm, but the tremor in her fisted hands betrayed her nervousness. She bent over Prince to examine his face. Something passed through her eyes and then she moved to a cart by the bed.

Prince didn't take his eyes off the doctor while she busied herself with gloves and lining syringes and other instruments on the cart. The woman didn't seem to age. He'd seen her the first time soon after being chosen to be a semental and her hair was as dark now as it had been then. Her figure, too, had remained the same, maybe slightly slimmer. Only a few wrinkles around her eyes gave away her age.

"I'm so tired. I didn't sleep well last night. Would you be so kind as to bring me some coffee?" she asked the nurse, who left the room right away.

"How are you, Linda?" Prince asked when the door closed behind the nurse.

"You'll never learn your place, will you? I didn't think I was going to see you again." She sighed heavily, leaning closer to him again after having nervously looked at the door.

"To be honest, me neither." Prince smiled at her. He shared a history with the doctor. The memories he had weren't completely pleasant, but Linda had always been humane, and he had paid his dues when asked. Not that he ever had any say in the whole process. The farm's activities were a cover up for the semen black market, and he was one of the most requested "donors."

"I missed you," she whispered near his mouth.

"Linda…" Prince moved his head before she could kiss him. He hadn't expected her to be sentimental, but in the past, she'd showed him kindness and that should've warned him. More than once, she had personally taken care of collecting the specimen from him. At the time he hadn't liked the probing. He had waited patiently to be done with it and be sent back to his cell.

"I know you've been beaten—"

"Things are different now." Prince carefully chose his words, thinking of how to deal with the doctor. He would have laughed at the situation if the consequence of his actions weren't potentially a matter of life and death.

"So, it is true, after all," she said, surprise in her voice, her dark eyes telling more than her words.

"What?"

"Rumor has it that you kidnapped the president's daughter." She said it as if reporting gossip, but her tone wasn't casual.

"I didn't kidnap her," Prince rectified Linda. He still got incensed by the accusation.

"Oh, I believe you. I saw the look in the Layan girl's eyes when she was talking about you. She pleaded the Priestess with her life. She cried for hours," the doctor said. "You were always different from the others," she added after a long pause.

He interrupted her, following thoughts of his own. "She was here?"

"It's what I just said," Linda answered, raising an eyebrow.

"Why was she here, in the infirmary?" Prince fought the straps keeping him down.

"The Priestess got carried away in reprimanding her." Again, Linda tried to make it sound lighter, but Prince's breath caught in his chest at her statement.

"*Why* was she here?" he repeated. What Linda wasn't saying was driving him crazy with fear. "Tell me. I need to know."

"Why do you want to know? She's back with her mother, and if the president is as smart as she looks, she'll never let her daughter out in the world again. Especially with the Priestess in homicidal mode." Linda stalled, taking several steps away from him.

"Please, tell me." He looked at her and hoped she could see his pain.

After a long pause, Linda slowly retraced her steps until she was standing right before him, her arms crossed under her chest. "The Priestess sent Pax here when it was clear she had been having contractions for several hours. I couldn't stop the contractions. It was too dangerous for her, and she was ready to give birth."

"How's she?" Prince's voice was a whisper. He kept his eyes on her.

"She's fine." Linda lowered her head to glance sideways.

"How's the baby?" he asked, terrified by the answer. *Please, tell me my baby's fine too.*

"A girl…"

The door opened with a loud thump against the wall before Linda finished her sentence. "Priestess!" She looked as surprised as she sounded. "I'm almost done preparing the worker for the procedure."

"Change of plans. I'm in a hurry and you should've done it already. My women will ship this *slave* to Ginecea," the Priestess said, while the black and gold soldiers shoved the doctor out of the way. "You've enough stored already—"

"But it takes only a moment!" Linda protested.

The Priestess ignored Linda's plea. Instead, she looked around, seething anger showing in her eyes. "I should've shut down this farm long ago." The Priestess left the room with her soldiers trailing silently in her wake.

Prince was carted around, strapped on the bed. His mind still anchored to Linda's revelation about his baby girl. More than anything, he needed to know how she was, how Pax was, and what was happening to them at the moment.

"This time I'll make sure this is your last trip," the Priestess said, looking directly at him, and the soldiers gasped.

He barely registered the Priestess had talked to him. He didn't care.

* * *

Prince arrived in Ginecea the same day. He didn't have a clear recollection of how long it had taken because he'd thrown up the whole time. Not only had the Priestess publicly spoken to him, but she had also let him fly on her jet. The soldiers put him in the cargo bay, moved several boxes against the bed, secured it to the wall with some rope, and forgot about him. The noise, the rocking, the cold, and the pain in his stomach all added up to make for a miserable experience. Whenever his body gave him a brief rest, his mind kept visiting old and new nightmares about the fate of both his baby and Pax. When the combination of sounds and movement stopped and the big door opened loudly, rolling on its hinges, he was left there until the rest of the cargo was disembarked.

"Did they bring back animals again?" a young fathered woman, wearing worker's clothes—brown one-piece suits made of heavy cotton—asked, walking toward him. "I'm tired of cleaning up their mess every time."

Prince wished for a moment he were an animal. He dreaded the moment when the woman would discover there was only him to clean after. Approaching steps announced the time would come soon enough.

"Another man. Disgusting. I can't believe the Bestiarium isn't full already. Where are they going to put this one? I have no idea," the woman said, freeing the bed from the wall.

"It isn't our business to worry about that. Besides, he already has a place arranged for him," an older fathered woman answered, and she directed a cold stream of water on the bed, hitting Prince full force.

He gasped in shock.

"At least the soldiers were nice enough to properly restrain this one." The older woman gave an appreciative look at the leather bindings tying him to the bed, and he felt humiliated once more.

"And it'll be easier to transport him." The other woman joined in and he had to close his eyes under their scrutiny. "Let's hurry, before the Almighty finds us slacking."

90

Prince listened to the conversation, trying to understand what was happening and why the two women were wearing clothes normally worn by men. The two kept hosing him down until they were sure he didn't stink anymore and finally pushed the bed with harpoons, directing it outside.

"Wait! You forgot to cover him. Someone could see," a third woman called from behind.

He heard one of the two apologize for the oversight, and a thick cloth was promptly laid on him.

"It always surprises me that we're in the middle of Ginecea and nobody's ever found out about the Bestiarium..."

"Shut your mouth! One day you'll regret it's so big. There're cameras everywhere."

Prince listened to the two women bickering for a while, but the warmth of the cloth sheltering him and the movement of the bed lulled him into a state of light dozing.

"Is this the cage?"

"Yes, this is the one the Priestess *herself* ordered to be cleaned for her newest addition."

Prince felt the cloth being removed and a dash of cold air rushed over his wet body. He saw the women staring at him with renewed interest.

"He doesn't look like much." The younger woman poked his side with the harpoon.

"Well, he must have earned the Priestess's attention if she chose for him one of the cages she can see from her private rooms."

Prince noticed, with mild interest, the knife in one of the older woman's hands, slicing at the bindings. His mind was fully focused on all the bits and pieces he was listening to. Slowly a picture was forming, and he remembered the Priestess's words about death not being punishment enough for him.

"Go inside," the older woman said, brandishing a gun at him to reinforce the order.

When he hesitated, more out of disorientation than a conscious act of rebellion, the other worker pushed him inside the cage.

"I really don't understand what makes this one special."

The words stayed with him when the two women left, and Prince found himself jailed again.

"You've made the biggest mistake of your miserable life!" Prince shouted with all the air in his lungs, staring at a big window with an intricate design on its windowpanes. Pain immediately propagated from his fingers, which were holding the metal bars tight, to the rest of his body. The electric shock left him in a state of disorientation and physical ache for several minutes, but it also revived him. Once his teeth weren't chattering anymore, he looked at his new abode. The barred cage faced a park that stretched as far as the eyes could see. He couldn't see the walls that must border the perimeter; green bushes and trees in full bloom composed a colorful picture. He wasn't alone. There were other cages scattered between the flowerbeds. Each one was different from the other: elegant, airy structures dotting the park resembling steel bouquets. Each one occupied by a young man.

"Hey, you!" Prince called to the closest cage.

The man looked at him with big, worried eyes, but didn't utter a single word in acknowledgment.

"Are you okay?" Prince hesitantly asked. He felt there was something amiss with the whole picture. The park was silent, not a single sound breaking the spell.

The slave was still looking at him, still silent, almost frozen in his stance inside his cage.

"Can you talk?" Prince asked. Then, when silence answered his question, he said, "You can't."

The slave nodded, and then he moved his head toward the other cages.

"They can't talk, either?" Prince followed the man's eyes and saw his other neighbors staring back at him with the same frozen postures.

The slave nodded again.

"Why?"

The slave brought a slim hand to his mouth and pointed at it.

Prince understood right away and recoiled at the thought. Automatically, his fingers went to touch his lips, his tongue hitting his teeth, and shivered. He felt sick and powerless. "NO!" he screamed until his cage became alive with the electric buzz, and he was silenced once more, by pain first and darkness soon after.

Time passed. Days? Weeks, maybe. The subtle humming of the electricity seemed a constant in his new life, except for when the women came. Prince never bothered to make an effort to memorize his jailers' physical features, but they brought food twice a day to the rest of the Bestiarium's inhabitants and once every other day to him.

The cages were hosed down daily. His was never cleaned. Cruel hands groomed the men once a week. Nobody lent him as much as a comb. The only consolation for Prince, given the circumstances, was that the Bestiarium was shielded from the harshness of the weather by a dome: opaque during the day and transparent at night. He wasn't under any delusion the Priestess had thought of the men's wellbeing. It was clear that respectable Gineceans knew nothing of this place and the Priestess wanted to keep it that way.

"He stinks," one of the anonymous jailers who brought him food said, pinching her nose.

Since the last time he had made an effort to remember, five meals had passed, ten days, and his cage was filthy. He used only one corner to relieve himself, but without water to clean the space and his body, the smell wasn't getting any better.

"Maybe we could—"

A second woman cut in, worriedly looking at the window. "Don't even say it! If *she's* listening, we're screwed."

Prince saw them scurrying away, forgetting to put the bowl of food closer to the bars. The women were disgusted by his appearance and normally came as close to the cage as their noses permitted. Usually, with a bit of struggle, he managed to grab the rim of the bowl. He stretched his arm, and then his fingers, reaching for his meager, unsalted rice porridge, only to find that the difference between starving for another two days and eating was just the length of a nail. Hunger pains prevented him from laughing at the situation. He watched his food rot before his eyes, but he didn't have tears left to acknowledge his personal predicament.

Prince started hallucinating before the next bowl of rice arrived. Vivid memories of Pax cooking started playing before his eyes. The texture and the smell of the food she'd prepared for him, nothing more than water and a handful of oats sometimes, filled his mind. The quality of the experience was such that he was soon lost in it. He evoked the way they both used to stir the contents in the pot over the stove, one of his hands over hers, while he told her about his day in the fields and what Randal and Remy had done. He heard her laughs at his tales. He felt the smell of her skin when he laid his chin on her shoulders and caressed her stomach with his free hand. Even in his addled state, he knew he missed her more than nourishment, and he realized he preferred never to be lucid again. Reality was too painful to bear.

"I want to show you my most precious specimen," the Priestess intruded in Prince's hallucination.

"Not now! I was having a good dream," Prince yelled, resented.

"And he still talks," the Priestess continued.

Prince saw other women walking after the Priestess. "Go away, all of you. I'm having fun here, and you're ruining my moment."

"Not for long, obviously. I like my pets silent. They're cuter to look at." The Priestess reached behind her and pulled someone before the cage. "Look at him. Do you still feel something for this animal?"

"Prince!"

He saw her then, rushing to him while her mother tried to push her back. It was nice to see her again, even as a figment of his imagination.

"Pax!" He touched the bars the same moment she did, and horror struck him when he saw the pain in her eyes. He then felt the electric current himself and realized it wasn't a dream.

"Stop it!" Prince shouted through clenched teeth. He saw Maurice Layan at her daughter's side, caressing Pax's shaking body. *No, the baby*, he thought, only to remember she wasn't pregnant anymore.

"I don't let anybody play with my pets. Even the ones I don't like are off-limits to anybody but me," the Priestess answered to something the president had said.

"Was it necessary to keep the electricity on when you knew we were coming?" Maurice Layan had created a shield around Pax with her body.

Prince paced, furious at the Priestess, furious at Maurice Layan who wouldn't move and let him see how Pax was.

"That was exactly the point. Your daughter's caused me a huge headache, and she deserves this and more. She's only alive because you pleaded for her. And I don't know why. I'd be ashamed to have a daughter like yours. Praise to the Almighty Goddess priestesses get to choose their heirs."

"She needs medical help," one of the guards escorting the Priestess commented, keeping her voice low.

The Priestess shrugged her shoulders and laughed. "A little bit of pain never killed anybody."

Prince watched, frozen in shock, while Maurice Layan demanded to see a doctor with panic rising in her voice. He wanted to scream at everybody, but knew the Priestess would take her revenge on Pax, and he bit the inside of his cheek. The guards started whispering to each other, and the Priestess kept laughing. Several minutes passed before Pax was finally carried away by the guards.

"We'll come back later, then. There's still so much I want to show you." The Priestess followed the somber procession without having lost her good humor.

Prince's legs buckled and he fell to the floor. He remembered he was supposed to feel physical pain, and it came back to him in a rush. White foam formed at his mouth, while he fought hard to stay awake. He focused on the hate consuming him from the inside and won his battle. He commanded his body to breathe and slowly rearranged his limbs on the floor, until his head was safely pillowed between his knees. Later, when he was able to sit without throwing up, he directed his thoughts toward Pax. She and the baby had been in his mind constantly, since the moment he had been whisked away from the farm. Linda's words about the baby girl had left him with questions that kept him awake at night, more so than the hunger and the beatings.

Now, he realized, he hoped she would have never seen him. He knew the physical pain would disappear, but seeing him caged like an animal, covered in his own filth, wasn't something she was going to forget. That was a pain she would never heal from. He could only imagine, from the stink he emanated, what he looked like.

"I'll make you pay for everything you've done to her!" he yelled toward the window as one single truth hit him. He hated the Priestess as much as he loved Pax.

CHAPTER 8

A cloudless night sky shone through the dome. Prince was still resting his head between his knees, mindlessly rocking. The other men had gone to sleep, but he couldn't rest. With his eyes closed, he sang the lullaby his father had taught him.

"Ego te amo," Prince repeated several times.

"Ego te amo, forever and ever." Pax's voice resonated in the calm night.

He opened his eyes to look at her, paler and skinnier than ever.

"Don't!" he said when she went for the bars—again.

Pax looked at her fingers, red from where they had touched the electrified bars. "I'd do it again, only to touch you for a moment."

"I miss you," he whispered.

"I'll do everything I can to free you from this nightmare." Despite Prince's distress, Pax carefully slid her slim hand through the bars, avoiding the metal. "I'll find a way," she said, stretching her fingers toward him.

"I'm sorry." Prince moved away from her touch.

"For what?" Pax's eyes darkened.

"I don't want you to look at me." He took shelter in the farthest corner.

"I fell in love with you without knowing what your face looked like. Remember?" Pax slowly retracted her arm, walked to his corner, and reached for him once again. "Let me touch you, please. I need to know I'm not dreaming."

"I'm disgusting." *I'm hardly dreaming material*, he thought, but he let her caress his skin.

"I could never find you disgusting. I've never seen anyone as beautiful as you. You stole my breath away the first time I laid eyes on you. You're my prince." Pax kneeled on the ground, arranging her body to be as close as she could to the cage without being shocked.

Prince took her fingers in his hand, minding his movements so that her skin wouldn't touch the bars. "Close your eyes and listen to my voice."

Pax smiled sadly and then shook her head. "I want to look at you. I missed your skin on mine. I miss your eyes on my body when we make love. I miss you."

"How are you?" Prince asked when he found that her words were burning his skin.

"I'm fine…"

"The baby?" He saw the pain etched in the darkness under her eyes and her hand furtively caressing her flat belly when she had answered.

"We had a baby girl," Pax said, her voice breaking along with Prince's heart.

"We *had* a girl…"

"Linda told me she had dark hair, like yours. She said she was too small, and her lungs weren't fully developed. They didn't let me see her. I begged them, but my mother and the Priestess kept me drugged and locked." She brought a hand to her chest and pushed over her heart, as if to stanch an imaginary flow. "I wanted to hold her, just once."

Prince's mind was stuck on the past tense. *We had a girl.* The words cut deep. He had hoped. He knew she was barely eight months pregnant, but he had hoped. He could've sworn his heart was bleeding and he ached in new and unexpected ways. His mind went on a treacherous loop, mixing bits and pieces of reality with fantasy. Images of their girl played before his eyes. Their baby girl with dark hair like his. The unborn daughter he had sung lullabies to and talked to so many times. The little girl he had seen grow in his dreams and become a copy of her mother. She was no more. He couldn't accept it.

"It's my fault. I shouldn't have antagonized the Priestess. Our baby would still be safe. I'm sorry," Pax continued between sobs. "Sometimes, I feel her. Sometimes, I wake in the morning and realize she isn't with me anymore. I still sleep on my back for fear of hurting her."

Prince needed to scream, to open his mouth and let the poison out. It was drowning him from the inside.

"I reached for you at night and wished you were there with me. I knew you were alive. You couldn't be—" She closed her eyes for a moment. "I believed I'd see you again." She raised her hand and turned it to show him the burns. "I'll wear these scars like jewels on my skin."

Every word she said pierced a dagger through the hole his heart had become. Then, her pain and his pain combined and became rage. Something stirred in his soul. Something powerful and blind. A feeling that frightened him. "It's not your fault. You didn't do anything wrong. The Priestess killed our girl, and I'll avenge her with my last breath. I promise you, I'll kill the Priestess."

"Oh, Prince…"

"I won't rest until she pays. From now on, there'll be no more tears." He looked at her, and something in his eyes must have shocked Pax, because she gasped. "No more sorrow."

She nodded, but remained silent.

"How did you escape the guards to come here?" he asked after a moment. Ideas were already emerging.

"One of the guards outside my room was at the farm when I lost my baby. She took pity on me and let me out when I asked her." Pax's expression was puzzled.

He didn't like the idea of having to rely on one of Priestess's women. "Does she know that you are here, with me?"

"Yes, I had to tell her—"

He liked that even less. "Why did she let you?"

"Not everybody is like the Priestess."

"Or your mother." Prince also blamed Maurice Layan for everything that had happened to them and for his daughter's death. He had never said anything negative about her before and felt bad when he saw Pax's reaction, but it was out and he couldn't eat his words. "Can you come back?" he abruptly asked a few seconds later, following his train of thoughts. He had to act on an idea that was quickly taking shape, and time was of the essence.

"I'm not sure. If the Priestess finds out—"

He cut Pax off, "Then... find as many sharp rocks as you can and bring them to me." Then changed plans in midsentence. "And, I could use a piece of rope."

"Sharp rocks and a piece of rope," Pax said and let go of him to execute his order.

"That one is perfect. I need a few more of that size." Prince directed her while she fetched stones of various shapes, but small enough to fit through the bars of the cage. "That's enough." He stopped her, feeling the urgency to keep moving with his plan. The sky outside the dome was lighter, and he thought he saw a shadow behind the Priestess's window. "Go, get the rope now."

"Give me half an hour." Pax blew him a kiss, retraced her steps, and silently disappeared behind a thick copse of trees.

Prince remained crouched in the same position, thinking of what to do next. The dome was alight with the morning sun when Pax came back. Bathed in the warmer colors, she looked more like her former self.

"It took longer than I thought. But here it is." She slid a skipping rope through the bars. "It's the only kind of rope I could find."

"It's exactly what I need. The wooden handles are going to be of great help. Thank you." Prince had heard the apology in her voice and saw Pax's eyes light up at his words. She was smiling, and he was assailed by memories of her. For a moment, only the two of them existed in the universe.

"What are you going to do?" she asked.

"I'll break free of here." He tried to sound reassuring.

Hope and dread colored her expression. "How?"

"There's no time to explain, but you must go back to your room and create a diversion long enough for me to find a way out of here," he said in a rush. The shadow behind the Priestess's window had moved, and he thought he saw a figure.

"What is it?" Pax was alarmed and followed his eyes.

"Duck behind that bush," he whispered, and Pax did as told without question.

A moment later, Prince heard running steps converging toward his corner. "Run," he said to her, hoping she could hear him.

"I love you," Pax's voice came through the greenery.

The bush shook and Prince knew she was on her way. He sighed in relief and focused on what he needed to do. Steps that didn't belong to Pax echoed on the path leading to the Priestess's quarters.

A few seconds later, a far, indistinct shape walked out of the shadows. No more than a moving speck. Prince tensed in anticipation.

"Is there anyone here? Mistress?" a guard called.

Come closer, he thought, readying his arm.

"Mistress?" The guard came into view.

Good. He rejoiced, seeing the petite size of the woman. The rock's sharp edges were cutting into his fisted hand. He steadied his breathing. *We had a baby girl.* He channeled the white, blind rage the words had summoned into something he could use and powered his aim with it. *We had a baby girl.*

"What—?" The guard was hit squarely on her right temple before she could finish the sentence. She fell on the ground, her legs angled toward the cell.

Even better, he thanked the Heavens for the small favor and threw the skipping rope outside, being careful at not touching the bars. After several attempts, the noose he had tied slid around the guard's booted ankle, and he pulled her closer. The woman was slim, but he hadn't eaten in a while, and he struggled to achieve his goal.

He didn't rest until the guard's leg came in contact with the bars. The sizzling sound of the electricity shooting through her twitching body told him she was going to be innocuous for a long while. He looked at the wooden handle he still held tightly and smiled.

Removing the gun from the unconscious guard proved more difficult than he had thought, but in the end, he managed to slide his arm between the bars without electrocuting himself. He had to move the woman's body to position the holster by the cage. His upper body ached with renewed pain at the effort, but time was running out, and he couldn't bother with it. Meanwhile, the rest of the cages had come alive with silent energy. The mute men were looking at him, fear in their constantly pained faces, asking questions he couldn't answer.

"I'll come back for you. I won't forget what happens here," he said to them. "I promise!" Prince saw several eyes trailing between him, still inside his cage, and the guard outside, and he knew his words sounded improbable. "I have help." He showed them the gun. Genuine interest replaced the general apathy in the men's demeanor. The moment didn't last long. Sun shining high on the dome, the constant humming of the electricity abruptly silenced, announcing the women were coming with their trays full of rice porridge.

"I'm going to skip my meal again," Prince grunted between his teeth.

One of the two workers heard him and approached his cage. Her eyes widened in surprise when she saw the unconscious woman on the ground. Her surprise became fear when she saw the gun he was aiming at her.

He brought a finger to his mouth. "Keep quiet."

But the woman didn't. Prince's finger automatically pressed the trigger, thanking Lucas for the time he had spent teaching him how to use a gun back at The City of Men. He wasn't sure where he had hit her, but the guard emitted a choked sound and crumpled close to the cage, not far from the first one. He wasn't happy about it. He would have rather obtained the keys without bloodshed. And a gunshot was loud. He waited for the inevitable.

"Malina? Where are you?" the other woman called.

"Here," Prince answered to bring her closer.

"Malina?" The woman's eyes widened at the sight of the motionless shapes by the cage. Prince lay still. *We had a baby girl.* The woman seemed to take forever to approach the cage. He raised his hand and fired.

"What—?" She looked at him in disbelief, then lowered her eyes to her midsection and brought both hands over a flowering dark stain.

He watched as her eyes rolled back. To him, it seemed to take forever, but eventually she sat by the cage and passed out. Her body was angled toward the bars, and he reached out to search her pockets. It wasn't easy. There wasn't enough space between one bar and the next to maneuver. The woman was close, but not close enough.

"Where are the keys?" Prince heard a commotion coming from the palace and redoubled his efforts. His arms were aching and his hands cramped, making every gesture difficult. He tried to steady his shaking limbs, but his fingers didn't want to cooperate. He wiped his forehead and tried again. And again. Finally, he made contact with the key ring hanging from the woman's belt. Something in his peripheral vision moved. He waited a second too long and the keys slipped from his fingers.

The first worker he had shot, not as unconscious as he had hoped, stirred and looked at him in confusion. "What the—?"

Prince hastily pointed the gun at her head. "Open my cage."

"I—" she started to say.

He lowered his aim and shot at her leg. "Open my cage." Prince's voice was steady as he pointed the gun back at the woman's head. "I won't ask twice."

The woman, whimpering in shock, reached for the key ring on the ground and slowly started to sort the keys, looking for the right one.

"Faster." Prince's finger slightly pressed on the trigger.

The woman fumbled with the keys, but eventually managed to open Prince's cage.

"Bring them inside." He made clear what he wanted her to do by pointing at the unconscious guard and worker lying just outside the cage. The woman complied immediately, dragging the bodies inside. The guard was already stirring.

Prince closed the cage. "Where's the closest exit?"

When the woman hesitated, he used the gun to deliver his request, but missed on purpose.

"A mile north of here you'll find an archway covered in roses…" The woman answered before fainting.

A siren blasted inside the dome, and he knew he had to run. Pax had done her job, but the diversion, whatever it was, wouldn't last forever. The Priestess wasn't an enemy to underestimate. It wasn't going to take long for her to discover their intentions.

Prince ran. Lungs exploding, he ran. Silent eyes followed his escape, and hands rose in salute. Fingers splayed high in the V of victory, and tears carved paths down faces that were finally smiling. Rage propelled Prince's legs when he would have collapsed, struggling for air. Images of a baby girl who would never grow up and mouths that would never talk fueled the hatred burning his heart. He stumbled and fell. Blood stained his frayed pants. Hands and knees on the pebble trail, he felt a vibration that started slowly and gained strength in a matter of seconds. Prince looked up and saw the men stomping their feet in a rhythmic pattern. He stood up, and for a moment, the rest of the world faded to a dim gray, but he put one foot before the other until he was running again.

When he found himself at a crossway between trails, the men indicated him the way, pointing at the right direction. Finally, the archway appeared.

"I'll come back," he said to one of them. The prisoner looked at him with eyes full of hope. "Let the others know."

The man, a mere boy, nodded and smiled.

"Thank you," Prince said to him. He brought his right hand to his heart and bowed to the boy.

"Thank you," he mouthed back and then pointed at the archway.

Prince wanted to say something more, but the men's stomping was quickly overpowered by angry shouting and shooting. The Priestess had figured it out. He went through the archway and found a gate hidden behind thick greenery.

"Let's hope I find the right one...," Prince said out loud, trying to decide which key matched the lock on the gate. The women noisily announced their arrival, silencing the men's attempt at rebellion with brute force.

He imagined the men shot for giving him moral support and his stomach folded in. "I hate you more than anything else in the world. I hate you, Priestess," he cried and went to press one of the keys inside the lock, hoping they were universal keys, when he heard the humming coming back to life. *Not now!* He could feel the electricity buzzing through the metal gate and swore. In his desperation, he would have chanced it and kicked the gate, but someone beat him to it. The gate burst open from the outside and almost hit him. He barely registered his name being shouted before he saw a plank of wood being hastily dropped on the ground. He was grabbed by two strong arms and yanked onto the street.

"Sorry, but you'll have to ride coach," a young woman Prince had never seen before said.

She forcefully rushed him inside the trunk of a car. The gun she pointed at him convinced Prince it was better to follow her suggestion. Everything happened so fast he didn't have time to react. He found himself nested in the warm darkness of the confined space before he remembered he still had a gun clutched in his hand. And he began laughing, a hysteric chuckle that, for a moment, erased any other thought.

"I'm Lexi. Pax's friend. She sent me here to help you." The young woman's voice came muffled through the carpeted wall of the trunk.

At her words, Prince's laugh died in his mouth and he stilled. He swore when the car abruptly swerved and was thrown from one corner to the other, hitting his head against a hard edge.

"Be quiet!" the young woman ordered him, and the car came to a sudden halt. "Don't move. Don't say a word. Don't breathe."

Something in her voice, her pleading tone despite the curtness of her words, made him comply. He heard the car window being lowered and steps getting closer.

The steps paused by the left side. "Mistress." A pause. "How can I help you?"

"I'm Lexi Corellis. I'm here for Pax Layan." The girl's voice was polite, but authoritative.

"We're on lockdown. By the Priestess's orders, nobody goes in or out."

"But the president's daughter just called me. She said she's been cleared by her mother... the president?"

"I need to talk to someone—"

"Oh, here she is. Pax?"

Prince recognized the sound of her gait and his heart jumped in his chest.

"Hi, Lexi. Thanks for coming to pick me up. My mother can't leave now. There's some sort of emergency."

"Mistress Layan, I'm sorry, but I can't let you go. I got precise orders."

"I understand, guard..."

He heard Pax's voice soften and imagined her smiling at the woman.

"Mirelle, Mistress, at your service."

"Thank you, guard Mirelle. My mother has given me permission to leave. She's busy with the Priestess, but I can call her so she can talk to you."

"I'm not sure—" The woman's long pause didn't promise anything good.

He started worrying and thought of using the gun still in his hand, when Lexi intervened. "Pax, I don't think is a good idea interrupting the president while she's with the Priestess. Who knows what kind of emergency they're dealing with. I wouldn't call if it were my own mother!"

"Well, Mirelle needs to be reassured I've been cleared..."

"But you're the president's daughter! I don't think a guard would doubt your word. Right, Mirelle?"

"No, of course not! I would never! It's just that my superior was adamant about guarding this gate. But I guess my orders don't apply to Mistress Layan..."

"Thank you, Mirelle. I'll remember to mention your name to my mother." The slightest tinge of relief colored Pax's voice and he hoped the guard wouldn't notice.

"It's my pleasure to serve the presidential family." The steps resonated at first louder when the woman walked by and then faded as she moved away from the car. Finally, the sound of a gate closing filtered through the trunk of the car.

Prince tried to fill his lungs with air, his heart beating wildly against his chest. After a moment of silence, one of the car doors opened and closed, and then the engine roared to life.

"Where is he?" Pax asked.

"I'm here!"

"There."

Both Prince and Lexi answered at the same time.

"Prince! Hang in there," Pax said, sounding closer to him, and then added, "Lexi, can you drive faster?"

"They can still see me from the Priestess's place. I can't go any faster without attracting attention. Be patient."

"Prince, are you okay?"

"I'm fine. Don't worry." Even through the wall, he could feel the anguish in her voice.

"How long do you think it's going to take the Priestess's guards to realize you just got away?" Lexi asked.

"Not long. I was right there with my mother and the Priestess when the siren gave the alarm."

"So that was the blasted noise I heard over the phone."

"Yes..." Pax's voice trailed off for a moment. "What is *that*?"

"It's a toy gun. What do you think it is?" Lexi laughed and then added, "I didn't know how he would react and there was no time for explanations."

Pax made a comment Prince couldn't hear. He had so many questions to ask and just listening to the back and forth between Pax and her friend wasn't enough. He felt the car slowing down.

"Okay, I guess going fast isn't an option anymore," Lexi said.

"What's happening?" Prince couldn't help but intervene in the conversation.

"The streets are crowded with the Priestess's guards," Pax answered him.

"News of his escape must be already out. The Priestess doesn't waste time," Lexi commented.

A few minutes later, Prince heard Pax and Lexi talking, but they kept their voices low and he couldn't hear what they were saying. The tone was agitated, though, and when the car stopped, one of the two swore out loud.

"Okay, stay calm and let me talk," Lexi said.

He didn't think she sounded like the one who should be in charge.

"Prince, please, don't make a sound," Pax pleaded.

From the panic in her voice, he realized why Lexi had wanted to take the reins of the situation.

"Everything's going to be okay." He couldn't yell, but hoped his words had reached her.

The pattern of sounds from the previous stop repeated almost perfectly. The window rolled down. Someone walked by the car and paused at the driver side.

"Where are you going?" an authoritative voice asked.

"Good morning, officer. I'm escorting the president's daughter to her marine residence."

He held his breath, but Lexi managed to talk slow.

"Good morning, Mistress Layan. Ginecea is closed until further notice. President's orders."

Prince cursed under his breath. This woman wasn't going to be easily played.

"But I'm going to visit my grandmother," Pax said.

Her voice portrayed the right combination of pure breed haughtiness and boredom. He was proud of her.

"I'm sorry, Mistress, but the President herself called to dispatch the order."

He could easily imagine the woman unapologetically shaking her head.

"My mother knows where I'm going. She told me to check on her mother since she's too busy to go." Pax tried once more.

"I can't let you go."

"But—" Lexi tried to intervene, but she was cut off by a ringtone.

"Wait a moment." The officer spoke at length with someone on the phone and then addressed Lexi.

"The president is looking for her daughter."

The officer's voice had a tone Prince didn't like. He hoped Pax wouldn't lose her head.

"I'll personally escort you back to Layan Mansion, Mistress, so your mother doesn't worry about you," the woman said with a final tone.

"I'll follow you." Lexi sounded resigned.

"You better," the officer cautioned.

A moment later, when the car was already in motion, Lexi commented, loud enough for Prince to hear, "We're screwed. What are we going to do now?"

Prince heard some commotion taking place inside the car. Lexi swore.

"Exactly what the good officer said," Pax whispered close to Prince. She sat in the back now, only inches from him.

"What?"

"We're going to Layan Mansion."

"Have you lost your mind?" Lexi asked and the car swerved.

"Careful!" Prince cried, trying to brace his body from hitting anything sharp.

"Yes, careful, Lexi. We don't want to attract unwanted attention, remember?" Pax sounded too composed, given the situation. She had gone from agitated to preternaturally calm in the span of a few sentences. She must be thinking of something.

Prince hoped against hope she was, because he was of Lexi's same mind, but refrained from voicing his thoughts. Having a conversation through the padded walls was difficult at best. With Lexi's nervous hand at the wheel, it was proving impossible.

"Ten minutes and we're home, my love," Pax's voice resonated even closer.

He looked up, following the sound of her voice, and saw her eyes peeking through a slit between the seat and the rear deck. "Home?"

"Pax, sit down and look ahead. The blasted woman is looking at you," Lexi called, a worried note in her voice.

Pax slid a finger down the slit and Prince took it, as if it were a lifeline.

"Don't push our luck," Lexi admonished her.

"The guard isn't following us that close. She can't see what I'm doing from there."

Prince savored the moment, closing his eyes and focusing on the texture of her skin, but the car slowed down and Pax wiggled her finger to let him know that something was happening.

"Get to the front seat, now. We're almost arrived."

Pax squeezed his finger and then left. He heard her moving to the front of the car. He left his hand stretched out, missing that small contact already.

"Lexi, act calm." The situation reversed, Pax instructed her friend.

"Easy for you to say." Lexi stopped the car.

Prince heard the sound of the window getting rolled down again.

"Thank you, officer. We'll go to the back entry now."

He admired the steadiness in Pax's voice, but wondered at her plan.

"Just a moment. I have radioed the presidential guard. They're coming to escort you inside as we speak."

"How prompt," Pax commented.

This time Prince could hear Pax's teeth clenching at the news.

"Here they are. Mistress Layan, have a nice day."

"You too, officer."

Prince endured the nerve-racking moment while other useless greetings were exchanged between Lexi, Pax, and several women who sounded concerned about the president's daughter's safety.

"Lexi is my guest, and she's coming with me," Pax stated when someone suggested to send her friend back.

"But we don't have Mistress Corellis on the guests list for today."

"Talk to Anna, then. She'll approve it."

Prince was sweating copiously and his own smell was nauseating him. A few minutes later, after a back and forth conversation between the guards and an annoyed woman who was answering only with yes and no, a verdict was reached.

"Very well, your friend has been cleared to visit. Mistress, follow us inside the garage, please," one of the guards said with clear censure in her tone.

Prince endured the last minutes of the car ride, wishing he could breathe fresh air before throwing up and giving his presence away. His stomach almost betrayed him, when Pax, perfectly on cue, told him to have faith that everything was going as planned. Despite his predicament, he smiled at her words and forced his body to behave.

"We got the welcome committee," Lexi said.

"Of course she's here…" Pax's tone was full of venom. "Prince, I'll be right back."

He heard both the driver's and the passenger's doors open and close.

"Anna, what an honor. You didn't have to leave the office for me. I know my way around the house." Pax's voice came from outside, but close to the trunk.

"Always a pleasure to interrupt my day for you, Pax," a woman answered.

Even in his distressed state, Prince heard the tangible tension between Pax and the woman.

"I only wanted to be sure you were okay. Your mother's been worried since you left the Priestess's place."

"You mean the garden of horrors?"

"I didn't like what I saw there, either… but you shouldn't have left the way you did."

"I couldn't stand it any longer and I called Lexi to pick me up."

"I understand it was stressful for you, but I had to pull all my strings to get you out of this one with the Priestess. Your sudden departure raised questions."

"And why is that?"

Prince had to give Pax credit. She sounded innocent.

"*He* escaped from the Priestess's place."

Pax's answer was immediate. "Good. I hope you never catch him."

"Do you happen to know anything about it?" Anna's voice was soft, but it was clear she suspected Pax of something.

"I'm here. Rest assured, if I knew where he was, I'd be with him, not talking to you."

Anna issued an audible sigh. "Pax, I'm not the enemy."

"I don't know why I tend to forget."

Prince had never heard her treat anybody the way she was treating the woman.

"I hope, one day, we'll mend this ridge…"

"I'm tired. If you don't mind, I'd like to rest."

"Sure. I'll check on you later."

"Don't bother."

"Pax…"Another loud sigh followed and then Anna said, "Lexi, it's always nice to see you."

"See you later, Anna. And thanks for letting me stay."

"I know Pax needs you. We'll talk." Clipped steps echoed in the silence and then dimmed to nothing.

"You shouldn't talk to her like that," Lexi said a moment later.

"You weren't there. She never raised one finger to make my mother see reason," an angry Pax replied. Then her voice softened and she whispered, "My love, hang in there a few minutes more and I'll let you out."

"I need fresh air." Prince was on the verge of fainting.

A cooler breeze swept through the trunk as Pax opened a crack. He gulped down air, feeling his mind clearing right away.

"Oh my, it stinks in there!" Lexi coughed out loud.

"My apologies, Mistress, I didn't have time to shower," Prince called out, unable to let it pass.

"We need Celeste," Pax said, ignoring the bantering.

"For?" Lexi asked.

"A change of clothes for a tall woman. Prince, I'll be back in a second."

Nothing happened for several minutes, and Prince ended up dozing off. He was startled by the trunk being opened completely.

"My Heavens! What happened to you?" Celeste came into view with a worried face and one hand covering her nose.

"Nice to see you, Celeste." Prince tried to smile at her, but his effort turned into a grimace when, raising his head higher than his shoulders, he saw black dots swimming before his eyes.

"Easy, my love," Pax said, her lips gently touching his forehead.

Prince felt two sets of hands helping him up and then lowering his legs out of the trunk.

"Just cover him with the blanket. We don't have time to fully change him. We can't stay here much longer," Lexi said.

Prince let the women drape a heavy, dark cloth around him and then followed them on unsteady legs.

"Faster," Lexi pleaded, several steps ahead, keeping a door opened for them.

Pax pulled him through the door when a voice resonated in the garage.

"Mistress? Is everything okay?" a woman called, voice coming from a distance.

"Yes, Floria. We were just talking. Thank you," Pax responded immediately and closed the door behind her. A long, well-lit hallway stretched ahead of them, containers full of clothes and recycling bins at regular intervals. "We're safe now." She looked at Prince and embraced him.

"Pax, I really need a shower." Prince wanted to take her in his arms more than everything else in the world, but he was conscious of the horrible spectacle he presented. He felt as if he were withering a beautiful flower with his filth.

"I don't care." Pax kissed him before he could move.

Prince was swept away by her mouth seeking him and simply gave in to the whirlwind of emotions taking hold of his mind. He forgot about the way he looked and smelled and felt only her skin getting closer and melting to his. His arms went around her, encasing her slim frame as he had done so many times, and kissed her back until she was breathing through his lungs.

"Ahem…"

The soft coughing was repeated several times before Prince realized what it was for, and then he wished both Celeste and Lexi somewhere else.

"You need to take a shower," Lexi said, face a bright shade of red, her eyes focused on the point of her shoes.

"You can use my bathroom," an equally flustered Celeste proposed.

Prince looked at Pax, both smiling at the same time, and said, "Yes, please."

CHAPTER 9

The warm water hit Prince's skin. He raised his face and let the steady jet wash away his shame. Gentle fingers caressed him while applying scented soap. Pax cleaned his body and kissed his skin while whispering loving words. When she had applied foam to every inch of him, she leaned on his chest and rested silently, caressing his back and soothing his sore muscles.

"I thought I was going insane without you," Prince whispered to her. He kissed her head and hugged her close. It always surprised him how they were shaped to match perfectly. Their bodies felt whole when together.

"I did." Pax's hands came together on his chest, and she placed them over his heart. "When Lauren tortured you, I went crazy. I wanted to kill them with my bare hands. And yesterday, when I saw you in that cage, trapped like an animal, I lost my mind. I guess the electric shock was a blessing."

"I'll make them pay. I promised you." Prince covered her hands with his. "Look at me, my love." He kissed her tears slowly. "Feel my heart," he said, gently pressing her hands with his.

"Every night I dreamed of listening to your voice telling me how beautiful I was. I dreamed of sleeping in your arms. And then I woke up." Pax left a trail of small kisses along his body, starting with his lips, moving to his jaw, the point of his ear, and then down his throat.

Prince shivered, and his hands left hers to caress her body. She was still soft, even after having lost so much weight, and her skin was reacting to his fingers. He reached down to her belly, and she, unexpectedly, moved away from his touch.

"Let me," he said without giving her an option. He gently probed, his fingers finding a ridge that wasn't there before. "What is this?"

Pax covered it with her hands. "Doctor Linda cut me to get the baby out. She told me our daughter was suffering, was too small to make it alone, and I wasn't strong enough to deliver naturally."

Prince knelt before her and let the water wash away the pain coming through his eyes. He kissed the scar, feeling the roughness marring her skin, without saying anything.

"When I came to from the anesthesia and my mother told me the baby had died, I didn't want to believe it. It was too painful to remain awake. Only the thought of you kept me alive."

"You shouldn't have been alone when we lost our baby. I should've been with you."

They stayed like that, mourning together, until a timid knock on the bathroom door intruded on their private pain. When they emerged, a warm meal waited for them on the table dominating the studio. Celeste had already left, and a note by the tray said she'd come back the next day.

Prince gulped down the food and mentally thanked Celeste.

"You're going to make yourself sick. Slow down," Pax said with affection, putting a hand on his arm.

"If you take care of me, I don't mind. You were a great nurse last time." Prince bent to kiss her. "I got to spend the night with you, remember? It was the first time we slept together." He had been caught in Sundial's main wing—looking for her—and punished for it, which had resulted in him being exactly where he wanted to be, in the infirmary conveniently located closer to the women's sleeping quarters. Escaping Linda's watch had proved simple. Running undetected through Sundial's maze was slightly more complicated.

"I was so scared you were going to die on me. And for giving you a piece of meat." Pax laughed softly.

"I was nervous that night." If he closed his eyes, he could still feel the exhaustion that had governed his acts and the dizziness caused from being in her presence. After having daydreamed of a moment alone with her, he was terrified when it finally happened.

"Why?"

"Because I couldn't stop thinking of you and worried you'd be disgusted by me."

"Weren't you worried I'd rat you out?"

"I didn't care about that. I only wanted to spend time with you. I got in trouble several times because I was found where I didn't belong." He reached for her hand on the table and brought it to his lips for a peck.

She tilted her head and smiled. "Did I tell you that at the farm I looked for you everywhere? I even asked to be moved from the recreation facility to the nursery to see you."

"That's why I couldn't find you! It took me several days to track you down." Prince laughed at the thought of them chasing each other around. "I kept checking for you at the swimming pool until I was caught red-handed."

"I think I fell in love with you that very first day at the farm. I couldn't know it then, but it was love at first sight." Pax got out of her chair to sit on his lap.

"I was a monstrosity. There wasn't a single inch of my skin visible under the bruises." He stroked her cheek.

"You looked at me." Pax got sidetracked by a slow kiss.

"I looked at you," he teased her, lowering his kisses down her throat.

"I have dreamed about your eyes ever since." Pax shivered and trailed her fingers across his chest.

"What about my eyes?"

"I love them."

"Good." Prince gently pulled her up and looked at the narrow bed across the room.

"Please," Pax said with the softest of whispers.

Their first rejoicing was quick and born out of love, sadness, and a multitude of feelings too complicated to explain. Prince fell asleep in Pax's arms, still inside her.

* * *

"My love, you're smiling." Pax's voice welcomed him back.

"Pax of mine," he answered, playing with the meaning of her name. He had dreamed of cradling a small girl in his arms, but didn't want to tell her.

"Are you hungry?" Pax showed him the new tray lying on the table. "Celeste just left it outside the door."

But he didn't care about eating, not right away. He only cared that Celeste had the good sense to stay away a while longer. "Come here."

Pax looked at him, her lips curved in a smile. Then she plucked several grapes from a deep dish, placed one between her lips, and approached him in bed.

Prince took the grape from her mouth and bit her lips playfully. "I need you, now."

Pax kept feeding him from her mouth, and when the last grape disappeared beyond his teeth, she started caressing him while he removed her clothes with renewed anticipation.

He tried to take his time the second time around, but a nervous intensity governed his movements. "I can't get enough of you. I can never have enough of you. I need you more than food and water."

She moaned in consent, and he was glad she could understand his necessity to be whole with her.

"It was torture to think of you, knowing I couldn't touch you," he whispered to her breast, kissing the nipple with the lightest of touches and enjoying feeling her labored breathing. He could barely think of what to do next. His hands traveled up and down her body, resting a moment longer where she was more sensitive and then starting again in a feverish frenzy. He turned her around to look at the rest of her body.

"I could sit here for hours admiring the way the light hits the length of your legs, and especially here..." His voice trailed when his fingers reached her softest spot, and she shivered. "Like the dunes of the desert."

Prince forgot his good intentions of going slow. "You're too beautiful," he said by way of explanation and gently joined their bodies with a sigh. He entwined his hands with hers while kissing between her shoulder blades.

"I love you," Pax said, head tilted sideways, her mouth seeking his.

Celeste gave them all the time they needed, and when she knocked on the door, Prince felt particularly thankful to her.

"Care for some news from the outside world?" Celeste timidly entered, but rested her back on the closed door, not daring to come closer.

"Yes, please." Prince smiled and showed Celeste the empty chair.

The girl didn't move. She struggled to look at them. Prince realized he was only wearing his pants, and that Pax looked disheveled, her hair sticking up everywhere and her shirt buttoned up at the wrong places.

"Well?" Pax raised an eyebrow, oblivious to Celeste's embarrassment.

"Well, it seems that the only safe place for you in Ginecea is Layan Mansion," Celeste answered.

"Is it that bad outside?" Prince asked.

"You have no idea." Celeste sighed. "Even pure breeds are being stopped and questioned. The city has broken out in pure madness. Outside is a nightmare. Farms and factories are being searched as we speak. Men are tortured on mere suspicion they know anything about you. Fathered women are being detained for the same reason."

"The Priestess must be mad," Pax commented, reaching Prince's hand under the table.

"She's out of control. I heard her own guards complaining when they thought nobody was listening." For a second, Celeste's eyes went to Pax and Prince's intertwined hands, longing showing in her faraway expression.

Prince felt sympathetic to the girl's reaction and released Pax's fingers. "Let's hope she loses her control completely."

"Where did you spend the night?" he asked as an afterthought.

"I slept in Pax's bed, alongside Lexi's in the library. Her empty bed wasn't going to pass unnoticed," Celeste explained. "No, nobody realized the body under the blanket wasn't yours," she added when Pax raised her brows once again. "You're supposed to have breakfast with your mother and the Priestess."

"She's here?" Pax raised her voice and then slapped her hand over her mouth.

"She came first thing this morning and asked for you. Anna's keeping her at bay, but I don't think she can hold the fort much longer," Celeste said with an audible sigh.

"I don't want to have to endure her presence." Pax looked for Prince's hand again and tightened her fingers around his.

"You should probably go. Don't make her wait. I'm afraid even your mother's power would prove useless if you keep angering the Priestess," Prince whispered to Pax.

"Just her physical presence makes my skin crawl. I feel sick talking to her." Pax locked eyes with him.

"I'll be here waiting for you to come back. Don't worry." Prince caressed Pax's face and kissed her lips. "You mustn't give her any reason to suspect of you."

"He's right. The Priestess is in a foul mood." Celeste put a hand on the doorknob.

"Go." Prince gently pushed Pax out of the chair. He watched her straighten her clothes, then exit the room, escorted by a nervous Celeste, and found himself alone and with time to waste.

Later, when the knock on the door intruded on his thoughts, he knew it was too soon for Pax to come back, and didn't dare asking who it was.

"Open the door. We know you're there." The knocking continued.

Prince grabbed a knife from the kitchen and glanced at the only window in the room. He swore under his breath when he realized there was no way out. The window opened on an inner courtyard.

"Open the door." The voice trickled through, muffled by the walls.

Something about the way the woman spoke made Prince uncomfortable.

"We could blast this damned door to pieces, but you don't want to attract attention. Am I right?" the woman reasoned.

Prince shivered at her words, but answering still didn't seem to be a good idea.

"You leave us no choice." A loud but short noise followed the words.

"I can't believe you had the audacity to hide here," Anna, President Layan's factotum, greeted a bewildered Prince, once the door was successfully relocated from its hinges. A small army of four of the Priestess's guards followed her inside.

"I live to impress you." Prince couldn't help but answer. His first reaction to a woman's presence never changed. He had learned to never show how scared he was. And, at the moment, terror flooded him.

"Do you also care to keep on living to impress Pax?" Anna asked.

Prince didn't deign the woman with an answer. He leaned on the kitchen sink, relaxing his stance, wondering about her choice of words.

"I hope you're going to follow us without problems." Anna sighed, confusing Prince more. "We don't have time for pleasantries, and I'm not going to beg you. Are you coming of your own volition or do you need to be convinced?"

"Why should I go anywhere with you?" Prince decided to humor the woman.

"Because Pax is going to pay for your foolishness if you don't."

Prince tried to decide what to do, when Anna covered the distance between them in the blink of an eye and stood to face him at a rather uncomfortable proximity.

"Don't think for a second I like it," Anna whispered when he automatically moved away from her. She cornered him against the wall, and one of the guards promptly pointed a gun at his head. "You could die this moment and I couldn't care less what happened to your rotting corpse, but Pax is another story."

"Stop talking about Pax," Prince spat.

The guard pressed her gun against his temple without saying a word.

The ringtone of a cell phone went off, and Anna brought a finger to her mouth as a general warning. "Yes?" she answered after drawing a slow breath. "No, we haven't found anything. The servant was mistaken... I know. Everybody's on edge these days."

Prince saw the guards looking at each other and then at Anna.

"I've just bought you time. Don't squander it." Anna turned to stare Prince in the eyes.

Prince silently nodded, although he still wasn't sure what to think.

"Put those on and don't make a noise," Anna ordered him, while one of the guards threw a bundle on the bed.

Prince walked to it, relieved to be at a safe distance from the women, donned a long tunic over his clothes, and waited for Anna.

"Grab the laundry basket and stay one step behind us," she said.

The guard who was still aiming the gun at his head lowered it and put it back in its holster, and then much to Prince's surprise, she said, "Right after me," without sounding insulting.

"Would you mind?" Anna asked as he hesitated a moment.

Prince moved along in line behind Anna and two of the guards at the front. The other two guards closed the procession. The women made a show of making small talk and laughing. They walked unhurriedly through the hallway. Prince saw servants walking by; some of them greeted Anna with obsequious words, but mostly, they lowered their heads in silent bows. Anna's presence and the Priestess's guards cleared the path until they reached a big hall with a double staircase.

"Mistress's room needs a new change of linens. Escort the new servant to the bedroom," Anna told the guard in front of Prince and left them at the base of the staircase, where she went right, and the guard diverted him to the left.

Prince's breath froze in his chest when he heard Pax's voice resonating in the air.

"*You*! I've been looking for you. You can't force me to stay in this house. I want to go to the coast. Ginecea is oppressive these days." Pax stalked down the opposite flight of stairs, followed by Lexi, when she saw Anna going up. The president and the Priestess trailed a few steps behind.

"I wasn't looking for *you*. What do you want, now?" Anna stopped and addressed Pax, her tone soft despite the harsh words.

"*Madame President* just told me that *you* think it's not a good idea for me to go to my grandmother's house."

Maurice Layan made a comment at her daughter's use of her title, and Pax angrily turned around to look at her. The Priestess scolded Pax. Prince waited for the retort to come, but fortunately, Pax ignored the woman.

"Pax, try to calm down," Lexi suggested loud enough for Prince to hear it from the other side of the staircase.

"Is it true?" Pax went down three steps to stop before Anna. Lexi shadowed her immediately, taking hold of her friend's arm.

"Of course it's true. Ginecea's under attack, and the safest place to be is Layan Mansion," Anna said and, for a moment, directed her eyes toward the other end of the staircase where Prince and the four guards were waiting.

"Kids these days don't know how to behave, and that's the parents' fault, I'm afraid. As the President of Ginecea, you should be an example, but..." The Priestess tsked and put a hand on Maurice's shoulder in a mockery of a maternal gesture.

Prince watched the whole exchange, unable to think. He still didn't understand Anna's angle, but he was sure the woman didn't want to hurt Pax. Revealing himself before the Priestess would do more damage to her than him. He'd almost reached the last step before the landing when Pax, following Anna's silent suggestion, looked in his direction and recognized him under the servant's clothes. Her eyes widened for a second and then she focused her attention on Anna again.

"So you're saying I'm stuck here with nowhere to go?" Pax's voice was angry, but steady.

"Yes, that's exactly what it means. As of this morning, I've given orders to close the schools all over Ginecea," Maurice Layan answered instead of Anna and then added, "Not only in Ginecea City."

"You must be kidding me..."

Prince didn't hear the rest of the exchange. The guard behind him hissed a, "Move, don't linger on the stairs," accompanied by a nudge of the gun against his right kidney, convincing him to obey the order.

He heard Pax raising her voice, and both her mother and Anna answering that she couldn't talk like that to an adult, but he couldn't turn around to see how she fared.

"Stay here until Anna comes back," the guard said, pushing him inside a room at the far end of the hallway.

Prince heard the door closing behind him and, for the hundredth time, wondered what was going on.

He looked around and saw he was in a bedroom. The dim light coming through the heavy drapery revealed a big bed and the pastel tones dominating the place. From the walls to the ceiling, everything was either a shade of pink or ivory, down to the accents. Breathing in and out to collect his thoughts, he went to sit on the small couch, this one pink-and-ivory striped. Then, between one deep breath and the next, his eyes lingered on a framed picture sitting on the desk. He recognized Pax immediately. A younger version of her lithe self caught jumping midair, a big smile on her face. Other pictures framed joyous moments in Pax's youth. He closed his eyes, head resting in his hands.

"Have you figured things out already?" Anna appeared from a lateral door. "The damage you've done? The foolishness of getting involved with Pax Layan?" She closed the door behind her. "The Priestess won't rest until she finds a way to make Pax pay for every slight she has committed against the women's sacred way of life."

Prince raised his head and wondered how he had let his guard down.

"This room is connected to my wing. Pax's ancestors, obsessed with safety, built Layan Mansion with several hidden passages," she said, answering his silent question.

"What do you want from me?" He felt tired.

"I already told you." Anna's movements betrayed her nervousness. She paced from the door to the couch, but she didn't sit. Instead, she turned and picked up one of the pictures, a faded image, framed in battered wooden filigree. "I used to spend lots of time with her. She was the sweetest child." She caressed the glass protecting the picture with her fingers and put it back on the desk. "For the longest time, I thought I didn't a need a girl of my own as long as I had her."

He fought his instinct to run toward the door, knowing it wouldn't do him any good, and hoped she wouldn't come closer again.

"I don't think I'll be ever able to accept you, but help me save her life and I won't hate you." Anna closed the gap between them and leaned to stare into his eyes. "From now on, follow my orders and don't get any ideas. That's what I want from you."

"I don't trust you."

"And, I don't trust *you*. But it doesn't matter at the moment. You can choose between coming with me and getting thrown in confinement. I'll do anything in my power to see that she's safe." Anna didn't blink. She straightened her back, moved aside, and opened the lateral door, leaving it ajar for him. "Shall we?"

Prince gave a last look at Pax's room and made his decision.

"Good thinking," she said and led him into the dark hallway.

Prince let the woman's comment go. "Where are we going?"

"Where I can hide you without fear of you getting caught by overzealous servants."

"And where is this safe haven?"

"Unfortunately for me, my apartments, where I keep the surveillance monitors for the whole house. Safest place if you want to hide someone."

"Are you going to tell Pax where am I?"

"I'm still debating that. It would be safer for her if she didn't know, but she has shown no regard for her life where you're concerned. I'm worried she'll do something stupid to find you."

They walked for a good five minutes, up and down stairs that seemed to go nowhere, until light from outside lit the hallway.

"Pax's great-grandmother, Rosie's mother, Darya, added a new wing between floors. Nobody comes here. That's why I asked to have this side of the building." Anna paused before a door, knocked three times, and then turned toward Prince. "There's someone eager to see you."

He opened his mouth to ask what she meant when the door opened and a familiar face appeared. "Well, this is a surprise."

124

"I must admit I couldn't believe my eyes when I saw you on the screen, sneaking around dressed as a maid." Lucas, a smile on his face, hugged him.

Prince didn't know if he wanted to laugh or cry. "Where've you been? What happened to you? You left me stranded in the desert with an army of desperates. How could you?"

"I didn't plan it—"

"This isn't the time for a chat. You'll have time to catch up later. Now, I need to explain a few things." Anna directed Prince toward the center of a big room and made him sit at a table. "I must count on your word. I can't redirect pure breeds to guard you without raising suspicions. Maurice isn't the same as she was before Claudine's death, but she isn't stupid. She'll notice anything out of the ordinary. She knows who works for her and in what position."

"I won't try to escape. Is that what you want to hear?" Prince asked.

"He isn't going anywhere without Pax. I assure you," Lucas confirmed.

"I hope you're right and I haven't misjudged you." Anna talked to Lucas, but her eyes were on Prince.

"I think I proved it to you in all these months spent here as your prisoner, haven't I?" Lucas asked the woman.

"Well, it was in your best interest—"

"And I'll be forever grateful."

Prince listened to the exchange without understanding what they were talking about.

"Anyway, stay put. I'll provide three meals every day and the promise that the Priestess won't find you. Are we fine?"

"We're perfectly fine." Lucas looked at Prince, who slightly nodded.

"I'll leave you to your chat, then. Don't try to contact me. I'll come back at regular intervals and brief you on what's happening out there. Lucas, you can explain the rest."

"Will do," Lucas said, sitting at the table.

Anna left, and Prince stared at the closed door for a few seconds before blinking. "Start talking, please."

Chapter 10

"Come sit." Lucas gestured toward a table in the middle of the spacious room composing the atrium of Anna's apartment. He took out a black, Spartan-looking chair—echoing in the clean form the spirit of the rest of the furnishing—and patted the seat for him. "The short of it is that I needed help, and Anna delivered it." He looked tired, and his fingers tapped the black table without rhythm.

"And the long of it?"

"We were ambushed in the desert and I almost lost Cordelia."

"Where is she?" He had almost expected to see her coming out from one of the doors opening into the room.

"Anna took her to a hospital that accepts fathered women. She presented Cordelia as one of her own maids and no questions were asked."

"What happened to her?"

"She was run over in the melee. I found her bleeding and unconscious. I'd have made a pact with the Priestess herself given the choice. I was lucky I got Anna instead."

"How did it happen? How she ended up there?"

"She was sent by the president to help the Priestess locate the fugitives. Maurice Layan wants us dead, and she trusts her secretary to obey her orders."

"What's the deal with Anna? I don't understand."

Lucas rested his chin on his steepled hands. "Anna's a reasonable woman, and she's realized the Priestess is pushing Ginecea to the brink of a revolution."

"She doesn't seem to like me."

"She doesn't like to see Pax suffering."

Prince shrugged. "Can we trust her?"

"I don't know her that well, but she saved Cordelia's life. And as I said, I'm forever indebted to her." Lucas paused, his eyes unfocused for a moment.

"I don't like it."

"Me neither, but I didn't have a choice. You'd have done the same if Pax were dying."

Prince shook the thought from his head. Images of her giving birth alone kept coming back. His hands balled up in two fists under the table. "When were you ambushed?" He needed to change topic.

"It happened the same day we left. We were scouting a stretch of desert that seemed promising for camping. It had several shallow canyons we could've used to hide during the day. I remember thinking we'd found the perfect place to let the kids and the elderly get a break. I went to take a closer look at a series of boulders that impeded clear sight of the northern side, and I left Cordelia behind for a moment. It was careless of me, and I'll never forgive myself for being so stupid. The noise still echoes inside my ears—engine roars and screams. The dust covered everything in a brown cloud. I couldn't see what was happening, and it was so fast…"

Prince laid a hand on Lucas's arm. "You couldn't have known."

"I should have. I heard one of the men who had accompanied me cry, and then another… By the time the screams stopped, I had barely moved a step and it was already too late for them. "

"We weren't equipped to withstand the Priestess's Army. They're organized, prepared, well-fed. We're nothing but a bunch of ex-slaves…"

"Still, I don't feel better knowing that." Lucas's hand went to massage his right arm. "Those deaths are on me—"

"What happened to you?"

"This is nothing. As soon as the sand settled down, I went looking for Cordelia, walking by the bodies covered in brown sand, and found her trapped under a car. I didn't know if she was still alive, but I didn't think. I moved her or the car—I don't know what I did, but I didn't stop until she was in my arms. And then I heard a woman ordering me to surrender or she'd shoot me. I begged her to save Cordelia. She could shoot me if she wanted, but she had to save one of her race."

"Was it Anna?"

"Yes, it was Anna. She commanded the guards to lower their weapons and checked on Cordelia. Not even half an hour later, I was strapped to the rear seat of Anna's car, Cordelia nested between cushions beside me. It was a long ride, and Anna insisted on driving, herself, commanding the rest of the Priestess's women back to Ginecea on their own."

"Why?"

"I was too dazed to notice how unusual the whole situation was, but I realized later that Anna wanted to talk to me without others listening."

"She wanted to know about the fugitives." Prince couldn't help saying it.

"Yes, among other things."

"What other things?"

"Again, at the time I wasn't questioning her reasons, but she had lots of questions about the women living in the City of Men. She wanted to know if we kept them captive and seemed surprised when I told her they stayed there on their own free will."

"You didn't say anything about the Caves, right?"

"No, of course not. I wouldn't betray the Priest. But, she never asked me about him anyway. She wanted to know about Rosie Layan, and when I answered that I didn't have a clue, she went back to the former subject. I don't think she believed me, but she was more interested in knowing why women would want to live in a man's world. She drilled me for hours about daily life in the desert. I told her only what she could've learned on her own and prayed it was enough to make her happy.

"Meanwhile, Cordelia's breathing had become shallow and I couldn't wake her up. Anna drove to Ginecea's outskirts, then told me to lie on the car's floor and wait. I looked as she dragged Cordelia out, leaving a trail of blood. I stayed inside that car for hours, thinking and praying to God, while swearing all along. When she came back without Cordelia, she only said, 'You're dead. I killed you when you attacked the fathered woman I was transporting in the car.' I only wanted to know if Cordelia was alive. I didn't care about anything else and I told her. 'She's going to be fine, but she won't leave the hospital for a very long time. You owe me,' she answered. I knew that."

"And then? Did she bring you here?"

"Yes, Anna explained what she expected from me, and I agreed. She wouldn't turn me over to the authorities if I agreed to give her more information about the estranged fathered women. She seemed obsessed with the subject, but it worked out fine for me. I thought that once we reached Ginecea, she'd toss me to the wolves, but I was still useful for something."

"You've been here the whole time? Doing what?" Prince lay back on the chair to take a look around.

"Satisfying Anna's curiosity for the most part."

"I don't understand. Why didn't you try to escape? If I were you, I'd already found a way out of this prison. There is nothing you can do for Cordelia from here."

"I'm not as young as you anymore, and I see things differently. And as far as Cordelia and I are concerned, we've learned a long time ago to put the greater good before us. I can't hold her hand while she's recovering, but there's a lot I can do for our cause from *here*, where I can gather invaluable information impossible to find anywhere else." Lucas stood up and told Prince to follow him into the next room. "Take a look," he said, pointing at a series of screens anchored to the wall. "Do you know what they are?"

"I've seen a room like this at Sundial. The guards called it the monitor room." Prince's escapades had given him knowledge other men didn't have. "How come there're no locks?" He had spent the better part of one night, several years ago, prying the lock open to take a peek at what lay behind a similar closed door.

"This is Anna's apartment. She's the only one who can access the surveillance room."

"She doesn't mind that you snoop about?" Prince could hardly believe that.

"She lets me use the whole apartment, no restrictions. I can also watch TV."

Prince took a better look at the monitors and saw that one streamed images of a room full of books. Pax was there with Lexi, sitting on a bed by the window, and Lexi was counseling her.

"Don't." Lucas took Prince by the elbow, making him turn around. "I know what you're thinking, but it isn't worth it. She's safer if you stay out of the picture, at least for now."

"I wasn't thinking—"

"Of course you were. Leaving this apartment to be with her is not an option. The Priestess is here every day. Sometimes she arrives unannounced and stays for hours. And her guards skulk around the whole time. Her Holiness's constant presence is why Anna is rarely in her apartment, and when she is, it's already late at night."

"But—"

"If the guards aren't enough to deter you, you better know that they aren't the only ones checking the perimeter. The moment you lay one foot outside the door, the Priestess's hounds are going to sniff your scent."

"Hounds?"

"Yes, four-legged, scary hounds. It's a recent addition. From what Anna has said, the president doesn't seem to be pleased by those creatures patrolling her house, but the Priestess has insisted."

"No going out, then..." Prince laid one hand on the monitor pointing at Pax. "But why does the Priestess think Maurice Layan needs such a level of protection?"

Lucas shook his head. "I don't know."

Prince's eyes went to one of the monitors where he saw Pax sitting on a small bed and Lexi holding her hands. "Do you mind giving me a moment?"

"Sure thing. We'll talk later."

"Of course." Prince didn't move for several minutes, staring at the colored wall of images without thinking. "How are we going to come out of this?" he asked the monitor. There was no audio, and he didn't want to call Lucas to fix that, so he stood there looking at Pax crying on Lexi's shoulder. "What are we going to do?"

Later, when he realized he had been staring at an empty room for a while, Prince went looking for Lucas. He found the man sitting on a low couch, reading a worn-looking book.

"Enlightened?" Lucas asked.

"What am I going to do?"

"You, by yourself, nothing. *We* prepare."

"Man, please. I'm in no mood for riddles. My head's already hurting."

"Come here. I'll show you how to watch the news on the TV." Lucas put the book down by his side and turned on the monitor resting on the opposite coffee table.

"I know how it works." Prince sat at the other of the couch and stretched his legs.

"You must've had an interesting life at Sundial," Lucas commented. "Here it is."

Prince looked at the screen changing from one serene scene depicting pastures and distant water to a violent war zone. Sounds accompanied the images. "What is it?"

"This is Ginecea, or better said, this is what's happening to Ginecea."

"Those women are dying."

"The Priestess has started targeting fathered women's villages she believes are favorable to the cause."

"What cause?"

"It turns out the City of Men wasn't the only place where fathered women escaped to live a different life. The Priestess's Army found dozens of villages where women were aiding escaped workers. We're talking about the poorest among the poor, women who had nothing to lose, whose social status was barely above the men."

"But I thought the fathered women were all treated the same way."

Lucas shook his head. "The last three presidents, helped by this Priestess—"

"Can't believe so much power is given to one woman. Priestesshood shouldn't be for life. Priestesses should be elected as presidents are. Not that it would make any difference for us, but still."

"I agree on both counts. Nobody should be able to hold an office for so long, and it wouldn't change our situation." Lucas caressed his chin. "Anyway, what was I saying?"

"The last three presidents, helped by the Priestess…"

"Yes, they have done their best to create differences among the fathered women. The ones who serve pure breeds are in the higher caste. At the bottom there are the ones who guard the slaves working at the sewer plants."

"You mean the waste plants?" He had heard of those places. There were rumors among the men. It was said men working there weren't treated as bad as on the farms. Waste plants were thought to be the best place for a man to end up, with the exception of the City of Men.

"Yes, that's the insulting name under which they're known. The women living there are considered low in status because they must interact with men the whole time—they can't contribute to the collective vote system."

"I don't think I've ever met one." Prince tried to recollect his memories of the various fathered women he had encountered at Sundial.

"You wouldn't have. Once a fathered woman is sent to a waste plant, it's a life sentence. They live at the very fringe of society, where the sewers and the recycling centers are. There are less than twenty sewage disposal plants in all Ginecea, and even fewer recycling centers, and they were built in hard-to-access places, where no pure breed would ever go. And, actually, now that I think of it, you met a couple who escaped from one of those places—"

"I still don't understand the point in showing those images to the rest of the population." Prince was too concerned with the ramifications of what he was seeing to waste time in gossip.

Lucas's eyes went to the TV screen for a moment and then blinked. "The Priestess thinks she's sending a message to the pure breeds that her way is the right way and that those women are endangering Ginecea."

"In reality, she has opened several minds to the wrongness of what she's doing and the danger she's putting everybody through," Anna said from the back of the room. "I knocked and waited, but you were too busy talking." She walked toward the TV, gave a good look at the news and commented, "It's getting worse." She sighed, loosened the collar of her blouse, and sat on one of the two chairs facing the couch with her back to the screen. "There's only so much I can stomach and talking with the Priestess doesn't help my digestion either."

"We must talk," Prince said before Anna could add anything to her soliloquy.

"Okay." She relaxed on the cushion, flattening the palm of her hands on the armrests.

"Did you grow a conscience overnight?" Prince studied the woman, hoping his words would upset her enough for her to drop her shield.

"No, I forgot I had one to begin with," Anna replied, curling and flattening her hands. A moment passed before she said anything else. Then she looked at Prince and he saw she had taken a decision concerning him.

"So, why?"

She held her gaze on him. "I'm trying to rectify a wrong I inadvertently committed several years ago."

"Why haven't you turned Lucas or me over to the authorities?"

Anna finally turned her head to face Lucas. "You didn't tell him?"

"I was coming to that." Lucas muted the TV.

"I'm one of them." Anna turned her chin slightly to the right and inclined her head toward the TV, where the images were getting bloodier.

Prince let her words sink in. "You're a fathered woman, not a pure breed. How is it possible? You work for the Layans."

"I've been working for Maurice for the last twenty years. But, not only that, I'm one of *them*, a wasted woman, as the other fathered women call us."

"I don't believe you," Prince said, turning to face Lucas.

"I can prove it to you." She stood up, unbuttoned one of her sleeves, methodically rolled up the fabric to show a large leather band—an engraved bracelet covering her forearm entirely—then removed it, turning her arm palm up. "Look at my arm."

Prince stared at the devastation on her skin. Anna's forearm was severely scarred by what must have been a crude attempt at burning letters and numbers on it. From the double lines creating an echo on the design, he knew she had struggled and tried to get away. The branding irons had been repositioned at least twice. Boys were taught by their fathers not to resist when the moment came for them to be numbered like cattle. Men had exorcised the practice by incorporating it in a rite of passage from childhood to adulthood. When he had come back from the infirmary, the other men had cheered him. He was fifteen, and for a brief moment before becoming a semental, he had belonged somewhere.

Anna moved and brought him back from his reverie. "What does it say?"

"Caron, and then there is an asterisk and three numbers." Prince couldn't help but bring one hand to the inside of his left arm, where the string of twelve numbers on his skin had defined his life as a slave.

"Caron is a sewage disposal plant. The asterisk is the tribe I belong to. The number signifies my place inside the tribe. Or it did, until I escaped."

"You're Maurice Layan's secretary." Prince shook his head and refrained from touching her arm. "Nobody ever noticed the marks?"

"I keep my arm covered when around people and I normally wear long sleeves. I say I burned it and I'm conscious about it."

"But how could you escape from Caron? And how did you get here? How did you get to become who you are now?" His eyes were on her marks, their hideousness hard to ignore.

Anna rolled down her sleeve. "I was helped by a prominent pure breed."

"How? And why?" he asked.

"Caron, like every sewage disposal plant, is led by wasted women, but once in a while, Ginecea sends someone to ensure everything is working properly. When left for long stretches of time alone, those isolated plants tend to become too independent, if you understand what I mean. The central government can't abide that, so they send pure breeds who drew the short straw and must get their hands dirty with us. I was pretty, and most importantly, at the right place at the right moment. Viola was much older than me and the most handsome woman I'd ever seen. It was easy for me to fall in love. I was lucky she reciprocated the sentiment. When it was time for her return to Ginecea and her wife, she couldn't leave me behind."

"How could she get away with that?" Prince was fascinated by the story.

A sad smile touched her lips. "She didn't, not completely. She managed to forge some papers and I became an adopted orphan, and thanks to those papers, I got accepted to a good private college, where I learned how to be a proper pure breed. I was young, smart, and determined to change my station in life."

"And she left her wife to be with you?"

"No, when confronted by her wife regarding the time she spent visiting me, Viola confessed she wanted a divorce. Her wife told her it would never happen and started investigating me. Viola chose to end her life before our story, and my past, became public knowledge. Soon after, Maurice Layan came to my college to recruit a secretary. I was recommended as the first of my class. I've never disappointed Maurice in my job." Anna paused.

Prince understood her pain and his voice was softer when he spoke next. "You said something about a wrong you intend to rectify."

Anna seemed taken aback by his gentleness. "When I left, my whole tribe paid for my actions. I didn't know. It came to my attention only recently, when the Priestess decided it was appropriate to show the massacre of defenseless wasted women on public television. Caron was one of the first plants to receive prime-time exposure, and I noticed my tribe wasn't on the roll anymore. I got worried and I quietly investigated. The Priestess ordered their extermination twenty years ago because they let one single teenager escape. So, you see now? I have my reasons to hate the Priestess and fight her tyranny."

"You do realize our goals aren't the same?" Prince crossed his legs and sank on the couch.

She nodded. "It will suffice. We have a common enemy in the person of the Priestess, and we both share sincere affection for Pax."

"I love her," Prince corrected Anna.

She raised one eyebrow. "Then prove it." But her tone wasn't as sharp as before.

Lucas stood up, massaged his legs, and said, "Now that we're better acquainted, I'll go fix something to eat."

Prince almost laughed at the awkwardness of the moment. "I'm hungry," he admitted, following Lucas to the kitchen.

"Anything for you?" Lucas asked Anna.

"No thanks. I needed some free-time from Her Holiness, but I must go back to help Maurice deal with her." Anna walked in the opposite direction.

"Did you talk to Pax?" Prince stopped her midway through the door.

"No, she went to the library as soon as she saw you. As I was about to excuse myself to visit her, the Priestess summoned both Pax and Lexi to join her for an afternoon tea. I came here, instead."

Prince nodded in acknowledgment and let her go. Anna saluted them and closed the door behind her.

"She's a good person," Lucas said once they were alone. Prince wanted to say several things, but ate the sandwich Lucas had prepared for him in silence instead.

Several hours later, warm golden light inundating the living room, Prince came out of the surveillance room and asked, "What time is it?"

"Dinnertime, already." Lucas was on the couch, a copy of the same book he was reading earlier in his hands, glasses perched on his nose.

"Did I spend the whole afternoon there?"

"It seems so." Lucas removed his glasses and smiled.

"I'll go insane." Prince's eyes adjusted to the brightness in the room. He could still see the images from the monitors dancing in midair where Lucas sat. *It was worth it, though,* he thought. He had been able to see Pax coming back from the gardens, walking through the long hallway, and finally going to rest in the library. When she disappeared from every screen, he decided to reemerge from the surveillance room.

"You'll find a way to spend the days."

"Is reading helping you?"

"This is a religious text. It's the story of how the Goddess came to power after defeating the God."

"Why would you read something like that?" Prince went to pick up the book Lucas put on the coffee table. It was an old copy. The red leather cover was faded and sported a few wrinkles. Anna must have read it at length. He leafed through the pages, when he noticed the inscription on the first one. It said "I'll always be yours, V." He closed it and immediately put it down.

"I realized men and women know so little about each other. We're kept in forced ignorance because, otherwise, it would be difficult to control us. But women are ignorant too. Their knowledge of Ginecea is limited to what the priestesses have decided is convenient for them to know. Thousands of years of misinformation and downright lies. Ironically, the current Priestess, in her eagerness to destroy whatever is left of the man population on this planet, has set in motion several wheels that are limiting her control over the fathered women and eventually even over the pure breeds."

"I can't find any sympathy in my heart for the guards who tortured me for years." Prince's memories were fresh, and if Pax hadn't crossed his path, he would have expressed his sentiment with stronger words.

"It could've been the other way around." Lucas shrugged one shoulder.

"Still—"

"Imagine a City of Men where women were treated like slaves. Imagine being told since you were a kid that women are impure evildoers. You'd grow up with the certainty that beating them is the appropriate response if they don't comply with your rules. Of course, you wouldn't give them the right to vote or to have a family. You wouldn't come close to them, right?"

"I'd give my life for a woman, so don't give me this crap. I'm not going to excuse any of the atrocities they commit every day against defenseless men. It isn't a what-if situation. I live on Ginecea, and I'm a man. It's as simple as that." Prince wanted to tell Lucas that he couldn't know what he was talking about since he was born and raised in the safety of the Priest's world, but stopped before he spoke the thought out loud.

"You could've been the one committing the atrocities."

He felt anger building up. "No, I wouldn't have. If you're a decent human being, you remain the same despite the situation."

"That's what the Priest always says," Lucas whispered and smiled at him.

Prince forced himself to cool down enough to keep talking in a civilized manner. He would never talk back to an elder. His father had taught him better than that. "I do agree with you that if men and women knew each other, this world would be a better place. And I also agree that there are good, even exceptional women out there. But we are at war now. "

"I'm in no danger to forget it, don't worry. I'm just trying to find a medium ground to analyze our current situation with fresh, unbiased eyes. I don't want, once everything is over, to commit the same mistakes women have being making since the dawn of time."

"This is the reason we need men like the Priest."

"And lots of them," Lucas finished. He touched his heart with his right hand and bowed his head.

Prince followed him in honoring the Priest. "I miss him."

Lucas opened his mouth to say something, but no sounds came.

"Changing topic… Is there any way to put the audio on?" Prince indicated the surveillance room.

Lucas nodded. "Right away."

They ate a light dinner and then Lucas went back to his reading. Prince, having nothing better to do, spent several hours staring at the flickering screens, hoping to catch Pax. He soon became acquainted with the mansion's geography and even started to appreciate the complexity of the additions to the main building. "We could live our whole lives here, and nobody would be the wiser," he commented out loud.

"That's exactly what I realized my first day watching the monitors," Lucas said from the living room.

"Hey, what's this?"

"What?" Lucas walked into the surveillance room.

"This." Prince showed him one of the monitors streaming from the gardens. Two people dressed in dark clothes moved from one tree to another, carrying something between them. "It doesn't look right."

"It's too dark—" Lucas let the glasses slide on his nose and took a better look at the screen.

Prince stood on the edge of the chair, getting closer to the images. "It's almost impossible to see their features, but from their posture, I'd say they are army."

"Priestess's people?"

"See how they move in complete silence? They know where the cameras are."

"You're right. And there're no dogs in sight. But what are they doing?"

"It looks like they are smuggling something out of the mansion." Prince pointed at the dark shape they balanced carefully between them.

"A pet?" Lucas scratched his chin.

"I don't think the Priestess is kidnapping kittens."

"Whatever it is, it's small." Lucas craned his neck and sighed. "I can't see them anymore."

"They're moving toward the back gate." Prince stood up and went to the end of the wall where one of the monitors was showing the duo walking in the frame. "Whatever they have trapped inside that bundle must be of some value, judging from the care they are taking in handling it."

"It moves."

"It does," Prince confirmed. He stared at the scene in fascination. Meanwhile, the two women had managed to avoid another monitor. "And… here they are." He pointed a finger to the next screen. "They are officially out of Layan Mansion, and not surprisingly, there's a black car waiting for them outside."

"Is that the Priestess?" Lucas asked, leaning closer to the screen.

"Wait, let me see." Prince leaned too, and then said, "Yes, it's Her Holiness herself."

"I wonder what she's doing."

"Nothing good, I'm sure." Prince watched the screen until the car disappeared into the night. He shook his head and then stepped out of the room to fetch a glass of water. "Do you want some?" he asked Lucas, but the man didn't answer back. Prince took his time to stretch his legs and breathe some fresh air, being careful to avoid moving too close to the windows.

"Wait, there's more." Lucas called him a few minutes later.

"What is it now?" Prince offered Lucas a glass of water anyway.

He tapped a finger on one of the monitors. "Maurice Layan just appeared running full speed into the gardens. She seems disheveled and is clearly upset about something."

"Where's Anna?" Prince asked. "Maurice Layan doesn't seem to move a step without her." He sat beside Lucas, his head moving from screen to screen. "Speaking of which…"

Anna wasn't outside. She was in the library talking to someone who was out of the picture. Prince straightened his back against the chair. He played around with the knobs on the desk, but wasn't happy with the result. "Why can't I hear anything?"

"The library is a big room, and the microphones aren't close to where she's sitting."

"I need to know who she's talking to," Prince said, frustration making him turn the knobs all the way up and down several times.

"You're going to break them." Lucas gently stopped him, putting a firm hand on top of his.

On the screen, Anna moved to the left, and Pax appeared along with Lexi. They were having an animated discussion, and bits and pieces of what they were saying came through.

"She just said my name." Prince jumped on his feet.

"Shhh," Lucas said, bringing one finger to his mouth and angling his ear toward the screen.

The three women moved across the room and, for a moment, their voices sounded clear.

"I want to see him!" Pax faced Anna, her chin up, her body ramrod straight, barely reaching the other woman's neck.

"It isn't safe. You have to listen to me. The Priestess wants to get rid of you, one way or the other. Don't give her any reasons, for Goddess's sake!" Anna looked down, but her expression wasn't angry or irritated. She looked concerned.

"Pax, she's right. Please," Lexi said, restraining her friend and making her move one step back.

At the same time, the three women turned around, different feelings showing in their faces. Pax was angry, her hands balled in two fists. A fourth woman, a nurse by the uniform she wore, entered the screen, and everybody moved out of the picture. Their voices became softer, and then there was only silence broken by static noises.

"I can't stand this—" Prince looked at Lucas and let out his breath all at once. "This seeing and not being able to do anything. A day hasn't even passed and I'm ready to break something. I'm not going to stay put and wait while I know she's a few rooms away, upset." He walked back and forth, covering the entire floor in only a few steps.

"She's fine," Lucas said, reaching for the glass of water waiting for him on the desk and offering it to Prince. "I don't think there's anything else to see here, and it's getting late. You should try to rest."

He accepted the water, drank it in a single gulp, and resumed the pacing. "I haven't done anything all day. My legs are getting restless, my hands are aching to punch someone, and my mind is about to explode." Prince waved at Lucas from the doorway. "I need to release some energy."

"Use Anna's gym." Lucas passed Prince and motioned for him to follow. He led him to an empty room that housed a rack of weights lying on the floor. "Knock yourself out, and when you're done, the next room on your left is the guest room where you're going to sleep."

Prince thanked him, went to the floor, and started an abs routine. When the muscles burned, he added weights to the mix. When he wasn't able to raise his head from the floor anymore, he closed his eyes and started kicking and scissoring with his legs.

"Are you trying to kill yourself?" Anna asked, looking at him from the door. She looked tired, her eyes red, a briefcase hanging from her right shoulder, weighing her down.

"I don't like being caged, no matter how big the cage is," he answered, letting his legs down with a thump.

"You should be grateful this cage is well-equipped." She set the briefcase on the floor, walked into the room, removed the heavy weights from his outstretched hands, and flexed her arms for several repetitions. "I used to run every morning for an hour straight, before Maurice announced she wanted to take a shot at presidency. I miss it."

"I'm going to see Pax, no matter what you say to me, or to her."

"Eavesdropping?" She raised one eyebrow, but she didn't sound upset.

"What else is there to do around here?"

"Cleaning my apartment? I had to send away my maids to keep Lucas a secret."

"I'm devastated for you." Prince sat down and stretched his muscles, starting with his calves and moving up to his quadriceps. "What about the guards who were with you when you came to kidnap me?" When he tried to arch his back to release his abs, a strangled moan escaped his mouth.

"I thought you were made of a stronger fiber," Anna said, her lips slightly curved up. "They aren't going to betray me. Don't worry."

He wasn't reassured by her words, but decided to let it go. "What's up with the Priestess smuggling something out of the manor?" Prince lay flat on his stomach, chin on the floor.

"When?"

"Around the time you were talking with Pax."

"What did you see, exactly?" Anna let the weights roll down from her hands and locked eyes with Prince.

He told her what he and Lucas had seen in a few sentences. "So what was that all about?"

"I'm not sure." Anna hesitated and then added, "I need to go talk to Maurice."

Prince observed how the woman left the room in a state of agitation, almost running. He went to the surveillance room and checked on her wake through the sleeping house. She looked as if she were getting even more upset from one screen to the other. He saw her entering Maurice Layan's bedroom without knocking on the door.

"Tell me it's not true," she yelled at Maurice.

The President of Ginecea was a heap on the floor, her head resting beside one of her bed's legs, her hands clutching what looked like a small pink blanket.

"What's this?" Anna yanked the piece of fabric from Maurice's hands and looked at it in disbelief. "It can't be." She shook the blanket. "You told me she died." She went to pick up Maurice, reaching for the woman's dress and yanking her up by the collar. "Maurice, I'm begging you. Tell me it's not what I think it is, please." Her voice broke at the end.

"She made me promise. I didn't have a choice. I did what I had to do to save her," Maurice said, sobbing between one word and the other.

"Why did you keep this from me? I could've helped you." Anna didn't release the other woman.

"She said she was going to kill both of them. I couldn't lose my granddaughter. You have to understand."

"Where did she take her?"

"I don't know. She said to me, 'I have great plans for her.'" Maurice's body sagged on the floor when Anna lost her grip on her for a moment. "Please, don't tell—"

Anna shut Maurice's mouth before the woman could finish the sentence. Her eyes darted toward the camera, as if she had only now remembered about it, and then she whispered something to Maurice before walking out of the room.

Prince stared at the monitor for a few seconds, then broke in a mad dash toward the door. In his haste he almost ran over Lucas coming out of the bathroom.

"Where are you going? No... You can't go out. Stop!" Lucas yelled.

CHAPTER 11

Prince heard the man's command after he was already in the hallway. He sprinted through the house, letting his memory play back hours of mindless staring at the monitors. He found the library on the first try, then went to the bed by the window and gently caressed Pax's arm. "My love, it's me," he whispered between kisses. "I need to talk to you. Follow me outside."

"Prince! How did you find me? Were you here the whole time? Anna didn't tell me where she was hiding you." Pax got out of the bed and took his hand.

"Pax, where are you going?" Lexi raised her head from the pillow and gasped when her eyes took in Prince's dark presence beside her friend.

"Cover for me. If anybody should ask where I am, say I needed fresh air, please?" Pax asked.

Prince didn't wait for Lexi to make up her mind. "It's important I talk to you in private," he said to Pax while pushing her out of the room.

"Pax?" Lexi called.

"It's okay. Don't worry." Pax closed the library's door behind her and then threw herself in his arms. "I was going crazy not knowing what was happening to you. Did they do anything to you? Are you hurt? I begged Anna, but she—"

"Our daughter is alive," Prince said.

"What—?"

"She's alive. Your mother and the Priestess lied."

Pax made a strangled sound and sagged to her knees. "It can't be."

Prince sat on the floor with her and took her head in his hands. "Look at me," he whispered close to her mouth. "It's true. She's alive—our baby girl is alive."

"How do you know?"

"Let's go somewhere safe." He helped her up, supporting her by the elbow, and walked her toward the end of the hallway where her bedroom was.

"What are we doing here?" Pax asked once inside, shooting a confused look at him.

He walked to the hidden door just a few steps right from her bed. "There's a passage behind this wall."

"What—?"

"Cameras are hidden everywhere in this house. It isn't safe to remain here longer than necessary." He opened the door to the dark corridor. "Anna showed me the passage this morning when she kidnapped me."

She stood at the threshold, surprise showing in her bewildered eyes. "How long has this door been here?"

"Probably forever. Not sure. Doesn't matter." He pulled her along and closed the door behind them. They only took a few steps inside before he softly pushed her against the wall and kissed her again, longer this time. "Our baby is alive. Nothing else matters," he said when he emerged from the embrace and then took his time to explain what he had discovered.

Pax listened, at first interrupting him with questions, but soon became speechless when things started to make sense.

"Say something." Prince worried at her reaction. He stroked her face with light fingers and hugged her tight to feel her skin against his. "Please, say something, my love."

"I need to talk to my mother." Her voice held a cold edge.

"I don't think it's going to help."

"She lied to me! She told me our baby had died when she was here the whole time. My mother let me cry for days, and her words of consolation were 'You'll have a proper one.' She looked at me and said she was sorry my baby girl hadn't made it, but things happen for a reason. She said that to me." Pax collapsed in his arms once again.

"Love!" Prince didn't let her fall. "No, no, no!" He shook her, and when she didn't react, he slapped her. "I'm sorry...," he whispered, panic swelling in his chest. She gasped, and he finally breathed.

"My mother's going to tell me where my baby is," Pax said as soon as she opened her eyes.

"This isn't the right moment." He gently helped her to a sitting position, taking care her back was firmly against the wall. He crouched in front of her. "I'm angry with the whole world, but right now, the only thing that matters is that I want to hold my baby. If your mother kept a secret from you, what do you think is going to happen when you confront her with the truth? I don't care why she did it."

"But I do." Pax was trembling.

"I understand you do, and you'll have your words with her, but not tonight."

"When, then?"

"When we get our baby back."

"What do we do now?" Pax slowly raised her chin and let her head rest on the wall.

A series of muffled noises reached them in the hidden hallway.

"Someone's knocking at my bedroom's door." Pax stood up and swayed.

"Easy." Prince steadied her.

"I'd better check it." She squeezed his hand and went back to her room.

Prince flattened his body against the wall and craned his head to listen. He heard the door in the bedroom open, steps walking in, and several voices talking all at once.

"I told them you couldn't sleep," Lexi said.

"We went looking for you outside, but you weren't in the garden," Anna continued.

"I was worried you'd left me—" Maurice Layan was the last one to talk. Her voice sounded broken, her words ending in a choked question.

"Mom, what's wrong with you?" Pax asked, her voice barely containing her rage.

"A bad night, that's all," Anna answered. "But now that it's clear everything's fine, we should all go to sleep. Don't you think, Maurice?"

Prince heard someone sobbing.

"Mom?"

"Can I sleep with you?"

"Maurice, it's better if you go back to your room. I'm sure Pax is tired and needs her sleep. Come, I'll accompany you. Maybe we can have a nice cup of steaming herbal tea along the way."

"I want to stay with my daughter."

"Mom…"

"Madame President, I could give you something to calm your nerves," a fifth voice said.

"Yes, Mom, you should take something like Nurse Sheila is suggesting, and then we can spend some time together tomorrow."

"Follow me, Madame President. Let's stop at the kitchen and have some chamomile tea."

"Good night, girls," Anna said.

Prince listened as the steps receded and the door closed.

"Where is he?" Lexi asked after a moment.

"He left." Pax's voice didn't betray any hesitation. "Let's go back to sleep."

"Are you okay?"

"Just fine."

Prince stood in the dark for several minutes after Pax and Lexi left; then he went back to Anna's apartment, where he found Lucas awake and waiting for him in the living room.

"So?"

"I'll have a long talk with Anna," Prince answered.

"About what?"

"About my daughter."

"You already know she died at birth—" Lucas paused at the noise of incoming steps.

"Is it so, Anna?" Prince asked the woman who had just entered the room.

"I came here as soon as I could. It's not what you think." Anna was having problems steadying her voice.

Prince didn't say anything; he stood there, his eyes on her.

"I didn't know anything. Maurice never told me the baby was alive and that she had her."

"I don't care about that. Tell me where my daughter is."

"I don't know. Maurice doesn't know. She could be anywhere."

"What are you talking about?" Lucas stood up and intruded in the discussion, physically creating a barrier between Anna and Prince. "You, sit and breathe, and, you, have a cup of water, or something stronger maybe," he said, gently pushing Prince out of the way.

"I'm as upset as you are."

Prince closed his hands in two fists, but refrained from acting on the impulse of hitting something, someone. "I don't think so, Anna."

"Does Pax know?"

Prince didn't even think to answer the woman's question. His expression was eloquent enough.

Anna shook her head and sighed. "She's going to do something stupid."

"Help us find our daughter."

"I don't know where the Priestess is hiding her."

"You've already said that." Prince followed Lucas's suggestion and sat on the couch.

"Think. Where could she have taken a newborn baby?" Lucas asked from the other side of the room, bent over a low table full of bottles, pouring some dark liquid from a decanter into three tiny glasses. "That will do." He walked to the couch and pushed one of the glasses into Prince's hand. "Have some."

Prince accepted the offering without questions. He gulped down the liquid and coughed.

"You'll feel better in a second." Lucas patted him on the shoulder. "Let's focus on the good news here. Your baby is alive."

"Yes, she is." Prince was still coming to terms with the revelation. Now that the adrenaline rush and shock were subsiding, he could feel the void in his stomach growing stronger. Something was missing and his rib cage was too small to contain both his lungs.

The dark liquid burnt a passage through his internal organs, releasing warmth in its wake. "What is it?"

"Cheap medicine." Lucas promptly gave him a refill.

Prince took a good look at the miniature glass, thought about it, and then brought it to his mouth, this time savoring the liquid. He saw Anna doing the same. "If you were the Priestess, where would you hide a baby?" he asked her, his tone warmer.

"The baby was born premature, so she needs medical attention." Anna's voice was almost too low to be heard.

Back at the corner where he was sorting through the bottles, Lucas hit the table with one of the glasses. "The Temple."

"Yes, it makes sense. It's the only place where there's a medical facility completely under the Priestess's watch." Anna went to fill her glass from a different bottle containing a transparent liquid, but her hands shook badly and a generous amount of the beverage ended up on the table. "I knew Claudine's death has obfuscated Maurice's mind, and her hate of men has grown to levels equal to the Priestess's, but I didn't think she could go as far as to hide the child from Pax."

"The question is what the Priestess wants with the baby, and why she removed her from this house tonight?" Lucas nursed his glass, letting the liquid slosh from one side to the other.

"Could she hurt her?" Prince had to ask it out loud.

"If she wanted to kill her, she'd have done it already." Anna went back to the couch to sit beside Prince.

He automatically moved away from her. "I'm going to the Temple."

"You don't know what you're talking about. The Temple is the Priestess's version of an inexpugnable fortress." Anna turned toward him and, in the process, lost half the contents of her glass on the couch.

"You're going to help me break in," Prince answered. "And we're walking through the main entrance." He helped himself to a third shot and then to a fourth right away.

"Okay, you want to ease it now, champion. You're not making any sense." Lucas gave him a worried look.

149

"Actually, I'm feeling much better." Prince moved toward the table once more, but Lucas blocked him midway through.

"You've never had alcohol before," Lucas stated.

"This is alcohol?" Prince tried to go around the other man, but Lucas moved with him.

"Okay, you're done for the night. Go have a shower and sleep it off. Tomorrow, we'll talk about your plan. Right, Anna? Tomorrow, you'll help him. Now go get some rest, you too," Lucas said, facing Prince and then Anna.

"I told you I'm perfectly fine." Prince managed to reach the table and take a swing from one of the bottles before Lucas realized what he was up to.

"You won't be able to go anywhere tomorrow if you don't stop drinking." Lucas placed both hands against Prince's chest and pushed him until he stood with his back to the wall. "Go to sleep, now."

Lucas's words penetrated Prince's fogged mind, and he slowly walked toward his designated room. The walls were moving before his eyes, and the floor got away from under his shoes.

"Do you need a hand getting up?" Anna was looking at him from far away.

"No, thanks." *Why is she being nice to me?*

"I'll help you find Pax's baby… your daughter."

"Why?" he asked, trying to rise from the floor and failing.

"Because what Maurice and the Priestess did goes against everything I believe is right. Nothing can justify kidnapping a child." Anna surprised Prince by extending one hand and grabbing his wrist, helping him up.

He looked at her with wary eyes but whispered, "Thanks," and found the guestroom's door after a few attempts.

Cold moonlight still streamed through the draped window when he woke up with one of the worst headaches of his life. He swung his legs off the bed and realized he was still wearing the tunic from the day before. He had gone a whole day without noticing. He threw away the garment and grimaced at the state of the rest of his clothing. Nausea hit him as soon as he put one foot on the floor. He half ran, half stumbled through the apartment, looking for the bathroom. He barely reached it in time. When, afterward, he was washing his face with big splashes of frigid water, he remembered with fondness last time he'd had to embrace the toilet. Pax had been there with him.

Coming out of the bathroom, Prince was feeling nauseated and famished. He wanted a glass of water and headed to the kitchen. Several minutes later, the nausea hadn't lessened, but the hunger turned out to be thirst, and although he was still tired, his eyes were wide open. The monitors in the surveillance room were on, their light casting a blue shadow under the door. *One quick look to see if she's sleeping well*, he said to himself and entered the room.

His eyes went immediately to the monitor set on the library, but Pax wasn't sleeping in the library or in her bed. Movement on one the farthest monitors on the left caught his attention.

"Let me go," she was saying to someone who was pointing a gun at her head. Her voice was strangely calm, given the situation.

Prince tried to remember where that monitor was streaming from, but it was too dark and he wasn't sure.

"Lexi's going to raise the alarm as soon as she wakes up."

"I wouldn't count on that. She's heavily sedated."

"My mother will look for me." Pax made a move to the right, but the other person followed her with the gun.

"Your mother is useless. I've been drugging her for months now. She's a puppet in the Priestess's hands."

"And so are you, Nurse Sheila." Pax stopped trying to outmaneuver the woman.

"I'm honored to be helping Her Holiness achieve her dream of cleansing Ginecea from its plagues."

Pax let the woman ramble some more and then asked, "And what about Anna? Have you drugged her as well or is she working for you?"

"The Priestess has thought of everything," the woman answered, a smile on her face.

"What do you mean?"

"I just delivered a letter to her from the Priestess, requesting your presence at the Temple."

"To do what?"

"The Priestess doesn't need to explain herself! Anna won't dare question Her Holiness's demands. And you shouldn't either. If it weren't for the fact that you're going to be of some use, I'd teach you some manners. The Priestess is right about today's youth." The woman scoffed in disbelief.

Prince stared at the monitor, hoping that someone would say anything useful to pinpoint their location.

"You should be grateful the Priestess has deemed you fit to donate blood for the Chosen," the nurse said, her tone bordering on hysteria.

Prince shivered at the woman's words.

"Chosen? What Chosen? There hasn't been a Chosen since before my mother was born." Pax stepped back, but the nurse followed her close.

"Yes, the Chosen has been elected. It's a glorious moment for Ginecea. Imagine how women will rejoice at the news."

"Yes, I'm sure it'll be great. But I still don't understand why you need me. How am I going to help the Chosen?" Pax spoke slowly.

"She is smaller than usual, and she needs a transfusion," the nurse answered.

Prince saw the expression in Pax's face change from incredulity to terror.

"You don't need the gun anymore. I'll follow, but tell me where we're going at least." Pax's eyes darted up for a moment.

"You'll know soon enough. Hurry up. Her Holiness is waiting outside."

The nurse accompanied Pax out of the screen. Several minutes later, Prince saw them walking out one of the garage's back doors and heading toward the gate. The same gate Pax had used to sneak him inside. Outside, the same black car he had seen the day before waited for them. No audio was available from that corner of the gardens, but Prince clearly saw Pax looking around.

Prince didn't hesitate; nausea forgotten and headache put aside, he strode to Anna's bedroom to wake her.

"The baby needs a transfusion, and the Priestess has taken custody of the blood bank," he announced to a dazed secretary.

"What...?"

"Nurse Sheila just kidnapped Pax because something's wrong with the baby. I don't know where they're going, but the Temple is probably our best shot." Prince opened the curtains, but the light coming in wasn't strong enough. "Anna, I need your help. Now." He came close to the bed, but refrained from taking her by the shoulders. He threw the glass of water she kept on the nightstand at her, instead.

"What did you do that for?"

"I'm desperate," he offered as an apology, and when he finally had her undivided attention, he explained what he thought was happening.

* * *

"We can't both fit in the trunk," Lucas said.

"I'll lie flat on the floor." Prince accepted one of the long, black dresses Anna had rummaged from her closet.

"You won't need to hide. You look like servant women," she said, adjusting the straps on his back to cover his form. "Try not to look so tall though." She loosened the fabric on his chest to create the semblance of fullness where there was none. "You know the drill, no eye contact and stay one step behind me."

The woman had explained how they were going to leave the mansion one too many times already, and Prince felt trapped in constant déjà vu, always waiting for someone else to do what he needed to do. "Yes, but if we don't go right now, the chances of being seen by someone will become a certainty."

To aggravate the situation, the woman hadn't told them her plan for when they arrived at the Temple. When he had asked her, she had answered, "I'll find a way." Prince's frustration had grown considerably in the last few minutes.

"Okay, follow me." Anna opened the door of her apartment, waited for the two men to get out, and then strolled through the hallway at a rather brisk pace.

"Slow down," Prince hissed from under the veil Anna had made them wear.

"You just said to—"

"He's right. Try to walk normally." Lucas gently touched her forearm. "You don't want to attract any attention."

"I'll try," Anna said, and her pace slowed.

"Better." Prince walked behind Lucas, holding a chest.

"Maybe I should talk to Lexi." Anna abruptly stopped in the middle of the hallway.

"I think we should move." Prince put one foot forward.

"Lexi's going to worry." Anna didn't move.

"Let her," Prince whispered angrily.

"No, we need all the help we can get, and Lexi could be of help."

"I'm not sure we have time to bring Lexi up to speed." Lucas stepped closer to Anna.

"And she's been sedated—"

Anna intervened before Prince could finish. "I'll wake her up."

He shook his head. "But—"

She raised one hand. "It'll take just a moment. Hide in here." Anna darted toward the right, opened a door that led to a small room, and left without giving them time to argue.

Prince and Lucas ran inside and closed the door. The light coming through the doorframe was enough to light the empty room.

"Sit. You look exhausted." Lucas gave the example, crossing his legs on the tiled floor. "How long did you sleep?"

Prince didn't answer; he was angry, his head had started pounding again, and he hated to be confined in a dark, empty room. It reminded him of everything he wanted to forget. He sat, however, and stretched his legs in front of him.

"Can I ask you about my son?"

Prince wasn't ready to talk about Randal, but he knew that sooner or later the time would come. "Why didn't you ask about him earlier?" Once or twice, he had almost prompted the conversation and then guilt had stopped him from saying the words.

"Because I didn't want to hear that he's dead." Lucas readjusted his body on the floor to face Prince, breathed a long breath, and then asked, "Is he?"

"No." *I hope he's still alive,* he thought, but Lucas read the line between his silences.

"What happened to him? Is he wounded?"

Prince explained how Randal and another young man had followed him back to Sundial and how he had lost track of them when he had been taken to the Bestiarium. "I shouldn't have accepted their help. I'm sorry, Lucas."

"Randal's stubborn," Lucas whispered.

"I noticed. He's also brave."

"So, tell me from the beginning what happened since I left."

Prince was relieved by the change of topic. He summarized what had happened to the rest of the fugitives. "At least all of them are safe, hidden in the Colony, far away from this madness," he said at the end.

Lucas had other questions, and Prince answered to the best of his knowledge, but after a while they remained silent, each with his own burden of heavy thoughts. Time stretched and they were still there, awaiting their fate. When Prince finally thought that Anna had sold them out and armed guards were going to take them to their execution, she came back accompanied by Lexi.

"I'm coming with you," Lexi announced, looking rather awake for someone who had been drugged.

"This isn't a shopping spree," he said between his teeth.

"I won't leave Pax," Lexi answered back.

"She's going to be our alibi." Anna led them outside.

"How?"

"It just so happens that I'd already scheduled a visit to the Temple. I sent my busy mothers a message saying they don't have to accompany me anymore. Everybody wins."

"And why are we coming along?" Prince couldn't help the tone.

"I need my maids."

"You need two maids?" Prince knew Pax was fond of her friend, but he could only see Lexi as another haughty pure breed.

"I work on one of the Temple's charities. I'm helping with the education of the poorest among the fathered women."

"Still, why would you need two maids?"

"Because, I've been collecting goods for the past two months, but I can't haul thirty boxes full of books and medicines by myself."

"We'll have to stop by Lexi's house to get the supplies and change cars. We need a bigger trunk to transport the boxes," Anna said.

"And, why does Mistress here need to be escorted by the President's secretary? What's your excuse for the road trip?" Prince asked her.

"I'm the charity treasurer, and Madame President *has signed a check* I must take to the Priestess in order to be properly cashed. The Priestess signs the necessary forms, but I take care of the money. Nobody else but me has the key to the charity's safe," Anna answered and then shushed Prince before he could reply. "There's always someone on duty in the garage." She then opened the last door at the end of the hallway and greeted someone on the other side.

"Good morning to you, Floria. No, thank you. I'm not going to drive my car. Can you bring us Mistress Lexi's?" Anna turned around and said to them, "As soon as she's back, enter the car and sit in the rear."

Lucas nodded, and when Prince didn't respond accordingly, he gave him a soft push.

"Right," Prince whispered.

The noise from the car's engine reached them, and Anna signed for them to follow. Prince lowered his head and did as told, hoping Floria wouldn't notice how tall the two maids were. He opened the car door and slid inside. Lucas went around and sat on the other seat. Anna and Lexi were safely in the front, the car already rolling out of the garage when the woman ran to stop them.

"What is it now?" Anna lowered her window. "Is everything okay, Floria?"

"I was just wondering if I can ask you a favor, since you are going to the Corellis's," she said, her hands nervously grabbing the window's edge.

"If I can, sure," Anna replied.

"I'd like to send greetings to one of the maids working there."

"Sure, who is she?"

"Her name's Aria."

"Aria?" Lexi asked, raising her voice.

"Yes, is there a problem?" The guard sounded taken aback by Lexi's reaction.

"No, no problem at all. Aria used to be my personal maid. She doesn't live at my house anymore. She got reassigned to my grandmother," Lexi said, her words hasty.

"That's why I haven't heard from her in while." The woman seemed to think about it for a moment. She opened her mouth to speak, closed it, then bowed and stepped back to let the car pass.

"Okay," Anna said, waved the woman good-bye, and signed to Lexi that they could go. "What's Aria's deal with Floria?" she asked Lexi as soon as they were out of the garage.

"How would I know?"

"There's no point in denying your affair with the girl. I know everything about it. Now, what's with her?"

Lexi turned toward Anna. "Did Pax...?"

"Your friend would never betray you. Remember when you both wondered if someone was listening to your conversations? You were right. So, about Aria?"

"I honestly don't know. She never mentioned she knew Floria."

Anna seemed satisfied by Lexi's answer. "Perfect, now let's go."

"If you don't mind," Prince added. He was feeling caged and helpless.

"There are steps to take in a certain order, if we want to succeed. Every small, insignificant detail could be important." Anna didn't turn. "Now, remember you're a maid and show me some respect."

Prince sat back and relaxed his head on the cushion. He would have never said it to her, but he was glad Anna, the haughty, efficient secretary, was back. For a long moment, he'd thought she wouldn't snap out of the confusion she had shown since learning about the baby. "Everything's going to be fine," he whispered.

CHAPTER 12

The ride was eventful—they were stopped several times by the Priestess's Army patrolling the streets of Ginecea City, but Anna's and Lexi's reasons to be out and about at such an early hour in the morning checked out and granted them passage. Prince and Lucas maintained a nervous silence the whole time. Despite the early hour, the streets were crowded, mostly military vehicles, and at any moment the woman sitting in the car next to theirs, driven by boredom and curiosity, could take a better look at the two maids.

Prince was too nervous to doze off, but closed his eyes and slowly repeated prayers he had learned long ago when he was a boy. He rhythmically tapped on his leg to keep count and tried to focus on that task. He wished he had the small chain of wooden beads his father had made for him, but as with every other material possession he had ever owned, the women had taken it from him. It was the first time in years he thought of the prayer chain. The memory came back to him as vivid as if he was touching it, the smoothness of the material against his palms, the pine scent reaching his nose every time he rolled the beads between his fingers.

As long as I have my memories, you can't defeat me, he thought, but it still stung. After all those years, he was a man now, but it still brought tears to his eyes to remember the scared, little boy he had been. And then, by association, images of a baby girl formed in his mind, and his stomach churned at the idea that someone could hurt her the same way he had been hurt. "Please, hurry," he said out loud to the women in the front.

"I tried to reach Pax, by the way." Lexi looked at him from the front mirror.

"And?"

"She hasn't answered."

Anna turned to look at him. "Her cell could be dead. Don't jump to any conclusions."

"Or she could be in the Priestess's presence and can't talk," Lucas said.

"I'll try again later."

Prince nodded and then angled his body to face the window. He wasn't fit for company. By the time they arrived at Lexi's house, he was so agitated that Anna, after having checked nobody was around, let him out of the car to breathe. He had just taken a few steps around the courtyard of the Corellis Mansion when Lexi called them to the back of a low building just inside the estate's walls. Hauling heavy boxes helped Prince finally relax. Half an hour later, a black truck was already exiting the main gate, on its way to deliver goods to the Temple.

* * *

Prince looked at the Temple's majestic entrance. Even behind the black veil, the light bouncing back from the mirrored surface covering the façade blinded him. They had reached the place with the last sunrays dancing in the sky and the sight was humbling. The Temple disappeared if he looked at it directly and reappeared around the corner of his eyes when he turned his head right and left. He had never seen anything so beautiful and so deceitful. It was impossible to determine the shape of the façade, blending with the sky almost seamlessly, but solid nevertheless, hidden behind the illusion.

"We are probably the first men to see this," he said, his voice but a whisper. He was both repulsed and fascinated by the sight. The Temple was the physical representation of everything that was wrong on Ginecea—a monument bloodied by the enslavement and systematic torture of an entire race. Still, it was a work of beauty. "I never thought I'd see it."

Lucas nodded at him and kept staring outside the window caught in the same spell. "The Priest told me about the time he spent in the Temple. He was born here, lived in this prison for twenty-two years, and I'm sure he never saw this."

An awkward silence followed Lucas's words. Prince wondered if women ever thought about what it meant to be a man. Maybe

Lucas was right. Women didn't know the whole extent of what happened behind the factories' walls.

Anna nervously coughed. "I'll make my presence known to the Priestess. Parading this check is going to grant me immediate entrance to her private apartment. *Maurice* has been particularly generous this time," she said, writing the check on the spot. "Madame President is firm in her desire to bring knowledge to the fathered women." She looked at the sum she had just written, signed it, and then commented, "It's all for a good cause."

"I'll wait for your call to drive to the storage facility." Lexi's fingers danced on the wheel.

"I'll keep the Priestess occupied long enough to give you time to unload the truck and find a place to hide them." Anna got out of the car and walked toward the exploding sun.

Although he knew there was a wall ahead of them, Prince was still surprised when a door opened and the woman disappeared behind it. As Anna had predicted, the check expedited the whole process of seeking an audience with the Priestess, and she called to give the okay a few minutes later.

Lexi drove around the building that was much bigger than Prince had anticipated and parked in an alley. She used the horn liberally to get attention, and he hoped it was standard procedure and she wasn't upsetting anybody.

"Look down," she ordered them.

Prince heard a sound resembling a metallic chain being rolled up, and then someone asked, "What do you want?" He raised his chin up, just to have a glimpse of their interlocutor.

"Delivery for Literacy Sans Frontier," Lexi answered.

"Did you schedule the drop off?" A woman walked toward the car.

"Yes, but I'm slightly earlier—"

"The crew's coming back later. I'm alone here. I can't help you." The woman raised her hands.

"That's okay. I brought my maids with me." Lexi pointed a finger at Lucas and Prince in the back.

Droplets of sweat ran down Prince's head, but he didn't move and tried to breathe shallow breaths.

"The crew should be present." The woman glanced at the two dark figures in the back and then turned to face Lexi again.

"I'm in a hurry and I have lots of medical supplies in the back. We'll still be here by the time the crew arrives."

"Okay, I guess. But you must stay until then and sign the forms."

"Don't worry. I won't leave without proof of my good deed. I need it to raise my GPA." Lexi backed up with the trunk facing the storage door.

"I'll be in my office." The woman, who had kept her eyes on the car the whole time, probably worried Lexi was going to smash it against the building, went back inside. A moment later, the metal door opened all the way up, and Lexi backed up some more.

"Let's do this." She turned toward the men and added, "I know what I'm doing. I've been here several times already."

Prince and Lucas cautiously opened the doors, and when it was clear the woman wasn't going to come out of her room for fear of being asked to help, they stepped outside and went to open the trunk. Lexi gave them a silent nod and then walked around the vast room that was only partially filled with crates.

"May I use the bathroom?" Lexi craned her neck over the office's door.

"You must go inside the building proper. Go to the first door on the right and then follow the blue signs on the walls. Here's the key. Lock the door after you when you leave the storage room—the Temple guards are paranoid about security, especially when the Priestess is home—and bring it back to me when you're done," the woman answered without leaving her table, where she was busy doing something on a small monitor.

"Thank you." Lexi came out holding in her hands a long chain with a small key dangling at the end. "Girls, do you need to go?"

Prince and Lucas went immediately after her.

"What now?" Prince asked as soon as they were outside of the storage room and inside what looked like a series of galleries jutting from a central hub. Each gallery had colored signs on the wall, as the woman had mentioned.

"Get a feeling for the place, and later, after you've helped me unload the majority of the boxes, you'll take one of these galleries and enter the Temple."

Prince had to admit that Lexi had thought things through. "Thanks," he said to her.

"I'd do anything for my twin sister. Now, keep in mind the green arrows bring you directly to the main building where the Chapel and the Priestess's apartments are, and you want to avoid that. Pink squares lead to the infirmary, and purple circles go to the nursery."

They stayed a few minutes out there, and then Lexi walked them back to the storage room. They worked for less than an hour, sometimes moving the same boxes around several times to give the impression the cargo was larger and required more time to be disposed of.

"The crew will be here any minute now. You can't stay much longer," Lexi finally said to them. She went to the office, dancing a nervous dance on her feet. "Sorry, must go to the bathroom again."

Prince heard the woman complaining, but Lexi came out with the chain. She hushed the men outside the storage room. "Don't get caught," she said, looking directly at Prince once they were safely in the outer hallway.

"Not in my plan," he answered.

"When you're safe and far away from here, tell Pax I want her to be happy."

Prince didn't expect her words. "I'll do that."

"What are you waiting for? Go." Lexi turned around to enter the bathrooms. She didn't look back.

"Where to?" Lucas asked after a moment.

"We follow the purple circles." He'd thought about it and if Pax was at the Temple, and he was counting on that out of pure faith, the only plausible place where she would be was in the nursery with their daughter.

"Purple circles it is, then." Lucas reached Prince's pace in a few steps.

The gallery was illuminated by cold lights set high on the ceiling and spaced at lengthy intervals, giving the place an eerie atmosphere, as if they were walking in and out pools of white and black. Once in a while, they passed recessed doors marked with symbols and letters.

Prince would have broken into a run, going from one purple circle to the other, but kept his steps under control, taking in details as he went. The doors opened only on the right side of the gallery, the letters were in alphabetical order, and the symbols varied from stylized flowers, to depiction of tools, to the more common sign of the bathroom. The place seemed to stretch forever; there wasn't an end in sight and the only company they had was the occasional whirring of cable lines bordering the floor.

Despite the gallery being roomy, Prince started feeling as if a gigantic throat were closing around him. The farther he walked, the less he could breathe. At any moment, women could come out from one of the doors and see them. Everything went a shade darker in a matter of seconds.

"Everything's going to be okay," he whispered to himself.

Lucas heard him. "Think about your family. Focus on Pax and the baby." He put a hand on Prince's shoulder, gently pushing him ahead.

My family, Prince thought and forced himself to breathe in and out until the dark spots dancing behind his eyelids withdrew. "My family," he repeated out loud.

"Yes, good." Lucas nodded.

The irritating sound of badly oiled hinges resonated through the gallery. Prince and Lucas stopped on the spot and turned, looking for the source of the noise. A door opened several steps behind them and women's voices filled the silence. Prince and Lucas were standing under bright light.

Prince frantically looked on his right and pulled Lucas with him toward the next black spot and into the archway of a recessed door. He flattened his body against the cold surface of the door and raised the veil until it covered his entire face. A soft rush of fabric indicated Lucas was doing the same.

Not now, not now, not now... Prince's heart drummed against his rib cage without control, his legs threatened to give up, and his ears were playing tricks on him because he couldn't hear anything past the noise of his own blood flow. *Not now, not now, not now...*

Time froze. He waited for the women to walk by and discover them, hiding like little kids who close their eyes and think that nobody can see them, but the seconds stretched and his fear became terror. *What if they walk right to this door?* For a fleeting moment, he felt the desire to laugh and then to scream. *Why don't you come already?*

And they came. Brisk steps and bits and pieces of conversation echoed above Prince's roaring heartbeats. And they left. A door, not far away from where he and Lucas were hiding, opened and closed. A moment passed, then a minute. Silence was restored in the gallery. Prince's legs finally won the battle against his mind and he collapsed on the floor, one hand trying to tear open the veil that was stuck to his mouth, the other pressing on his chest to push his heart back inside.

"They didn't see us." Lucas's voice mirrored the bewilderment Prince's felt.

"We should hurry." Prince commanded his wobbly legs to straighten and then he leaned against the door when all the blood in his body rushed downstairs.

"Take it easy." Lucas held him by the arms.

"I don't have time for that." Prince pushed his heels on the floor, wiggled his fingers, made small circles with his head, and pressed forward.

"We did it once. We can do it again," Lucas murmured, keeping up with the new stride.

"Let's only hope the next door doesn't open in front of us." Prince started silently reciting the prayers his father had taught him. He wasn't a believer, but the words echoing in his mind felt good.

They walked fast at first and then ran. Still, there was no end to the gallery. Prince knew, from recent observation, that the Temple was a big facility, but they should have arrived somewhere by now. Maybe he had misunderstood Lexi's words and the gallery didn't end to the nursery. Maybe they had already passed it, hidden behind one of the many doors. He kept running, dragging along Lucas, wondering if they were on a fool's errand. And even if they found the nursery, what then?

"One step at the time." Lucas took his arm again and softly squeezed it.

Prince hadn't realized he had talked out loud, but nodded and sped up in a twirling of black fabric flying around his body. Every time he saw one of the recessed doors, his heart skipped a bit.

"Look!" Lucas yelled.

"Don't yell!" Prince yelled back, but he looked and stopped running. Ahead, far away but in sight, there was an arch, and beyond the arch there was a flurry of activities. Whatever it was that place was full of women. They needed a plan. "Come here." He directed Lucas toward one of the recesses and hid in the dark. "I can't think straight," he answered the man's silent question. "We walk there," he said after a while.

"Okay."

They adjusted their dresses, raised the veils up to cover their mouths and the facial hair darkening their jaws, slowed their run to a leisurely stroll, and several minutes later, two tall servant women walked through the archway.

"Walk as if we have a reason to be here," Prince whispered to Lucas, hoping the women were too busy with their own tasks to bother giving them a second look. At first glance, the place, bright and smelling of cleaning products, was another hub from where galleries radiated from. *Great*, he thought, the familiar feeling of despair filling his mind. Then he saw the galleries had signs indicating where they led. A brief scan of the tags revealed him what he needed to know. "Neonatal Emergency" was written in bright red letters on one of them. "There." He directed Lucas to his left.

A loud, but not unpleasant noise echoed through the big hallway. A moment later, doors opened and closed and they watched as a river of women flooded the place. Prince and Lucas got caught in the human stream, but managed to walk against the current and turned toward the Neonatal Emergency. A woman kept the door opened for them as they entered a smaller hallway painted in calming blue tones. The repetitive sounds of rustling wind and rain came out of speakers on the walls. Windows and clear doors opened on the hallway, revealing several rooms containing rows of cradles, some of them hosting babies. In one of the rooms, there was only one cradle, and he couldn't help but pause and take a better look at that solitary baby. His eyes moistened when a tiny hand emerged from a blanket. "It's so small," he said in awe. The hand balled up in the tiniest fist and a loud wail followed.

A woman, dressed in nurse garments, appeared in the room and went to check on the baby. Prince and Lucas flattened against the column between one window and the next. A whirl of the black dresses must have caught her eyes because Prince heard steps coming closer to the window. The nurse paused for the longest moment mere inches from where he was standing, and then went back when the baby redoubled her effort to attract attention.

They crouched low and walked out of the way, reaching the end of the hallway where there was a solid and menacingly closed door. There was nowhere else to go but behind that door. The woman announced in baby talk that she was going to fetch a bottle and that she was coming back soon. Prince hoped the nurse was going back where she had come from, but the steps echoed closer and louder instead of getting away from them.

He pushed the door open without thinking. He and Lucas had just entered a dim-lit room when he saw several bottles lined up on a counter, a table with food displayed on it, two fridges, a big sink, and a stove. They had found the kitchen. Beside one of the two fridges, there was a dark space indicating a storage room, probably a pantry closet. "There!" *Let it be big enough to hide both of us*, he prayed.

They had just reached the safety of the storage, which was slightly larger than a broom closet, when the nurse entered the kitchen singing a lullaby. She stayed in the room longer than Prince deemed necessary to fill a bottle with some warm milk. She was walking out, still singing, when a phone rang. He wanted to scream in frustration. Not only the woman didn't seem to be in any hurry to do what she had to do, but the rings came from the wall by the storage entry.

"Neonatal Emergency," she announced with her sweet voice. "No, the Chosen hasn't eaten yet. I was preparing her a bottle just now." A small pause, and then she said, "I had to send the donor to sleep. She didn't want to leave the baby, but I told her the Chosen was getting better already. There is no need for her to be here."

The conversation continued on more personal tones, but thankfully, the nurse remembered the baby's milk was getting cold, which in turn led her to linger in the kitchen to warm the bottle, again. More annoyingly, the singing had resumed. The door opened abruptly and someone else stepped in.

"The baby's crying! What's taking you so long?" Pax's imperious voice stopped the singing right away.

"I understand your concern, but I assure you, Mistress Layan, your attitude isn't justified. The Chosen is under my personal care. I was appointed by the Priestess herself for this task, so please, let me do my job without interfering," the nurse answered.

"I heard you on the phone!"

"Her Holiness's aide was asking about the Chosen. Do you have a problem with me answering her?"

Prince heard the last sentence, but didn't have time to think that Pax spoke again, her anger spiking up with each word.

"I want to be sure she's fine. That isn't hard to understand, or is it?"

"Mistress, with all due respect to your name, you seem to forget that, although you were selected to be the Chosen's donor—I'm sure given your pure blood—you're only an instrument in her wellbeing. In other words, you're just the donor." The nurse matched the coldness in Pax's tone with some of her own.

Prince heard the door being slammed back in its place and the nurse commenting out loud, "She believes that since she's the president's daughter she can do and say whatever she wants."

The door opened and closed one more time and he and Lucas were finally left alone to collect their thoughts.

"Good news is we found both of them," Prince said and then with an exasperated sigh added, "Bad news is we have nowhere to go but here." He slowly stepped outside the storage area, only to be surprised by the door opening again. He hadn't heard the steps approaching and was caught standing between the two fridges, disbelief on his face that he had gone so far only to fail miserably.

"It's me." Pax ran to him. "Don't worry. After the scene I've just made in the nursery, I don't think the nurse is coming after me." She closed the distance between the door and Prince in a second, nodding in acknowledgment when she saw Lucas.

Prince was confused, but her presence was enough to make him feel better.

"Lexi called me. Sorry I couldn't answer earlier—" Pax showed him the cell phone she was holding. "And, I thought I saw two tall maids walking through the hall. I'm so tired I could've been hallucinating. Then the nurse was taking forever to get out of here and I got scared."

"You look so pale." Prince took her in his arms.

"Baby needed lots of blood, but I'm fine. You should see her, my love. Our baby is small, but she's just perfect. She has your dark eyes."

Prince's throat closed and hugged Pax tight, taking in the familiar scent of her skin that had the power to calm him. "Is she going to be okay? What did she need the blood for?"

"The pediatrician says she's strong for being born so small, but she's anemic."

"What's that mean?"

"She has a reduced number of red blood cells because she was born early."

"Is that dangerous?" Prince wasn't sure he had understood what she was talking about. His father had taught him to read and write, and at Sundial, he had stolen books from the women's library, but his knowledge of the human body remained lacking.

"The pediatrician explained it's fairly common in premature babies, but since they found a good donor, she'll be fine."

"Thank the God," Prince whispered. Then a bigger picture formed in his mind. "We can't take the baby anywhere else. She wouldn't make it outside."

"Maybe not now, but we'll think of something." Pax looked him in the eyes and tried to smile.

"Maybe Anna will find a way," Lucas said.

"Maybe." Prince couldn't smile back, but tried to soften his expression.

"Lexi couldn't explain everything on the phone, but she did mention Anna. Is she in it, too? Is it true?" she asked, surprise in her face.

"It's true. She's here at the Temple, and at present she should be stalling the Priestess to give us some time to rescue you and the baby." Lucas sat at the table. "My legs are refusing to support the rest of my body. I'm going to faint any moment now."

"It's okay. I don't think I can stand much longer myself." Prince turned to face Pax.

"You're fine. Take five. The nurse isn't coming back. I told her I was going to the kitchen to fix something to eat and that I didn't want to be disturbed."

"We should find a safe way to communicate with Anna." Prince plucked a few red grapes from the fruit bowl. He was famished.

"Can you call her?" Lucas took an apple and carved a good chunk out of it with a single bite.

"Yes, I guess there's nothing strange if I call her to ask how my mother is faring. I don't think the Priestess would be suspicious." Pax opened her cell phone.

"Wait." Prince put a hand on hers, closing the phone she was holding.

"Let's think what you want to say in case the Priestess *gets* suspicious." Lucas went for a second apple.

The cell phone rang and took everybody by surprise.

"I guess we don't have time to worry about that." Pax showed them the caller ID. "Hi, Anna. I'm fine."

Prince took Pax's other hand and slowly stroked it. "It's okay," he whispered, locking his eyes with hers. He felt her body relax under his touch.

"Oh, you're here at the Temple! When did you arrive?"

Prince tried to imagine what was happening on the other side of the conversation and why Anna had called.

"Lexi's here, too? Oh, right, the Literacy Sans Frontier project. I forgot she had a drop-off scheduled on these days." Pax removed her hand from his and went around the kitchen looking for something.

Lucas seemed to understand what she wanted. He put down the half-eaten apple and went toward the cupboard drawers, opened in rapid succession three of them, and found pen and paper. Pax took them, went back to the table, and started writing.

There is something wrong with Anna, Prince read. He looked at Pax, but she shook her head. *I don't know*, she wrote while talking at the phone.

"I'll have to ask the Priestess," she said to Anna. "It's late anyway."

Prince's ears caught the soft noise of steps approaching the kitchen. He put one finger to his mouth and then signed to Lucas to follow him back inside the closet. Someone entered the room in silence, approached the kitchen table, moved a chair, and sat down.

"Okay, see you later." Pax ended the call, the sound of the cell phone being closed a neat click. "What do you need, nurse?" she asked.

"The Chosen is peacefully sleeping, and while I was looking at her, I realized that we should, at least, be civilized toward each other. I guess we started on the wrong foot, but first and foremost, we both have the Chosen's wellbeing in mind. What I'm trying to say is that I'd like to start over with you," the nurse answered.

Prince groaned under his breath and leaned his head against the wall behind him. Lucas bumped his elbow.

"I'd love that, too." Pax's voice came distorted, but it didn't sound sincere to Prince.

The nurse didn't think the same. "Thank you, Mistress. I'm one of your mother's bigger supporters, and I hated the idea that we couldn't stand being around each other."

"I'm probably crankier than usual."

"Well, you did donate a great quantity of blood. I was surprised you didn't faint."

"I don't faint easily." Pax's tone was suddenly darker.

Prince's memories played back the last time she had fainted before his eyes, and the time before. And he remembered, once again, why he hated the Priestess with all his heart.

"I must admit you're one tough young lady, Mistress."

"Thanks."

"Hungry?" the nurse asked.

"I'll finish this apple. My mother's secretary called while I was trying to decide what I wanted and now I'm too tired—"

"Nonsense. You need to eat. I'll fix something for you. I must prepare something for myself anyway before the Chosen wakes up for the next feeding."

For several long minutes, Prince only heard kitchen sounds—chopping, cutting, and washing, mostly done in silence. Pax and the nurse were busy preparing their dinner.

"Do you think I'll be needed much longer?" Pax asked after all the cooking preparation had ended.

"The Chosen is having an amazing recovery. You should've seen her just an hour or two before you arrived. The Priestess was desperate. The time before—"

"The baby was sick before?" Pax interrupted the woman.

"Oh, yes, several times, in fact. But the other episodes were easily kept under control. The anemia is something that just happened. But, between you and me, with all the blood the pediatrician draws every day to test her, I'm not surprised she ended up needing a transfusion. I told her once. But, what do I know? I'm but a nurse."

"Why does she need so many tests?" Pax seemed to read Prince's mind.

Barely daring to breathe inside the small closet, side to side with Lucas, he was aching to ask his own questions.

"She's small even considering she was born premature. Her lungs weren't fully developed and she needed a machine to keep her lungs working. It's a miracle she's alive, I'm telling you. She's a resilient girl. She'll be a great priestess one day." The nurse's voice reached lyrical tones on the last sentence.

Prince, putting together the woman's words, was starting to picture an image he didn't like. He couldn't believe the Priestess wanted anything to do with his daughter.

"Anyway, the worst is passed. The Chosen's put on some much needed weight, and her vitals are perfect. My guess is that the pediatrician will keep you around for another day or two, just to be on the safe side, and then you're good to go."

"Sounds good. Thanks for the sandwich," Pax said.

"Time's up. Let's go check on her. Are you coming?" the nurse asked after a long silence.

"Sure, right away."

Prince patiently waited a few seconds before leaving the safety of the closet.

"We're trapped. Let's finish what we started." Lucas reached for the loaf of bread left behind on the table and cut some cheese from a platter.

"The nurse didn't clean up after herself." Prince took in the details of the untidy kitchen.

"And you're surprised why?" Lucas put two slices of cold meat between the bread and cheese.

"We can't stay here much longer. Someone's coming to clean."

"Again, we're trapped." Lucas turned his head toward the only exit.

"Just a sec. I've forgotten my phone on the table," Pax said out loud, entering the kitchen and looking at them with a worried expression. "Anna was trying to warn me about something, but she had to end the call," she whispered in a rush.

"We'll find a way to leave, but I want to see the baby first." Prince hadn't thought about saying that, but it sounded right.

"It's too dangerous, and you just told me that someone could come any moment now." Lucas put down his meal and stared at Prince.

"I want to see her." Prince stared back at him.

From the outside the nurse called Pax. She went out before the woman would come any closer.

"You're making no sense," Lucas said softly.

"If it's the last thing I do, I want to see my daughter."

"It *is* going to be the last thing you do if—"

"It's going to be the last thing I do anyway…"

"Don't talk like that."

"It's true." Prince shrugged. He felt tired.

He watched as Lucas ate what was left of the women's meal. He tried to nibble at the bread, but his stomach clenched down, refusing to let anything in. He set to wait for Pax to come back, nervousness possessing his body.

Finally, Pax's head appeared at the door. "Hurry," she whispered and led them out. "The nurse just went to report to the Priestess. I don't know how long she'll be gone. And I'm worried the next shift will start soon. You must go now. There's a door just outside the Neonatal Emergency that opens into a small backyard. You can lock it from the inside. Wait for me there."

Prince kissed her softly and then ran inside the nursery where the solitary crib was. He had no doubt it was his daughter's. The Chosen.

"There isn't time," Lucas hissed under his breath.

"I'll meet you there. Go." Prince waved his hand and didn't wait for the man to answer back. He leaned on the crib and moved aside the white blanket. Words failed him at the sight.

"Isn't she perfect?" Pax murmured by his side.

The baby chose that moment to open her eyes, as dark as his, and look at him. A small hand hooked on his finger.

"You can't give up on us. We need you," Pax said to the baby, then took her from the crib and gently placed her in his arms.

"She's so small." He was worried he was going to hurt her by just holding her tiny body.

"Look, she loves you already."

The baby cooed, snuggled against his chest, and the corners of her lips curved up.

"Is she smiling?" he asked, unable to do anything else but stare at her.

"She is. I hadn't seen her smiling…"

A knock on the glass made them jump. Prince's first instinct was to cover the baby inside his arms, but it was Lucas, who hadn't left.

"If you want to help your family, you must leave, now." Lucas's words came through the glass distorted, but clear enough.

"I don't like what the Priestess wants to do with our baby," Prince, his back to the glass, said to Pax.

"Go, or it will be all for nothing." Pax pried open his arms to extricate he girl. "Go. Wait for me in the backyard. We'll think of something."

Lucas, tired of waiting, barged inside the nursery and dragged Prince outside. "I understand your feelings. I do." He pushed him through the hallway. "But you haven't eaten or slept for some time now, and your judgment is clouded."

Prince started to protest, but Lucas shushed him and added, "I know you aren't big on following orders, but you'll make an exception now."

Prince closed his mouth and raised his veil over his face, leaving only his eyes uncovered.

"Good. Now, I'll open the door and I'll check if the coast is clear. You stay with me." Lucas gave him a last look, turned around, opened the door ajar, put his head through the crack he had created, waited a moment, opened the door some more, and stepped outside, one hand holding Prince's sleeve in a tight vice.

They were in and out of the main hallway in a matter of seconds. The door marked with a stylized flower opened to a small, internal backyard. "So, this is what the sign stands for," Lucas commented when they were safely inside their new haven. He drove the lock into place and sat on the mossy floor with his back to the door.

CHAPTER 13

"When Randal was just a child, he used to climb everywhere. One night, he didn't come back home. We looked for him for hours. The Priest didn't go to sleep until we found him."

"Where was he?" Prince sat on a bench facing the door.

"Lying at the base of a low cliff he was trying to conquer. He'd fallen and lost consciousness. When I saw him, I thought he was dead. I remember the moment as if it were happening now. I decided that living wasn't important anymore. It was like a switch inside my head. A moment there was light, the next pitch dark."

"Then what happened?"

"Then he opened his eyes."

"Why are you telling me this?" Prince plucked a blossom from the flowerbed and brought it to his nose.

"Because, a few moments ago, before you held your daughter, you had the same expression of a man who doesn't care anymore."

"I'm fine. It was just a moment."

"You better believe it because now you have both Pax and the baby depending on you keeping your head firmly in its place."

"Why are you here, with me?"

"You can't make it alone."

"Why aren't you marching toward Sundial to rescue Randal?"

"It's been in my thoughts since you told me about him. But even if I find a way to reach Sundial, what then? I must help you first. If we don't defeat the Priestess, there is no hope for my son, or for any other man."

"You think I'm here to defeat her?"

"I know you hate her enough to try. That's why I need you focused on your task."

Prince raised his legs and laid his head on the bench. "Sometimes, I think hate is the only fuel powering my body." He closed his eyes for a second. He only wanted to raise his family far away from Ginecea, and the Priestess, and all the women who thought of him as something evil and base. He wanted to see his baby daughter grow. "How could the Priest remain sane through those long years?"

"The Priest was alone all his life. In a city full of people, he was completely alone."

"This place reminds me of the Priest's gardens. There's even a koi pond there." Prince indicated the small basin of water brimming with colored life.

A soft knock on the door made Lucas jump.

"It's me, Pax."

Lucas unlocked the door and let Pax in.

She went to sit on the bench and took Prince's hand in hers. "The Priestess has just released me from donor duty. The nurse was ordered to draw enough blood in case the baby needs more, but once that's done, probably tomorrow morning, I'm free to go."

"And the baby?" Prince asked.

"I can't stay here with her without alerting the Priestess that I know whose baby the Chosen is. And she isn't ready to leave the Neonatal Emergency yet."

"As long as the baby is under the Priestess's care, she's safe," Lucas said.

"I know, but the idea of leaving our daughter with that monster makes me sick." Prince was getting restless. He was on the verge of collapsing, but his mind wouldn't let him relax.

Pax's cell phone rang. "Lexi? Where are you?" she asked.

Prince listened to the conversation without focusing on the words being said. He was trying to plan an escape route, but he felt trapped once again. "What? Slow down, I can't understand what you're saying. Lexi?" Pax stood up, her face suddenly pale. "Lexi?"

Prince and Lucas stood up as well.

"Lexi's just been taken in custody by one of the Priestess's guards. Before her call was ended, she managed to tell me Anna's already in custody, and the Priestess has given direct orders to chase down two tall maids. The guards have permission to shoot on sight." Pax went back and forth in the confined space between the flowerbeds, the pond, and the bench. "This is madness. Any maid taller than average could be killed. The Priestess doesn't care about fathered women's lives anymore. She's deranged."

"How did she discover us?" Prince asked.

"I don't know. Doesn't matter." Pax froze, her face betraying the inner turmoil. "We have to run away before they put the place in lockdown." She reached for the door; then she turned, a sudden thought lighting her eyes. "I can't leave the baby now. The nurse hasn't collected more blood yet—"

"You're staying." Prince stopped her hand from turning the handle.

"But what about you?" Pax asked slowly, grabbing him by his shoulders. "I don't want to leave you…"

"Our daughter is more important. I can take care of myself—she can't. She needs you." Prince raised her chin with a finger to force her to look at him. "And I'll feel better knowing you're both safe. The Priestess won't do anything to you, because she needs you too."

"But—"

"We'll find a way to be together, but right now, you must stay with her." Prince hugged her close. "You're tough."

The siren announced the end of the shift. Pax and Prince broke the embrace, pain etched in their faces. "You can do it, with or without me," he whispered to her.

"It's now or never." Lucas looked at the couple with sorrow.

"Kiss her for me." Prince caressed Pax's cheeks, pressed his forehead against hers. "I love you both more than life itself." He kissed her, wiping her tears with his lips.

"Now!" Lucas was calling him from the outside. "Prince!"

"Go," Pax murmured with what was left of her voice.

Prince felt physical pain tearing at him when he was forced to leave her embrace for the cold air of the hallway. He found himself outside, propelled by Lucas's strong arms.

"I'm sorry, but you weren't cooperating," the man said.

Heads low, bodies bent, and veils up, they entered the flow of women busy walking toward their next destination. Prince focused on the task at hand and moved forward as if he knew where he was going. The next turn, he made up his mind and followed a group of women, among whom there were several servants clad in dark garments as they were.

"Stop where you are," a guard ordered, aiming her gun at them.

The whole group of women obeyed the command like a herd of sheep. Prince touched Lucas and they followed suit making sure to blend, semi-hidden by the rest of the black clothes.

"You, step forward." The guard was looking at Prince.

He didn't move. After a long moment, the woman in front of him thought the guard was talking to her and moved aside from the group. Another woman, an older servant, slowly walked toward the guard to confront her. "What do you want from her now? Another shift? Her blood? Leave her alone."

A chorus of comments followed the older servant's words. "You pure breeds think we can go without food and rest for days!" someone yelled.

The guard was taken aback by the servants' reaction. "Stop where you are. Do as I say or I'll shoot you." Despite her intention to look in charge, she stepped back, fear showing in her halting movements.

The older servant defiantly moved forward. "I'm tired of young hotheads like you giving me orders." After a moment of hesitation, a few of the other dark-clothed women took courage and went to assist their newly appointed leader. The women wearing suits and lab coats moved aside, adding confusion to the already tense situation. Prince and Lucas swiftly moved with the latters, partially hiding beside the shallow columns decorating the hallway.

"All of you, I said move back!" The guard started swinging the gun in a long arch meant to encompass the whole company. Her nervous finger pulled the trigger. A shot resonated in the crowded hallway, the noise echoing from the high ceiling and back to the floor. There was silence one moment and chaos the next. Screams and cries filled the air.

"Halt!" Other guards arrived. More guns were pointed at the defenseless crowd. Fathered women ran in every direction as shots were fired in rapid succession.

Prince saw the older servant fall and soon disappear under a stampede of terrified women looking for safety. He and Lucas joined the herd and ran with them. There wasn't time to ask where they were going, and there wasn't any certainty that the women themselves knew what they were doing. More than once, hoping they would make the right decision, they had to choose which group to follow, since the women split several times. They went in and out of the main gallery, sometimes passing through labs and internal gardens, only to return to the central hub. Two hours later, after having left the gallery for good, they finally reached the end of their journey.

Prince looked around at the place and recognized a dormitory. It was roomier and better taken care of than the slaves' equivalent, but had many similarities. A central room opened on several dozen cubicles. The cubicles didn't have bars to keep the occupants inside, but they didn't have doors for privacy. The beds were bigger than the slaves' crude cots, but they were the only furniture. The real luxury was the big table at the center of the larger room. Fathered women were allowed to eat together. Judging from the variety of food displayed on the table, their fare must have been much better than what he had gotten used to eating at Sundial.

The women scattered around, some of them hurried to their places, while others split between the central room—where at a second glance there was also a kitchen—and a hallway that probably opened to the bathrooms. Prince and Lucas found themselves stranded in the middle of the central room with nowhere to hide. A few women stayed behind to take a better look at them sticking out of the crowd with their barely concealed height and countenance.

"Welcome to the Temple chapter house. You can remove your veil now," one of the servants said. The others came closer.

Prince and Lucas exchanged glances.

"If we wanted to rat you out, we'd have done it already." The servant reached for a chair, sat, took a slice of bread from a large plate, and waited patiently for the men to do something.

Prince was the first to lower his veil and then open the dress on his back to step out of it. It was futile to fight and he was tired from the long run. He imagined Lucas was exhausted too.

"Who are you?" the servant asked, her voice calm. Two women joined her at the table.

Prince looked at Lucas for guidance. The man nodded.

"We're ex-workers far away from home," Lucas answered.

"How far?"

"Several days."

Prince thought the exchange between Lucas and the woman was strange. She looked at ease talking to men, and that wasn't normal. None of the women seemed concerned with their presence.

"Are you one of the Priest's men?" the second woman asked.

Prince recoiled at the question. "I don't know what you're talking about."

"Relax, everybody here knows about the Priest and the City of Men," a third woman added, checking the fruits on the platter.

Prince hastily scanned the room for cameras. His throat was parched and the light in the room was too bright.

"My aunt told me tales about a place where men and women were free to be together and how they had equal rights. She told me she knew where it was, and she would've shown it to me one day, but she disappeared and we never heard from her again." The woman offered him a slice from the apple she was cutting.

"My cousin escaped from Ginecea several years ago to live with a man. The Priest welcomed her. She used to send messages to the family, but she hasn't in a while. There are rumors," the second woman said.

Meanwhile, the room had filled with the rest of the inhabitants. Prince shivered. So many women all in the same place reminded him of a lynch mob. Not so long ago, back at the City of Men just mentioned, he and the Priest had faced an army of women only to be stoned and sent to death. If it weren't for Pax and Lucas, who had helped her, he wouldn't be alive. He gingerly looked at the piece of apple and waited until the woman ate her portion. Someone put a cup of steaming coffee before him.

"Drink. You don't look well."

He finally decided he didn't have any power to change the immediate future and accepted the beverage with whispered thanks. The hot liquid entered in his system in a matter of seconds. He looked at Lucas and at the rest of the company, then finally relaxed and listened to the tales being told.

"Is it true the president destroyed the City of Men?"

Prince lowered his head, vivid memories of the carnage playing before his eyes.

"Yes, it's true, but most of its citizens escaped." Lucas answered for both of them the questions that kept coming after that statement.

Prince, his mind finally working and his stomach full, didn't interrupt Lucas. He kept to himself, taking in all the questions and answers and forming a picture about those fathered women, which was both fascinating and hard to believe. The more he learned about Ginecean social strata, the more he had to admit Lucas was right. Ginecean society was built upon layers of compartmentalized lies. Every social stratum kept ignorant about the others by the centralized authority of the Priestess. Even the president was probably kept on a need-to-know basis by Her Holiness.

The fathered women in that room didn't know anything regarding the destruction of the City of Men firsthand. They weren't allowed to watch television. What they knew came from their more fortunate relatives who worked as maids for pure breed families. Those luckier women had better lives and once in a while, they sneaked a peek at their employers' televisions. They had known about the sewage plants' massacres the same way. Everything worked by word of mouth in their world. They weren't slaves like the men, but they weren't free, either. Among the fathered women, there were further differences that were becoming clear to him while they talked about their shifts.

He was sure pure breeds didn't know about the fact that their maids' distant relatives—who were forced to work with the men— didn't have sick days or vacations, or that if they didn't fill their quota, they didn't receive food. Pax didn't know anything of that sort. She wouldn't have abided such disparities.

And at the bottom of the feeder were the men, who knew the least. They were needed to keep Ginecea alive and didn't know how important they were. Without them, there were no women. The only ones with the full knowledge were the priestesses. One single person who inherited the truth from her predecessor and who, in exchange, would teach the next one to hate and enslave men. A never-ending cycle of pain, sorrow, and prevarication perpetuated by one woman.

"The Priestess has my daughter," Prince said, managing to silence the crowd.

Countless eyes turned to look at him.

"She has lied to my companion, told her our baby had died in childbirth." His voice broke and he accepted another cup of coffee.

Lucas came close to him and laid one hand on his shoulder.

"The Priestess is keeping my daughter here at the Temple," he finished. "She has plans for my baby…"

"Is your daughter the Chosen one?"

He nodded, grateful he didn't have to explain. "I want her back. I want my companion back. I want my life back." He lowered his eyes on the table.

A few hands joined Lucas's in giving Prince physical comfort. "We'll help you." It wasn't one voice. All of them said it, some out loud, some whispering.

"It's time we take things in our hands." The woman who had asked the first question offered her outstretched hand. "I'm Magdalene."

Several hours of continuous talking and presentations later, Prince had heard more than he could possibly remember about the Temple chapters, as the fathered women living there called themselves. A barrage of names—Lucille, Marcia, Erika, Dana, Simone, Laura, Carole, and others he didn't understand—descended upon his ears. He tried to match the names with the faces, but it was getting late. The only woman in the room he wouldn't easily forget was Magdalene. She had surprised him earlier on by welcoming them. The others were a big blur in his mind. Still, each and every one of them had a story to tell, and he listened patiently. Some of the information was of vital importance and he made an effort to keep his eyes open.

"I was sent here soon after I was born. I was maybe a week old and some pure breed bureaucrat decided I was going to work at the Temple. I was raised here. It could've been way worse. This isn't bad. I could've ended up at the sewage plants. As a Temple chapter, we've the *privilege* to serve the pure breeds who serve the Priestess," Magdalene explained, playing with a long necklace that had a black stone pendant.

Prince had been looking at the pendant for some time, his eyes following the hypnotic movements and feeling more and more tired, but when he heard the way she said the word "privilege," he couldn't help but smile. Meanwhile, the night had almost become morning.

"Of course, the Temple chapters are not allowed before Her Holiness's presence."

"You never saw her…?" Lucas said, half question, half statement.

"We see her more than we'd like. The point is, she doesn't see us. We are but a buzz in her hearing. I wouldn't be surprised to discover she doesn't know how many of us live here."

"And we are strictly forbidden to enter the Temple proper," a Lucille added.

"Why?" Lucas asked.

"It's said there are workers there," Marcia, or Carole, answered.

"Probably sementals." Prince was interested in hearing more, despite how tired he felt.

"Yes, sementals. We don't know why the Priestess keeps so many of them here when she can't stand the idea to be in the same room with a fathered woman." Magdalene finally took the reins of the conversation.

Prince began to understand why priestesses did the things they did. They had perfected a foolproof method to feed bits and pieces of truths and lies to the Ginecean population. The current Priestess didn't want anybody she couldn't trust close to the men imprisoned inside the Temple. She couldn't risk a simple fathered woman discovering why she needed her livestock nearby. "Well, you are in a better position than the pure breed guards who works at Sundial, anyway. They have to deal with the *workers* all day long."

"The pure breeds who work as guards at the farms are there because they did something to displease the Priestess. It's a penance of some sort," Magdalene said, embarrassment in her face.

"That's what you have been told?" Lucas asked.

"It's common knowledge…" Marcia, or Carole, answered when Magdalene didn't follow.

"Of course it is," Prince said. Another lie. *Let's divide the pure breeds among themselves as well.* The Priestess was everything but displeased by the pure breeds working at Sundial. Cruel, greedy women like Caren and Lauren were the very pillars upon which Ginecea had been built by generations of priestesses. The truth was that Her Holiness needed to keep the women who worked for her at farms like Sundial, which was in actuality a sperm bank, shielded from the rest of the pure breeds. Prince's head was overflowing with data he was slowly putting together. There were connections that were easier to make, and others more subtle to understand—what the Priest had revealed to him about the incognito had shocked him into silence then—but he thought, for the first time in his life, that he knew what he was meant to do. At the moment, he was too tired to talk about it.

It was already morning, according to the clock on the wall, when Prince retired to a vacant cubicle and finally lay down. As he put his head on the pillow, he was already sleeping. His mind didn't rest, though. He dreamed about his innocent daughter, and in his dream, she was already a priestess and she hated him more than anything else in the world.

"You cried and trashed in your sleep the whole time," Lucas said when they sat for breakfast, or lunch, or early supper.

Prince looked around, his eyes sleepy. It was difficult to say the time of day with his back to the clock since the chapter house didn't have windows. He filled his plate with fruits and bread and silently ate. He didn't have to explain to Lucas why he couldn't sleep peacefully. "There won't be another Priestess reigning over Ginecea," he answered instead, saying out loud his last thought.

"And how do you plan to do that?" Magdalene sat at the table. Several other women joined, eager to hear his answer.

Prince made an effort to remember some of their names, but his mind didn't cooperate. There were so many of them, and he still felt an atavistic uneasiness in their presence. Although, the night before he had noticed how Magdalene had hesitated before saying it was a punishment to be sent to work where the workers were. It spoke well of her.

He resorted to the energizing effect of the coffee to focus on what he wanted to say. "I intend to set you free from your status of lesser citizen."

"We are fathered women." Magdalene raised one eyebrow.

"A fathered woman and a pure breed are different only by the way they are raised." Prince let the words sink in.

"I don't understand. We are *fathered* women..." Again, Magdalene's voice faltered and she didn't add the obvious, "*We are a lower breed because men's semen was used to conceive us.*"

"Our semen is used to create men *and* women. Technically speaking, all women on Ginecea are fathered." The reaction to Prince's words wasn't what he had expected. Angry stares cooled the atmosphere.

"I don't believe you," Magdalene said, clearly trying to steady her voice, and every other head nodded in consent.

Prince thought it was the saddest thing they couldn't even think it was possible they were worth more than what society had told them.

"Sundial, the farm where I'm originally from, isn't just a nursery for exotic plants. Orchids aren't the most precious goods they produce. Sundial is the Priestess's semen factory. She uses sementals like me to restock her fridges with new specimen."

"But, sementals are used to produce... semen. I don't understand what you are trying to say."

"What do you know about Sundial?" Prince gently asked the woman—she was one of the women who had spoken the night before—sitting behind Magdalene.

"What you just said–that Sundial is famous for the orchids. There was lots of talking about a new hybrid several months ago. I know because a friend of mine is close with someone who works there," the Temple chapter answered without hesitation.

"See," he said to Magdalene. "There's a reason why you know about the plants in great detail, but you don't know anything about the lab where I was taken every day of my adult life to make deposits." He waited for the woman to say something, but she remained silent. "Why the secrecy about Sundial?"

Some of the women murmured something, but nobody offered an answer to his question.

"I'm a semental and I come from Sundial, which as far as everybody knows, is a nursery. I understand your confusion. I didn't know any better myself." He felt that by repeating the concept the women would understand, but they were still staring at him. "The Priest, the man who escaped from Tarin and built the City of Men, is President Maurice Layan's father." He dropped the bomb and looked around to see the effect.

Every single woman in the central room started talking at the same time. It was chaos. Magdalene was the loudest, but it wasn't possible to make out her words.

"The Priest himself told me about his daughter," he stated and then looked at Lucas to confirm his words.

Lucas nodded. "Yes, what he's saying is the truth. I've known the Priest my whole life and he told me his story."

"Why would you tell *us*?" Magdalene asked, a mix of reverence and disbelief in her voice.

Lucas shrugged. "Why not? It's time to start revealing old truths. Given the situation on Ginecea, I don't think the Priest would mind."

Prince listened, incapable of moving, taken by the tale the man was unraveling, as was everybody else. He already knew the story, but there was something to say about the passion Lucas put in his words. More than an hour passed, but nobody took a break or left the room. At the end, Lucas's eyes were bright, and several women audibly sniffed away their emotions.

"So it's true," Magdalene said, a few tears rolling down her cheeks.

"Yes, the Priest was the first one to uncover the truth about Ginecea."

"We could've known long ago," another woman commented.

"The times weren't right. The Priest was alone, struggling to survive in the middle of the desert. All his energy went to build a safe haven for men and women. Nobody would've believed him anyway," Lucas said, his tone angry, pain etched in his face. The mood in the room changed accordingly and nobody dared to say anything else about the Priest. "He did what he could and did a great job with what he was dealt."

After a long moment of awkward silence, the women regained confidence and started asking questions. Prince and Lucas alternated in answering them, trying to be specific and direct. It was difficult at first to maintain a coherent train of thoughts. But those women were eager to know and kept asking all the questions they had never thought they could ask in all those years.

"It's still hard to believe," Magdalene said, several hours later.

Prince's head was aching and his throat was parched. "We are all being defrauded of our lives."

"So, what now?" she asked.

"Now we'll spread the story," Prince answered. "You'll quietly talk about what you've just learned with every other fathered woman you meet."

"Yes, we must reach every factory, every plant, and every chapter house." Lucas hit the table with his fist.

"Every fathered woman deserves to know the truth." Magdalene looked lost in her thoughts.

"We're going to fight the Priestess," a woman proclaimed.

"We don't have an army like the Priestess has," another murmured.

"We don't have weapons!" someone from the back said.

"You're both right, but between men and fathered women, our combined numbers exceed the pure breeds." Prince raised one hand to silence the barrage of comments his statement ensued. "We are so many and they are but a few. If we are united against the Priestess, she won't have a chance."

"He's right. Ginecea isn't prepared to defend itself. Over the years it's grown complacent." Magdalene stood up, her eyes bright. "Look at us. Yesterday, we rebelled against one of the Priestess's guards. It's never happened before, and we didn't even know what we know now. We're ready."

"The Priestess won't even see us coming." A unanimous chorus of cheers and laughs was abruptly stopped by furious pounding on the door.

"Open to the Priestess's Army!"

CHAPTER 14

"They're here for us." Lucas was the first to react. "If they take us now, we're dead."

"I won't let them." Magdalene took Lucas's arm and made sign at Prince to follow her.

Lucas and Prince looked at each other, wondering where the woman was taking them. The place was an enormous, albeit comfortable and luxurious, prison. There were no windows they could see, no other entrances apart from the door where the Priestess's Army was waiting for them.

Magdalene walked without hesitation toward the wall opposite the door. She went for the heavy-looking cupboard and removed two platters from the second shelf; then she put her whole arm inside the space she had just created and pushed. While the pounding on the door became frightening, another sound filled the room: the chirping of well-oiled mechanisms.

"We're going to knock down the door if you don't open in three."

A sudden whoosh and the cupboard slowly started rotating on itself.

"One…"

Magdalene pushed the cupboard to hasten the process.

"Two…"

Prince and Lucas lent a hand.

"Now go. Follow the tunnel," Magdalene yelled to be heard over the commotion of women screaming all at the same time.

"Thr—"

They were already inside.

"Push from your side to put it back," Magdalene said.

"—ee…"

The cupboard went back all the way and the two men were left in the dark. From back inside, screams and the sound of gunfire reached them.

A sense of constriction immediately took over Prince, but the thought of Pax and his daughter made him forget where he was. After a deep breath, he extended his arms in front of him and moved a tentative step.

"I can't see a thing," Lucas said behind him.

Prince reached out to the side and found something. He laid his hands on what appeared to be a wet, crude wall and moved forward with more confidence. "Follow my voice."

They walked, nothing changing in the geography of the place, if not for scurrying sounds that kept them company for a good while.

"This tunnel goes forever," Lucas said some time later. "It must have taken years to build a tunnel like this, nobody being the wiser. I wonder how they managed to get rid of the soil and rocks they dug out of here."

"Those women are... different from what I expected." Prince kept walking one slow step at the time, his hands carefully searching for obstacles ahead. "They sure are resourceful."

"In my experience, I found that resourcefulness is definitely a trait of their sex."

"The only woman I've ever been around is Pax, so I wouldn't know."

"Well, she *is* a woman." Lucas laughed.

"I only saw her as a woman at the beginning. After, when I got to know her, it didn't matter anymore which sex she was. She's just Pax to me. I'd fall in love with her anyway." Prince paused for a moment to stretch his right calf.

"You got something worth fighting for."

"I know." After that, Prince didn't feel the need to share any more of his thoughts. He resumed his slow procession, the tip of his fingers chafed by the abrasive walls. Dark thoughts kept appearing at the edge of his mind and he sent them away. He had a plan. He only needed to remain alive long enough to see it brought to completion.

"I guess, by word of mouth in a month or so, the news will reach the majority of the fathered women." Lucas, following his own train of thoughts out loud, interrupted the silence.

Prince blindly nodded. "Once they know, it'll be easier to convince them to ally with the men and fight the Priestess."

"In actuality, they'll fight Ginecea." Lucas was having some trouble breathing.

Prince had noticed that the night before. Not during their escape through the Temple's gallery, but when he was talking to the women. Lucas had been out of breath soon after they had started talking, and he was sitting. Prince hadn't thought anything about that since they had just run for two hours to save their lives. "Are you okay?"

"Just fine."

Prince didn't think the man sounded fine, but let it go. "What the—?" Even at his slow pace, he found the impact painful.

Lucas bumped into him and swore. "Just found the end?"

"Yes, headfirst." Prince checked the bump already growing on his forehead.

"Can you feel any handles?"

"Just a moment." Prince touched the solid wall that had just stopped him in his track. "I can't find anything and it doesn't feel like a door." He moved his hands up and down, fingers carefully brushing the surface. "Wait... Found something."

"What?"

"There's an opening on the bottom and I can smell fresh air coming in. We have to kneel down and crawl."

Lucas emitted a sound, expressing how much he liked the idea.

"At least it's short. I can see the end from here." Prince went on his hands and knees, his eyes adjusting to the dim light shining at the end of the duct. He didn't have to endure the confined space for long. After no more than fifteen minutes, he reached outside and discovered it was already night.

"Where are we now?" Lucas asked, looking around.

"I have no clue. We're lucky the moon isn't covered by the clouds. Otherwise, it would be pitch black." Prince took a moment to breathe some fresh air while keeping an eye on a formation of dark clouds moving fast through the sky.

"We have to move. We can't stay here." Lucas walked a few steps back and forth, making a circle.

"Shhh." Prince stopped Lucas. "Listen. Can you hear it?" A feeble, but continuous noise that became louder in a matter of seconds. "Is it a car?"

"It seems so."

"Go back." Prince had one foot already inside the tunnel.

They crouched in the small space. "Our freedom didn't last long," Lucas commented.

"Let's hope the car goes away soon." Prince sat on the crude floor, his hands crossed and his head touching the ceiling.

The car got closer, then slowed down and stopped by the entry of the tunnel; the exhaust fumes from the engine filled the space. Prince held his breath, but when he opened his mouth to let some much-needed air in, he started coughing along with Lucas.

"Hey, you! Come out." A woman appeared, peeking from the outside.

Prince and Lucas flattened their bodies against the walls.

"I don't have all night to wait for you to decide what you want to do. Get out now, or I'll leave you here." The woman squinted and added, "I know you're there. Magdalene sent me to rescue you."

Prince tried to decide if it was a trap.

"I've things to do, places to be. I tried, but I didn't find you. I'm leaving. Bye." The woman moved out of the entry.

"Wait, we're coming. Give us a second." Lucas decided for both of them. "Sometimes you have to trust your instincts," he whispered to Prince. "Or have some faith."

"I'm not the most religious person," Prince answered, although just recently he had resorted to praying.

They crawled back outside to confront a young woman who was looking at them with interest.

"I'm not sure you're worth rescuing, and I'd really hoped you wouldn't come out of that hole, but I owe a favor to Magdalene and I always pay my debts," she said. "Ready to go?" She showed them her car with a flourish of her hands.

"When you are," Prince answered.

The woman went to her car and opened the passenger's door. "Would you do me the honor?" She wasn't happy.

Prince couldn't help but sigh. The night was getting interesting. A rescuer who didn't want to rescue them and a bump on the head that was triggering another headache. *At least I slept,* he thought.

"I'm Aria." The young woman turned on the engine without looking back to see if they were inside.

She's already trying to lose us. Prince sat and closed the door just in time. Lucas hurried up, his left leg still outside.

"The faster we get away from here, the better chance we have they won't catch us," Aria explained, barely softening her tone.

"Where are we going?" Prince thought the girl's name was somehow familiar.

"To my employer's estate. Nobody's going to look for you there."

"And where is it?" Lucas relaxed on the seat.

Prince envied the man's calm. He was sitting on the edge of the seat, trying to decide if he wanted to cry in despair or laugh in hysteric fits. He did neither.

"In the country, seven hours north. You were lucky I was here. Milady Corellis sends me to the Temple to deliver messages to Magdalene once every two or three months. And this time I was so looking forward to spending the night..."

"You work for the Corellis family?" Prince couldn't believe the coincidence.

"I used to work at the Corellis Mansion in Ginecea, but I was sent to rusticate with Milady several months ago."

"You're Lexi's Aria," Prince stated.

"How do you know Lexi?" Aria turned around to face him.

"I'm Pax's companion."

"You're what?" Aria hit the brakes, and both Prince and Lucas flew forward, bumping their faces against the front seats.

"What I told you, but keep driving, and please, never do that again." Prince massaged his jaw.

"Before I got *relocated*, Lexi told me there was some kind of trouble with her friend, but... Wow, I'd never thought Pax Layan was into men," Aria said and then added, "No offense, I'm just surprised."

"None taken." Prince sat back on the seat. "I must tell you something," he said, not completely sure it was the smart thing to do.

Lucas put a hand on his arm to caution him from saying anything else. "She's already hostile."

Aria heard the comment. "I've good reasons to be hostile." She accelerated. "I'm waiting. What were you saying?"

"Lexi is at the Temple."

Lucas groaned in disagreement. "Was that necessary?" he whispered to Prince, lower this time.

"Tell me something I don't know. She's the reason I wanted to stay overnight."

"You knew she's there?" Prince didn't understand.

"Of course I knew. Lexi and I've been planning this date for months. We've tried to match my message delivery duty with her charity work several times already, but it never worked out. I haven't seen her in such a long time. I thought tonight it was finally going to happen... if I didn't have to drive you around."

"It probably wouldn't have worked anyway."

"Is there something else?"

"Yes..."

Lucas let out his breath out loud at Prince's admission.

"Okay, get it over with. You're making me nervous." Aria turned to give Prince a sideways look.

"I will, but please don't stop driving. Lexi was taken into custody by the Priestess's guards." He braced his hands against the back of the front seat anyway.

"Do you have anything to do with her situation?" Aria didn't stop, but she slowed down considerably.

Again, Prince debated what was best, but decided the right thing to do was to be honest. "I'm afraid that I do."

"Tell me what happened."

Prince summarized the last two days in less than ten minutes, but then he had to go back and forth trying to explain how things had been set in motion and why he, Pax, Lexi, Anna, and Lucas had come to the Temple. At the part about the incognito, he expected her to have a strong emotional reaction, but she kept listening in complete silence, her face a mask difficult to decipher.

"Now everything makes sense," Aria said when he finished talking. "So that must be what Lexi wanted to tell me…" She paused for a long moment, then sighed. "Right before I was exiled, Lexi sent me a message saying she had important news and that she couldn't wait to see me. I didn't expect her to run to my room soon after, but that's what she did. 'Our life is going to change for the better,' she told me as she entered my bedroom. She didn't have time to add anything else. One nosy maid, seeking to better her position, had seen her sneaking in and warned her mothers. A few minutes later, we got caught in each other arms and that was enough. The same night, I was sent away. I would've been thrown out and left without resources if she hadn't interceded on my behalf. Goddess only knows what she promised her mothers to spare me the streets… or even worse, a sewage plant. I haven't seen her since." Aria's hands shook as she nervously controlled the wheel.

"I'm sorry." Prince reached out his hand to touch Aria's shoulder, but stopped halfway through.

"It's not entirely your fault."

Prince saw her face in the rearview mirror. She was silently crying. The sight was made even sadder by the fact she was trying hard not to sob.

"Do you want to go back and try to rescue Lexi?" Lucas asked.

"I understand if you don't want to carry on with driving us tonight. Just leave us somewhere where we can hide." Prince was already thinking of what to do to survive the night.

"As much as I'd like to throw you outside and turn around to see if she's fine, there's really nothing I can do without making her situation worse." Aria quietly cleaned her tears with her sleeve and then stepped on the accelerator.

"Thanks," Prince said, his hand landing on the headrest of the front seat.

"Don't thank me. I'm not doing it for you."

"Still." Prince could understand the woman's rage. She was as powerless as he. "I'll do everything in my power to rescue my family and the people who helped Pax."

"I'll make you stick to your words." Aria looked at him from the rearview mirror, her eyes ablaze with passion.

Prince's lips curved up. "You and Lexi make quite a couple." He saw her smile back.

"So the ride is going to be long and hopefully uneventful. Entertain me. After all the talking you've done, you still haven't explained how on Ginecea you and the president's daughter met," Aria said.

"Pax came to Sundial for a summer camp. I *worked* there."

"And?"

Prince told her the details. He talked for hours, explaining how he managed to escape his cell just to get a glimpse of Pax and what happened when the guards got hold of him. He even showed Aria and Lucas the scar on his neck just under his right ear, attesting to his bravado. He skipped the part regarding his second visit to Sundial. Those memories still made him want to scream. And he could barely talk about the Bestiarium. If not for the fact he had promised to go back there, he would have erased the whole experience from his mind.

"Now, tell us about this Milady Corellis who's been exchanging messages with Magdalene and who's going to host two ex-workers," he finally asked her.

"Milady Corellis, Lexi's grandmother, is something... I'd never expected to happen to me. She's an interesting lady who's trusted me with secrets that could ruin her life if they got out." Aria paused, her voice colored with a hint of respect. "If it weren't for the fact that I haven't seen Lexi in months, I'd even say that being sent away from Corellis Manor was for the best."

"You got my attention," Prince said.

"Milady is very sensitive to human rights' issues and she's been working underground for some time now to change our society."

"Is that right?" Lucas, who had been dozing on and off for a good hour, was now awake.

196

"I can't wait to meet this Milady of yours." Prince's extremities were going numb. He slowly worked his hands and ankles in slow circles, forward and backward. He had learned the trick in solitary confinement when he was a boy. Usually the cell wasn't large enough to walk his cramps away, so he had found how to ease his growing pains. Next, he bent his neck right and left.

"I'm not sure you're going to meet her, actually."

"You haven't told her we're coming for dinner?" Prince asked.

"Milady is serious about not leaving traces. She makes me deliver her messages by voice only, and we never talk on the phone, unless for short daily tidbits."

"Is she going to throw us out?" Prince pinched the arch of his nose. He could see the first lights of the day blooming on the night sky. He didn't know how long Aria had been driving, but they were probably close to their destination.

"At least we'll be seven hours away from the Priestess." Lucas shrugged his shoulders and reclined his head once again on the headrest.

"Let's not get ahead of ourselves. I said I was going to hide you in Milady's property, and I *am* going to hide you in Milady's property. If you get to meet her or not isn't important." Aria pushed on the accelerator.

"Too tired to drive?" Lucas leaned toward the front seat. "Not that I'm offering to take your place. I've never driven a car."

"Me neither." Prince thought that driving a car was something that could come in handy.

"Yes, I'm tired. I've been driving the whole day, and now also the night, but we're close and I want to lay my head on a pillow. We're less than forty minutes away." Aria exhaled a long breath, rolled down the window, and stuck her head outside for a moment. "Much better."

Prince followed her example and his mind cleared and so did the darkness outside. The morning promised to become a bright day. He could now see the landscape rolling away. He had never seen the country before. It was a wide expanse of low hills and winding paths, with trees and bushes bordering the road. There was a small river cutting the fields and a few small buildings with thatched roofs. It was a calming sight. "What time is it?"

Aria checked her watch. "Five past six, right on schedule."

"I could live here," Prince said, his mind already projecting images of Pax and their baby there with him. "I'd be happy here." He remembered he had said the same thing at the Colony and, for a moment, wondered about Carlos and the people there.

"I had the exact same feeling the first time I woke up at Milady's house. I opened the window to let the sun in, and my heart exploded. My favorite part of the day is working at the orchard, tending to the fruit trees. One of the maids working at the house taught me how to make preserves. With Milady's blessing, I've started building my own cottage. It's just one room, but it's mine."

"You have your own house?" Lucas asked.

"I thought only pure breeds could own property, unless you lived in the City of Men where the Priest has seen to change that."

"Every woman working for Milady is paid and owns her place."

"I've never heard of anything like that." Lucas embraced the front seat.

"As a humble fathered woman, me neither. Before going to live at Milady's, I couldn't even think it was possible. I told you, if Lexi were here, it would be perfect."

Once more, Prince envisioned his own idea of perfection. He could see Pax and the baby playing outside their small cottage. He would build a swing for the baby and a hammock for Pax. He had seen the swing and the hammock for the first time back at the City of Men—one of the men working in his crew had built them for his sons—and he had wanted one of each since then. He would sing lullabies to the baby under the big tree with the silver-white trunk.

"Does anybody in Ginecea know?" Lucas asked.

"I don't think the Priestess would like that." Prince saw in the distance a hill covered by luscious vegetation. He leaned on the open window and rested his chin on his forearms. A sudden noise caught his attention; thousands of birds flew away from the trees on the hill and formed one big, ever-changing cloud in the sky.

"Several people know of Milady's village, but they think it's just another of her pet projects. The Priestess has been informed, but she doesn't think it's anything to be worried about. Milady's grown a reputation of being eccentric, and she's cultivated it over the years to suit her goals. Nobody takes her seriously. Not even her daughter, the Ambassador." Aria turned the car on a small, rough road. "Five minutes and we're home."

Prince sat straight back on the seat and closed the window. He focused ahead, eyes glued to the sight. A wooden fence bordered the road with roses crawling over it. Sitting on the posts, there were blue birds. The birds flew away and he saw the village lying on the right side of the path, nested between majestic trees. There were more cottages than he could count, slim roads connecting several larger buildings, and women hurrying everywhere. Some of them carried woven baskets full of fruits and vegetables, others tended to small animals. "I thought it was something... smaller."

"That's what everybody thinks. When people hear the word *village,* they dismiss it as wishful thinking. Milady lets everybody believe she's delusional. The Ambassador and her family never come to visit. But look at what she has accomplished here." Aria stopped the car at a wooden gate, went to open it, then drove all the way to a square. "Wait for me to come back. I'll inform Milady I'm here, and I'll ask if she wants to see you."

Prince took a good look around. "I'd never thought to say this... but I'm starting to think that there're women, other than Pax, whom I'd probably like as human beings," he said, one hand rubbing his chin, and then added, "I hope Milady isn't going to ruin it for me."

Lucas laughed, walked several steps to waken his legs, and then turned back. "I'm impressed by all of this already."

Some of the women looked at them, surprise showing in their faces.

"They aren't screaming." Prince raised one hand and saluted two girls walking their way. The women changed their course at the last moment to avoid a full frontal with Lucas, who was looking at the scene with an amused expression, but their eyes widened and they nodded at him.

"I wouldn't be surprised if some of those girls have never seen a man up close." Lucas smiled.

Low murmurs and sideways glances followed as more and more villagers saw them. Prince leaned against the fence by the gate and set to enjoy the people watching. Maybe it was the open air, maybe it was the realization that those women weren't going to attack him, but his mind relaxed. He breathed deeply, inhaling scents he wasn't used to. The tree looming over the gate had slim, long leaves that when crunched between his fingers left a foreign smell. It entered his nostrils and went down into his lungs, opening a path of freshness. The grass under his feet was green, wet, and soft. He found the discovery fascinating. Years spent in the Desertica Region had shaped his mind to believe everything was dry and a shade of brown.

Maybe an hour later, Aria emerged from one of the biggest buildings, a larger version of the cottages with a tiled roof and a wraparound porch. She wasn't alone. Another woman followed her outside, one arm safely on Aria's. From a distance, Prince noticed the woman's slow gait, but she was fit and tall. They took their time to walk, and he took in other details. The woman had something that reminded him of Lexi, but she was something else altogether. Milady's face was handsome and terrifying, much more like the Priestess's. S*he did ruin it for me, after all*, he thought.

"Lucas, Prince, come meet Milady Corellis. She wishes to personally welcome you to the Village."

Brief acknowledgments by both parts and then Aria gently removed the woman's hand from her arm and walked toward them. "She wants to talk to you in private," she said to Prince.

"Me?" He didn't want to be alone with that woman.

"Prince, it's your name, right?" Milady signed to him to come closer.

Aria gave him a push, but he braced his feet on the ground. "Yes, it's my name," he answered, raising his chin ever so slightly.

"I'm not going to eat you. Relax." Milady walked toward him, and to his utmost surprise, she put her arm under his. "I don't have much balance these days and I don't like to use a cane. It makes me look older, and I don't feel a day over forty."

He didn't like the contact and couldn't help but shiver. He also wasn't used to chatty women, or at least he wasn't used to women who wanted to strike a conversation with him. And, for the nth time, he was reminded of how he didn't consider Pax a member of the opposite sex.

"You are the Layan girl's companion I've been told. Is it true?" She resumed her slow walking, forcing him to follow her.

"Yes."

"And you have a kid with her."

"Yes."

"And the kid's been chosen to be the next Priestess."

"Yes."

"Do you know why your daughter is the Chosen one?" Milady asked.

Prince stopped walking and turned to face her. "To punish Pax for her perversion?"

"I'm sure making your companion suffer was a nice addendum, but that's not the reason. It doesn't have anything to do with her."

"Then why kidnap a child and tell her mother she died?" Prince kept his eyes locked on hers.

"It's you."

CHAPTER 15

"It's me what?" For a moment, he thought the woman standing before him was not well in her head. Maybe the people thinking she was delusional were right.

"It's you the reason why your baby has been elected to be the Chosen. Pax Layan as the vessel was a most fortuitous coincidence."

Prince didn't comment on the last statement. He didn't understand the woman's choice of words.

"Has anybody told you why you're named Prince?" she asked, taking him aback, again.

"My father gave me this name."

"And what was his name?"

"I… don't know. I don't remember," he answered. Shame filled his thoughts and he hated the woman because of the way she made him feel.

"Don't feel bad. It doesn't surprise me that you don't know your father's name, but I can answer the question for you."

"What do you mean?" *She's going to tell me he didn't have a name, but a string of twelve numbers.*

"Your father's name was Prince, and your grandfather's name was Prince, too. All your direct relatives have had the same name."

"I'm not following you, Milady," he said, feeling compelled to add her title. He disliked her even more for that. She made him feel like a scared boy again.

"How could you? That is not the kind of information a slave, pardon, a worker has access to," she amended gently. Milady's lips came up, not a smile, but a hint of what she would look like when she decided to smile. "I know it sounds horrible. We are talking about your name, after all."

"So I gather you've a fascination with names."

"No, I don't. But I happen to know something about you—through your name—that very few people on Ginecea know." The hint of a smile came back, and with it, her eyes lit up.

I'm a nice, entertaining diversion for her. Prince kept his thoughts for him.

"You are of the semental line used to make priestesses." Milady sat on a wooden bench. "You don't believe me?" She raised an eyebrow to challenge him.

Prince stared at her, but didn't utter a word. He hadn't decided yet if he wanted to contemplate what she had just told him.

"I'm sure at your farm the women took very good care of you."

"Up to a point."

"Were you a troublemaker?"

"I stood up for myself," Prince corrected the woman.

"Feisty, another trait of your type. You're engineered that way."

He felt offended by her words, but decided to let it pass. "What do you mean I make priestesses?"

"Literally what I said." Milady kept her eyes steady on him, as if she were studying his reaction.

Do you want to know what I know? He wondered. "I'm a semental. The only women I *make* are fathered." He was conscious of being in the presence of a pure breed whose family decided good and bad weather on Ginecea. No amount of eccentricity on her side could make him forget how powerful she was.

"My age is such that I don't play games anymore. If I trusted you enough to reveal a truth of a magnitude that could destroy Ginecea, you'd better show me the same respect."

Prince felt all the weight of her words. Despite his intention to look in control of his emotions, he looked down at the grass.

"One of my greatest passions has always been history. I've been researching Ginecea's origins all my life. As a birthday gift when just a girl, my mothers gave me a book about mythology. I was hooked from page one. There were these incredible stories about a war of epic proportion between a goddess and a god, and how they'd loved each other at the beginning. But they were too different—they were wrong together. The goddess finally realized she was a slave of her base emotions and declared war on her former lover. It is said the god didn't react kindly, but the goddess was valiant, her heart pure, and she won. She enslaved the god and swore to take revenge on all his progeny."

"Interesting tale, but slightly prejudiced," Prince murmured, his eyes still avoiding hers. "And the version I heard was different."

"Oh, I'm sure men have their own version of this story. Anyway, let me finish. It gets more interesting, and even more unfair. The goddess decreed love between women and men impure and stripped all the women who had sided with the god of their souls. The goddess called them fathered women and forced them to give birth to men to remind them of how base they were. But the fathered women were still women after all, and the goddess couldn't find in her heart the strength to treat them as the men."

"Lucky them," Prince said.

"I'm sure the fathered women share your sentiment. Anyway, there is an interesting fact that made me think the first time I read the story. The goddess was pregnant when she started fighting the god. The first priestess was born soon after. I remember that, when I read it the first time, I thought the whole story didn't make sense. You see, I'd been taught about the holy birth of pure breeds, and I couldn't understand how the goddess could be pregnant without a wife."

"Did you ask your moms about that?" Prince couldn't help to ask, happy he had found his wit again.

"I did, as a matter of fact." Milady chuckled. "But they didn't give me a satisfactory answer. And I've always been the curious type. I became quite obsessed with Ginecean mythology. My personal library was composed of rare texts, most of them ancient, and some of them just forgotten in friends' attics. People knew of my interest and they thought it cute to encourage me. I was the only sixteen-year-old who was gifted, for her debut ball, a first edition of the *Holy Book of Goddess*. I studied it until the spine, already tattered, disappeared into dust. But I wasn't satisfied with what I'd found. I started studying history instead. I thought that maybe I'd found my answer there." Milady paused.

"I guess you found them."

"Yes, I did. And, you, my dear Prince, are part of the answer."

"If you say so." He didn't like the way she had said his name. It sounded like a mockery.

"I do say so, and for a good reason. Your name is short for 'principal,' as in the first in order of importance, the best of the herd."

"Thank you for the compliment." Prince's eyes narrowed into two slits, her words fueling him with the necessary strength to feel offended.

"Don't hate me. I'm recalling the passage verbatim. Anyway, sometimes it pays to be a book enthusiast and to have very few friends, real or imaginary. I was given access to public libraries and private collections with the same ease, and I spent all my free time researching. It was only a matter of time that I'd stumble upon something interesting. And when I did, I was old enough to realize it wasn't wise to come public with my discovery."

"What did you find?" he asked.

Milady smiled a full, white teeth show. "One day, I was bored— I hadn't found anything interesting in a while—and I asked a close family friend, who owned one of the oldest collections of medical texts in Ginecea, if I could take a peek at her library. I was charming and she said yes. Nobody ever took me seriously, not even then. I was regarded as a weird, young pure breed, but in a nice way. My pedigree was the key to open any door. Anatomy wasn't my cup of tea, but I thought, why not? What I found that day changed my view of right and wrong.

"I was sipping my favorite drink—pink melted sorbet—from a tall glass, when I saw with the corner of my eyes a spider coming down from the ceiling. I jumped on the chair, sending the sorbet everywhere. I was mortified; several ancient, priceless medical texts were now a sickly shade of pink. I remember I removed my sweater to mop the books. I turned around to see if I spread sorbet anywhere else, and here it was, gracing the cover of a book half hidden by a layer of dust that predated the library owner's date of birth." Milady took a pause and cleared her throat.

Prince generally liked a well-told story, but he was getting impatient and didn't care for the details.

"The book was older than old. It was ancient," the woman explained.

Prince felt offended, once again. *I'm not stupid.*

"There were pink sorbet stains all over the fore edge. I opened the book to clean it inside and imagine my surprise when I saw it."

"Saw what?" He felt his irritation mounting.

"It was a semental anatomy text. Nobody had touched it in decades. Actually, nobody had probably entered that library in decades. I leafed through the pages, looking at the pictures, and found them well painted, but what caught my full attention was a chapter named 'Principals and how to raise them.' That day I did something I'd never thought of doing before. I stole the text." Milady shivered, her eyes bright, savoring the memory.

Prince thought how he felt every time he had gotten away with something and couldn't help but understand her.

"I read it from cover to cover in two days, devouring words I'd never heard before, keeping a dictionary by my side, but to no avail. The terminology in the text was either obsolete, or simply not meant for pure breeds' eyes. What I understood was that principals—also shortened to *princes*—were sementals with a different status among slaves. The priestess personally supervised that the lineage was kept pure, and that no gene alteration was introduced. At the time, I struggled with the medical terms, but I borrowed and studied anatomy manuals until I could understand the basics. Again, family and friends thought it was my next phase, and as long as I kept myself out of trouble—as other pure breed girls, among them even the President's daughter, your Pax's grandmother, were on everybody's mouth for their wild behaviors—I was good. By the age of eighteen, I was an expert in the art of principal breeding and there was nobody I could talk to about that."

"How did you put together the facts that a principal is a special semental who has something to do with the Priestess?" Prince had heard lots of things lately, but he couldn't accept the idea that Milady was telling the truth.

"It was written in the book. As I told you, at first I didn't understand. I didn't have the right knowledge and maturity to decipher what was being said hidden by obscure terms and strange turn of phrases. My fancy for mythology gave me the key to uncover the secret code. There was a passage where it was said how the princes' seed blossomed into fruit for the sterile daughter of the goddess, but it needed to be tended by a worthy vessel. The next passage was all about how to choose said vessel."

"You are saying that the Priestess matches her designated principal with one pure breed of her choice?"

"Yes, but while there can be several young pure breeds who can be the worthy recipients, there is only one principal for every generation."

"I don't understand… If what you say it's true, why the Priestess has tried to kill me more times than I can remember?"

"My guess is that she had stored enough of your semen already. And then it turned out, even more conveniently, that a young girl from the Layans, one of the most venerable and respected families in the whole Ginecea, was pregnant with *the* principal's daughter. You must admit, from the Priestess's point of view, it was almost impossible to pass such opportunity. So she lied to the mother and took the girl for her."

"But my daughter was kept by Pax's mother until she was taken away from her."

She shrugged. "I don't know about that."

Prince walked back and forth for a few seconds, still unsure of what to think. He kicked a small pebble, and then another, but his mind didn't clear. He had a chaotic twirl of ideas fighting for supremacy, and none was winning at the moment.

"So, what I thought was going on at Sundial isn't entirely true." Prince was fine with what he knew; he didn't want to fit other ideas in his mind. "I was sure I'd uncovered the women's big secret: a semen factory where a good specimen was stocked for the discriminated pure breed."

"In a way, you're right. Although Sundial is specialized in raising principals, to have a whole farm just for one fancy semental at a time isn't good business. And principals' births are strictly regulated. A principal is kept dormant as long as he isn't needed. Whenever they aren't needed, normally because a priestess has already been born, principals are used to create the next eligible specimen, and if the boy survives, his father's services are no longer required."

"What happens to the father then?

"They are retired."

"I see." He had already known that answer. "Did my father *make* this Priestess?"

"No. He would've been too young for that. And, on top of that, to ensure good genes, the next priestesses' donors never share blood ties with the former. So it's safe to say your grandfather wasn't used either to procreate Her Holiness."

"How do you choose the principal?"

"Princes come from a selected breed of men. And for every Priestess, there is only one prince, as I already told you. Every generation is bred differently to achieve the genes' maximum variety. It's not a coincidence that priestesses are strikingly beautiful."

Prince didn't share Milady's opinion of the Priestess's beauty. The woman represented everything he hated and he couldn't find her beautiful. "How did I come to be the next prince?" he finally asked.

"Principal lineages are alternated. It was your lineage's turn to be chosen."

"Okay, but how was my paternal lineage chosen?"

"One of your ancestors must've been an exceptional specimen, and his semen was implanted in an equally exceptional fathered woman."

"Wait, are you saying that fathered women are involved in the process? I thought you said pure breeds were used—"

"We are talking about two complete different things. A principal is conceived by another principal and a fathered woman. A priestess is conceived by a principal and a pure breed."

"What about the byproducts?"

"What do you mean?"

"I'm talking about the boys and girls who are conceived in the wrong order. What happens to the boy who is conceived by the prince and the pure breed, who should've been a girl?"

"Here is where Ginecean gynecology has reached its fullest potential. There aren't any byproducts. Only the right embryo is conceived and brought to full term. I'm not a scientist, but what I understood is that there are methods to ensure the gender of the child with extreme precision. In the book there was a whole other chapter about the countless experiments done in the past and how gynecologists were looking for a way to keep as many viable embryos as possible. They managed to reduce the margin of error to zero so they didn't have any waste. Cleaner and more elegant. You must give credit to a millennium of breeding studies."

Prince snorted at the last statement, but let her finish. "Anyway, we were talking about your ancestor and how you came to be. What was I saying...? Oh, yes. Your lineage has been kept unaltered through controlled breeding. Principals are the equivalent of the men's pure breeds. At the end of the anatomy book, there was a list with the serial numbers marking sementals as principals. And again, even if you are a prince, it doesn't mean that, as a result, you're going to collaborate toward the creation of a priestess. So, in other words, you were born with the right genes and at the right moment."

"Or at the wrong one, better said. I don't care to be special."

"Given your circumstances, yes, I must agree with you. But at least you know your daughter is taken good care of. I know she's kept like a goddess."

"Again, I don't care about her being treated differently from any other child. She should be in her mother's arms, by my side." Prince felt the familiar pain squeezing his heart.

"I didn't mean to belittle your pain." Milady patted the bench to invite him to seat.

"No, but thanks. I can't sit now. I need to clear my mind." He was full of nervous energy.

"I understand. It's a fascinating subject for me, and I could talk for hours about the wonders of preordained breeding, but I see I gave you more food for thought than you had any desire for. We'll finish talking later. Now, why don't you earn your meal like everybody else does at the Village?" Milady slowly stood up, but her legs looked unstable. "Can you help me?"

"Sure." He surprised himself saying this. "What do I have to do for a meal around here?"

"You look like a strong guy. There are several cottages' roofs that need to be mended."

"I know a thing or two about thatched roofs."

"Then you could prove yourself useful after all." Milady chuckled.

Prince accompanied Milady back to Aria, who was deep in conversation with Lucas.

"Prince is going to help you repair some roofs." Milady left his arm to take Lucas's. "I'll show you the orchard where you can help with wood cutting."

Prince looked at the woman and his friend slowly taking the path winding through the houses and disappearing, as if they were old acquaintances. "Sometimes I envy how he seems perfectly at ease in women's presence."

"You've been raised to believe we're evil. It's not entirely true." Aria gestured for him to follow her. "Come, there's some work to be done."

* * *

The sun was setting low on the horizon. Prince had finished repairing a young couple's cottage wall. It had crumbled to pieces the night before, after a deluge of water had poured down for hours. At first, the two women tried to contain the damage by patching the holes with plastic sheets, then realized it wasn't helping and left the cottage to its doom. He and Lucas gave them shelter in their room inside Milady's cottage.

Milady had been generous with them. Although the Village was a women-only environment, Prince and Lucas were treated with respect. Milady had seen to that the first day; she had called a meeting and informed the villagers they had two guests, no need for further explanations. Two long weeks had passed since then.

"Done. You can go back to your house tonight," he said to the young couple.

"Thanks," the two women answered at the same time. They were young and very much in love. Prince had caught them exchanging effusions every time they thought nobody was looking. A bittersweet emotion filled his heart at the sight.

"Prince?" Aria was calling him from the other side of the cottage.

"I'm here." He stepped out of the cottage's shadow to greet the woman.

"I have news," she said, a somber expression darkening her face.

"Have you heard from Lexi?" His heart quickly jumped in his throat. He knew she was as worried as he was. They talked during their breaks about Pax and Lexi.

"No, nothing from her, but Milady was just checking the news and she found out about an uprising at the Temple."

He started running, Aria following him closely. He reached Milady's so quickly he could barely breathe. She was waiting for him at the door and Lucas was already by her side.

"What do you know?" he asked, blood ringing in his ears.

"The president announced a few minutes ago she successfully took control of the rebels who had occupied the Temple."

"What rebels?" He was afraid to ask.

"It seems the fathered women of the Temple chapter house have been fighting the Priestess's Army for the last two weeks." Milady made a sign to go inside where she could sit. They entered the small living room opening to the porch. A gentle breeze moved the curtains, inflating like white sails.

"For the last two weeks?" Prince helped her on the chair with the raised cushion the woman used to rest her back on.

"Ginecea didn't divulge the news until the situation was under control," Milady answered.

"Did you see any images?" Aria went to sit on the low stool by Milady's chair.

"Yes, there was a short piece showing the chapter house's quarters in flame."

"Any deaths?" Prince thought of Magdalene and the other fathered women who had spent a night and a day listening to what he had to say. He felt guilty he couldn't remember their names, but their eyes, bright with wonderment at his words, would stay with him forever.

Lucas shook his head. "I arrived as the piece was ending, but—" He was pale and taking long sips from a glass full to the rim with an amber liquid. He looked at Prince and sighed. "Have some." He gave the glass to Prince, who accepted the offer and gulped it down.

"The president said it was an inevitable bloodbath. Unfortunately"—she gave Prince a sad look—"none of the fathered women living at the chapter house escaped death. She clarified that she tried to negotiate with the rebels, but that in the end, regretfully, they didn't give her any other option. Special Forces were sent to help the Priestess's Army and were given orders to use explosives after the fathered women refused to surrender. The final attack lasted less than a few minutes. She finished, declaring that no act of mutiny against Ginecea and the Priestess will be tolerated and that from now on swift justice will be dealt." Milady talked slowly, each word weighing her down in the chair.

"Do you know if anything happened to the Temple's inner quarters… and the medical facility?" Prince was pacing to and from the porch, listening to Milady and creating his own images of the Temple's massacre. The glass of liquor he just drank hadn't entered his system yet.

"No, the president didn't mention anything else," Milady answered and then asked Aria if she could bring her some water and an analgesic for her headache.

"When we left, Pax, Anna, and Lexi were still there. What happened to them?" Prince murmured, unable to talk any louder, his voice choked. "What about my baby?"

"I don't know," Milady said. "I called my daughter, but I couldn't ask if she knew anything about Lexi. Supposedly, Lexi is attending college. Or at least, this is what I officially know."

"What did your daughter say?" Aria was back with the glass of water, her hands trembling and her eyes red.

"My daughter told me everything was okay and that they hadn't heard from Lexi in a while because she's busy with midterms, but they were going to visit her in a month."

"Anything could happen to her in a month. If something hasn't happened already!" Aria cried, and both Lucas and Milady tried to calm her. "Don't you see? She could be dead… like the fathered women."

"Don't say that." Milady leaned to embrace Aria. "My little Lexi is well. Nothing happened to her. Do you hear me? She's fine."

"I can't stay here." Prince was starting to feel the first effect of the alcohol, but judging by the fact that he couldn't breathe, it wasn't enough to dull the edge of the fear paralyzing his mind.

"Let's go outside. Some fresh air will help," Lucas proposed, one hand on his shoulder to guide him to the porch.

"No, I can't stay *here* at the Village. I must go back to the Temple."

"You can't—" Lucas started.

"I need to know if Pax and the baby are fine."

"They could be anywhere," Lucas said.

"You must think this through." Milady had one arm around Aria's shaking body.

"I'll go with you." Aria raised her head and looked at Prince.

"Aria, you're going to get yourself killed, and for nothing." Milady shook her head.

"Wherever the Priestess is, so Pax and the baby, Lexi, and Anna must be." Prince went outside and inhaled deeply. The calming effect of the alcohol had finally kicked in and he felt dizzy, but he didn't need it anymore.

"You don't know that for sure." It was Lucas's turn to pace furiously around the room.

"I know nothing for sure, but what else can I do? If I don't do anything, I'll drive myself crazy."

Milady commanded everybody's attention back to her by raising one hand. "We need to find where the Priestess is, and then we'll know where the Chosen is. The Presentation is scheduled for the next month and the Priestess isn't going to let the baby out of her sight."

"What's a presentation?" Prince asked. He had probably heard about it, but never paid any attention to the women's rituals. The woman's world could have been on another planet altogether for how much he had used to care. Now, he wished he knew more.

"Presentation is when the Chosen is officially presented to Ginecea. It's a big celebration that lasts three days. Ginecea City is illuminated the whole time. Pure breeds wear only white clothes to symbolize rebirth and parties are given in five of the most ancient households. The rest of the citizens, mostly the fathered women who don't work in any of the big five, roam the city, inebriated on cheap liquor sold at street carts that abound for the occasion. A Presentation doesn't happen frequently. I don't remember the last one. I was but a girl when the current Priestess was chosen."

"I have to find my daughter before this happens." Resolution settled in Prince's heart and he found some peace in the decision.

It was easier said than done, he discovered soon enough. A whole week passed. Seven full days he worked as a handyman, went back to his room, ate, and hoped he could sleep without having nightmares. Sometimes his wish was granted, but more often than not, he woke up screaming. A few days later, Lucas ended up asking Milady if he could sleep on the couch in the living room. Prince checked the news every day, but nothing relevant was said about the Priestess's whereabouts. Nothing more was said regarding the uprising that had taken place at the Temple. Ginecea was carefully giving out information, and the majority of the news was unimportant; the most anticipated interview with the president the next week was cancelled due to Maurice Layan's hectic schedule. Penny Ron appeared ticked off when she released the press announcement, but she smiled for the camera and blew kisses to the fans. A rerun of some silly show took the vacant slot.

"Something's going on, and it must be big," Milady commented one afternoon when Prince, Lucas, and Aria had joined her in front of the television. Usually their shifts ended later, but the weather was inclement and the wind prevented them from doing anything else outside.

"The Priestess is manipulating the media to cover up whatever is happening out there." Aria had taken the habit to peruse the newspapers until they fell apart. She checked every article, looking for inner meanings and words out of place, sometimes reading until the wee hours of the morning and then worked without any rest. "Look here. Two entire pages on the importance of matching colors of your bedroom's windows draperies with your coverlets. Pure breeds can't be so stupid as not see what is going on. Something horrible happened inside the holiness of the Temple not even a week ago, and it seems nobody cares anymore."

"The Priestess doesn't want anybody to care," Milady corrected Aria.

"Still, how come nobody is asking questions?"

"Again, even if they're asking questions, and I know we aren't the only ones with a brain, the Priestess is doing a great job in keeping everything quiet." Milady changed channels until she found what she was looking for. "Let's see if they say anything here. This is a small, family-owned television company, whose owner I know from college. Layla Bertrand is one of the few friends I've ever made and among even the fewer number of friends I'm still in contact with."

They all stared at the screen, frozen on an image depicting some Ginecean shores.

"I like the musical choice," Prince said after a moment. "What are we looking at, exactly?"

"The Maritime coast," Milady responded drily.

"What were we supposed to look at?" Prince's mood hadn't improved after a week of relative inactivity. He had been doing his designated chores around the Village, but in his mind he was wasting time. He should be chasing down the Priestess.

"Independent news. That's what I was hoping to watch. This channel started broadcasting a little while back. I spoke with Layla one or two months ago, tops. She would've told me if they were shutting it down." Milady kept looking at the TV for a while and then asked Aria to bring her the phone and her contacts book. Three phone calls later, it was clear that Layla Bertrand wasn't reachable to explain. "Well, whatever the Priestess is doing goes deeper than I first thought."

Prince listened to the older woman, his own thoughts becoming darker and darker. "I think I waited long enough. It was a pleasure to meet you, Milady, and I'll be forever grateful you gave me shelter when I needed it, but it's time for me to leave."

No amount of reasoning both by Milady's and Lucas's side had the effect they hoped for. Prince, helped by Aria, who was equally ready to go, prepared a bag with food rations and a first-aid kit.

"I'm coming with you. I'm not going to leave you alone," Lucas said an hour later, passing items along between Aria and Prince.

"No, I've been thinking about it, and it's better if I follow one trail while you follow another. You should go to Sundial and see what you can do to save Randal and Remy. Aria and I will find Pax and Lexi. We'll travel by car, all together, and then split when we're close to Sundial. You'll stop there, and we'll continue toward the Temple."

"Are you sure this is the smart thing to do?" Milady asked Aria.

"I'm sure it isn't." She tried to smile at the older woman, but it looked forced. "I have the car full of boxes and I'll say they are for Literacy Sans Frontiers. The Priestess is doing her best to show that everything goes as usual. She'll let us inside the storage facility, and from there, we'll find a way to see what's really happening."

"You don't sound as convinced as you want me to believe, but I'm not going to argue a moment longer. Just, please, be careful and if you see Lexi—"

Aria interrupted Milady, saying, "When I see Lexi."

"Very well, when you see Lexi, tell her how much I miss her, will you?"

"I certainly will tell her that, Milady."

Prince watched as the two women said good-bye to each other. He saluted Milady, lowering his head, a show of respect he had never thought of giving to a woman, unless forced by a whip. The most sacred sign of respect for a man, the right hand over the heart salute, he had reserved for Pax and Pax only, until now.

"Come here," Milady said, reaching for him.

Prince was unprepared for the woman's show of affection and remained speechless for the duration of the embrace.

"When all is done, bring your baby daughter here. I'd like to see her. I'd like to see you again." Milady released him.

"I'll see you soon." Prince couldn't think of anything else to answer back.

"It's a promise."

"It's a desire," he said, and with that, he turned to leave.

Aria raised one hand to stop him. "Wait a second," she whispered. "I heard something…"

Lucas, who had left the room to pick up his bag, rushed back in. "Hurry, we have to hide."

Milady and Aria looked at him with a silent question, then Milady went to the window and said, "Go to my bedroom and wait there. The Priestess just arrived."

CHAPTER **16**

Prince and Lucas didn't have to be told twice; they were already out of the room when someone knocked at the door. Lucas went straight to Milady's bedroom, but Prince had a sudden thought and retraced his steps to retrieve Aria. He peeked around the corner and immediately stepped back and flattened himself against the wall at the sight of the Priestess standing in the center of the room. Even with her back to him, she exuded arrogance and dominated the place as if it were her own. Aria was frozen before the woman, her traveling bag dangling from her elbow.

"Going somewhere, maid?" The Priestess's voice was sweet and controlled.

"She's just coming back from a hike," Milady answered for Aria.

Heels clicked on the floor tiles. "Hiking in this kind of weather is for crazy people. Are you crazy, maid?" The Priestess made another comment Prince didn't catch and then said, "Do you mind if I use this chair? This cushion looks comfortable and my back is hurting."

"Please. Would you like something to drink?" Milady asked.

"What happened to you, Raya?"

Prince was surprised to hear Milady's birth name.

"What's wrong?" The Priestess's voice was calm.

"Almost nobody calls me by my given name anymore. I've been Milady for so long it actually sounds wrong to be called anything else."

"Well, my dearest Raya, we were friends at some point, and friends call each other by name, right?"

While the Priestess talked, Aria must have tried to step out of the room because Prince heard soft steps inching dangerously close to where he was hiding, and at the same time, the Priestess raised her voice. "Maid, don't even think of it. Stay where I can see you." The woman paused and then continued, "What was I saying? Oh yes, that you and I were friends."

"I wouldn't call our acquaintance a friendship. You were the Priestess even then." Milady flinched. "To what do I owe the honor of having Your Holiness in my humble abode?"

"You wound me with your words and your coldness. When did you forget about me?"

"I don't recall there was a lot to remember to begin with. Anyway, although I'm truly ecstatic by having you here, I'm still perplexed about the reason for your unexpected visit."

"Do I have to have a reason to visit an old friend?"

"I don't live around the corner from the Temple or your home, and I doubt the mighty Priestess has time for a joy ride in the country side."

There was a longer pause, then the Priestess continued as if Milady hadn't talked at all. "You were one of the few pure breeds I ever called by that name: friend. I was a lonely girl and you were so vibrant. Everybody liked you and your little quirks. I remember how much I enjoyed listening to you. You were so smart and always with a book in your hands. Sometimes I followed you to the library and you never noticed me. I never told you, but I fantasized about marrying you. Of course, I knew it could never happen. No happy ending to the Priestess's tale, no 'They Lived Happily Ever After' for me. I was made to memorize the Priestess's code of conduct when I was barely four years old. While you were left to your books, I had to study how to repress any womanly desire. I've always wanted to be you. To be with you. And now, you're not even happy to see me. I've traveled the whole day to be here."

Prince was mesmerized by the Priestess's tale and didn't think to join Lucas in the bedroom, but kept his body against the wall, hidden by the doorjamb.

"Which reminds me, what are you doing here?" Milady asked. A chair was dragged for a few counts.

"Why don't you sit with me?" The Priestess's voice was uncharacteristically gentle. "Don't you remember how good we felt in each other's company?"

"You've changed so much," Milady answered.

Prince noticed how Milady's tone had changed along with the implicit admission that she and the Priestess were more than acquaintances as she had earlier stated.

"I've matured and become what was expected of me, but you've also changed. The Raya I knew and held so dearly in my heart would've never treated me the way you're treating me now."

"The Raya you knew was someone you've idealized all these years."

Prince's mind filled with more questions. *Milady Corellis, you left out a few things when talking about your youth.*

"Monica, what do you want from me?" Milady asked.

"For you to call my name once more. Oh, the rarest of treats. For this only I'd have gladly traveled from one end to the other of Ginecea."

Prince was shocked by the Priestess's confession.

"Monica, please!"

"The irony was never lost on me," the Priestess said and then laughed.

"What irony?"

"Do you know what my name means?

"I don't think so."

"Can you guess the origins of my name?"

"No, I can't."

A few steps and then the sound of a chair being moved to accommodate someone.

"Of course you can. You know everything."

"Please—"

"My tutor seemed fit to give me a name whose roots were deeply planted in the men's language. Shocking, isn't it?"

"That I didn't know—"

"Nobody does, of course. Although, I later discovered it was done on purpose, so I'd never forget my true calling."

"I don't understand," Milady said, her voice tired and tinted with a sad undertone, similar to the one Prince thought to have caught in the Priestess's.

You two must've been close, he thought, surprised he was still eavesdropping on a conversation that sounded too private to be of any use to him.

"My name means The Lonely One. Isn't it a source of endless amusement?"

"I don't find it funny."

"Because it isn't," the Priestess answered, but she was laughing. "I am the loneliest woman of all Ginecea, because I am the *only one*. There's only one priestess at the time. I was never meant for love. I've never experienced the caress of a woman or the gentle kiss of a lover."

"I'll ask you one more time. What are you doing here?"

"The question is another. Why would you go hiking in weather like this?" Aria must have been unable to talk, because the Priestess added, "Did you think I forgot about you?"

"I sent her to fetch something for me." Milady sounded uncomfortable.

"You meant a lot to a small, confused girl. Don't ruin the few pleasant memories left to me. If you can't tell me the truth, please do me a personal favor and don't say anything at all," the Priestess said to Milady, then, "Where were you going?"

"I was preparing for a long drive," Aria answered, her whisper betraying how intimidated she was.

"Where were you going?" the Priestess asked again.

"To the Temple."

"To do what?"

"I've some boxes for Literacy Sans Frontiers."

"And you were going to drive the whole night to bring the boxes to the Temple," the Priestess said, as if savoring the words in her mouth.

Prince could imagine the woman smiling her cold ghost of a smile.

"Do you really think I'm stupid?"

Nothing else was said for several heartbeats. The sound of metal clinging against glass echoed in the silence and startled him.

Prince heard Aria gasp out loud and then she said between sobs, "Magdalene's pendant—"

"You didn't expect she was still alive, did you? I see you have a television set. Didn't you watch the news? President Layan did an excellent job in restraining the rebels. I'm proud of Maurice. She'll soon reach her true potential as President of Ginecea."

"What happened to Magdalene?" Aria asked.

"She died, of course, but not before telling me about your little mail delivery service."

The metallic object, the pendant, was dragged on a hard surface and produced a strident sound.

Prince remembered the black stone medallion he had seen Magdalene playing with, and his eyes filled with tears. As the Priestess had just told Aria, the news about the woman's death didn't come as a surprise, but it still affected him.

"What was the purpose of these exchanges? What were you planning?" the Priestess asked.

The chair was moved and soft steps followed. "You don't have to answer—" Milady spoke in a reassuring tone.

"We were friends, nothing more."

"I don't believe you. Friends wait for the mail to arrive. They don't drive eight or nine hours to deliver it in person. Unless there isn't any written mail to deliver, but a much safer voice message."

"Magdalene and I... were in a relationship," Aria said.

"Magdalene was married."

"I was the... other."

"Not even the dead's memories are sacred anymore. I can't believe your brass. You, a sorry maid, are talking to the Priestess, lying through your teeth. Your life is worth nothing. I can dispose of you any way I want, and right now you're making my decision to erase you from the face of Ginecea so much simpler."

"I'm telling the truth. I went to the Temple any time I could to see Magdalene." Aria sounded frantic.

"You are one of the poorest liars I've ever met. Guards!" the Priestess called. Loud, booted steps filled the silence. "Take her outside and kill her."

A scuffle followed the Priestess's order. A chair was tossed on the floor. More sobbing.

"Please—" Aria cried.

"Monica, call them back. Stop this madness now," Milady said. She was breathing hard.

"Why?"

"Why, you ask me? Because you've already had your justice. You keep killing fathered women at the rate you're going and in a year or two there won't be any left. Leave this girl alone. She didn't do anything to you."

"You see, this is where you're wrong. This insignificant maid of yours was conspiring against me, helping the rebels with funds and information."

"She didn't do anything of the sort. You're getting paranoid—" Milady stopped in midsentence.

"Don't insult me by saying you didn't mean it. You aren't the only one, after all. But I happen to know Magdalene had someone from outside the Temple helping her cause. And look at the coincidence that this young, lovely maid used to visit more than she had any business doing so."

"Aria's just confessed she was Magdalene's lover."

Prince heard how Milady's was voice less steady than it had been a moment before.

"Aria. Why does her name sound almost intimate in your mouth? Is she your lover?"

"For the Goddess's sake, she could be my grandkid."

"You wouldn't be the first to get caught in the net of youth's charm. She's pretty."

"You're being crass, and this time, I truly mean it."

"So, we're back to square one. If you confess, I'll be merciful. I see my old friend Raya here has a soft spot for you," the Priestess said.

"There's nothing else I can add to what I've already said," Aria answered.

Prince could only imagine how scared the girl must be and yet she had just refused to save herself to protect Milady.

"Then there's nothing else I can do for you. Guards, you know what to do." The Priestess's tone was final and this time there was no resistance, just the fading sound of the booted steps and the softer ones circling the room.

"Milady, tell her I loved her." Aria's words came from a distance.

"Monica, I'm begging you. Reconsider what you're doing, please. This girl is innocent."

Prince hated to hear Milady pleading.

"The rebels desecrated my sanctuary with the help of this *innocent* girl. She knew what she was doing and now she'll pay for it."

The distant echo of what was happening on the porch reached Prince.

"On your knees," a woman commanded loud enough to be heard inside the room.

Prince couldn't help imagining Aria facing the death squad and silently cried.

"Stop it!" Milady screamed.

"Raya, don't get involved," the Priestess softly said, her tone in contrast with the moment. "I already got what I came for."

"No, you haven't," Milady answered.

"Don't do it," the Priestess admonished Milady. "I'm telling you, I have everything I need. Now I can return home, satisfied of how my day ended."

Prince waited for things to unfold and felt nauseous.

"It was nice to see you." The Priestess's voice contained a tinge that Prince failed to recognize. It was longing, fear, and anger.

He heard her clicking heels hit the floor tiles with a rhythmic pace.

When the walking stopped, the Priestess said, "Get ready—"

A chair was moved, almost thrown out of the way. "Wait, I can't let you do it."

Prince wanted to peek at the scene, but didn't dare.

"Of course you can. And I strongly suggest you to leave it that way since it's not for you to say what I can or I can't do." The Priestess didn't sound pleased by Milady's stubbornness.

"I know I don't have any power over you, but this is not right."

"You forget that *I* decide what's right or wrong on Ginecea."

"I haven't forgotten, but—"

"You must let it go before it's too late." A pleading tone colored the Priestess's words.

"I can't let it go."

"Why not, for Goddess's sake?" Rage replaced the former sentiment.

"Because, I simply can't."

"Don't…"

A few steps echoed and then Milady said, "Please, look at me."

The Priestess remained silent and Milady added, "I can't let someone else pay for my actions—"

Aria cried from outside, "No!

"I'm telling you only one more time—stay out of it," the Priestess said, one word at a time.

"I can't."

"Shut your mouth before it's too late. Don't say another word."

"Aria followed my orders. The messages she was delivering to Magdalene were mine."

"Raya, please, stop now."

"I've been helping the rebels for some time."

"For the last time, stop talking!"

Prince heard the plea in the Priestess's voice and hoped Milady would obey.

"I'm sorry, Monica."

The Priestess emitted a sound that could have been a silenced cry. "Guards, come back."

Prince would have sworn she heard her sobbing. He was peeking over the doorjamb before he realized what he was doing. Both the Priestess and Milady were facing outside. The guards—at an angle to him—were waiting for orders. He should have flattened back against the safety of the wall, but he couldn't.

"Raya…?" The Priestess didn't turn.

Milady straightened her back and faced the guards, who had raised their guns. "I'm not going to ask for forgiveness. I know what I was doing goes against Ginecean laws. Your laws. I only ask you to let me die with some dignity."

"No!" Aria shouted. "Let me go. You can't kill her!"

"Aria, I'm glad I could get to know you. I'm only sorry I got you involved in something too big—"

"Why did you do it?" the Priestess abruptly asked, still not turning.

"Knowledge made me conscious of all the wrongs in our society and I couldn't just stand and watch. I had to do my part."

"Books have always been your true passion. I used to be jealous of them. I thought you should've paid more attention to me. I was right."

"You aren't the first one to tell me so." Milady relaxed her stance.

"And, Raya, you were wrong before. You always had power over me," the Priestess said. She made a sign over her shoulder to the guards to proceed. "Not in the face," she said, walking to the window. She leaned on the windowsill, her head out of the room, one with the darkness of the night.

"Monica, I hated that you were the Priestess with all my heart, and I did notice when you were in the library." Milady had the last word.

The shot resonated in the small room.

A hand covered Prince's mouth the same moment a scream fought to get out.

"Shhh," Lucas whispered to his ear. "There's nothing we can do for her." He pushed him back to the wall.

Prince couldn't close his eyes, the tears falling freely. The last image he saw etched itself on the blank wall before him. He blinked, but the scene was still there. Milady lay on the floor, Aria by her side, and the guards stood against the walls, waiting for new orders. The Priestess was still looking outside, her body shaking.

"Move!" the Priestess ordered. "You too. Get out of here."

Scuffling, dragging, a piece of furniture was moved. Aria begged to be left by Milady's side.

"Outside! All of you!"

A door was forcefully closed. Eerie silence followed.

"I tried to protect you. All these years, I let you have your fun. Why did you have to repay me like this? Even tonight, I was going to let you get away with everything. You should've let the maid take the blame. You were a precious flower. She's nothing but dirt." The Priestess sobbed. "May the Goddess let you rest in her arms, my beloved."

She softly cried for a long while. Then the door was thrown open. "Look at what you did! Look at her!" The Priestess's command was answered by Aria's distressed and unintelligible words. "You should've died, not her. I didn't come here to kill her. I came here to warn her I knew what she was up to."

By now, Aria was crying uncontrollably.

The sound of harsh blows against flesh made Prince wince. The beating only stopped when a loud crash indicated Aria's head must have hit the floor.

"Check if she's still alive," the Priestess ordered.

"She's breathing."

"Then shoot her."

Prince strained against Lucas's hold. The man shook his head. Prince readied himself for the gun to fire and take another life.

"No, wait."

He wanted to scream.

"She doesn't deserve the reprieve of dying now. Not anymore. If I have to live with this memory, so will she. Cripple her." The Priestess's steps echoed in the room for the last time.

The gun rang out twice. Aria came to her senses, only to scream an agonizing wail.

Prince acted without thinking once again and Lucas put more pressure on his hold. "Wait. We're all dead, Aria too, if the Priestess catch us," he whispered.

Prince couldn't hear Aria anymore and that scared him more than her laments, but he nodded.

They stayed hidden until the last car engine rumbled through the night. Only then, the first villagers came to check what had happened. Lucas was still holding Prince against the wall. When the preternatural silence in the room was broken by several voices screaming in shock, Lucas finally released him.

He ran to help Aria, who hadn't yet regained consciousness, and pushed away the women who were standing over her and Milady.

"Take her to my bed," he said to Lucas. "You, fetch some hot water and everything you can think of to remove the bullets from her legs," he asked the closest woman.

The girl nodded. "I'll go to the infirmary."

Once they laid Aria on the bed, Prince ripped apart her pants, starting from the ankles, but she was so pale he thought she was dead. Then he checked her pulse and found it, faint but steady. "Stay alive. Lexi will kill me if I let you die," he said, freeing her legs from the bloodied fabric. "Where's the water? I need to clean the wounds."

"I'll go." Luca left for several minutes.

Prince stared at Aria with nothing to do but wait for Lucas and the girl who had gone to the infirmary, and several thoughts crossed his mind. Pax and his baby were a constant presence, but now the idea that he wasn't prepared to protect them terrified him. Maybe that day, now it seemed so long ago, Milady had been right. As long as the baby was under the Priestess's protection, she was fine. He hated the thought, but it was true.

"Prince?" Aria stirred, then moaned in pain.

"Stay put. Don't move or you'll lose more blood."

Lucas came back with the water almost at the same time the girl came back with a first-aid kit. Prince looked at what was inside the kit and saw it lacked real anesthetic. Aria would have do with plain painkillers and a good dose of alcohol that Lucas went to retrieve from the living room. Meanwhile, he and the girl washed Aria's legs and then moved them, one at the time, to check on the damage the bullets had inflicted.

"The one on the right leg went through, but the one on the left is still inside," he said to Aria who seemed to listen, but her eyes were unfocused and her breathing shallow and uneven. "Clean her where she needs to be cleaned, please," he asked the girl. He couldn't bear the sight of Milady's blood smeared all over Aria's face.

"Have you ever removed a bullet?" Prince looked at Lucas, hoping the man would say yes.

Lucas shook his head. "In any case, my hands aren't steady. I could cut her bad."

"No, I'm sorry. I've never done anything like this," the girl answered when Prince turned to her with the silent question.

"Okay, Aria, you're stuck with me."

"You'll do just fine," she said, her words accompanied by a choking rattle that scared everybody in the room.

"We're wasting time. Do something, already," the girl said, eyes wide and full of tears.

"Here you go, Aria. Drink some of this," Lucas said, bringing to her lips a glass full to the brim with a clear liquid. "This is so strong it'll knock you out in a matter of minutes. Have some more. Yes, like this, good." He coaxed her to drink until the glass was empty.

"Save some for me." Prince's whisper was meant for Lucas's ears, but Aria heard it.

"I told you, you'll do great," she said to Prince, trying to make it sound light. "We'll drink to my health later." Another rattle shook her chest. "I feel fuzzy already. You better start digging the bullet out."

"Put something in her mouth." Prince looked around to see if there was anything they could use.

"Like what?" the girl asked.

"Like a towel or a belt or anything she can use to bite when—"

"I'm wearing one." The girl promptly removed her belt from her pants and handed it to Prince, who put it in Aria's mouth.

"I'll be quick. I promise." Prince looked at Aria, saw that the color in her face had gone from white to gray, clenched his teeth, and took a long breath. "Here we go."

Later that night, he lay in bed, eyes wide open, still shaken by the experience. Aria was a strong woman and had tried not to scream, but when he had to insert his finger deeper inside her leg to excavate the bullet he couldn't find, she emitted a frightening sound, then went still and fainted. His hand started trembling and Lucas had to apply pressure on his arm to steady him. "Give me some alcohol, now," he said to the man. Lucas didn't argue.

Back at Sundial, he had patched so many men with wounds, cuts, burns, and the occasional broken bone, but normally, for anything more serious, the women took the workers to Doctor Linda. A man was valuable to the farm only if working; the sooner he got better, the sooner he was earning his right to be kept alive. Prince couldn't imagine what had been like for the Priest, alone in the desert with nothing. If he had felt respect for the man before, now he thought of him as a living legend.

"What do I have to offer Pax and the baby?" he asked to the night.

"What every spouse offers his or her companion: love," Lucas answered.

"I'm sorry. I didn't mean to wake you."

"I was already awake. Milady's death and Aria's agony won't let me sleep either. There's no point in waiting for that to happen. Let's go for a walk. Maybe some fresh air will help."

"What if something like that happens to the baby, and I'm not ready to help? What if Pax needs me?" Prince donned a sweater without turning on the light sitting on the nightstand and, with the room bathed by the silvery light of the moon, went to open the door that led to the backyard. He kept it open to let Lucas outside.

"You've just become a father. It's perfectly normal to be worried. I remember when Randal wasn't even born I became paranoid about every single thing that could harm a baby. I drove everybody insane for months. Then Randal was there and I added new items to the list of things I should've removed from the house." Lucas closed the door behind him and shivered.

"My situation is different," Prince said, walking on the path he had tended to just a few days before.

"Of course it is. Every situation is different, but when a kid is added to the equation, the worries are universal. You'll do fine." Lucas closed the jacket to the neckline.

"Look what I did today..." Prince couldn't help but remember how his hands had trembled when he was trying to locate the bullet inside Aria's leg.

"Exactly my point. Look what you did today. You saved Aria's leg, and probably her life. Nobody could've done better. I couldn't. That girl couldn't. You did. When a problem was presented, you rose to the occasion."

Prince listened to Lucas, his heart growing lighter with every step. He almost tripped over the corner of a tile, pushed it down with the heels of his shoes, and followed the path to the street. There were one or two tiles sticking out that he had meant to even out, making it flush with the ground, imagining Milady having trouble walking on them, but now it didn't matter.

CHAPTER 17

"I'll do it, but you have to wait for me. I'm still coming with you." Aria was barely awake for twenty minutes at a time, but she hadn't changed her mind in the last day.

"Please, be reasonable. You're in no condition to travel and won't be for a while." Prince paced the claustrophobic space of Aria's bedroom. He came every four or five hours to check on her. She had woken the day before after sleeping for almost two days.

"Aria, we need to go." Lucas was changing the dressings on her legs. The wounds weren't bleeding anymore when washed.

"I know you've been waiting… how long now?" Aria was trying to drink some water from a glass, but she needed Lucas's help to bring it to her mouth.

"Four days." Prince's emotions had been all over the place the whole time.

"Another day and I'll be ready."

Prince and Lucas gave her a look that at any other time would have been comical, but now only conveyed frustration from both parties.

"Tomorrow, we go. And I'll teach you to drive on the road."

"You must be hallucinating," Lucas said, carefully touching her forehead. "And yet you don't have any fever."

Aria actually laughed. "There's nothing around us for hours. You'll both have plenty of time to practice on the road before we reach the next inhabited place."

"I was talking about your ill-conceived stubbornness." Lucas went to refill her glass.

"You'll be a burden." Prince glanced at her legs covered in bandages, now clean for the first time.

"I promise I won't." Aria pushed against the pillow to straighten her back and grimaced.

"We know you don't want to be, but…" Lucas set the glass on the nightstand and helped her up.

"Okay, maybe tomorrow is too early. But if you leave, I'll find a way to follow you the day after." An air of resolution dawned on Aria's face. "Or the day after that. And you can't go far on foot—"

"I'm sorry, Aria, but I think we should leave tonight," Prince said. Although she was right, he'd had enough of the conversation already.

"I still have a contact inside the Temple. Milady had sympathizers among the pure breeds, too."

"A pure breed can be sympathetic to your cause, but I bet she'd call the guards as soon as she realizes who we are." Prince was even more convinced it was time to leave the Village.

"I wouldn't be so hasty in judging people if I were you. You don't know this person."

"And you do. Would you trust her not to betray us?" Lucas asked.

"I've trusted her with my life every single time I went to the Temple, so it's a yes to your question."

"Okay. We'll stay for another two days. Then we'll leave. You'll come with us only if you're better. Understood?" Lucas patted the bed, careful not to touch her legs.

"How can you promise something like that?" Prince raised his hands to the air, despair settling in his heart. Maybe he wasn't the best equipped to keep his family safe, but he couldn't wait a second longer to put things in action to see Pax and his baby. As long as he was doing something to expedite the process, he felt less anxious. But in moments like this, when nothing was working in his favor, he felt the urge to haul rocks and run for hours. He couldn't do either.

"We need two days anyway to form a plan." Lucas arranged a plate with some fruit cut in small pieces. "Eat something, then rest. You need to recover fast." He gave Aria a fork and held the plate for her.

Prince stormed out of the room and went for a stroll in the backyard.

"Apart from the contact inside the Temple, we still need her. Two men can't travel alone. If we're caught, Aria is our pass." Lucas had followed him outside.

He was so out of sorts he hadn't heard him coming. "Do you think I don't know that?"

"Her dressing is still clean, and she tried to move her legs while we were talking to her. It's not ideal, but we'll have to wait."

Four days later, they were ready, more or less, to take leave of the Village.

Prince accompanied Aria, who was hopping on one leg, to visit Milady's tomb. The Village had a small cemetery that had been erected when, a few years earlier, one of the villagers, an older woman rescued by Milady from a cruel employer, had died of natural causes.

"I think she would've liked it," Aria commented before the small mausoleum composed of a pile of rocks piled one on top of the other, creating a willowy design.

"Lucas and I chose the rocks—"

"I know the meaning of this sculpture. The Priest's rock garden has become famous among the fathered women." Aria accepted his help to sit on the flat stone that blanketed Milady for her eternal sleep. "When I told Milady about the custom of erecting a rock sculpture to commemorate someone's memory, she said it was touching and beautiful." She opened the heavy bag she was carrying on her shoulders—she hadn't let Prince alleviate her burden—and retrieved a big book from it.

Prince read the title on the spine. The Holy Book of Goddess. Milady's priceless first edition.

"Among all the books she'd ever owned, this was her favorite. I've seen her holding this book so many times I lost count. 'This is where everything started,' she told me once. 'If you know how to decipher the words, here are the answers to everything you'd want to know about Ginecea and more.' I'm sure she'd be happy to know I gave it to you."

Prince was surprised by Aria taking his hands to deposit the book on them.

"Read it and fulfill your destiny," she said.

"What destiny?" The book felt heavy in his hands.

"I know about your name. You were born a principal. Be what your name states. Be the better one and lead Ginecea to freedom."

"You're asking the impossible. I'm just an ex-slave." When it came to describing his station in life, the word "worker" could never convey the truth.

"The Priest was an ex-slave too, and look what he's done with his life. Follow his example and you can't go wrong."

Prince felt uneasy considering a comparison between the Priest and himself. "I don't think I can accept this. I think Lexi is the person you want to give it to," he said, pushing it toward Aria to take it back.

"Lexi doesn't need it." Aria gently refused the book. "Milady's greatest legacy is in her personal library. She wanted knowledge to spread like a fever sweeping across Ginecea. The faster it infects this beautiful land of ours, the better our kids will live. When I first confessed to her why I'd been sent in exile to the Village, I thought she was going to punish me, a fathered woman who'd dared to raise her eyes too high. Instead, she let me talk and then she looked at me and said, 'You and Lexi aren't the first, nor will you be the last ones to suffer for love. But who decides what's right and what's wrong when love is at stake? I don't. Only your heart does.'" Aria caressed the flat stone and several tears fell on it; she wiped them at first, then laid her head on the slab and silently cried until a small puddle formed.

Prince let her express her pain. He had already paid his respects to Milady, several times in fact. During the eight days he waited for Aria to get fit to travel, after his workday had ended—he was helping a villager build a small storage attached to her cottage—he had taken the habit of talking to Milady. It was peaceful there. A ridge and a small body of water separated the cemetery from the Village. The girl who had helped Prince and Lucas tending to Aria's wounds had told them Milady had chosen that piece of land for the cemetery because it was her favorite place.

"She'd spread a blanket under this tree and read for hours," the girl had said, pointing at a majestic olive tree.

The decision to lay Milady to rest under that tree had been unanimous.

I hadn't had the honor and pleasure to meet you earlier, but I want you to know you made a difference in my life, and I'll never forget you, Prince thought, tears swelling in his eyes as well.

Aria reached for his hands. He slowly helped her up, balancing her unsteady body.

"You're still too frail," he couldn't help but say. Although they had already discussed at length about her resolution to travel, they hadn't changed their respective opinions on the matter.

"Just lightheaded, nothing more." Aria leaned on him, her face pale. "Better now."

"Then let's go." Prince still hoped she would change her mind.

"Just one last thing," she said, enlarging the opening of her bag, looking for something else inside. "Here it is. This will be my parting gift for Milady."

Prince looked, mildly intrigued; she had turned her back to him, so he couldn't see what she was doing.

"Farewell, friend. You'll be missed." Aria wiped one last tear and said, "Now it's time to go fulfill her dream."

Prince helped her walk away, but before leaving, he turned to look at the tomb. Aria had added something at the base of the stone sculpture: a small book carefully wrapped in plastic and further protected by a transparent bag. Prince went back and built a safe haven with some rocks to prevent the book from being ruined by inclement weather.

"It's the book she gave me the first night I arrived here. I learned its words by heart. I want people who come here to visit her to have solace from reading it," Aria explained, clearly pleased by what Prince had just done.

"What's it about?"

"It's called *The Book of Love*. It's about the God and is said to be the *Holy Book of Goddess*'s companion. Milady said she always thought the author must have been a slave, although nobody in Ginecea would admit anything of that kind. It talks about acceptance of all that's different and the power of forgiveness. It says that there're no differences among human beings, men or women, and that love is always pure. Not a popular topic among pure breeds." Aria laughed. "Anyway, it helped me tolerate the long days without knowing anything about Lexi. It gave me hope."

Several hours later, when the Village was a distant dot on the land and the sea was in sight, Prince was deep in thought. As promised, Aria had taught them the rudiments of driving, and faithful to her words, the road seemed rarely traveled. In the beginning, he listened intently to everything Aria was saying regarding breaking, accelerating, avoiding hitting objects on the road, and after a while, he relaxed. When it was Lucas's turn to stay behind the wheel, Prince stopped paying attention and his thoughts drifted automatically to Pax. He remembered her talking about her own driving experience when she had left everything behind to look for him in the middle of the desert. She knew she was pregnant and she had embarked on a mission bigger than herself to be with him.

His mind occupied by reliving all his memories of Pax, Prince barely noticed time changing from day to night. He only emerged from his world when they got dangerously close to running out of fuel, and Aria instructed Lucas to drive to the closest station, being careful to only stop if there weren't other cars on the road. They were lucky. The moment Lucas got back inside, a car appeared around the curve, slowing down to stop and refuel. Prince and Lucas immediately lowered their heads, but it wasn't necessary.

"Nobody in their right minds would think I'm in a car with two men," Aria said once they left. She was right. During the whole road trip, the few cars they passed didn't check them. Drivers looked at their car, but didn't see them.

Several hours later, they reached their destination after nine hours without a single hitch. "Here is fine, close enough to send the signal, but far enough in case the wrong eyes see it. Stop there on the ridge overlooking the Temple," she told Lucas. "We're back where everything started." She looked at the distant lights looming ahead of them.

For me it started long ago, Prince thought, but asked instead, "Are you sure your contact is coming?"

Aria shrugged. "If she's still alive, yes." She reached for her bag and pulled out a candle and a lighter. "It'll take some time before she can reply to the signal."

"If she replies," Prince said, while thinking that they had relied too much on Aria's plan.

"Have some faith." Lucas was resting in the back seat, his legs stretching outside the window.

"Again, not so much the type." Prince sat sideways to talk to both Aria and Lucas. "How long does it normally take before this woman replies?"

"When you say the word 'woman,' it sounds derogatory. I must remind you that you fell in love with one and that you happen to have a daughter." Aria rolled down her window to wave the lit candle outside.

"According to him, Pax isn't a woman," Lucas said, laughing.

"Well, a man she is not." Aria looked at Prince.

"I love Pax. She could be anything, and I'd still love her. Same goes for my daughter. And I'm sorry if you were offended, but I must say I don't see you like a woman anymore either." Prince felt cornered and didn't like it, but Aria had a point.

"Is that a compliment?" she asked, a smile visible on her face lit by the waving light of the candle.

"I've become to think of you as a friend," Prince admitted.

"Well, thanks, likewise." Aria blew the candle and leaned on the opened window to scan the darkness.

After twenty minutes of waiting for something to happen, Prince got out of the car to walk away his nervousness. "You didn't answer my question before. How long can it take for this contact of yours to answer? We can't stay here forever," he called from behind a bush where he had sought some due privacy. The night was particularly dark and he couldn't see the car from there.

"I wouldn't be worried about that," a voice answered, too close and too feminine for his liking. "Now, do me a favor. Get out of there, keep your hands where I can see them, and tell me why I shouldn't put a bullet in your head."

"I can do the first two things you asked, but regarding the third, I don't know... I like to live? Is that the correct answer?" Prince walked out of the bush with his hands raised in the air, hoping that the woman, in her mid-thirties and wearing the black and gold uniform of the Priestess's Army, wasn't trigger-happy.

"Lorna?" Aria appeared at his side and stood close to him.

"Aria?" the woman asked, her voice almost happy. "Is this yours?" She indicated Prince with her gun.

"Technically speaking, he isn't," Aria answered, and then when the gun moved lower and closer to Prince's body, she added, "It's okay, Lorna. He's with me. He's a friend."

"*He* is a friend?" Lorna repeated. "Have you lost your mind?"

Prince wanted to yell to Aria, "I told you so," but thought better of it.

"No, I haven't lost my mind, and, yes, he's a friend. And he was also a friend of Milady," Aria said.

"*Was?*" Lorna lowered the gun to the ground.

Prince inhaled deeply, his jaws sore by having clenched his teeth to a grind.

"Milady is dead," Aria said, her voice breaking on the last word.

"Dead? What do you mean dead? When? How?" Lorna forgot about Prince right away.

"The Priestess killed her—" Aria started explaining, but she couldn't go any further. "Please tell her," she asked Prince, who was startled by her request. "Please, tell her. I can't," she repeated, taking his hand in hers to draw some comfort.

"Let's go sit," Prince proposed to the two women. They went back to the car where he and Lucas were officially presented to the pure breed, and then he told Lorna what had happened at the Village.

Lorna—Lieutenant Lorna as it turned out—listened to him, asking confirmation from Aria any time she couldn't believe what she was hearing. As the tale drew to its end, the pure breed looked devastated. "What are we going to do now?"

"We're going to finish what she started. We can't let her sacrifice go to waste," Aria answered, her voice steadier.

"I need to know if Pax Layan and the Chosen are at the Temple," Prince finally asked.

"What do you want with them?" Lorna asked, suspicion on her face.

"He doesn't mean any harm to them. Don't worry." Aria went on explaining how everything was related.

Prince listened to his own story told by someone else and agreed wholeheartedly with the pure breed when she commented, "Unbelievable."

Lorna didn't seem shocked by the revelation about the fact that both fathered women and pure breeds were conceived by using men's semen.

"Pardon me for pointing this out, but for being a pure breed and all, you seem particularly cool with this piece of information." Prince couldn't help but question Lorna. Aria had been explaining detail after detail, and the woman had asked all sorts of questions about Milady and the Village.

"I was one of the few privileged guards who work in the inner circle at the Temple. I also know about Sundial and other places like it."

"There're pure breeds who know about that?" Lucas asked, a fraction of a second earlier than Prince.

"Well, there must be someone the Priestess trusts. She can't do everything by herself. But, no, although I work inside the inner circle, I'm not officially privy of that kind of knowledge."

"So, how did you know?" Prince asked this time.

"I stumbled upon medical records not meant for my eyes. In the beginning, what I read didn't make a lot of sense and I discarded what I saw without a second thought. But then several months later while I was on duty at the obstetric guard, I overheard a conversation behind closed doors I shouldn't have heard. The things the two doctors were saying were heresy, and my first impulse was to run to report them to the captain. I thought she would know what to do. It was too big for me to handle. I was about to call my superior officer when another woman entered the conversation. It was the Priestess. I almost fainted right there and then. She knew everything. Not only that, she was giving the two doctors orders on how to improve birth rates and stuff like that. I was so upset I didn't know what I should've done next. I went to talk to the captain, but at the last moment, I realized nothing good would come from telling her what I heard."

"How can you live with that kind of knowledge and not do anything about it?" Prince's voice betrayed his feelings toward the woman.

"It's easy for you to judge. My world was collapsing and I felt there was nobody who would understand. I felt both guilty and disgusted. Guilty because I've been raised to never question the Priestess's authority—disgusted because I couldn't look at the fathered women without thinking that we pure breeds are the biggest scam on Ginecea. I went crazy and lost my job in the inner circle. I was lucky enough that Captain took pity on me and didn't send me away. I was relocated to work in the storage area," Lorna said, her voice lower with each word until at the end it was just a whisper.

Aria continued where Lorna stopped. "It was then that we met. I was doing my usual rounds for Milady, dropping off medical kits for Literacy Sans Frontier and hoping to see Lexi, when I struck up a conversation with this lonely guard. She was extremely polite and never treated me with contempt because I was a fathered woman. From that moment on, every time I came for a delivery, I looked for Lorna. Almost six months later, I invited her to visit me at the Village. She did and she met Milady."

"Milady changed my life." Lorna wiped one tear dangling from her eye. "She told me things I'd never thought a pure breed of her station would say, and I confided in her. She didn't think I was a traitor of my race. She showed me passages from books, and I felt free to think for the first time in my life."

"You never told me what you knew," Aria said. "I'd heard bits and pieces from Milady, but until I met Prince and Lucas, I'd never put things together."

"Milady and I thought times weren't ready for the truth to come out. Too many lives were at stake. Milady was worried that an uprising of fathered women would end in genocide. The Priestess was still too powerful, and the pure breeds would've fought for their rights to go untouched." Lorna sighed. "We had this conversation with Milady so many times. When the first attacks on the fathered communities working at the sewage plants started, my conscience shouted too loud to ignore. I couldn't keep the secret anymore, and I told her. We decided that I could test the waters and see if there were other sympathizers at the Temple."

"I imagine it wasn't simple," Lucas commented when Lorna paused for a moment.

"No, it wasn't simple at all. I didn't even know how to broach the subject without giving myself away and being accused of heresy," Lorna answered Lucas.

"I introduced her to Magdalene, and she helped Lorna find other likeminded people while building a net of fathered women and pure breeds who can trust each other with their lives." Aria offered the others a swig from a bottle she retrieved from the side pocket. "I thought we were going to need something strong, sooner or later," she explained sheepishly.

"Thank you. You were right." Prince took the first gulp.

"I regret not having confided in Magdalene. She should've known. But I was worried about her reaction at such news, and the movement wasn't as organized as Milady wanted. In the end, nothing mattered. Magdalene is dead. Milady is dead…"

"We told Magdalene and the other women of the chapter house. She knew. In the end, it did matter. She died knowing her blood was as pure as yours," Prince said and let a long moment pass, respecting the two women's desire to mourn their friends, but then he had to ask again the question that had started the conversation. "Can you tell us where Pax Layan and the Chosen are?"

"And Lexi Corellis," Aria added.

"They're not here. The Priestess left first thing this morning. The presidential family left with her, the president's assistant, and also Pax Layan's friend." Lorna looked at both Prince and Aria with an apologetic expression.

"Where did they go?" Prince was holding his breath.

"The chauffeurs were complaining that the Priestess had ordered them to drive nonstop to Sundial."

"We'll never make it to Sundial. We barely made it here with the second tank of gas, and I've spent all the money I had." Aria leaned against the window and rested her head on the glass.

Prince remained silent. He did not want to succumb to despair, but it was getting harder. He was just an ex-worker and didn't know anything about surviving in any environment that wasn't a farm or a desert. He had never worried about putting gas in a car. And yet here he was stranded two days away from the place he needed to be, and he felt completely lost.

"Maybe..." Lorna spoke, but Prince was drowning in bleak thoughts and didn't hear what she was saying at first.

"That could work," Aria said, her voice more cheerful than a minute ago.

"Well, we don't have anything to lose at this point." Luca looked at him, waiting for him to contribute to the discussion.

"What could work?" he asked, not daring to hope.

"There's the night train leaving in less than an hour. I'll start my shift at the storage facility in twenty minutes, and I can add a few more crates to the cargo." Lorna opened the passenger door. "You have to decide now. There isn't lot of time."

"Where does the train stop?" Lucas asked.

"Along the way, it stops for fifteen minutes at Sundial. I'll add to the log that an additional shipment is to be delivered there. So?"

"And what happens when we're dropped off at Sundial? How do we make it out of the storage facility?" Prince imagined being discovered by a startled guard and shot on the spot.

"I already said I have someone at Sundial who can help. Time is running. Yes or no?" Lorna asked.

"Yes, add two crates to the log," Prince answered without a moment of hesitation.

"What do you mean two? There're three of us," Aria said, but she didn't sound ready to fight. She sounded tired.

"You're not coming." Even Prince, whose mind had been far away the whole trip, had noticed how worn out she had looked. "You can't travel any farther."

"Nonsense, Lexi is there and I'm going..."

"No, you aren't. Not this time." Prince shook his head.

"I'm sure Lexi wants to see you alive and well," Lucas softly added.

Prince was glad Lucas had stepped in; he couldn't find the strength to keep asking Aria to do something he wouldn't have done in her position. He heard the two of them arguing back and forth longer than Prince thought necessary, but with every passing second, Aria lost ground until she had to agree to the inevitable conclusion.

"But I managed to come here." She tried one last time.

Prince understood her sentiment and was glad not to be the one who had to make that decision, but allowing her to be stuffed in a crate for two days was akin to murder for her. She needed someone else to decide in her place. "You're going to be of more help if you stay behind and help coordinate people spreading the truth."

"I agree with him," Lorna said, and both men turned to look at her at the same time, the same stunned expression on their faces. "You aren't fit for the ordeal they're going to go through." She met their eyes and silently apologized. "It's true," she whispered to them and then continued facing Aria. "Someone has to stay and help me. I can't do everything myself. I don't trust anybody else to carry my messages. The Priestess's paranoia has reached dangerous levels and she seems to be more alert than ever."

"I guess you have a point, but I feel I'm failing Lexi... I pushed myself to get better only to rescue her." Aria went to massage her legs without thinking. When she realized it, she grimaced in defeat.

"Lexi doesn't want you to die for her," Lorna said.

"But I would gladly," Aria answered, forcefully moving away her hands from her legs.

"Yes, but not while trying to reach her." Prince smiled at her. "That would help nobody."

"Aria, this is a war where everybody must do their part. Yours is to get better and build a net of trusted, knowledgeable women we can count on when the time is right," Lucas said.

"And we also need a good pair of eyes and ears inside the Temple." Prince put one hand on her arm. "So please don't get caught."

"I don't want to rush you or anything, but I have to inform my contact at Sundial that she just requested a last-minute order of medical texts from the Temple's library. It's late and we have to go to the storage facility to properly wrap them for shipping." Lorna pointedly looked at the wheel.

Prince's lips turned up at the image Lorna's words evoked. He saw Aria doing the same.

"Okay, okay, you convinced me. *But* I'll reach Sundial as soon as I can," Aria said.

Prince and the rest let her have the last word.

Finally, they left the safety of the ridge to travel to the storage facility. Once there, the next hour passed in a blur for Prince. He watched as things happened to him. Lorna told him what to do and he complied. She explained how the plan would unfold once they reached Sundial, but, first of all, he had to crouch inside the crate she was showing him and hold his head with his hands to soften the tossing and turning he was going to experience once the porters started hauling the cargo onto the train.

Prince gave a brief look at the temporary prison before climbing in. It was small and it scared him to have to spend any time inside. "Okay." He inhaled a big breath and dove in.

"See you soon," Aria said.

Prince tilted his head upward to give her a nod. "Sooner than you think."

"Good luck." Lorna helped him tuck his limbs inside and lowered the lid. Not even a full minute later, she told someone. "All yours."

Prince felt the crate being pushed and then heard a woman swearing.

"What are they sending to Sundial this time? A slab of granite?" the woman asked. "I need the hand truck for this one."

A moment passed, then Prince felt his crate being lifted.

"Hopefully, there isn't anything fragile inside." He heard the woman say, and almost at the same time, his crate was shifted and dumped. He almost cried out at the impact, but managed to bite his bottom lip instead.

"I don't care. Just help me out. There're two more I haven't checked out, and we're five minutes late," another woman said.

A big push followed.

Prince heard hurried steps and someone shouting from a distance. "Hey, you, it says fragile on top of that. Be more careful." Lorna's muffled voice reached him.

"Does it? Oh, it does, my bad. I didn't notice. Thank you for telling me, *Lieutenant*."

Prince detected the mock respect in the woman's tone and prepared for more rough handling as soon as Lorna left. He was right. He felt the exact moment when Lorna left the room, but fortunately his crate reached its final destination after only two pushes. He thanked Lorna for wrapping a heavy blanket around him.

A few hours later, he also thanked her for the bottles of water she crammed between his body and the blanket.

"When you've finished the water, you can still use the bottle," she had said slowly.

It took Prince a moment to realize what she meant.

"You won't be able to get out until you reach Sundial twenty-six hours from now. Two guards stand on duty the whole time. They never leave the cargo hold. I recommend you use the bathroom now, and do it fast because the crew is coming." Lorna had indicated a bush just outside the storage facility. Prince and Lucas had hastily followed her suggestion.

"I hope you aren't claustrophobic," she had told him before lowering the lid of the box and hammering it safely down.

"I'll manage," he had answered while thinking, *I'm terrified by dark, closed spaces.*

Once the noises and the bickering ceased, announcing that the women had finally loaded the last crate on the train, Prince was left with his thoughts, enough water to survive two days, and several packages of hard crackers Lorna had thought to toss in at the last second. He was grateful for that, too. It wouldn't do to arrive at Sundial and not have the strength to get out of his shipping container.

Then, a few minutes later, when the warm darkness of his temporary home became a reality, Prince realized what he had just done. "Sweet Heavens, I hope I didn't just kill myself. Pax needs me. My baby needs me. Please," he murmured over and over again.

He had placed his life into the hands of a pure breed, a woman he had just met, and never argued with any of the things she had asked him to do. Not even being closed inside a tight wooden box had made him wary of her intentions. When the train started rolling and a low hum reverberated through the wooden walls, he thought he had failed Pax, echoing Aria's fear. He didn't care anymore about being tortured. Physical pain he could stand. But being the reason why his family would suffer was unbearable.

He started losing his mind rapidly. This was worse than solitary confinement, and he had been in and out of those damp cells enough times to know. It was so hot he couldn't breathe and he started hyperventilating. *My heart is giving in*, he thought, gasping for air. *I'm drowning without water*. But, he didn't faint. Image after image of Pax and the baby dying at the hands of the Priestess because he hadn't survived the train trip played in his mind, accelerating his heartbeats to new speed. He fought hard to regain control over his emotions. "I'm not going to let anything happen to my family. Nothing," he repeated under his breath until the words became a mantra and suited his fears. "I'm not afraid of this. This is nothing compared to what I had to endure since I was a baby. This is nothing," he whispered, his forehead firmly pressed against the coldness of a bottle of water. "I'm stronger than this. Adversities made me stronger. The Priestess made me stronger."

Prince made an effort to focus on happy memories, Pax the center of them all. The first and the last time he had seen her. The first time he had made love to her. The first time he had held his baby. He went back and forth between those memories, concentrating on details to make them more real. The first time he had seen Pax she had just showered, her wet, cascading hair leaving a dark halo on her shirt. She had smelled of fresh water and lavender-scented soap. He knew it was lavender because Sundial had a butterfly pavilion full of them where he had been sent from time to time to tend to the plants when it was harvest time. *The women should've showed me more respect. I'm a blasted principal and they made me work as a gardener*. He laughed at his attempt at sarcasm, but it didn't make him feel better. His thoughts returned to Pax and how her eyes had grown wide when she had seen him on the floor while Caren and Lauren beat him. And he could remember as if it were happening now, how she had apologized to him when he had been forced to serve her at the women's table. Pax had said "I'm sorry" to him, looking him in the eyes. No woman had ever done anything remotely close to that. At best, women had used him. At worst, they had beaten and violated him. No woman before Pax had ever showed him respect.

Hours passed. The air in the crate became unbreathable, the warmth suffocating, and the physical urges couldn't wait. Prince's mind relaxed. At long last, the desire to hold Pax and his baby won over his claustrophobia.

CHAPTER 18

"Sundial, next stop!" A voice woke Prince from a hazy torpor.

"Prepare the cargo," one of the two women guarding the compartment said.

Prince tried to put together his thoughts, but as soon as lucidity returned, he regretted it. With full consciousness came violent surges of pain through his limbs. He couldn't move. Not even his toes. Every single part of his body ached and it felt as if thousands of needles were piercing his swollen skin. He cried, his mouth safely biting the palm of his hand. He had learned that trick long ago. Never let women catch you defenseless or in pain, they would remunerate your weakness with a healthy dose of beatings to make you stronger. He had several bite marks on his hands and arms attesting to his success in hiding his moments of weakness. He now linked crying to physical pain and biting. He was proud of that. *I'm stronger than all of you.*

Before he regained control of his aching body, the train stopped. His mind went blank, and all his fear came back. It was the moment of truth. "Please, please, Heavens above, let Lorna be a decent human being, please...," he whispered against his hand. "Please, please, please..."

The sound of a metallic shutter being rolled up interrupted his mental begging.

"Do you need any help?" a woman called from outside.

"We'll start dropping off the lighter boxes, but then, yes, we need the hand truck with the heavier load."

"The usual cargo?"

"There was something added at the last second."

"Strange. It doesn't say anything on my log. What is it?"

Meanwhile, Prince felt his box being moved.

"I don't know... something fragile, anyway. It says here on top."

He heard a hurried set of steps. Someone had just arrived. "Thank you, Meli. They're for me. Please be careful," an out-of-breath voice Prince thought sounded familiar answered.

"Good evening, Doctor Linda. What are those?"

Prince released the breath he was holding. Linda was Lorna's contact at Sundial. He was elated and at the same time felt he was going to throw up. He was ready for Lorna to fulfill his worries and hadn't considered, despite his pleas, she was going to help them.

"Medical texts I need to study," Linda said.

"And since when are books considered fragile? Lieutenant Lorna pulled another one," one of the guards said, and the other laughed out loud at the statement.

"Actually, these are rare texts, coming straight from the Priestess's personal library. I would've written 'fragile' in golden letters myself," Linda commented, her voice getting closer to Prince's box. "I hope you didn't let anything happen to those books. I wouldn't want to be the one to apologize to Her Holiness about the state of her rare manuals."

"No, of course not. We treated the goods with the utmost respect, as if they were our babies."

"I'm sure you did."

Prince felt a hand tapping slightly on the lid, but didn't dare answer back. He couldn't be sure it was Linda.

"Where do you want the boxes, Doctor?"

"Right in my study. I need to start on my research tonight."

Prince felt his crate being lifted and then heard the sound of wheels. The smoothness of the ride told him he was being transported on the hand truck the women had earlier mentioned. A thump followed. He hoped it was Lucas's.

"Just these two crates, Doctor?"

"Yes, thanks."

The ride was fast and without incident; the guards chatted the whole time while Linda kept quiet. In less than ten minutes, all motion stopped and Prince's box was lifted again.

"There, right there. Thank you."

"We can help you unpack if you're in a hurry," one of the women proposed. She didn't sound excited about it.

"Oh no, don't worry. You're both tired and I saw that there're lots of boxes to haul to the storage. I can manage, but thank you."

Prince waited impatiently for the guards to leave and for Linda to open the blasted crate, feeling he couldn't wait a fraction of a second longer imprisoned in that space. The moment stretched on, and he was sure that half a minute passed, then more than a minute. *What's happening? Linda, why don't you free me from this cage already? What are you waiting for?* His hands were already pushing on the lid when he heard Linda talking.

"Good Evening, Priestess."

"Good Evening, Linda. Do you have the results from the lab?" The Priestess's voice had a sobering effect on Prince. He lowered his hands to his lap and hoped his heart wasn't beating too loud.

"I do…"

"And?"

"And you didn't need to come here. I was going to report to you when you paged me."

"Good thing I did, then. Otherwise, we would've run around looking for each other." The Priestess nervously chuckled.

Prince thought both women sounded off.

"Yes, good thing you did."

"Anyway, what's the result of the blood test?"

"It's positive," Linda answered.

"Thank the Almighty Goddess…"

What's happening here?

"So the baby is a match," the Priestess finished after a long sigh.

"Yes. As I thought—"

"When can you start the procedure?" the Priestess asked, her voice happier and lighter than a moment before.

"If the Chosen is stable, at the earliest, tomorrow morning." Linda's voice wasn't as carefree as the other woman's.

"Thank you for the great news. Now I can rest my mind. I haven't slept in two days."

"I can give you something to help you relax, if you want," Linda said, her words slow and deliberate.

"That would be great. I can't function like this. I was terrified…"

Prince heard the sound of footsteps and drawers being opened and closed.

"Take two now, and if you don't fall asleep in the next hour, call me, and I'll send you another two."

"Thanks, Linda."

"Just my job."

"Ginecea is in your debt."

"Don't mention it. It's not like I'd let a child die," Linda said, dismissing the Priestess's thanksgiving rather hastily in Prince's opinion.

She was being reticent because he was listening, and he was starting to get more and more worried as the conversation progressed. They were talking about his daughter needing some procedure, and their preoccupied tones and hushed words were an ominous sign.

"Have a good night," the Priestess said, her voice coming from farther away, probably already at the door.

"And you as well."

Prince heard Linda's fingers nervously tapping on his box.

"And, Linda…"

He swore against his hand firmly shutting his mouth. *Leave, already!*

"Yes, Priestess?" Linda's tapping against the box intensified.

Linda, stop now.

"I apologize for my outburst earlier. I let my worries and my temper have the upper hand. I see now that you were right in keeping the baby alive. Thank you for being sensible. You're my Chosen's savior."

Prince shivered at the way the Priestess marked his daughter as hers. His stomach knotted and he thought he was going to throw up all over the box's walls. *I hate you.*

"I… don't know what to say… I don't deserve such honor from Your Holiness."

Don't grovel before this monster.

"You don't have to say anything. Lately, I've had to make difficult decisions and the baby's health has been a constant worry, day and night. As my physician, I'm asking you to allow me a private moment of weakness without judging me," the Priestess said.

Don't fall for the act. She's a monster, nothing more.

"If you need anything, just call me. I'll come to you," Linda said.

Finally, the sound of steps faded away and a door was closed.

Prince tapped on the ceiling of the crate. "Linda, get me out of here."

"Be patient just a moment longer. I want to be sure she isn't coming back." Linda's voice echoed inside Prince's box. "Okay."

He was blinded by the light coming in when Linda removed the lid.

"Oh my sweet Heavens, it smells like you're rotting from the inside in here," she commented as soon as he moved to get out.

"Hi, Linda, nice to see you." Prince was aware that his look mirrored his smell.

She went to open Lucas's box without saying anything else.

"Hey? You in there?" she called after a long moment.

"Is something wrong with Lucas?" Prince asked, emerging with great difficulty from the cramped space. His legs didn't want to cooperate and he ended on the floor, hitting his head against a chair leg. Fortunately, it was light and moved without opposing much resistance to his head. Nevertheless, it did hurt.

"Are you okay?" Linda came to his side, her hands already probing his head.

"I'm fine. Don't worry about me. Lucas? Answer me, man!" Prince half stumbled, half walked toward Lucas's box. Lucas was unconscious, barely breathing, an unhealthy sheen coloring his now-pale skin. "Do something!"

"We have to get him out of there. Help me."

Prince took Lucas's limp body by the armpits and heaved him out. His own body wasn't functioning well yet. He ended on the floor again with Lucas sprawled on top of him. Linda moved Lucas until he rested on the floor.

"What's wrong with him?"

"Twenty-six hours closed in there. That's what. I'm surprised you didn't faint." Linda went to a nearby table, opened a drawer, looked inside for a few seconds, and then picked something small and came back to Lucas's side. She moved a little bottle under Lucas's nose until his eyes fluttered with rapid movements. "Here you are. Good. Breathe in and out slowly. Can you hear me? Nod if you can."

Lucas tried to open his eyes, but his eyelids kept falling.

"You'll feel better in a moment. Just hang in there, will you?" Linda left again and went to fetch a bottle of water. She opened it, dropped several spoonfuls of what looked like white powder inside, and brought it to Lucas's lips. "Sip a little bit of this."

Prince shot her a puzzled glance.

"Don't worry. It's water and sugar, nothing more. You could use some, too. If you can stand, go and prepare some for yourself. I need to stabilize him first."

Prince pushed his heels to the floor and hauled himself up using the nearby chair for support. His head swayed at the effort, but eventually, he managed to keep himself upright. He walked slowly, tentatively putting one foot in front of the other until he reached the table where Linda kept some plastic bottles neatly arranged in rows. Close to the bottles were several small jars.

"The one on the left by the red book," Linda said without looking at him.

Prince took the spoon resting by the book. "How many?"

"Three should suffice."

He fixed his beverage, then gulped the sugary water in one single motion. "I need more," he said and went for it. After the third glass, he felt some of his brain functions working again—funny he hadn't even noticed they weren't until that moment. With clarity of thought came a better grip on his body. The needle-like pain left his limbs in a matter of minutes and he caught wind of his own smell. "I need a shower."

"You do. Door in front of you. Splurge with the soap, please," Linda said, but her voice was kind.

"Sorry for the mess." Prince indicated his box. "I used the empty bottles, but—"

"Well, your physiology allows you to use bottles for something, at least. After an entire day inside a wooden box, I would've done so much worse." Linda laughed at some image she was concocting in her mind. "Yep, way, *way* worse."

Prince went straight to the shower stall without stopping at the basin. He didn't want to look at the mirror until he was decent. He turned the water to scalding hot and let it wash away his grime. He was ashamed someone had seen him covered in his own filth, and for a long moment, the memory of the Bestiarium and the mute boys still imprisoned there lingered in his mind. *Nobody should be subjected to that.*

"Are you okay?" Linda called from right outside the stall. Only a thin, opaque glass wall stood between them. It didn't feel right to him that she was there. When he didn't answer right away, Linda opened the door.

"What are you doing?" Prince snarled, closing the door on her shocked face.

"I was checking on you." Linda threw a towel inside the shower.

He took it, and after summarily drying his skin, he draped it around his waist and came out.

"It's not that I haven't seen you naked before," she said, puzzled.

"It's not that I had a choice before."

"Okay." She raised her brow. "Here's your bag. I suppose you thought of bringing a change of clothes with you." She passed the bag to him and then stepped back and leaned on the sink.

"Thanks," he answered, still upset. "Do you mind?"

Linda looked at him, her thoughts clear, but she moved away from the sink. "Lucas needs my help." She closed the door harder than necessary behind her.

Prince quickly dressed and left the bathroom. Lucas was still on the floor where he had left him. "Lucas?"

"Hey there," the man answered, his voice low. "The ride didn't agree with me."

"He didn't have enough fresh air coming through the cracks." Linda was intently looking inside Lucas's crate. "And he's highly dehydrated." She showed Prince Lucas's almost-full bottles. "Why didn't you drink?" she asked Lucas, bringing to his mouth some water.

"I felt dizzy from the beginning, and then I don't remember a lot. It was hot and I felt tired." Lucas tried to pull himself upright, but swayed as his eyes clouded over.

"Easy." Prince crouched by the man's side and helped him straighten his back against the wall behind him.

"You could use something stronger to get you back on your feet." Linda approached Lucas with a syringe.

He gave her a terrified look and instinctively brought his knees to his chest.

"Don't worry. I'm not going to kill you. It's just a tonic."

"It's okay. You can trust her," Prince said, surprising himself.

Lucas gave her another wary look, but raised his arm.

"Thanks for the vote of confidence." Linda stroked Lucas's arm and gently pushed the plunger. "You should feel better almost right away." She kept her eyes on him and smiled when his expression changed and he visibly relaxed against the wall. "Like I said."

"Did you know stuff like that existed?" Lucas, looking more lucid and stronger than a mere minute ago, asked Prince, who nodded.

"He knows firsthand what I was going to inject into you." Linda went to throw away the syringe.

"It's the medicine that keeps beaten workers alive when the guards' exuberance gets out of hand," Prince said drily.

"I couldn't let you die, could I?"

Linda's words reminded Prince of the conversation he had recently heard. "We need to talk about what you and Priestess said."

"I wouldn't go there if I were you." Linda was busy cleaning stuff from her table.

"I'm not going to let it go."

"Sometimes it's better not knowing." Linda rearranged a row of bottles one time too many; several bottles rolled on the table and fell down to the floor before she could stop them.

"I must disagree. I've recently discovered that knowledge is power." Prince went to pick up some of the bottles. "I want to know what you were talking about."

"It doesn't concern you."

"I know my daughter is involved."

"I don't know what you're talking about," Linda said, her eyes staring at the floor.

"I know everything about this place. I know the Chosen is my baby who supposedly died in childbirth."

"You're putting together bits and pieces of what you heard. You're just guessing. And it's not what you think." Linda refused to look at him, even when he went to stand right before her.

"Linda, you're wasting time. How long do you want to play dumb?"

"How dare you talk to me like this?" Linda finally raised her eyes, fire brightening her face.

"I know I'm a principal." Prince took two steps back and gestured toward himself with his hands. "I know why I was kept alive when every other worker would be long dead by now."

"I'd keep you alive, anyway," she murmured, then bit her lip.

"Linda, you're Lorna's contact here at Sundial. You're harboring two fugitives, one of which the Priestess would be more than happy to see tortured and killed. Why are you acting like this? I don't understand what you're doing." Prince was getting angry and he wanted his questions answered.

"I'm trying my best to protect you," Linda said.

"Protect me from what? You aren't making any sense."

Lucas moaned and started breathing heavily.

"Lucas?" Linda crouched beside him and laid one finger on his wrist. "This isn't just dehydration. Do you know if he suffers from anything?"

"No—" he started to say, then remembered that in other occasions Lucas had been short of breath and overall out of sorts. He told Linda of Lucas's past troubles. "What is it?" he asked when she shook her head after listening to his chest.

"I think it's his heart." Linda stood up and paced back and forth several times.

"You're making me nervous." Prince stopped her by grabbing her arm. They both jumped back. "I didn't mean to scare you."

"It's okay," she said, but walked a step farther back toward the wall.

"It wasn't my intention to touch you." He raised both hands.

Linda grimaced. "I know."

"Can you do anything for him?"

"Very little I'm afraid. I'd need to run a whole battery of tests I can't do here and taking him to the infirmary is too dangerous. Caren and Lauren drop by every now and then, and I can't predict when they'll sneak in my office or apartment."

"What do you mean?"

"Things have changed at Sundial. No one has any privacy anymore. We're all subjected to unannounced visits from our beloved manager and her spouse. Caren and Lauren have recently tied the knot with the Priestess's blessing. Everyone was surprised by the unexpected honor bestowed upon the couple. It makes you think, doesn't it?"

"So, we aren't safe here."

"No, I'm sorry." Linda smiled sadly.

A soft knock on the door interrupted them.

"Linda? Can I come in?"

CHAPTER 19

Prince rushed to open the door. He didn't think. His brain deserted him the moment he heard Pax's voice. She was in his arms before anybody could object. He didn't care if someone else stood in the hallway. The thought briefly sojourned in his mind, but was gone the moment he was sure she was real. "I missed you," he whispered to her, his lips touching hers in a feather-light kiss.

Pax whispered his name, her hands on his hair, her mouth seeking his. "I missed you," she said back after a moment.

They didn't care there were other people in the room, their embrace growing more intimate.

"Pax?" Linda called. She had to repeat herself several times. "Pax? What are you doing here? Is something wrong?"

"Pax, are you okay?" Prince put some distance between them, just a fraction of space, to be able to talk.

Pax looked at him, her eyes focusing again, and her expression went from ecstatic to worried.

"Is the baby okay?" Prince asked, putting her at arm's length.

"She's still sleeping," she answered.

Prince almost breathed in relief at her words; then he saw both Pax's and Linda's face. "She's still sleeping... Is there something wrong with that?"

"She's lethargic." Linda walked toward Pax.

Prince automatically moved one step back, still keeping Pax harbored in his arms. "What does it mean?"

"She can't seem to wake up on her own. She's been sleeping a lot lately," Pax answered.

"Why?"

"It could be several different things. We're still testing her to be sure," Linda answered, holding onto the words a moment too long.

Prince read through what the doctor hadn't said. He let go of Pax, but retained her hand in his. "The Priestess was saying you can save her," he said, squarely looking at Linda. "Is that right?"

The doctor didn't answer his question, so he repeated, "You know I heard you talking about it. Tell us how you're going to save our daughter."

"Did she say that?" Pax looked at Prince with frantic eyes. He nodded. "Can you save our baby?" she asked Linda, and suddenly, her voice contained a note of hope.

"Yes... I think there's something that can be done for the Chosen," Linda admitted, but her voice didn't convey the same hope Pax was showing.

"The Priestess mentioned something about a match."

"What match?"

"It's complicated. You don't want to know the details, but the important thing is that something can be done for the Chosen." Linda slowly retraced her steps.

"Don't call her that!" Pax yelled at the same moment that Prince asked, "Who's the match?"

"Yes, who's the match? You tested me already, and I wasn't a good match you told me," Pax said.

"We might have a donor for the Chosen."

"What donor? I already gave her my blood, and what do you need a donor for?" Pax jerked out of Prince's grip and went to confront Linda.

"Things seem to be worse than we expected."

"What things? You haven't explained anything!"

"Tell me what's wrong with our daughter." Prince joined Pax, forming a united front facing the doctor.

"She has a genetic blood disorder."

"It can't be!" Pax cried, and Prince asked, "What's a genetic blood disorder?"

"It's an ailment that gets passed through the parents' genes," Pax answered his question. "But I'm perfectly healthy, and look at him!" She turned toward Linda.

"It's something that rarely happens," the doctor said.

"Explain." Prince couldn't stand the cajoling anymore.

"You're both carriers. I'm sorry…"

"What do you mean?" Prince asked.

"I should've tested you, but it's so rare nowadays and workers are closely screened… I'd never thought… and both parents must have it to give it to the child. Who could think of that? I didn't. So rare."

"You aren't making any sense." Pax took hold of Linda's arms and shook them.

"The Chosen needs a bone marrow transplant." Linda looked at Pax first, and then her head moved to face Prince.

"What is it? Can I help?" he immediately asked, his thoughts fluctuating between despair and hope and back. He wanted to shake the doctor into telling him everything he needed to know, but kept his balled hands by his sides.

"No, you can't help." Linda shook her head.

"But, you have a donor. Who's the donor?" he asked once again, barely restraining his hands from raising and pinning Linda against a wall. He forced himself to push his rage and worry out of his body with several deep breaths.

"Someone who's similar in genetic makeup to the Chosen." Linda lowered her eyes on the floor at the statement.

"And who is it?" He understood little of what the woman was saying and cursed his condition as an ignorant man.

"I can't tell you. I'm sorry. The only important thing is that the Chosen has a good chance to reach maturity if we act now."

"You can't tell us—why?" Prince already knew she wasn't going to answer, but he had to ask.

"My life is in jeopardy already. Accept my answers. Nothing good will come from looking for the truth."

"You must be kidding! *You* say not to ask any more questions and to be happy with that! *You* just said our baby has a good chance of reaching maturity, implying that could not be the case if nothing is done. *You* said she got whatever she got from us, then tell us not ask you what it is! It's our baby you're talking about. It's our little, precious daughter, for the Goddess's sake, Linda." Pax enumerated every "you" with her fingers, angry tears falling down her face.

Prince turned to embrace her and started stroking her hair. He was shaking too. "I want to see her," he said.

"Absolutely not!" Linda put a hand on his arm.

"You already said I have to be on the move, anyway." Prince jerked his arm to remove Linda's hand and brought Pax closer to him.

"I said that, but—"

"Here, there, somewhere else… What's the difference if I have to move around?"

"The nursery is heavily guarded, and—"

"So, it's the last place they'd expect a man to be," Prince finished.

"I don't think you've thought that through." Linda was looking at him, eyes wide.

"It's packed with guards. She's right, and the Priestess comes and goes every hour," Pax murmured.

"I know Sundial by heart. I can find my way without being detected by the guards. Don't worry." He kissed her softly, silencing her reply.

"I still think attempting something like this is pure madness."

All of a sudden, Lucas cried out and everybody turned toward him.

Prince was the first one to reach his friend, who was moaning and thrashing on the floor. "What's happening to him?"

"I need to take a better look at him…"

"What? What do you think is it?" Prince looked at Linda, her mouth open, her eyes staring at nothing.

"We're going to use the morgue," she said and moved to the door, as if her words were enough explanation.

"Wait!" Prince went after her and stood before the door. "What do you intend to do?"

"I normally perform autopsies in the morgue. No one will question me if I take a dead body there."

"Okay…"

"I'm going to fetch a stretcher that can hold both of you."

"Both of us?"

"Yes, move now. I don't have time to explain." Linda went for the handle, forcing Prince to jump back.

"I hope you know what you're doing."

"Lock the door behind me." She was already out the door.

Prince obeyed and then he and Pax stayed silent for a moment, looking at the closed door staring back at them, then Lucas cried and they were both at his side.

"Hang in there, man. She's going to make you feel better. You'll see," Prince said.

"Lucas, don't worry. We aren't going to leave you alone." Pax sat by him, one hand on his shoulder.

"I'm in a lot of pain. I can't breathe," Lucas whispered and his voice sounded distorted.

"Everything's going to be okay." Prince caught Pax looking intently at him, her lips curving up slowly at his words.

"He's right, Lucas. Everything *is* going to be okay," Pax said, her free hand seeking Prince's touch.

Prince, despite the situation, wanted to be alone with her. One look at Lucas's pale face and he felt guilty at the thought, but the simple touch of her fingers brought him somewhere else entirely. A place where problems didn't exist. "I love you," he mouthed to her.

"I love you," she said only slightly louder, her fingers tracing circles under his wrist.

"Do you want me to get out of the way and give you some privacy?" Lucas surprised both of them.

Prince and Pax laughed, the moment gone, but a different lightness had taken its place.

"Feeling better?" Prince asked.

"No, I wouldn't say so, but I had to stop you before you did something I really didn't want to see." Lucas's mouth stretched in a thin smile.

"You're in a lot of pain." Pax wiped the sweat from his forehead.

"I think I told you that already, didn't I?"

"Is there anything we can do for you?" Pax asked.

"For starters, you could stop looking at each other the way you are, then some water would be nice. My throat feels like sand every time I try to swallow." Lucas made a failed attempt at pushing his feet on the floor; he went limp for a second.

"Hey, what do you think you're doing?" Prince restrained Lucas by holding his head. The man was shaking and felt cold to the touch. "I think he's about to faint," he said to Pax, who was crouching beside Lucas with a glass of water. "Mix some sugar in it." He showed her the table and she executed his suggestion without a question.

"Okay, little sips now. Good," he said when Lucas finally opened his lips. Lucas seemed to regain some color, but it was hard to say if he was getting any better, given how pale he still was.

"He's too cold," Pax said. She stood up, her eyes looking for something, and when she saw it, she walked resolutely toward it. She stood before the linen closet for a second and then started removing items, throwing them away until she found what she needed. "Here. A blanket or two should help a little." She walked back with her outstretched hands full. "Lift his head up," she asked Prince, and while he gently moved Lucas off the wall, she wrapped the man with a colorful quilt and then added a second for good measure.

"He's already sweating a lot by himself," Prince murmured. He wasn't sure that covering Lucas was a great idea, but he understood Pax's need to do something, to feel useful, and didn't press the point. He did loosen the blankets around Lucas's throat though.

"How long does it take to find a stretcher?" Pax was pacing from one end to the other of the room. "Can we even trust her? She's been keeping things secret here at Sundial for so long."

"Don't worry. The doctor won't rat us out. She's dead if the Priestess discovers what she's been up to," Lucas rasped, surprising Prince and Pax.

"You feel any better?" She went back to his side to fuss with the blankets.

Lucas managed to free one of his arms from the cocoon and gently moved her hands away. "Yes, I'm much better. Don't be so worried about me. I'm made of a stronger material than you think." He even made it sound true.

Prince could still see through his bravado—the man was scared.

Three knocks on the door, repeated in rapid succession by another two, were followed by Linda's voice announcing she was back. Prince went to open the door, making sure he stayed behind it.

"Ready?" Linda asked the trio once she parked the stretcher in the middle of the room. "You'll have to squeeze your bodies together, but once we cover you with the linen, nobody is going to check underneath." She removed the white, folded cloth. "Okay, put Lucas on it, and then you follow," she said to Prince while uncovering Lucas.

"I need some help," he admitted after having trying to lift Lucas from the floor and failing. "Even from you, big man," he said to Lucas, who smiled at him. Eventually, with help from both women, Prince arranged Lucas on the stretcher.

"Your turn now." Linda nodded at Prince.

He climbed on the stretcher and lay flush with the other man.

"Get closer to him. It must look like one big body once you're covered." She moved Prince's arms and legs until they were attached to Lucas's. She opened the cloth that cascaded to the floor. "It's the biggest size, thick and heavy. It wouldn't do to cover you with a see-through sheet. It took me forever to find it."

"I was wondering why it took you so long." Pax absentmindedly caressed Prince.

Prince held his breath for a moment, but Linda didn't seem to notice Pax's tone.

"Now, leave one hand outside the linen," she ordered him. "Yes, dangling just like that, perfect."

Prince felt a moment of unexpected peace when the whiteness of the linen colored his vision. It was heavy as Linda had said, more canvas than linen.

Pax squeezed his hand. "I'm here."

He squeezed back.

"Going out, now," Linda announced, her voice betraying her nervousness.

Prince clung to Lucas. "Don't get any ideas," he whispered to him.

"I wouldn't. She seems the jealous type."

He hated being transported like that. It made him feel like a small boy once again, but he tried to relax his muscles and lay flat under the white tent.

"We're in the hallway now," Pax said.

Prince had a good idea about their whereabouts since they had just left Linda's place. He smiled. Pax made him smile for the silliest things. He wondered if he had ever felt joy before meeting her. He hadn't, not like that.

"Keep your voice low," Linda said to her.

"Sorry." But she didn't sound sorry.

"Just walk by the end of the stretcher as if you're helping me move it around. If we encounter anybody, let me do the talking. You look... not well, and I'm worried someone's going to ask you something. Actually, avoid eye contact just in case." Linda's voice was monotone.

"As you wish," Pax answered in the same tone.

Prince saw the milky-white haze of brightness around him dimmed and sputtered until it became complete darkness. "Did someone turn off the lights?" He tried to maintain his voice as low as possible.

Neither Linda nor Pax answered. They had stopped pushing the stretcher. He recognized the approaching sound of reinforced boots stomping on the stone floor.

He felt Lucas stiffening and his breath became irregular. "Lucas?" Prince lowered his voice a notch. "Lucas? Relax. I'm sure it's nothing."

"Don't talk," Linda said.

Prince wasn't sure if the woman had meant it for him or for Pax. It didn't really matter.

"Doctor?" a familiar voice asked from a distance.

Lucas was now shaking.

"Try to breathe slow and calm down or we're screwed." Prince lowered his voice even more, praying Lucas could still hear him. He slowly, carefully moved his hand and touched Lucas's forearm.

"Is that you, Linda?"

Lucas stopped shaking and Prince almost starting trembling himself. He recognized the voice and hoped he was having a nightmare.

"Yes, it's me. Is that you, Caren?"

"Yes, and who's with you?" The boots resonated louder.

"Pax Layan is with me. Can you tell me what's happening?" Linda said.

"Mistress Layan, what are you doing here?" Caren's voice came closer yet.

"I needed something for a headache," Pax answered after a moment of hesitation.

"What's going on?" The doctor brought the conversation back to topic.

In the dark, Pax's fingers sought Prince's hand and he couldn't help but feel better at her touch. He automatically put his hand under the safety of the linen when a cold cone of light spread unwanted brightness around.

"Electricity is down, but I sent Lauren to check on the generator."

"Mice again?" Linda asked.

"Probably, like last time."

Prince listened attentively as the woman's boots echoed on the floor and then stopped too close to the stretcher. "What do you have here?" The cone of light moved around and then stopped on the linen, at Prince's shoulders height. The light went up on down on the contour of his body twice before it stopped again somewhere between him and Lucas.

"I have to autopsy this body."

Prince mentally congratulated the doctor on keeping her voice under control. He hoped Pax could do the same.

"Did something happen today? I wasn't notified of any accident with the workers."

"No, no accidents in the last few days. This worker was old. He should've been retired sooner." Linda made it sound as if she was annoyed.

"You know we need the workforce. And why waste an autopsy on this one?"

"I'm required to perform autopsies on dead workers every six months." Linda kept her voice bored.

"Your lucky day, ah."

"Yes, you could say that. I can't wait to get this over with. Do you think it'll take much longer to provide electricity to the lower level?"

"My priority is to bring the electricity back to the infirmary and then to the fridges."

"But the morgue can't stay without electricity for long."

Prince felt the woman moving around the stretcher and almost recoiled when a gust of air cooled his left ankle, and then a hand touched his skin with an impersonal caress.

"Look. It can't stay out of a fridge for long." Linda's words accompanied the touch.

He lay still, forcing his heart to slow down and hoping Lucas was lucid enough to understand the situation.

"Disgusting. Why did you show it to me? You know that when it comes to the workers I have a weak stomach. I can barely tolerate them when alive. Cover it."

Prince's ankle was released and the linen covered it. He almost sighed in relief. Lucas hadn't moved. He was barely breathing.

"Well, you don't want this to become even more disgusting, I'm sure," Linda said.

"Okay, okay, I'll..." Static noises covered the woman's last word. Prince heard Caren asking someone when the electricity would be back on, but he couldn't make out what the other answered. The only thing clear was that Caren didn't sound happy about it.

"Tell you what. Take this to the infirmary and use the fridge there until Lauren finds a way to put everything back together."

"I can't use the fridge in the infirmary. Are you crazy?" Linda was convincing in her indignation.

"I've just been told it's going to take a while."

"How long?"

"Quite a good while longer than a corpse can be safely stored outside."

"How can it take that long to repair some animals' damage to the cables? I'm not using the infirmary fridge to store a dead body. It's not hygienic."

"Linda, you'll do it."

"I see. Using your power again?" Linda's emotions were showing through her words.

Something else is at play here, Prince thought. *Let's hope Linda is smarter than confronting Caren on whatever ground they're fighting.*

"You're being unfair. You know as well as I do that, back then, I didn't have a choice but force you to… cooperate."

"That's your own excuse. If you want to believe that, good for you, but I'm not ready to forgive you. And in the end I was right, and you and all the others were wrong."

"And I even admit that, but…"

"You admit that now."

"I do. Now, can we move along?"

"Fine."

"Let's start this again. Lauren is doing her best, but it's still going to be a while before the power is functional throughout Sundial. Now, please stop arguing with me. I don't like being in the dark with a dead worker. If you could do me a favor and follow me, I'll safely escort you and Mistress to the infirmary."

"For the record, I still think I should take the corpse to the morgue and wait there for the electricity to come back." Linda tried one more time.

Prince felt the stretcher being moved forward. Lucas stirred.

"Linda, you and Mistress Layan must go to the infirmary."

The stretcher stopped abruptly, moving Prince and Lucas forward. He let his body follow the motion and his arm slid over the edge. Thankfully there wasn't enough light, and he rearranged his legs closer to Lucas's. It wouldn't do to have a corpse with an odd number of limbs sticking out from under the linen.

"So, you're ordering me around, despite what you just said."

"I'm sorry, but I can't let you go by yourself."

"Very well, we'll go to the infirmary. Let me pass," Linda said.

The stretcher moved backward.

"I'll escort you."

"Don't be ridiculous. We can manage ourselves," Linda insisted, her voice now seriously darkening.

Stay calm. Don't confront her, Prince thought. *Nothing good is going to happen from confronting Caren.*

Silence stretched for a few seconds and then he heard someone sigh, and soon after Caren said, "No, you can't. As much as I'd like to turn around and mind my own business, it's just me here at the moment and I must make sure you and Mistress Layan are safe."

"Why wouldn't it be safe to walk to the infirmary by ourselves?" Pax asked.

"What's going on?" Linda added.

Booted steps paced back and forth, then abruptly stopped by the stretcher once again. "Fine. Do you want to know something? It wasn't mice that ate the cables. Someone cut the power lines from the outside."

"Who did it?" The doctor pulled the stretcher toward her.

They were moving backward. Prince felt nauseous and wondered if Lucas felt the same, but he hadn't given any sign he was still conscious. Prince was both relieved and worried at the thought that Lucas had fainted.

"Who was it, Caren?" Linda asked once more.

"There's no need to yell for everybody to hear," Caren cautioned her.

"So?" Linda lowered her voice.

"Workers, who else?"

"The other day, I heard some of the nurses talking about it." Pax intruded in the conversation.

"I didn't think it was already in the open. Lauren and I are trying so hard to contain the rumors. Obviously, we should do a better job."

"Word of mouth is the fastest means of communication on Ginecea," Pax said. "How long this has been going on already?"

Yes, how long, Caren? Prince forgot for a moment where he was, completely taken by the conversation.

Caren was silent.

Aren't you going to answer, Caren?

"This isn't the first time, right?" Pax asked.

"This is the third time this month alone. I'm trying to keep things quiet, but women are getting scared," Caren finally answered.

Prince took in that last piece of information and hoped they would talk some more.

"Recently, two of my nurses resigned. They both told me they had family business to attend to. I thought it was an unlucky coincidence," Linda said. "But now it makes sense. I've been wondering about all the power outages…"

"Five guards asked permission to visit relatives, and after a few days, obligations and whatnot appeared from thin air. They aren't coming back. I'm not deluding myself. Tomorrow or the day after tomorrow, something else is coming up, forcing them far away from Sundial. Five women I have known since they were girls." Caren's voice came soft, but her words were clear.

The situation is ripe.

"You can't ask people to stay."

"I know, but I thought I knew my women better."

"You only know a person's true colors in times of crises."

"Still painful nevertheless."

The stretcher halted and Prince experienced a moment of reprieve from the motion sickness.

A door was opened and the stretcher moved again. Suddenly, a dim light shone under the linen. Prince's moment of relief was short lived.

"Caren, finally. I've been waiting for you for the better part of the last hour, and I see that you're not alone," the Priestess said.

CHAPTER 20

Prince felt Lucas stir and mentally thanked Linda for taking the extra time to look for the heavy cloth covering them. The women's voices sounded dangerously too close to the stretcher, and Prince did not have to warn Lucas not to move because the man's body went rigid beside his.

"At your orders, Priestess," Caren meanwhile had said.

"That's what I thought—that you were at my orders, but it doesn't seem the case anymore," the Priestess replied, venom in her voice.

"Have I ever disappointed you, Your Holiness?" Caren sounded wounded by the Priestess's words.

"Not yet, but things aren't working the way they're supposed to. So my disappointment is just around the corner."

"I'm doing my best," Caren said.

"Your best is not enough."

"I'll try harder to please you."

"Please, do that."

A moment of silence followed. Prince felt steps moving on the floor. The dim light filtering through the canvas threads was obscured by a big, menacing shadow.

"And what's this?" the Priestess asked.

Prince saw a smaller, pointed shadow hovering over his head. Something poked him in the shoulder. He stopped breathing.

"Dead worker," Linda said.

He heard a sharp intake of breath. "Dead worker? Here? Why, for Heavens' sake?"

"Ask Caren. It wasn't my idea. I was taking the corpse down to the morgue when she intercepted me."

"Yes, thank you for mentioning it. You forget to say how I found you in the dark where you could've been easily ambushed. Instead, I safely escorted you and Mistress here."

Heavily sweating, Prince commanded his body to lie still. The pointed shadow appeared once again in his line of sight and the canvas was lifted and tented above Prince's face. He shut his eyes.

Someone coughed. "Linda?" Pax called, her voice coming from the right side of the stretcher. "That smell. Is it normal?"

The canvas was released almost at the same time Pax talked.

"The corpse is already decomposing. I should've gone to the morgue," Linda said.

"But at the morgue there isn't any electricity." Caren started. "And it wasn't smelling a moment ago—"

Linda hastily interrupted the woman. "Do I have to spell it out for you? Again? The infirmary isn't—"

"I have had enough of the two of you bickering like spoiled children." The Priestess didn't raise her voice, but both Linda and Caren desisted from arguing any longer.

"My apologies, Priestess."

"It won't happen again..."

"Stop. Talking." After a moment of silence, the Priestess continued. "Good. Now, I won't tolerate having a corpse in the same area where the Chosen and I are."

"The Chosen is here?" Pax asked.

"Of course she's here. I wasn't going to leave her alone in the nursery where there's no electricity. Anyway, regarding this... find proper storage for it."

"Right away," Linda answered promptly. "Pax, could you help me move the stretcher to the next room?"

"Sure."

"I can help you. There's no need to trouble Mistress to double as nurse." Irritation showed in Caren's voice.

"No, I've waited long enough already for you to show up to just leave again. I'm sure Mistress doesn't mind," the Priestess said, close to the stretcher.

"Mistress can't wait to be of use." Pax's tone was deadpan.

Prince sighed in relief when the stretcher was finally wheeled away from the Priestess's oppressive presence. A door was opened and then closed, and dimmer light pervaded its closeted space. He could feel his sweat pouring out with the combined heat of Lucas's and his body under the canvas.

"Hang in there," Linda whispered.

"What are we going to do?" Pax worriedly asked. "We can't go back there, and we can't stay here forever. This is too dangerous. Caren or, Goddess forbid, the Priestess could enter with whatever excuse and take a good look at the 'corpse.'"

"Let me think for a moment."

Prince heard the sound of hurried steps pacing back and forth just around the stretcher.

"Linda?"

"I'm thinking."

"Do it faster."

"Shhh."

"At least stop pacing. You're driving me crazy," Pax said, her voice higher.

The pacing stopped. "It could work," Linda murmured.

Prince tried to hold back a sneeze, but failed.

"Don't move. There's a window that opens on the room we just left and the Priestess is looking at us," Pax warned him. "Linda, the situation could get worse any moment. Elaborate, please."

"The OR has a locked fridge. It's big enough to contain a body and I have the only key. Once there, we'll think of something else."

"Okay, let's go to the OR."

"Be ready. We'll go through three different rooms to reach the OR, so expect more people wandering around asking questions about our presence," Linda said.

The stretcher was stopped twice along its way toward the promised safety of the OR. Doctor Linda, as expected, was asked several times what she was doing wheeling around a corpse. She repeated the same story, growing more irritated with each telling until she almost yelled at the last woman who dared ask her if she needed any help. The OR was reached without a hitch after that.

"Lock the door," Linda commanded.

"Are you sure?" Pax asked.

"Do you want to argue with me?"

"Not at all."

The sound of a door being locked reached Prince's ears.

"Well, in an incredible turn of events, we're exactly where we should've been in the first place." Linda was already uncovering Lucas and Prince.

Prince swung off the stretcher, unable to wait a moment longer. "There isn't a single part of my body that isn't aching."

"I've seen you faring way worse. Don't complain." Linda dismissed him after a cursory glance and went to check on Lucas, who wasn't moving. "I need him on the operating table."

"Lucas, can you put your feet down?" Prince looked at him, and when Lucas shook his head, he reached under his shoulders and lifted him until he was sitting on the stretcher.

"Give me a moment." Lucas closed his eyes. "The room is spinning."

"Nothing to be worried about." Linda took a stethoscope from a hook on the wall and went to listen to Lucas's heart. "I'll make sure I check that everything's fine."

"Am I going to die?" Lucas's question made every head in the room snap to attention.

"Why are you saying that?" Prince was the first to talk, followed by Pax.

"Don't even think about it."

"Lucas, let me do my job." Linda smiled. "And, please, let's not jump to conclusions. Shall we?" She made sign to Prince to help Lucas down on the stretcher again. "Can you haul that machine over here?"

Prince followed her pointed finger and saw the machine sitting at the far end of the room. "It's heavy." He pushed it from one corner to the other. "What is this for?"

"To look at Lucas's heart. I used it on you once or twice."

"I don't remember." Prince walked around the machine and went to lean against the wall facing the stretcher.

"You were unconscious, that's why." Linda plugged the machine into the closest socket.

Pax walked to Prince and put one hand on his arm. He liked to feel the familiar weight, but sensed her tension hiding under the affectionate gesture. "Is everything okay?"

"Just perfect," she answered.

"Whenever I'm with you it's perfect," he whispered to her, and her body relaxed in his arms.

Their moment of reprieve didn't last long. "Need help here," Linda called.

In two strides, they were by the stretcher.

"What do you need?" Pax asked.

"Can you prep him for me? Just clean his chest and then put the gel on it." Linda was looking at Prince.

"*I* can do it. As I said before, Mistress wants to be useful." Pax intercepted the tray Linda was already passing to Prince.

"Have you ever done it before?" Linda skeptically raised one eyebrow.

"Doesn't sound so complicated," Pax replied while kindly opening Lucas's shirt to spray water on his chest. "You need a shower." She smiled at him.

Lucas attempted to smile back. "I was busy feeling bad, not like someone else—"

"Do you want me to draw you a bath?" Prince asked in mockery.

"Yes, please, and sprinkle some rose petals in it while you're at it."

"Okay, now lie down and try to relax. I'm going to take some pictures of your heart. It won't take long." Linda scanned Lucas's chest in slow circles, resting on each spot for several seconds. She looked at the monitor the whole time, but didn't let a single comment out, her forehead relaxing and tensing depending on what she saw.

"Can you tell me something... anything?" Lucas finally asked.

"Well, we have the typical good news, bad news situation. Although, in your case the good news calls for celebration. Which do you want to hear first?" Linda looked at Lucas, waiting for his answer.

"Good news first." He didn't hesitate.

"It's not your heart."

"That's great," Pax said.

"You can clean him up. I'm done." Linda waited for Pax to start removing the gel from Lucas's chest. "Yes, it's very good news."

"But?" Prince couldn't help asking before Lucas did.

"You must've had a lung infection some time in the near past, and it wasn't properly cured." Linda moved the machine out of the way and sat on the edge of the stretcher, forcing Pax to step back.

"So he just needs an antibiotic, right?" Pax found her way back to Prince and snuggled against him.

"Yes, a long course of antibiotics would do the trick, but I can't cure him without alerting the Priestess about what I'm up to," Linda said.

"What do you mean? Aren't you the one running this infirmary?" Pax asked.

"Yes, but per the Priestess's new orders, only pure breeds have the right to be cured of serious ailments."

"What?" Prince raised his voice, only to be shushed by the other three.

"Yes, I must have written permission to restock my medicinal pantry and prescribe antibiotics, and the woman being treated checks and signs a form, which Caren must validate. She's the one appointed by the Priestess to keep the keys of the medicine locker. And Lauren takes stock of the supplies. Quite efficiently, I might add, as I recently discovered."

"It's insane," Pax murmured.

"I completely agree with you. Now, the problem is that I don't trust the women here to lie for me—" Linda looked at Pax as if she had just appeared in the middle of the room. "Would you...?"

"Of course, I'm feeling something in my chest already," Pax replied, giving Lucas her biggest smile yet.

"Thank you," Lucas mouthed.

"I suggest you cough when you're near the Priestess, and try to look weak and tired," Linda said to Pax.

"I'll do my best." Pax coughed. "Like this?"

"Less like *that*, and more like *this*." Linda gave a convincing example of coughing.

"Now, the problem remains of where we're going to stay... That door can't stay locked forever," Prince said after they had talked a while about the new development of Lucas's health.

"For tonight, this is your best hiding place. It's late, there are no scheduled surgeries, and nobody is allowed to loiter here anyway. Tomorrow, there's a... thing I've got to take care of, but even if the procedure is less than an hour long, you'll have to disappear way before I start."

"I might know the place..." Prince admitted, although he wasn't happy about sharing his hideout with Linda. He looked at Pax, and she nodded.

"Where is it?" the doctor asked.

"Just outside the OR, as a matter of fact."

"I see... And how long have you known about this place?"

"I don't think is relevant," Prince answered.

"Maybe you're right. Actually, it's better if I don't know anything about it." Though Linda didn't look happy with that. "Anyway, I can't stay much longer. I'll come back early tomorrow morning."

"Before you go, I need to ask you something." Lucas pushed himself up, looking directly at Linda.

"Okay."

"My son and another young man are currently Sundial's *guests*. Do you know where they are kept?"

"They were with me when I was caught last time," Prince said.

"I know who they are." Linda's answer was immediate and that scared Prince. Workers received the doctor's care only when in serious need of it.

"Where are they? Are they okay?" Lucas asked.

"They're alive," Linda answered before Prince had to come up with something.

Lucas murmured a prayer of thanks.

"They're in solitary."

Lucas's eyes grew wide. "I need to see Randal."

"One step at a time... but I'll see what I can do," Linda said.

"It's all I ask."

Linda gave Lucas something to relax, helped him bathe in the adjacent bathroom, had him changed in nurse's garments, and waited until he fell asleep. Finally, she instructed Prince about what he needed to do in case he had another attack, repeated the safety procedure rules several times, and then turned toward Pax to say, "Time to go. Start coughing."

"I'll be back in no time." She kissed Prince.

"Be careful." He held her tight for a moment before releasing her to the doctor.

"You shouldn't come back here." Linda moved aside to let Pax pass. "What if the Priestess starts looking for you later tonight?"

"I'll explain I went for a walk."

They were out of the room, and as soon as the key was turned to lock the OR, Prince started worrying while listened to them still bickering behind the door. He didn't like the way Pax and Linda were confronting each other. They were back after less than an hour, but he had driven himself crazy imagining the worst scenarios. They were still arguing, but at least Linda carried a bag with the medicines Lucas needed.

"I've my reasons." Linda closed the door behind her, her face showing irritation.

Pax immediately went to his side. "So do I."

"If anything happens to you, I will be held responsible before the president."

"I'll take care of her," Prince interjected.

Linda's eyes darkened for a moment, but then, looking at Pax, she said, "*You*'ll take full responsibility for whatever happens."

"Sure, no problem," Pax answered, snuggling farther inside Prince's embrace.

Linda scoffed, but without another word, she went to wake Lucas to give him several pills, talked to him for a few minutes, and finally left.

When the soft click announced the doctor had closed them inside the OR once again, Pax turned around to give Prince a kiss. "I thought she was never going to leave. We're finally alone."

"Well, technically we aren't," he said, smiling at her. "We must wait just a moment longer—"

"For what?"

"You'll see in a second. I promise." Prince made sure Lucas didn't need anything, then dragged Pax to the other side of the room and opened a small door between two tall cabinets that almost hid it and led her into a small room.

"Is this your secret place?" Pax kissed him, darkness surrounding them.

"No, this is just the broom closet—" He moved his hands across the wall until he found the knob he was looking for. "Still here." He turned it around and a door opened. "Welcome to my *thinking room*." He led her inside the hidden space and closed the door behind them. "It should be here—" He went to his knees and fumbled in the complete darkness for a few seconds, looking for the spare candle and lighter he had left there a lifetime ago. "Let's see if it still works." He smiled when the flickering flame of the candle illuminated the small space. "Not much of a retreat, but it's private."

"I told you so many times already, I don't care where we are as long as we're together." Pax was in his arms before he could reply. "Goddess, I missed you. Baby was sick, and I wanted you with us."

Her face was illuminated by the dim light, and he saw the deep line edged along her mouth and between her eyes. "I'm here," he could only say, a barrage of feelings fighting for supremacy. They soon found their way on the floor. "It's probably dirty."

"I wouldn't care if it were on fire." Pax grabbed his shirt and removed it with frantic hands. His pants were following suit when a sudden wailing broke into their privacy.

"It's a baby crying," Pax said, her hands leaving his body.

Prince brushed her hair away from her face. "Are you sure?"

"Yes, there's a baby crying on the other side of this wall." She sat, closed her shirt that somehow had come loose, and leaned toward the wall to lay her ear against it. "Are there kids at Sundial?"

He brought a finger to his ear, then pointed at the wall and whispered, "Not that I know of."

She frowned. "Our baby—?"

"No, it can't be her. The infirmary is on the other side of the OR." The baby's cries made him sick to his stomach.

She briefly relaxed, then softly tapped the wall. "What's there, then?"

Prince thought about it for a moment, trying to remember the layout of the place. Then the memory of one of his escapades came back to him. "There's a storage room that opens both to the adjacent wing and to the gardens." Once, he had saved his hide by using that room to flee from a group of angry guards chasing him.

"The gardens? It can't be. We aren't at ground level."

"Sundial was built following a natural slope. This side of the facility borders the gardens. South of here is the nursery with the orchids. Remember when we escaped the fire?"

Pax nodded. Then she shook her head. "But there's a baby on the other side of this wall," she repeated. "This baby must be our daughter's age, because they cry the same way."

Prince thought about what she had said and shivered, imagining the small, defenseless child waiting for someone to attend to her. "I know this room and the storage room have a thin wall in common—"

The baby started crying louder, a desperate whine that echoed inside the *thinking room.*

"We can't leave the baby there," Pax said, resolution dawning on her worried face.

He had reached the same conclusion. Every cry elicited a strong urge to do something to alleviate the child's suffering. But Sundial's geography wasn't on their side. "It isn't that simple. The safest way would be to go there from the outside—too many chances to be caught by guards if we try to walk to the storage through the hallways connecting this wing to the other. But even so, to reach that room, we'd have to go out of the OR, back to the main building, and out through the gardens—"

"*We* can't go, but *I* can."

"You could, but I don't want you to go by yourself."

"We can't just let the baby—"

Prince shushed Pax. "Listen," he mouthed, one finger on his lips.

The bay wasn't crying anymore. All of a sudden, a woman's voice humming a lullaby filled the silence. "Good boy," she cooed in a childlike voice.

Prince's stomach relocated to his throat at hearing the woman's words.

Pax turned to face him, her eyes wide. "It's a boy?"

He nodded, speechless. "Why are they keeping a boy there?" She grabbed his hand. "What's a boy doing at Sundial?"

The woman kept humming.

"Maybe she's his mother and she's hiding him from Caren and Lauren," Pax said.

Prince wanted to believe it was true. "Yes, she must be a fathered woman." If he and Pax had fallen in love and conceived a baby, other men and women could too. He pulled her to him and caressed her head, only then realizing how bad he was shaking.

On the other side, a door open and closed, the humming stopped, and the baby started crying again.

"Your Holiness, you startled me." The woman's voice sounded familiar to Prince, but his mind had gone blank at the first two words.

"Is that... Linda?" Pax whispered.

"There was no need to come here."

He recognized Linda's voice above the baby's cries and nodded to Pax.

"You know I don't like to leave things unchecked. Especially when me and mine are concerned."

The Priestess's statement sent a chill through Prince's spine.

"What's going on?" Pax mouthed. She was looking at him and he shook his head, unwilling to voice his fears.

"No need to be worried. I have everything under control," Linda said.

"I hope so. My Chosen's fate is in your hands." The Priestess sounded worried. A long pause. "Is it ready?"

"The *boy*'s grown stronger in the last few days. I made sure he had the right—"

The Priestess interrupted Linda. "I don't care for the details. Just tell me if it's ready or not for the procedure."

"This is a baby we're talking about, Your Holiness!"

"He is merely a tool. A lucky tool at that. The Goddess gave him the privilege of being the Chosen's twin to serve a purpose, and that is what he will do. He is a means to an end for the most powerful woman in Ginecea. Now, tell me. Is it ready?"

CHAPTER 21

Prince heard the words and couldn't believe what he had heard. Pax looked at him, the same horrified expression on her face. *It can't be*, he thought, while she said it out loud. Silence on the other side followed her outburst. She gasped and then brought both hands to her mouth. He pulled her back to him. His own heartbeats ringing in his ears, for a second, he thought they had been discovered.

"He will be ready for the spinal tap tomorrow morning," Linda finally answered.

He didn't know the meaning of what Linda had just said, but fear gripped his heart. Pax let out a sob against his chest. The baby stopped crying. The two women resumed their talk.

"Let me know if anything changes."

"I will, Priestess."

"One more thing—"

"Yes?"

"You must save the Chosen."

"I'm a doctor, first and foremost."

"I have no doubts about your professionalism as a doctor. What I'm saying is that I don't care what happens to this one as long as you save the Chosen."

A long pause, some baby noises, and then Linda answered, "I understand," with the same tone as someone who didn't understand at all.

"You've already disobeyed me once on his account. Although I admit your disobedience proved useful, you must never forget I won't tolerate insubordination twice."

"There's no need to remind me, Your Holiness. I'm well aware I'm alive only because my act might save the Chosen's life."

"Then you'll do whatever it takes to save her."

"No doubt about that, but—"

The boy cooed.

"He's a principal…"

"I don't care what it is. It can't be used anyway since he shares the Chosen's blood."

"But principals are so rare and precious—"

An abrupt noise, like a fist hitting a hard surface, filled Prince's small space. "I said I don't care about this… slave." The Priestess's voice rose to an angry pitch. "He resembles the Chosen too much."

The boy cried again.

"Why is he doing that?"

"You may have scared him. It'll take a few minutes to calm him."

"I'll leave you to your task, then." A door opened and closed with more strength than necessary, sending the boy into a fit.

The lullaby resumed. Linda's steps were loud and clear. She was walking back and forth, her voice growing sweeter.

"She's rocking the baby to sleep," Pax murmured. "She's rocking *our* baby to sleep. I had twins. We have a daughter and a son. Everybody lied to me…" She leaned against the wall, head in her hands, sliding all the way to the floor.

Prince stared ahead, anger slowly building up.

"Prince?" When he didn't react, she tugged at his leg. "I can't deal with this alone. Say something."

He couldn't. Tears of helplessness streamed down his face, his fists balling up by his sides, the need to tear down something growing stronger.

"It should be me!" Pax clung to his leg like a lifeline, releasing a sob and then another. "I should be rocking my boy to sleep, not her." She was getting agitated, her voice louder. "You stole both my babies from me. You, and my mother, and Anna, and the Priestess. I hate all of you."

The lullaby abruptly stopped. Linda's steps came closer to the wall. "Pax?" she called. "Oh, crap."

"Bring my son to me," Prince said, his voice barely controlled. When Linda didn't answer back, he repeated, louder, "You bring him here now, or I'll come through this wall."

"Prince?" Pax was looking at him, her eyes showing how worried she was.

He felt a twinge of pain at seeing Pax scared by his reaction, but couldn't stop himself from punching the wall. "Now!"

"I'm coming. I'm coming. Stop it. You're terrifying him," Linda answered, the baby crying in the background. Steps resonated softer until they faded into silence.

Pax touched his arm with a feather-light caress. "Please..."

Prince looked at the wall, now sporting a serious dent, then at her. "I'm sorry. I don't know what happened to me."

"You don't have anything to apologize for." She snuggled against him, forcing his body to relax around her.

"I... scared myself. Something ugly overcame me." Droplets of blood trailed down his knuckles and he saw his hand was still fisted. He swiftly cleaned it on his pants to hide it from her.

"It's okay. The moment is gone. Let's go back to the OR."

He followed her, his heart racing as if he had run, his hands flexing to release the energy that had built up again. *The moment isn't gone.* "Give me a second. I need to wind down," he said when they reached the OR. He went straight to the bathroom and its shower stall. There, he collapsed on the wet tiles, under cold water, and cried. He couldn't remember if he had ever cried so much in all his adult life, but let the tears fall without restraint, sobbing, gasping for air, unable to sit up straight.

When he finally raised his eyes, Pax was there looking at him from outside the stall, the wet lines running down her face mirroring his. "My love," she murmured, then stepped inside the shower and cradled him in her arms, rocking him back and forth, kissing his tears, mixing them with hers.

"Our baby boy is the donor they were talking about," he said, voicing the obvious.

"I know, my love. I know."

They stayed in the shower until it became unbearable sitting under the falling water, then slowly helped each other up, shivering in their wet clothes.

"Pax, Prince..." Linda was there, staring at them from the bathroom door. "I didn't mean to intrude, but I couldn't find you."

"Where is he?" Prince asked, walking past her and dragging Pax with him.

Linda didn't have to answer. The baby, wrapped in a thin cotton blanket, was peacefully sleeping inside a bassinet resting on the floor. The boy brought one minuscule thumb to his mouth and started sucking it with a satisfied noise, his lips imperceptibly curved up. His other hand moved and went to rest on his head, where he latched it on his brown, curly hair, his fingers moving in circular motions. One of his eyes half opened, revealing a dark-brown pupil, and then closed again, followed by a louder sucking of his thumb.

"My baby." Pax fell to her knees by the bassinet, brushing her son's small head with one hand and wiping away her tears with the other.

Prince stood paralyzed before them, not daring to come any closer and touch him. All the rage he had felt until a moment ago—gone, only a profound sense of wonderment left. He kept looking at the small miracle that was his son, unsure if he was dreaming. "He's so small. Why's he so small?" he asked Linda.

"He isn't small. He's fine," she answered, leaning over the bassinet.

Pax protectively shielded the boy and softly whispered. "My baby boy." She took him in her arms and opened the blanket to see him better. "He's perfect," she said after a short examination of his small hands and feet. The baby burrowed his head on her wet shirt and found her bare skin, poking his nose against it. "He's hungry." She smiled at him and caressed his cheek.

"There's some milk left in his bottle." Linda went to the bassinet and retrieved it from a lateral pocket. "Here."

At Linda's words, Pax's expression clouded for a moment, but she accepted the bottle and gently touched the baby on the cheek to make him turn toward it. A moment later, he started feeding from it and she visibly relaxed, her eyes focused on his every little movement.

Prince looked at the two of them together, Pax hunched over the baby, who was now sucking from the bottle with noisy gulps, her arms cradling him in a soft embrace, and thought it was one of the most beautiful sights he had ever seen. He unglued his feet from the pool of water he was standing in and lightly padded over to them. "He's our son." He put one arm around Pax's shoulders and bent to kiss the boy. "I love you," he whispered to him, inhaling the baby's scent. It felt good, familiar. He turned to fold them completely inside the shield of his arms. "I love you," he said again, this time to Pax.

"I'm sorry, but I need to take the boy back to... his room," Linda said.

"Our son isn't going back to the storage room." Prince left his back to her. "Don't worry. I won't let her take him anywhere," he whispered to Pax.

"You don't understand. The Priestess ordered a guard outside his room. She isn't going to risk—"

"Why on Ginecea would the Priestess order such thing?" Pax asked, moving out of Prince's embrace and forcing him to finally turn around.

"She's worried I'll try something." Linda lowered her eyes.

"Something? Like what?" Prince pulled Pax back.

"Like trying to hide him again." Linda picked up the basinet from the floor and put it on a table, where she rummaged through a bag attached to its back. "He needs to be changed. Do you want to do it?"

"Of course I'll do it," Pax answered, snatching the diaper Linda was holding.

"Explain your part in all of this." Prince went to the table where Pax had laid the boy.

"It's a long story," Linda said.

"Start from the beginning." He moved around the table to keep a hand on the baby while Pax changed him.

"The only thing you need to know is I kept him alive against direct orders."

Prince raised an eyebrow. "Why?"

"Why?" Linda repeated. "I can't believe you of all people are asking me why."

"What does she mean by that?" Pax paused for a moment and raised her eyes to look at Prince, leaving the baby with one chubby leg outside his jumper.

"Why did you disobey the Priestess? I want to know." He finished dressing the baby.

"What do you think I am? A monster?" Linda's voice was growing louder.

"You still haven't answered me." He gave her a hard look. "And I suggest you lower your voice."

"I'd never kill anyone. I never have and I never will. A baby? There's no power on Ginecea that would force me to harm a baby. Any baby."

"Thank you," Pax said, holding the boy close to her.

"I'm a decent person." Linda walked toward the table, but didn't come close to Pax. "He likes to be caressed on his back, in small circular motions." She mimed the action. "Like this."

"I should be the one telling others what he likes, not you." Pax stepped farther away from Linda as if she was worried the woman was going to touch her baby.

"I know this must be painful for you, but believe me when I say that I did the best I could given the circumstances." Linda softened her voice.

"You've no idea how painful it is… all of this. First, I was told my baby girl had died, and then I discover I had twins, and thank the Goddess they are both alive. I know I should be thankful, and I am, but it's hard for me to forget that you were as guilty as everybody else in hiding the truth from me."

"I couldn't do anything different."

"Why? Why did the Priestess take it so personally?" Pax asked.

Linda hesitated for a moment, then looked first at Prince and then turned toward Pax. "The Priestess took it very personally, but not for the reason you think. Your baby girl has principal's genes and your boy wasn't expected at all."

"My girl has what?"

"His genes." She nodded in Prince's direction.

"Of course she does! Who else's?"

The doctor sighed. "Prince carries the genes that make priestesses."

"This is a joke, right? She's joking." Pax turned toward Prince. "Tell me she's joking."

"As far as I know, she's telling the truth," he said.

"Prince is short for principal, as in the semental with the extraordinary traits, the best specimen—"

"I got it, thank you," Pax interrupted Linda. "Is it right?" she asked Prince again.

"Lexi's grandmother told me so." Prince raised his hands in sign of peace. "I didn't know anything about it myself, and I don't think my father knew either."

"Wait, what did you say? Did you just mention Lexi's grandmother?" Pax gave him one puzzled look.

"There wasn't any time to tell you what happened, but the short of it is that Lucas and I were saved from the Temple by Aria—"

"Lexi's Aria?"

"Yes, the same one, who brought us to the Village—"

"Milady's pet project," Pax supplied.

"The Village wasn't just her pet project," Prince softly said.

"Wasn't?" Both Linda and Pax asked at the same time.

"The Priestess had her killed." He decided to be direct. "I'm sorry," he added after seeing the expression on their faces.

"Milady Corellis is dead?" Linda asked after a long moment of silence. "She didn't answer my last call..."

"I must reach Lexi. She should know." Pax went to sit on the closest chair, absentmindedly rocking the baby in her arms.

"Where's she? And Anna?" Prince asked.

"The Priestess sent both back to Ginecea," Pax answered. "But at least Anna managed to minimize the damage by lying through her teeth and telling the Priestess exactly what the woman wanted to hear." She smiled at the thought, then froze. "I wish I had her gift." The baby cooed and rearranged himself inside her embrace.

"He needs to—"

"Do *not* tell me what he does or doesn't need," Pax snapped at Linda. "Anyway, you were explaining to me this thing about... principals."

"At Sundial we've been studying eugenics for decades—"

"I don't know that word." Prince frowned.

"Eugenics is the science of improving a population by controlled breeding." Linda didn't seem comfortable talking about that.

"So you have only the traits you find desirable," Pax added.

"There're several eugenics centers spread through Ginecea, but only one specialized in breeding principals. Sundial is that one."

"But how is it possible nobody knows about it?" Pax asked.

"Until now, it was a well-guarded secret. Only the Priestess, Caren, Lauren, and I know the exact details of what happens at Sundial. The other women working here, like our dear botanist Marion, think we smuggle semen. It has worked fine."

"And now, you told us."

"He already knew anyway. And I'm sick of pretending what we do here is right. Hiding the truth to keep a whole race enslaved is the real abomination. I've had doubts all my life, but the Priestess's recent actions have helped me a great deal to clear my conscience from any sense of guilt. The last straw was when she ordered me to kill him." Linda looked at the baby. "I realized we've all gone too far. If murdering a baby is seen as a minor thing, we as a society don't deserve to live."

"Was my mother involved in the decision of...?" Pax held the baby closer to her, unable to say the words, kissing his head.

Prince looked at her and saw how heartbroken she was. "Pax," he murmured, laying a hand on her shoulder.

She tilted her head to his side and brushed his hand with her lips. "I need to know."

"No, your mother didn't know you had twins. When they brought you to me, you were already unconscious and your mother was hysterical. I had to calm her before looking at you. I gave her something and ordered a nurse to take her to another room. Meanwhile, you'd started bleeding and so I went to check if the baby's heart was giving any sign of distress. I found two heartbeats instead. The Priestess came soon after, asking me to perform a DNA test on the baby as soon as she was born and didn't want to leave. I didn't want to tell her what I'd just found out, but your condition worsened. The twins' heartbeats slowed. I had to perform a cesarean section before it was too late for you and the babies. The Priestess stayed there"—Linda indicated a spot on the opposite wall between two bookshelves—"and didn't move until I was done with the procedure. 'Not a word with anyone,' she told me. She waited until the DNA test came back positive and then told your mother you had a baby girl." She paused for a moment, went to take a bottle of water from the table, and drank from it. "Your mother is another victim of the Priestess's lies. Her fragile mental state—and I've the feeling that she's been under the influence of drugs for a while—allowed her to believe everything she was told. The Priestess probably blackmailed her. I don't know the details, but I'm sure she was very convincing—"

"We went back to Layan Mansion not even a week after I gave birth, and my mother never told me anything. She looked at me and lied about everything," Pax said, talking over Linda who hadn't finished her tale.

"You weren't in any condition to leave the infirmary and the Priestess was waiting for the test results to come back. I tried to buy you some time by stalling the exams, but the Priestess was in a hurry to leave. I begged her to let you stay with the babies, explaining to her that they were too small and needed their mom to survive. She wouldn't listen. 'He was never born,' she said, looking at the boy in disgust, and I couldn't believe my ears. 'Make it so,' she ordered when I said I didn't understand. I looked for a safe place to hide him right away. I was too worried the Priestess would ask Lauren to carry out her orders."

"He's been in the storage room the whole time?" Prince asked, his eyes on the baby peacefully dreaming in his mother's arms.

"Yes. I thought nobody would find him there."

"But he was all alone in the dark with nobody to hear his cries." He shivered at the image he had just conjured, his hand reaching out to caress the small head. The baby smiled in his sleep. "What if he was in pain or if he needed anything?"

"I went to check on him often—"

"What if he was scared?"

"I did the best I could for him." Linda looked tired. She went to sit on a chair facing Pax and Prince, her hands holding her head. "It was so hard keeping him a secret. Sometimes at night I slept in the storage room, especially his first two weeks... Then Caren saw me coming back one morning from the gardens and she wouldn't let it go. I invented a lover, but I was terrified she didn't believe me, and I didn't go to see him for several hours. When I finally could, he was lying still in the crib. "

Pax sobbed. Prince took his baby's hand in his, feeling the need to be reassured he was alive. "What had happened?"

Linda didn't seem to hear his words and she wasn't looking at them. "I picked him up thinking he was dead," she said, her sobs joining Pax's. "His small hands were cold and I started stroking them. He was so small in my arms."

"What had happened?"

"I don't know for sure. It could've been so many different things, but he moved in my arms and I came back to life myself. That's when I realized I couldn't support the Priestess and what she represents anymore."

A long silence descended on the room, the only exception the baby's soft breathing.

"What are you going to do to him?" Prince finally asked.

CHAPTER 22

"We could lose both our children today." Pax was restless, refusing to sit down with Prince, her feet dancing on the floor.

They were back in the secret room behind the OR closet, this time sharing their space with Lucas. Prince and Pax had spent the better part of the night talking with Linda, but in the end, they had let her take their son with her. It had been several hours ago in the wee hours of the night. Morning had come and they hadn't slept. Shadows danced before Prince's eyes and the flickering light of the single candle illuminating the small space didn't help.

"It's not going to happen." Prince leaned his head against the wall. He was tired, his nerves threatening to jump at any moment.

"She'll save them," Lucas said. The second energizing shot Linda had administered him had entered his system and he looked much better. He had walked to their hiding place helped by Prince and stumbled only once.

"How do you know?" Pax's eyes locked on Lucas and he lowered his head.

"I'm sure—" Prince wanted to reassure her, but wasn't sure of anything himself. He had never felt such level of anguish. When he thought he could feel no more pain, here was the proof he was wrong. His children were fighting for their lives and he couldn't do anything to help. He wasn't allowed to be with them, to hold their small hands when they needed it most. His hatred for the Priestess renewed once again.

"How can you be sure?" Pax asked, her hands trembling.

Prince looked ahead, eyes swelling with tears he didn't want to shed in front of her. For a moment, he wished he were alone to scream until he had no voice left. "I am because it can't be otherwise." But he said it too low to be heard.

"Linda has kept your boy alive against all odds." Lucas put a hand on Pax's leg and she finally sat down. "You must have faith she'll do her best for both your kids."

"I can't breathe. This room is too small." Pax stood up again and started pacing from one end to the other of the small quarter.

"Pacing won't help. Sit with me and I'll massage your shoulders. Try to relax your mind. It's going to be a long day. " Prince was affected by her nervousness, but he had been trying to keep his own at bay for several hours now.

Pax slowed down, but didn't sit. "I can't. I can't stop thinking about what Linda said. Our baby girl's only hope of surviving is by having a transplant from her *brother*."

The more Prince thought about it the angrier he got. *It isn't fair,* he kept repeating to himself. The fact that he couldn't share his worries with Pax made him even angrier.

"What if we've just sent him to…?"

"Don't," Prince murmured. "Please, don't say it." *I don't want to hear about it. I'm too scared as it is. A parent shouldn't have to make such decisions.*

"I didn't mean to—" Pax crouched beside him, took his hands in hers, and kissed him softly.

Steps resonated from the storage room. Linda's voice came through the wall. "Keep him warm and check his vitals."

"They're taking him." Pax couldn't help but sob.

"She's going to save them both," Prince repeated.

Lucas murmured something to soothe Pax and Prince, but they weren't listening.

A knock on the wall startled them. "I gave you my word. I won't let anything happen to them," Linda said, her voice coming from the other side as a low whisper, but still loud enough to be heard.

Prince took Pax in his arms and let the moment pass. He couldn't speak, his mind a chaos of thoughts governed by fear. He cradled her, needing the act for himself—the rocking movements giving him an anchor to reality. Linda had made clear the risks his kids were up against if nothing was done. His daughter was destined to live a miserable life, never to reach adulthood, and his son was now under the Priestess's radar. She wouldn't let him live unless she needed him to save the Chosen's life. Linda had also made clear the risks to the babies when she performed the surgery. She had given them details about every single thing that could and would happen. But in the end, they had released the boy in her hands, unable to make a decision that would favor one of the children over the other. This way they both had a chance. And yet, it didn't feel right.

"I'm scared," Pax said, her head pressed against his chest.

Prince didn't say anything, his frantically beating heart speaking for him, while thinking all along, *How are we going to survive this if...?* He had asked Linda to explain every aspect of the surgery, committing to memory even the words he couldn't understand. "They'll start preparing him any time now."

"When are they going to harvest his bone marrow?" Pax asked.

"Linda is going to wait for him to be asleep," Prince automatically answered. He knew she had heard Linda's explanation, and she understood the procedure better than he did, but he was aware of her need to say things out loud and be reassured about what was happening. "Don't worry. He won't feel anything."

He silently waited for what seemed like an eternity, trying to imagine what they were doing in the OR. When he couldn't bear the wait anymore, he left the hidden room and glued his ear to the wall of the closet attached to the OR. He heard Linda asking for a nervous central system catheter and crawled back to the hidden room to report. "They're going to infuse her with his bone marrow." He took Pax in his arms. Most likely, not more than an hour had passed from the beginning of the procedure, but it was already too long for him. "Stay calm or you'll do something stupid," he said under his breath several times and then stood to shake his tingling limbs. He wouldn't dare challenge his luck twice and go back to the closet, but it took all his strength not to barge through to the other side.

"Prince?" Pax was looking at him, her eyes red and swollen.

He bent down to brush her head with his lips. "Just talking nonsense. Don't worry. I'm exhausted and my brain isn't working. I'll close my eyes for a moment." He lowered his body to the floor and brought her down with him. His need to hold her was stronger than his weariness, feeling that without her physical support, the floor would swallow him whole, imprisoning him in the darkness beneath. But even with her body close, he couldn't relax.

"What do you think is happening now?" Pax asked after a while.

"Both babies need to stay sedated for another hour or two after the procedure."

"Do you think he's going to suffer a headache?"

"No, that's why he needs to be sedated and sleep it off. The less he moves the faster he's going to recover." Prince didn't mind repeating Linda's words if that helped Pax pass the time. It helped him too, having to think about her and how she felt. He was also grateful to Lucas, who had said nothing since the ordeal had started. Another word about having faith and Prince would have exploded.

Without warning, a knock on the wall adjacent to the OR closet made both Prince and Pax startle.

"It's me."

Reassured by the Linda's voice, Prince opened the door for her. The doctor looked tired and his heart skipped a beat. "Linda...?" His voice choked, and the false courage that had sustained him until a moment earlier left him.

"Are they...?" Pax was shaking.

"They're fine," Linda said, walking inside in the already crammed space to touch Pax's arm in a reassuring gesture. "Everything went according to plan. The kids are sleeping peacefully." She seemed to think about something, then looked at both Pax and Prince, hesitated for a long, awkward moment, and said, "The Priestess has just left, and I sent everybody else away to keep the room quiet. Do you want to see them?"

Pax was out of the door before anybody could say anything.

"Thank you," Prince murmured to Linda and then followed Pax. He didn't even know what he was doing; his feet seemed to fly over the floor, tears obfuscating his sight. He stopped before the twins' cribs and fell on his knees. "Thank the God..."

Pax followed him to the floor "Are you sure they're okay?" she asked Linda, her head turning from one bed to the other.

"They're twins. I'm confident she won't reject his marrow. Only time will tell, but I'd be surprised otherwise."

Prince laid one hand on each bed, touching his kids with the softest of caresses. He wanted to take them both in his arms and never let go. Their shallow breathing was punctuated by the slow rising and falling of the thin sheets covering them. "Why don't you cover them with something warmer? A blanket?"

"Is she shivering?" Pax echoed his worries, her hand side by side with his gently stroking the girl's head.

"They aren't cold. The temperature in this room is kept constant." Linda walked toward the head of the cribs, stethoscope in hand, and bent to check on the girl—forcing Prince and Pax to move their hands. "Her heart is beating just fine." She then lowered over the boy, repeated the auscultation on his small chest and smiled. "He's a warrior."

Prince felt Pax stiffen in front of him, her hand reaching out to reclaim her baby boy. He leaned forward and brought her closer to his chest. "We're together," he whispered to her and she relaxed her stance. "Nothing and nobody will separate us from our kids."

Pax brought one of his hands circling her waist to her lips and brushed it with hers. "I know." Then she turned looking for his mouth. "I know."

Prince was aware of Linda looking at them, but he didn't let her ruin their private moment. "I'll fight for our family." He returned Pax's kiss, sealing his promise.

Linda emitted a throat-clearing sound and walked away in a hurry, leaving them alone.

"Finally." Pax moved out of Prince's embrace to stand up, fetch a chair, and drag it by the cribs. She sat between the two sleeping babies, a satisfied expression on her face.

He looked at her, marveling at how she could become a different person in the blink of an eye. "You're beautiful." And she was with her red eyes circled by dark half-moons, her hair limp, and her pale, tired skin. She had an inner fire that was hard to ignore and he could feel she was keeping it at bay while caressing their kids in slow circular motions. When her eyes locked on his, her intensity burning him, he was reminded of how strong she was, of everything she had done to be with him.

"I'm nothing if I don't have you with me," she said, her unfaltering eyes on him, her fingers softly massaging the babies.

Prince was shaken by a sudden spell of shivers and hugged her knees, his head on her lap. "It won't happen again."

They stayed in silence, savoring the gifted moment, their babies sleeping on either side, until Linda announced with a cough she was coming back.

"The Priestess is on her way. She wants to be present when the Chosen wakes up." She approached the girl's crib, visibly trying to maintain distance from Pax who was looking at her in angry silence. "I must ask you to go hide, now," she said when neither Pax nor Prince made any attempt to leave the room.

"Come." Prince straightened his legs and pulled Pax upright along with him. "Don't let the Priestess touch our boy." His words came out as threat more than a request, leaving out the implicit "or else."

"I won't," she answered without raising her head from the cribs. "Take some water with you." Still in the same position, her eyes focused on her patients, she indicated two bottles arranged on the shelf close to the door.

Prince grabbed them with a "thanks" and walked Pax back to the semi-darkness of the hidden room where Lucas was waiting for them.

"So, how are the kids?" He was crouched on the floor, his sleepy voice betraying he had been awoken by their intrusion.

Prince went to sit on the opposite wall, anchoring Pax to his side. "They seem to be fine."

They talked a good while longer, more to pass the time than for the sake of conversation, but the endeavor proved useful nevertheless. The three had finally time to recount what had happened while they were separated. Meanwhile, the thought of the Priestess in the same room with their kids never left Prince.

Echoing his worries, Pax asked, "Why doesn't she leave already?" She couldn't stop tapping her foot on the floor.

Prince put one hand on her knee and gently forced her to slow down. Particles of dust whirled all around them and he sneezed.

"My mouth is dry and my throat is itchy." He opened one of the water bottles, and after taking a long gulp, passed it to Pax.

"You look a mess," Lucas said, who had regained much of the strength in his voice and looked better.

"Thanks." Prince tried to kick him, but his movements weren't sharp.

"You should try to take a nap."

"Yes, we should, but someone must stay awake." Prince felt his body weighing him down, his eyelids heavy.

"I've rested enough. I'll guard the fort," Lucas joked.

Prince leaned against the wall, found a position that allowed him to stretch his legs, reached for Pax, who understood what he wanted and snuggled against him, surrounded her with his arms, closed his eyes, and let his mind drift away.

* * *

Something woke up Prince. He made an effort to open his eyes. Someone was shouting. The words came from a distance, muffled and unintelligible. Pax stirred. She was lying on his legs and trapping him to the floor. "Pax?" He gently moved her upright, her head lolling and her limbs wrapped around him. As he tried to extricate his arm from the tangle their bodies had become, she doubled over like a rag doll. "This isn't right," he said out loud, but he wasn't sure she could hear him. "Lucas?" The candle's flame was at the end of its life, but it was immediately clear they were alone. He went to open the door and found it unlocked, then stumbled inside the closet and saw the sliver of light coming from the door opening onto the OR, ajar as well. The shouting resumed, clearer and closer. "What the—?" Then he recognized the voices—Lucas's and Linda's. A mix of disorientation and headache fighting for dominance in his head, Prince balanced against the wall with unsteady hands, and putting one foot in front of the other, he slowly reached for the door. "Stay here." He turned and squinted at the darkness of the secret room, looking for Pax to be sure she had understood. She had curled up in the corner and was softly snoring. The image made him smile and he almost went back to her to sleep off this weariness when a louder shout brought words that scared him.

"You should've told them." Lucas was mad.

"I couldn't." Linda's voice by contrast had dropped.

"You didn't even try!"

"I—"

"What did you do to us?" Prince had crawled from one room to the other, feeling his mind slowly clearing. He was now fully upright, although still using the wall as a guide, and facing the two who were looking back at him with different expressions. "What is it?" he asked Lucas, wanting to erase that pitying look from the man's face. "What. Is. It?" The roar escaping from his lungs had the effect of vanquishing the last remnants of disorientation still clouding his thoughts.

"Please forgive me. I had to." Linda let herself on a chair, her shoulders down, defeat written all over her.

"You had to do what?" Prince stepped in the middle of the room, forgetting he needed support, and was at Linda's side in a heartbeat. "Tell me." His body betrayed him and he fell on his knees before her.

"I did it for your sake." Linda's hands reached out to caress his hair.

"Don't touch me and start talking." Prince slapped her hands away and put some distance between them, moving toward Lucas.

"Sit," the man proposed while dragging a chair from a corner. He left it beside Prince and then came back to take another for himself, sat on it, and crossed his legs.

"I'm fine." Prince was getting angry and didn't want to cooperate. He stood with his hands on the back of the chair, drawing strength from the act.

"She drugged you."

"Why?" Prince had figured that out already.

"You would've done something stupid." Linda refused to look at him, her eyes firmly on the floor tiles.

"What are you talking about?" Prince cursed himself when, belatedly, he took a good glance around the room and saw what should have been worrying him all along. "Where are the babies?"

"Try to be calm," Lucas said, one arm across Prince's chest to restrain him.

Prince, who hadn't realized he had walked back to Linda, was now hovering over her, his body trembling in pent-up rage, his hands balled in menacing fists, ready to land on the woman. "What did you do with them?"

"The only thing I could to insure everybody would survive." Linda's terrified eyes were now on him. "The Priestess had already told me she was going to take the Chosen with her, and I couldn't risk you walking in here once you realized what was happening. I had to make sure you were out long enough to give us time to remove the kids from this room."

"Where's my boy?"

"The Priestess has taken him with her as well. Just in case she needs him again."

Prince shivered at the cold meaning of the woman's words and swore. "Where are they now?"

"I'm not going to tell."

Prince lost it and grabbed Linda by her scrub, shaking her hard.

"Prince!" two voices yelled at once.

He didn't release Linda. "Tell me where the Priestess took my kids."

"Prince, stop it!"

One hand landed on Prince's arm and when he saw who it belonged to, he jumped back, releasing Linda with a cry. "Pax—" He was shaking from head to toes, unable to articulate a coherent sentence.

"I did it for you... I didn't want you to die. You'd have put yourself in harm's way... I didn't want to lose you forever." Linda was crying, big sobs covering her words.

"Where are my kids?" Pax's voice was cold and low, almost a rumble.

Prince looked at her, shielding him from the doctor with her body.

"The Priestess didn't tell me." Linda shook her head and cleaned her face with the palm of her hand.

"I don't have time to beg." Pax moved one step closer to the woman, making her wince.

"Tell us now." Prince was at Pax's side. The two of them a wall towering over Linda.

"I don't know." Linda's eyes darted from Prince to Pax and back.

"I think she's telling the truth," Lucas said, stepping between them.

Prince swore again and crouched low, taking his head between his elbows. "How long ago?"

"She left the OR half an hour ago," Linda answered.

Prince stood up and turned to draw a punch through the wall. The physical pain hit him hard, but it didn't help him with the urge to release his anger on Linda. He punched the wall several times before the skin on his knuckles split and he felt the blood covering his hands and weakening his fists. "I curse you."

Linda gasped at his words and brought her hands up to cover her face. Prince wanted to shake her until she hurt, but he didn't move from the wall, his back squared against it to support him from falling.

"Did she leave Sundial already?" He heard Pax asking Linda. "Did she?" Pax repeated louder, one finger under the doctor's chin to force her to look up.

Nobody heard Linda's answer. A siren blasted through the room, drowning any other sound. Prince looked at Pax ready to bolt toward the secret room when the OR door burst open with a kick. He pushed Pax toward the closet, hoping she could reach their hideout in time. "Run!"

"No!" Pax took a moment too long to ensure he was coming with her by pulling at his shirt, and they both got caught in the middle of the room.

Prince automatically stepped in front of her, readying himself for the fight, when he saw their assailants and exhaled the air trapped in his lungs. Relief passed through his features at the sight of a ragged army of beaten men bursting into the room.

"Dad!" Randal was at his father's side before anybody had recognized him.

"Randal?" Both Lucas and Prince exclaimed at the same moment.

Prince stood aside, leaving the two of them space, and took a good look at the other men. "What's going on?" he asked the closest, a man in his forties he knew from his former life as a worker at Sundial.

"We're taking the farm," the man proudly answered.

"How?" Prince felt his heart swell at the mere idea.

"We outnumber the women ten to one, that's how!" The man gave Linda a long, intimidating look.

The doctor didn't seem to have any fight left in her and, although she looked frightened, she didn't make any attempt at fleeing. After having jumped straight up when the siren had started, she sat down again as if waiting for her doom.

Prince spared her a thought, but had more pressing concerns to address. He was thinking about the man's words about the ratio between men and women at Sundial, something he knew well already. Back in his days as a troublemaker, he had gotten away with a lot, mostly because there weren't enough guards to supervise every corner of the farm twenty-four-seven. "Why now?"

"Because it's the right time. Half of the guards have left already. Remy and I were abandoned in our cells without food and water, and nobody came to check on us for two days," Randal said, moving away from his father's embrace to salute Prince. "I wasn't going to give them the pleasure of dying without a fight."

A low moan escaped Lucas's serrated lips, his face white. "Randal, my boy, I was afraid I'd never see you again... If anything happened to you..." He took his son's arm by the elbow to bring him closer to him again.

"Dad, don't worry. I'm here and I'm fine."

Prince saw Lucas take in the map of bruises discoloring his son's skin from face to arms and felt for the man.

"How did you escape?" Lucas's voice came out broken and he pulled Randal in a tight embrace.

"It seems the women have been deserting this place for a while. Sundial's falling apart and there aren't enough hands to keep up. The locks in our cells were rusty and didn't close properly. At first, armed women took turns guarding us, but as time passed, it became erratic. Sometimes there was someone in the morning, but nobody else in the afternoon, only to see a disgruntled woman coming for the night shift. When I realized they were understaffed, I started making plans, and while trying to force the lock, I discovered it was worse for wear. Every time we were left alone, I pulled at my chains until they came undone, then I used the metal bowl they had left for my food to beat on the lock. It took me two days, but had I known they weren't coming, I'd have yanked open the door way sooner without worrying I'd alert the women." Randal almost laughed at the last statement. "I wouldn't have bothered with niceties. Anyway, when it was clear nobody was coming, I threw caution to the wind and finished breaking the lock in a hurry. Then I freed the other men. Some hadn't seen the light of day for months."

"Where is Remy?" Prince asked.

"Safe, downstairs—"

"You stormed out of the dungeons without anybody stopping you?" Linda asked. Some color stirred back in her features, but her body still slumped against the chair.

"We were already on the second floor before someone came to greet us." Randal didn't move his eyes from his father. "And then we were running everywhere, calling the men to join us and spread the news. You should've seen their faces, Dad!"

"Did you see the Priestess?" Pax squeezed Prince's hand in hers.

He felt the subtle tremor shaking her echoing his own.

"No, but I came here first thing to ensure we had medical supplies in case we needed them. The last thing I was expecting was to find my father and you here." Randal smiled at Lucas, eyes bright.

"She could still be here," Prince murmured, not daring to hope. "We must go."

Lucas nodded and made a farewell gesture with his hand.

Prince, followed by Pax still holding his hand, started running in earnest, leaving the OR without a second glance. Room after room they opened doors only to find them empty. On two or three occasions, they encountered women, but they were too scared and simply moved aside to let them through.

"Where is she?" Pax kept asking, sometimes running ahead of him to scout two places at once.

Please, be here, Prince thought the whole time, looking for the now-familiar shape of the Priestess. His eyes changed focus any time he saw anything moving, near or far, trying to let everything in for fear of missing a crucial detail that could lead them to her. He looked at the same time inside the interminable hallways and outside the windows, until he saw it: a sudden gleam of metal reflecting the sunrays.

"There!" He pointed to the middle of the gardens outside, just right of the recreational center.

The helicopter was preparing to take off, its blades rotating at full speed, two women protecting the Priestess while fighting several men pressing close.

"Where are the kids?" Pax opened the window as if to get closer to the scene. "We're too far away," she cried.

Prince looked down at the ground and, for once, blessed Sundial's architecture. He moved her aside from the window, and without announcing his intentions, jumped. He fell, hands and knees protecting his body, rolling down the green slope under the window. He was at the bottom of the small hill a few seconds later, then stood and ran without stopping.

A soft thud on the grass, the sound of a sliding body, and Pax was at his heels a mere moment later. Prince could hear her steps and her ragged breath, but didn't turn around. It was now or never. The moment the Priestess flew away with their kids, he knew there was nothing else they could do to get them back. His baby girl would become the next priestess, and his boy would be dead. His lungs exploded in his chest, air cut through his throat like shards of glass, the muscles in his legs shot pain, but Prince ran, focusing all his rage on the woman stepping inside the helicopter.

"Priestess!" His voice managed to rise above the noise made by the blades and the engine. He called her until she turned around and saw him.

"You!"

He didn't hear her voice, but read the Priestess's lips and was rewarded by the expression on her face.

"You..."

He was now closer and could see the way her mouth trembled at saying the word and he drew strength from it. His legs doubled the effort and he flew over the path, leaving Pax behind.

"You can't be here," the Priestess said, making the mistake to wait a second more than necessary.

Prince was on her before she could close the helicopter's door. He used one hand on hers to prevent her from sliding the hatch, and he pulled her out with the other.

Someone shouted from the inside, and the Priestess shouted back she needed help and—after the first moment of surprise—she was herself again. She planted her feet on the second step of the movable stairs, squared her stance and looked at Prince defiantly. "You are nothing but a temporary nuisance." Her lips curved up as she spat on him.

Prince didn't wince nor release his grip on her arm. Without saying anything, he kept staring at her while tightening his fingers around her skin. When he saw the expression on her face change from arrogant to worried and then again to pained, he squeezed tighter.

The Priestess screamed and kicked in every direction; the front of her pointed shoes made contact several times with Prince's shins, giving her a small reprieve from his hold.

"Priestess!" A woman holding a gun and wearing the uniform of a pilot appeared behind her.

"Shoot him!" The Priestess wheezed out and thrust her most vigorous kick the same moment the pilot pressed the trigger.

As he was falling backward, his right leg giving in—the Priestess had hit his right knee with the heel of her shoe—Prince heard a loud noise and felt his hair singed by the passing bullet.

"Give it to me." The Priestess yanked the gun from the woman's hand and pointed at Prince, but he scampered under the helicopter to reach the other side. "Look for him."

"I can't see him."

The Priestess screamed in frustration at the woman's answer. "Look better."

Prince carefully kept his body flush to the fuselage of the helicopter.

"He must be underneath."

"Get him."

Prince strained his ears to catch what the women were saying. He needed time to recover from the hit that had left his knee throbbing. "Not the right leg," he murmured under his breath, needles painfully stabbing the injured part. As if on cue, the right calf cramped. He had stressed the already weak ligament to a breaking point. He hadn't had any time to acknowledge the damage until now. His legs threatened to collapse under his weight, and he anchored his feet on the skid and his fingers on the first jutting piece he found, which it was the pilot's door handle.

"Never mind." He heard the Priestess say, too close and too calm. "Let's get out of here," she added, and the sound of the cabin door being closed followed soon after.

Prince turned his head slightly to the right and saw her looking back at him from behind the safety of the window glass with a satisfied gleam in her eyes.

"Don't move," she mocked him.

The helicopter's roar intensified. Prince felt the vibration through the metal wall of the fuselage, raised his eyes and saw the pilot at her seat, focused on the dashboard. Desperation and pure, undiluted anger took possession of his senses. He forgot the knee, the cramps, the fact that he could barely drag breath inside his lungs, and lowered the handle while the helicopter was attempting to take off.

"What are you waiting for?" The Priestess's voice cut through the deafening noise of the engine.

The pilot swung toward Prince to push him out, but he was faster and punched her in the face repeatedly until she didn't move again. Still outside, his body leaning over the still woman, he pulled the key out of the ignition and the helicopter went silent, its blade slowly losing speed. A moment later, he climbed over the pilot, took her gun, and jumped inside the cabin, where he found the Priestess trying to hide something with her body and another woman, a nurse, by her side. "Move," he said, his voice a hoarse whisper, his hands supporting the gun.

The Priestess grabbed the nurse by the arm and jerked the woman in front of her, using her body as a shield.

Prince's gun was mere inches from the woman's face.

"Please, don't kill me," the nurse cried, trying to move out of the way, but kept firmly in place by the Priestess's strong hands on her forearms.

Prince felt sick. "Give me my kids."

The Priestess blanched. Her mouth opened to say something and then immediately closed with an unintelligible sputter.

"I know they're there. Step aside and let me take them with me and nobody gets hurt today."

The nurse started sobbing. "Please, I've a young daughter back home."

"Shut up or I'll kill you myself." The Priestess angrily pulled one of the nurse's arms.

The woman's cries didn't stop, if anything she seemed to be on the verge of a panic attack and started screaming.

"Stop!" the Priestess yelled even louder.

A feeble cry reached Prince's ears from behind the Priestess. She heard it too and forced the nurse to follow her to better hide the source of the sound.

The sudden movement brought the nurse in contact with the gun barrel. Her eyes terrified, she gave one last cry, shuddered, and passed out in the Priestess's arms. Before Prince had time to react and take advantage of the situation, the Priestess let her go to grab hold of something behind her.

"Get out of here." Her back straight, she looked at him with a new resolution showing on her face, her eyes bright. She raised one hand and showed him what she was holding. "It's enough sedative to kill him." Prince focused on a syringe pointed at a bundle semi-hidden inside one of two bassinets strapped on the cushion behind her.

Prince looked at her and knew she wasn't bluffing. He raised his hands, gun high toward the ceiling, and stepped back to put some distance between them. "There's no need to harm him." He hoped she would remember she needed the boy, but the look in her eyes was deranged. "I'll throw it away." He slowly reached back with his armed hand toward the opened driver door. He tossed the gun away before the Priestess would command him to release the weapon to her. A soft thud came a second later.

"Out!" The Priestess lowered the syringe to the baby until it rested on his small arm.

"Don't! I'll leave." Prince retraced his steps and was almost climbing backward to get out from the driver door, when he saw the malice in the woman's eyes and the way the needle was prickling the boy's skin.

"Out," the Priestess repeated, her voice soft and suddenly too calm, her hand shaking, the needle sinking lower and creating a small indenture in the small arm.

The boy's scared cries resonated magnified tenfold in the small space.

Prince looked at the scene, not daring to break the eye contact—as if in keeping the woman in his sight would keep things under control—tormented by the decision he had to make.

"Too late." The Priestess's hand hovered for a moment, her thumb moving on top of the plunger.

He screamed and jumped in the small, crowded space of the cabin to push the syringe out of the woman's hands, but she was faster and pulled the boy out of the basinet while keeping the needle too close to him. Prince stopped where he was. "Please, don't harm him. He didn't do anything to you."

The Priestess didn't acknowledge his words. She emitted a guttural sound while holding the boy, who was crying at the top of his lungs, put the dripping needle against his throat and started laughing. "I always win."

"Not this time." Pax's voice came from behind, loud and clear, a split second before a gunshot echoed in the confined space.

The Priestess closed and opened her eyes, blinking rapidly, shock emerging from beneath her madness, her laughing frozen in a distorted grin. Howling in pain, she collapsed on the floor, falling on the nurse, who was starting to stir.

Prince jumped ahead to catch the baby before he too went down with the woman. Then once the boy was safely nested in his arms, he raised his head and turned toward Pax, who was emerging from the driver seat, still holding the gun he had thrown out.

"I saw her... and our boy. He was crying. I shot before I could think what I was doing." She was shaking, the gun in her hands bouncing up and down.

"You did the right thing." Prince slowly stood up, cradling the baby.

"I aimed at her legs. I'd never put our son in any danger," Pax explained, looking back at him, eyes wide and brimming with tears. "I'd never do anything—"

"I know." Prince gently took the gun from her hands and in the process gave her the baby to hold. "I know."

"If she'd moved—" Pax hugged the small bundle and brought her lips to the boy's head.

"But she didn't and you saved him." He wanted to take both of them in his arms and reassure her that everything was fine, but the nurse was struggling on the floor to free herself from the Priestess who was thrashing around, her hands clasping the right leg. "I'll take the girl."

"You aren't going anywhere." The pilot, disoriented but awake, was brandishing what looked like a piece of a pipe with one hand. She pointed the pipe at Pax's head and swung it toward her.

The woman's movements weren't fully coordinated and Pax moved out of the way.

"Stop or I'll shoot her," Prince said, looking straight at the pilot, but aiming at the Priestess's injured leg. Years of physical abuses and consequent infirmary visits had given him a crude knowledge of human physiology. Linda had told him once that guards weren't allowed to shoot at certain parts of the body for fear of losing a worker. The femoral artery was one of them.

The pilot looked at him as if he were an exotic animal who had just talked. She sneered, took another swing at Pax, and almost hit the baby. The fine hair on his head bristled by the air shifting. Pax yelled in pain when the pipe made contact with her collarbone and she fell backward. The pilot took advantage of that and raised her hand for another blow, her aim directed at the small head.

Prince charged the pilot before the woman realized he had moved. He struck her with the muzzle of the gun repeatedly, his anger finding release in the act.

"You can stop," Pax whispered from the floor.

Prince blinked, once, twice, and looked down. The pilot was bleeding from a deep gash on the back of her head, face white, eyes closed, her body limp against the driver seat. He was holding her by the lapels of her uniform, and when he opened his fingers, she crumbled without a sound.

The nurse, now kneeling behind the Priestess, her back to the second bassinet, started shouting nonsense. The mic, still in the pilot's hand, came alive with a low buzz.

"They're coming for you," the Priestess growled, pressing on her wounded leg with both hands.

Prince walked past the Priestess, moved the nurse out of the way with a push, and grabbed his daughter's bassinet by the handle.

"Stop, now!" the Priestess commanded, the pain making her voice sluggish and weak. "Pax Layan, listen to me! You'll pay for this. I promise you."

"You can't leave the Priestess," the nurse said to Pax. "Are you insane? She needs your help. She's wounded." She went on and on, her hands on the Priestess's shoulders.

"My army will be here in a matter of minutes." The Priestess angrily slapped the nurse's hands. A gust of wind brought inside the cabin the distant sound of approaching vehicles, and she smiled a perverse parody of white teeth and mad eyes. "See for yourself."

"Mistress, help me." The nurse stood up and attempted a step toward Pax.

Prince raised the gun at her, and the woman sat rather clumsily by the Priestess, muttering a long string of curses under her breath.

Pax ignored both the Priestess and the blathering nurse and turned toward Prince, silently asking him for directions, the cars loud and close.

Prince gave a good look at the gun hot in his hand. Then his eyes went to his baby girl crying and in need of comfort. "Let's get out of here."

CHAPTER 23

"I swear I'll make you regret this." The Priestess, fixing her gaze on the boy, spat in Pax's direction.

Prince saw Pax flinch at the Priestess's threat and he felt a cold shiver running down his spine. "Open the door," he ordered the nurse. When the woman did not move, he pointed his gun at her once again. "Open the door, now."

The second time, the woman scrambled to her feet and complied.

"Useless coward," the Priestess said.

The nurse emitted a low whimpering sound like a beaten animal and returned to her side.

Prince followed Pax outside. He was still on the top step of the mobile stairs when he saw the first car driving around the corner of the building, speeding toward them. "Run!" He took the girl in his arms, abandoning her bassinet, then stashed the gun inside his pants' rear pocket and took Pax by the elbow. "To the recreational facility."

They ran, the babies crying in their arms, with at least two cars chasing after them. Prince didn't turn to check how many there were, doubling his efforts to reach the wall in front of them, a welcoming door looming ahead. He heard at least one of the cars stop, probably by the helicopter to provide first aid to the Priestess.

"Prince!" Pax's voice was silenced by the sound of cars' breaks being hit.

The acrid smell of engine fumes reached Prince's nostrils. He reached for the gun and blindly shot several rounds at whoever was chasing after them, while at the same time pushing Pax ahead of him and propelling her closer to the door, now within reach. "Get inside."

"It's closed," she cried.

He was at her side in a moment and went to try the handle.

"It doesn't open!" Pax kicked the metal surface of the door in frustration.

"Move aside," he told her. He handed her the girl, removed the gun from his pocket, aimed, and shot at the lock. The blast sent the kids into another bout of loud crying. He heard Pax lulling the babies with whispered words. "Go, go!" He left the door opened for her and then closed it behind him, his back to it. "Find something to barricade it."

Pax looked around, the big room semi hidden in the darkness. "There's nothing here."

"The fridges in the back room have wheels. Run!" Prince squatted and planted his back firmly against the door. The pounding started a mere moment later.

"Open the door!" A woman beat on the door with something metallic.

"Pax, hurry—" Prince was almost dislodged from his position by a more aggressive attempt at breaching through. For a moment, the door opened. He drew the gun and shot through the crack.

The women screamed in surprise, but were otherwise unscathed. The door slammed shut. With his back firmly against the metal door, Prince cursed at his mistake and tried to remember how many shots he had fired, but soon realized it was a useless exercise since he was unsure how many had been shot before he got the gun. He tried to remove the magazine to check, but another blow reminded him he had to focus on keeping the door from being ripped from its hinges.

The sound of wheels approaching gave him some strength, but his right calf was cramping badly. "I can't stall them much longer." Sweat soaked his back, making it difficult to maintain the stance. "Pax!"

The door ajar, Pax arrived with one of the fridges and a large piece of wood.

"Where did you leave the kids?"

"In the back room."

"Open in the name of the Holy Priestess."

Prince didn't lose any time pushing the fridge against the door. "Give it to me." He took the wood from Pax's hands and hit the wheels to bend them, then used it to jam the fridge in place. "I don't know how long it's going to work."

A violent blow dislodged the fridge.

Prince swore under his breath. "We need another one." He looked back at the room.

Pax understood and hurried to haul a second fridge back while he engaged in a battle of strength against the women.

His hands on the fridge, he pushed to close the metal surface on them, mentally thanking the round of renovations that had recently taken place, probably soon after the fire that had savaged the farm, with the result of upgrading the old wooden door to the sturdier metal wall.

"Here..." Pax, out of breath and white as a ghost, was back with the fridge and a larger piece of wood.

Prince immediately pushed it flush with the other and repeated the procedure of bending the wheel and jamming the piece of wood so that the fridge would not budge. From the other side, the women were getting angrier, judging from the blasphemy being spat at every blow.

"They can't go on forever," he whispered for Pax, who was looking at the door with terrified eyes.

"Are you sure?"

"Let's not wait to find out." He took her hand and ran to the back room. One look at the deserted place and his heart summersaulted in his ribcage. "Where are the kids?"

"Safe." She went straight to open a closet and unwrap the babies from a soft blanket she had used to cover and pillow them.

They were finally quiet and seemed to be dreaming, their faces composed in peaceful expressions. Prince felt a pang of remorse at having to jostle them back to their harsh reality.

"Where to?" Pax handed him the boy.

"This way." Cradling the baby close to his face to inhale the boy's clean scent, Prince walked to the wall dotted with the row of fridges and moved two of them aside to expose what looked like an electrical panel. He saw Pax's puzzled look and pressed his open palm on the right side of it. A soft click and the panel opened outward. "Custom built," he explained, showing her the tunnel looming darkly behind. He stepped inside, one leg after the other, through the small opening, searched the rough brick wall for the switch, lit the place, and then took the girl from Pax so she could climb over the edge and get inside as well. "This is what happens when you leave your slaves unattended. They tend to leave spaces between rooms, which in turn creates hidden hallways that run through the whole length of the farm." He pulled the panel back in its place and walked in the opposite direction with Pax following a step behind.

"Ingenious," she said after a few seconds of silent jogging.

"Thank you." The tunnel smelled of mold, and some of the smoke from the fire lingered in the air, as if it had become one with the walls, but he felt better at every step he took.

"Was it your idea?'

"Yes." He had asked the workers assigned to build the room to make an upgrade for him. They had liked it so much they hadn't stopped at the recreational facility. "When the women gave orders to remodel the back room into the new semen bank, I thought we were going to be caught, but your presence in the farm actually helped us cover our tracks."

"How so?"

"Caren and Lauren were so focused on impressing you—"

"My mother. Caren and Lauren were bent on having Maurice as guest of honor for the orchid's celebration thing, or whatever it was."

"Anyway, busy fawning after you, or your mom, none of the women noticed the panel."

"Now I see how you could go from one place to the other without being caught by the guards."

"That, and the women thought they could manage a place like Sundial with a handful of them guarding over us." They had reached a fork in the dark; two different hallways opened at opposite angles. Prince made a swift decision, turned on two switches, but merged right without pausing. A distant, muffled sound echoed through the ceilings and reached his ears.

"And to think Caren's so proud of her managing skills." Pax's voice sounded labored.

Prince turned around long enough to make sure she was fine. "Her own pride was my biggest ally." He heard the sound again. Closer, easier to identify. He felt relieved when he saw the stairs leading down and took them two at a time. Only one level down, but the air was already colder and moister. He had never particularly liked sneaking in and out from there. His throat always closed because of the closeness and dimness reigning over that tunnel.

"Where are we now?"

"Under the gardens. We just left the recreational center. Heading toward the men's cells. We will exit in my old cell." Prince didn't want to worry Pax, but once on the floor, he commanded his legs to redouble the pace.

"What is it?"

It was not necessary for Prince to say it out loud. The women were pursuing them, shouting threats. It was soon painfully clear the trick of lighting both hallways wasn't going to save them. "Take him and run."

"No—"

"There isn't time for this now. Run to the end of this hallway and then turn left twice. Keep going until you face a dead wall. Feel the bricks with your hands, find the lose ones, and push them to open a passage large enough for you to get inside my cell. Wait for me there." He took only one moment to give her a kiss while he passed her the small bundle, then reached for the gun and tucked it in her pants. "I don't know how many rounds it's got left, but neither do they. It will scare the women away if they catch up with you."

"What about you?"

"You need it." He gave the two kids a kiss. "Don't turn around." He pushed her away from him.

Pax had a moment of hesitation, but then one of the voices grew closer. "Promise me you'll come," she hurried to say.

"I promise." He watched her as her back disappeared around a corner and then turned around and ran toward the woman. He saw her before she saw him.

The Priestess's soldier, profusely sweating in her elegant but cumbersome black-and-gold uniform, stared at him in utter surprise. He charged his left leg with all the strength he could muster and kicked her squarely in her stomach with the heel of his foot. He almost fell backward when his right leg started shaking, but managed to stay upright and throw a series of fists, but only hit her twice in the face.

After the first moment of shock at seeing Prince attacking instead of fleeing, the woman regained her footing and defended herself. "You'll die today," she snarled, looked at him, seemed to think for a split second about the best course of action, and then drove her reinforced boot against his right leg.

Prince wasn't fast enough to dodge the vicious blow that left him crippled. He fell to his back before he could extend his arms to soften the impact.

"What were you thinking?" The woman had drawn her gun out of the holster and was aiming it at Prince's head.

Not now, he thought. Images of Pax and his kids played before his eyes. Without warning, he kicked at the woman's ankles and pushed until she lost her footing.

A guttural sound of outrage escaped the soldier's mouth while she stumbled backward. Prince was on her immediately, pinning her down with his body and slapping her gun away.

"What...?" The woman's eyes darted toward her gun, but it was outside her outstretched fingers' reach.

"You should've left me alone." Prince circled her throat with his hands and pressed until her eyes closed and her body went limp under him. He let go right away and jumped to the side, a strong urge of throwing up possessing him, then looked at the woman lying at an odd angle.

"Klea? Are you there?" a faint voice called from the recesses of the hallway; the sound of running steps followed immediately.

Prince's head snapped to face the incoming soldier, his heart beating fast and his lungs aching to draw fresh air. "Not today, not now." He picked up the woman's gun from where it had fallen, waited for the other to appear from around the corner, then aimed and pressed the trigger.

The woman, a younger soldier, probably Pax's age, disbelief showing in her wide eyes, crumpled to the ground without emitting a sound.

318

Prince saw the red stain instantly widening on her chest in a wide circle. His first reaction was to throw away the gun, but he thought better of it and started running. He didn't know if there was a third or a fourth woman and he couldn't waste any time looking behind. Hoping his legs weren't going to give out, Prince breathed deeply and forged ahead. The last part was agony on his battered muscles, but he didn't stop putting one foot in front of the other until he saw the dark opening of his cell.

"Stop where you are." Pax's broken voice came as soon as he reached the threshold.

"Pax? It's me." He couldn't see anything in the pitch-black surrounding him and stumbled on the bricks disseminated on the floor as soon as he stepped inside his former residence. Light filtered in from both the hallway and the tunnel, but it didn't seem to reach inside. It never had. Uneasiness grabbed him at the familiar smell permeating the place. Pax was at his side before he could call her name again. "Is everything okay?" He felt her trembling and went to touch her face, her arms, along her body. "Are you okay?"

Pax did not answer him at first. Instead, she put her arms around him and silently demanded he did the same. A few seconds later, when he had enclosed her in his arms and kissed her crown, she finally said, "I heard the gunshot and I was the one with the gun... I was the one holding the stupid gun... while you were getting shot." She was shaking and her words were but a whisper.

"I took a gun from one of the soldiers. I think I killed both of them," Prince said, not wanting to give details about what had just happened, but at the same time feeling the need to purge himself of the sour taste in his mouth. "I need to rest for a minute."

"Come here." Pax took him by the hand and led the way to the opposite corner.

He could hear their kids softly breathing and some warmth crept in his heart. "Are they still sleeping?" he asked, carefully sitting on the floor and reaching out in the dark to touch them, guided by the feeble silhouettes created by the outside light. His fingers found a small foot sticking out of the thin blanket, and for a brief moment, he felt his spirit lift at the sensation.

"They are." Pax scooped closer to him.

Prince accommodated her head on his shoulder.

"All I want is to be left alone to live with you and our kids. I don't want anything else. I don't need anything else." Pax sighed, raised her hand up to lower his head, and kissed him softly. "We have the right to be happy."

He kissed her back while pulling her in his lap, and for a moment, the rest of the world disappeared from his mind, his hands roaming over her body and awakening memories of a time when she wasn't skin and bones. He remembered when Pax's smile hadn't been sad. His eyes adjusting to the artificial twilight, he saw the outline of her face. "My beautiful Pax," he murmured to her lips, his arms crashing her to him.

One of the kids cooed, the softest of sounds, but both parents turned their heads toward the noise. When it turned out to be nothing more, they laughed softly.

Prince rested his forehead on hers, out of breath and barely able to talk, several different urges playing havoc through his body and mind. His mouth was on hers when another sound interrupted them.

"Check those cells. I'll go check the next hallway." Caren's voice came from outside, just a few steps left from where they were.

"Okay." Lauren. Heavy footing on the stone floor.

Prince saw a cone of light illuminating the floor of his cell.

"Heavens, but this place stinks of men," Lauren commented, lingering a moment too long on the spot, the cone of light moving around the cell to reveal its interior.

Prince froze and felt Pax do the same. He didn't dare move his hands from her waist and left his face hovering a breath away from hers, his eyes darting to the side where the babies were sleeping. *God and Goddess, please keep them silent.*

The cone of light moved dangerously close to his feet, but he resisted the impulse of bending his knees. The point of his right shoe was illuminated for a brief moment. He stopped breathing and stilled his leg.

"There's nothing here," Lauren said.

Prince waited until the light moved away in a big arch that illuminated the rest of the cell and its ceiling; he opened his mouth to inhale only when the sound of Lauren's boots announced she was walking away. At the last moment, probably for old time's sake, the woman decided to give the metal bars of the next cell a taste of her beating stick. The harsh, explosive sound reverberated through the deserted hallway and inside the cell, grating on Prince's frail nerves while bringing back his physical pain. He felt the movement at his side before the wailing started. His hands went to calm the baby, but the other cried before he could do anything.

"What the…? Caren, come here, there's—" Lauren was back, her hand guiding the light without hesitation and revealing Prince and Pax hunched over the darkest spot of the cell. "You! And you…? Caren! Run, you want to see this." She was already pointing a gun at them. "Move aside and let me see what you got there."

"Take me and leave her alone," Prince said, his own hand trying to reach the rear pocket where he had put the gun.

"Raise your hands in the air where I can see them. You too, Mistress." Lauren spat Pax's title as if it were a swear word and slowly walked inside the cell, keeping them well illuminated and under the aim of her gun. "If you have any weapons, release them now," she said to Prince while making a show of moving closer. "I'll put a bullet in her head and nobody will be the wiser."

"I've a gun in my rear pocket and I'll give it to you." Prince lowered his eyes to his pants to let the woman know what he was going to do.

"Go ahead, but remember, I'll make you clean her brain off this wall if you as much as sneeze without my blessing." She rested the gun on Pax's right temple and took pleasure in grazing her skin with the barrel. "Throw it outside."

Prince showed Lauren the gun and then let it slide past her legs and out in the hallway.

"Now, move."

Prince stepped out of the way while the woman forced Pax to the floor. Lauren gave a good look at the two bundles, casting the bright light on the babies and eliciting another round of crying.

"I knew it." She was satisfied and a greedy expression shone on her face. "You really are stupid."

"Please, don't hurt them," both Prince and Pax said at the same time.

"What do we have here?" Caren's shadow darkened the hallway.

"You won't believe who I found hiding like rats in the sewers."

"Mistress Layan and her slave." Caren towered from the outside, her hands lying casually on the bars, calmly taking in the scene.

"And the Chosen."

"The Chosen is here?"

"Yes, can you believe these two idiots?"

Caren stepped inside the cell, walked to the corner, gave a good look at the babies now squirming under the bright light, swore, and stepped outside again to use her cell phone.

Prince tried to listen to the conversation, increasingly worried by what was going to happen next, but the kids were still crying. A sideways glance at Pax confirmed she was as nervous as he was. Still training her gun on them, Lauren turned toward Caren. He inched imperceptibly closer to Pax until their bodies touched and felt her hands moving behind her.

The kids ceased their wailing. "Do you want both kids?" Caren was pacing outside the cell. She hissed something to Lauren, who immediately focused back on Prince and Pax. They both froze.

"And what about the slave?" Caren paused for a long moment, and then started talking again interjecting yesses and noes every other word, getting agitated as the conversation went on for several minutes. "Understood," she finally said and turned around.

"So? What is it?" Lauren, already forgetting the previous command, tilted her head toward Caren.

Prince saw the opportunity and moved one step ahead to partially cover Pax. It was enough for her to move freely and finish what she had started before Lauren, sensing there was something going on, fixed her eyes once again on them.

"The Priestess didn't give me permission to kill the slave—"

"But, why?"

"She wants to do it herself." Caren kicked the wall and a cloud of dust was the result. "And we're to bring him, the babies, and the Layan to her immediately."

"Let's get this over with, then." Lauren made to reach for the kids, but was stopped by Pax's cold voice.

"Don't get any closer to my kids."

"Don't you dare call the Chosen your daughter." Lauren inched forward.

"Stop where you are."

"Or what?" Lauren laughed and turned her back to Pax. "Can you believe her?" she asked Caren.

Caren first smiled back and then frowned. "Lauren—"

"Give your gun to him." Pax pressed her gun against Lauren's temple as the woman had done a few minutes earlier. "How do you like it now?"

Lauren let her gun fall on the floor and Prince picked it up.

"Don't touch a single hair on her head or I'll kill you." Caren was livid.

"You too, give him your gun, now." Pax forced Lauren on her knees.

"It's okay, love," Caren said, her voice shaking as she unwillingly got rid of her gun, throwing it at Prince who caught it in midair.

Lauren went to the floor and, without looking, outstretched her armed hand toward Prince's general direction. "You'll pay for this."

"Get in line," Pax murmured.

"What do you think is going to happen now?" Caren was looking alternatively between Lauren and Pax, seemingly refusing to raise her eyes to Prince. "You can't believe you can pull this off."

"Shut up." Pax, gun firmly pressing on Lauren's head, said to Prince, "Let's go."

"Let's go," he said back, thinking fast of where the next hideout was. "You two, step inside that cell." He pointed with his free hand at the dark pit opening in front of them.

"You got to be kidding..." Caren snorted and shook her head.

Pax retracted her hand enough to hit Lauren, who screamed in pain as the barrel made contact with her temple. "I said shut up." She grabbed Lauren by the elbow and helped her up. "Next is a bullet."

Caren swore but walked inside the cell, followed by a bleeding Lauren.

"Use the handcuffs on her." Prince kept his eyes on the two women and couldn't help but feel a dark enjoyment in the current situation.

Caren hesitated a moment.

"Do you need encouragement?" Pax asked.

Prince noticed the light in Pax's eyes and saw her hate pouring out, raw.

Caren must have seen it too because she hurried to tie Lauren's wrists together and then to the wall. "I'm so sorry, my love," she whispered to her when the lock clicked in place. She handed over the keys before Pax could ask. "Satisfied?"

"You have no idea," Prince answered instead, about to begin to tie Caren to the wall when he realized both women were looking at something behind him. He followed their eyes and saw her: one of the two Priestess's soldiers he thought he killed had followed them and crept inside the cell.

"There's a gun on the floor!" Lauren yelled.

Prince saw the gun he had been forced to throw away resting by the column just outside the entry of the cell and sprinted toward it, but the woman was closer and grabbed it before he could close his fingers around it. He cursed, angry and tired of the whole situation, rolling out of the way and up again, ending back to back with Pax, facing the newcomer. "Don't take your eyes off Caren," he said to Pax while he steadied his stance and aimed at the soldier.

A long, silent moment passed before anyone said or did anything until one of the babies moved.

"Take them!" Caren ordered the soldier.

"Don't move!" Prince screamed, shaking the gun toward the woman.

After a brief moment of surprise, the kids cried, realization dawned on the soldier as she understood what she had been asked to do, and she ran to the dark corner.

Prince pressed the trigger at her first movement, but the safety was on. "No!" Anger grew inside him. The soldier reached his kids before he had time to remove the safety and shoot again.

"Keep your gun on them," Caren ordered the soldier.

He looked at Pax, who had left her position the moment the soldier ran toward the corner and was now staring ahead, her eyes terrified as she watched the woman aim at their kids.

Caren calmly put one foot in front of the other and stood before Pax. "They aren't going to survive the day and I'll tell the Priestess you killed them," she said, a sick, perverted smile lightening her cruel traits.

Prince listened to her, knowing the game had gone too far and the woman had been waiting long enough to exact her vengeance. Knowing she was reckless.

"So small, defenseless." Caren was standing by the soldier before the two bundles, the babies crying softly, scared by the noises. "You shouldn't have touched my wife." She spared one last glance at Pax and then put her body in front of the soldier, shielding the woman from everybody else's eyes and aim. She whispered something to her and then said out loud, "Do it."

Prince was already on Caren when the shot resonated in the hallway, but as he put his hands around her throat she collapsed on the floor, a low gargling sound escaping her mouth. He didn't spare a moment and moved to the soldier, his whole body pushing her against the wall and away from the corner. The woman screamed in pain when he smashed her hand against the bricks over and over again until she let go of her gun, which he promptly collected. Pax's sudden cry caught his armed hand midair ready to silence the soldier; his head snapped to face the inevitable. "Are they...?" He couldn't say the word, but looked as Pax knelt and let the gun slide from her hold, her hands to her mouth trying to smother the sobs raking her chest, her body rocking in slow sways. His hands clutching the two guns by his side, he stayed frozen on the spot, unable to cover the two steps required to reach Pax, her head now tilted to her shoulder and her fingers touching the thin blankets covered in blood.

Prince fell to his knees. He looked at the two guns weighing down his hands and couldn't remember how they had ended there. Crying and shouting echoed all around him, but he couldn't focus on the words. His eyes fixated on Pax hunched over their babies, her back to him and the rest of her body swallowed by the dark shadow of the cell corner.

"What did you do?" Lauren was crying, her hands outstretched in a vain attempt to free herself from the shackles pinning her to the wall. "Let me go."

Prince's attention swayed her way for a moment, but it didn't last. His right hand moved by its volition and pointed the gun at Lauren.

"Let me go to her, I'm begging you..." she said, heedless of Prince's threat.

His head foggy, he tried to focus on Pax's cries and what she was saying.

"Don't let her bleed to death." Lauren stopped thrashing around, her head hanging low between her shoulders.

Her words collided with Pax's whispers and Caren's moans. The only one silent was the soldier, who had curled up in a ball by the wall, facing the hallway.

"Let me do something for her. Don't let her die like this," Lauren pleaded.

"I want you to shut up," Prince said, but without any conviction. He looked at his hand still pointing the gun at Lauren and wondered why he hadn't pressed the trigger.

Suddenly, the soldier tried a mad dash back to the tunnel where she had come from. "Stay where you are." The soldier stopped immediately. His other hand aimed in the soldier's direction. He didn't waste a second glance at her. His heart was broken by the sight of Pax emerging from the shadow with the boy and the girl cradled in her arms, blood everywhere.

"Goddess be blessed," Pax was repeating, kissing the babies on their small legs, arms, cheeks, heads, caressing and rocking them in her arms.

"Caren!" Lauren screamed.

"She isn't breathing," the soldier said from the corner.

Prince felt something warm wetting his knees and realized he hadn't moved. His eyes followed the dark stain sliding on the slanted floor until it reached its final destination, the drain slit running parallel to the cells. The thick liquid accumulated at the edge of the drain and then started to fall over. At the beginning drop by drop, but soon it poured down in one single, dark-red stream.

"Goddess be blessed."

"You killed her."

Prince followed the stream to Caren's still body. Her clothes were covered in blood from the waist down.

"Goddess be blessed."

He looked at Pax, his heart slamming against his ribcage.

"You murdered a woman," the soldier said, disbelief in her voice.

"Caren, my love." Lauren's voice was hoarse.

"My babies... My sweet babies..."

A soft cry followed by a flurry of motion silenced all the voices.

"Pax—" Prince whispered, moving closer to her.

She looked at him, big tears staining her face in stripes of white and red where her hands had smeared blood on her skin, and nodded. "I defended my babies. I didn't let her do anything to them."

"They're alive." Senses came back to him in a rush of overpowering feelings and he finally cried, body doubled over by searing pain, stomach heaving in waves.

Pax moved then, bringing the kids to him, to let him see them for himself. "It isn't their blood."

He already knew it by then, but needed to hear it. "They're alive."

"Yes, yes, they are." Pax angled her precious cargo toward him. "Look."

Prince looked down at the tangle of bloodied blankets and tiny limbs and the girl chose that moment to look up at him, her lips curved in a smile. His armed hands came to his mouth, palms crossed over his lips, as he started sobbing in earnest, mirroring Pax a few minutes earlier.

"Prince!" Pax screamed.

A shadow fell over him and the babies. He reacted without thinking and fired the gun at the soldier. The woman collapsed where she stood, the brick she had been holding landing by his left shoe.

"Caren... Caren..." Lauren mewed, oblivious to what had just happened.

Prince looked around, concentrating on hearing beyond Lauren's laments. The sound of angry, incoming boots stomping was soft but unmistakable. Someone was looking for them and wouldn't stop until they found them. "Where are you?" He had to wait a few interminable seconds before the sounds became clearer. "They're coming from there," he said to Pax, indicating their former escape route. He let out a curse, straightened his legs, and helped Pax up. "Give him to me." The boy, passed from her arms to his, was pleased by the change and made a gurgling sound, leaving Prince wanting to slow down to look at him and commit to memory his perfect features, the way he smelled, the color of his skin—resembling so much Pax's after a day in the sun.

"I know," she said and smiled.

He nodded. There wasn't any need for words between them anymore. "Back into the farm is our only hope."

"Okay." Pax stood on her toes to reach his mouth and gave him the softest peck, then repositioned the girl snugly against her chest and charged ahead, passing Lauren without a glance.

"Why don't you kill me?" the woman asked, for a moment her former, haughtily self.

"You were never so kind to me." Prince hadn't wanted to waste any time and talk to Lauren, but memories of past brutalities emerged, summoned by her request. "'You don't deserve to die and get it over with'—your words. It must have killed you that I was a principle and you couldn't get rid of me." He walked away, ignoring the string of insults she bestowed upon him, feeling lighter every step he took until he was able to sprint into a run. *I'm soaring above all this pain and misery,* he thought, lungs working at full capacity and muscles stretching beyond safety, the ever-present frown between his eyes relaxing.

"I'll lock it," he explained to Pax when they reached the stairs leading upstairs and asked her to hold the boy for a moment. He put the guns in his rear pockets.

The metal gate that separated the upper floors from the cells sat open, partially out of its hinges and rusted. Prince tried to move it, but it had been a while since anybody had oiled it and it was heavy. Loud screams for help echoed in the high-ceilinged hallway and he knew time wasn't in their favor. Angry voices followed soon after. He redoubled his efforts, planting his feet on the first step of the stairs, hands firmly grabbing the bars, and pushing the gate with his shoulders until it moved enough to be hoisted properly inside the hinges. Once the gate was in its place, rust falling off the structure where the frame connected with the hinges, Prince applied all his strength to move it until it slowly turned on its axis all the way to the other side.

"Stop where you are!" a soldier ordered. She was armed to the teeth and running at full speed.

"Go upstairs," Prince implored Pax while he fumbled with the rusted latch. He cut his fingers and scratched his nails, but the latch wouldn't cooperate.

Pax was almost out of shooting range when the soldier decided they needed to be persuaded. Prince judged that the woman missed on purpose. Pax was still the president's daughter and she was holding the Chosen. But there wasn't going to be another warning. Desperation gave him the boost he needed and the latch was driven home when the second shot was fired. Diverted by one of the metal bars, the bullet singed the skin on his left cheekbone and encased itself inside the wall behind Prince's ear. One of the guns fell from his pocket.

"Prince!" A muffled sound coming from upstairs reclaimed his attention.

Ear mercilessly ringing, he yelled, "I'm here," reached for his remaining gun, and returned fire at the fast-approaching soldier, who was ready to discharge the whole arsenal she was carrying. He made sure the latch was going to stall the woman long enough for him to escape and ran up the stairs at full speed, while she reduced the underlying walls to a sieve in her frustrated attempt at killing him.

"That gate isn't going to hold her and her reinforcements much longer," he said once on the landing where Pax was waiting for him, balancing the two kids in her arms. He took the boy and ran. Giving her a sideways glance without breaking stride, he saw the way Pax was looking at him and reached for his face only to find blood dripping down. "I was lucky."

He led her through the hallways, thankful she trusted him and didn't ask what his plan was. He didn't have one—just keeping them alive as long as he could. He knew Sundial by heart, but the women weren't playing by the rules anymore. He didn't know where to expect to see them next. His heart pumping with adrenaline, terrified he would make a mistake and drive them headfirst into a trap, he kept pushing them up and down the whole farm, hoping to find a way out. Twice they skirted a close encounter with the Priestess's soldiers, and twice they managed to escape by sheer luck. Every time he brought them closer to an exit, they had to run in the opposite direction, deeper and deeper inside the farm they were so desperately trying to leave.

"I can't run anymore," Pax cried, stumbling and almost falling when the heel of her shoe caught the raised corner of an uneven tile he had just avoided at the last moment.

They were back on the second floor. For the last half an hour, Prince had been trying to reach the part of the wing that hadn't been rebuilt after the fire. Remembering what they had already done once, he was hoping they could jump down on the ground from one of the rooms facing the slope. "We're almost there. I promise." He took her by the elbow and felt her body sagging for a moment. Without asking, he took the girl from her. Pax was skin and bones and weighed next to nothing, but they wouldn't go far if he tried to take her and the babies in his arms. They needed to rest, eat, and drink. The babies needed to be checked by the doctor. "Everything's going to be fine."

"Where are the men? Where did they go?" Pax had brought both of them to a stop, her breathing a labored, rasping noise. "Give me a second." She crouched and lowered her head between her knees.

"Somewhere outside, I guess." Prince didn't have time to think about anybody but them, and the kids had been crying for an hour already and he was worried there was something wrong. But he couldn't voice his thoughts, which were becoming increasingly darker. A sense of despair was sapping the last of him.

"They must be hungry." Pax tried to stand up. "They had a bottle last night and then nothing else after the surgery—" She looked at him, her eyes full of fear. "Linda said the surgery went fine, but—"

Prince didn't let her finish the thought. "They're hungry." Jostling both kids and the gun he was still holding, he gave her a hand. "Let's find some milk for them."

"Linda keeps the baby formula at the infirmary." She teetered on unsteady legs, but squeezed his hand and gave him a tentative smile.

"You sure it's the only place where we can find some milk for them?"

"That's the only place I know of."

He caressed her arm and decided they didn't have any other choice. They had two kids in need of medical attention, and sooner or later, that would have been the only logical decision to make. Better sooner.

"Where is everybody?" Pax struggled to keep the pace, but didn't complain and didn't ask to stop again.

Prince didn't answer, his senses focused on every sound out of place and every movement around the corner. But there was none to detect; an unsettling, peaceful silence greeted them everywhere they went.

Finally, a few steps from the infirmary, he heard voices.

He had expected to find someone there, but didn't slow down. The babies were now quiet in his arms and that scared him more than their crying. Their breathing was shallow, their heads following the undulating rocking of his fast stroll, their hands limp by their sides. *I should've come here earlier,* he thought, terrified at the idea it was already too late. He kicked the door panel and broke through the infirmary. "I need help!"

By the voices spilling outside in the hallway, he had half expected to be greeted by a posse of angry women—not the Priestess in one of the small rooms opening into the emergency, laying on one of the infirmary beds. Her injured leg was propped up and freshly bandaged, her hands tied on her lap. She screamed at Linda and Lucas, who stood at the door, Randal watching from a safe distance just outside of it, armed with a rifle and relaxed.

"You!" The Priestess's face flushed crimson at seeing Prince and Pax, her first instinct to jump out of the bed to reach them. The moment she lowered her legs on the floor, pain transformed her features in a distorted mask and she screamed, a toe-curling scream that silenced the low muttering in the emergency room.

"Take a look at them." He hadn't slowed his stride at the sight, bringing the kids under Linda's nose without acknowledging the Priestess's presence or her voice, which was now a shrill offense to his ears. "Now." His eyes, more than his words, conveyed the urgency. "They've been this way for several minutes," he whispered to the doctor, being careful at giving Pax his shoulders.

Linda lowered her eyes on the kids, said something under her breath, and then closed the door to the Priestess's room behind her, shutting the woman's angry words behind her as well. "Bring them here." She strolled toward one of the beds in the middle of the emergency room. "You, out," she ordered a man who was lying there and at the same time made sign for Prince to lay the kids there.

The man limped off the bed, giving Prince the formal salute, right hand on the heart.

While approaching the bed, Prince's eyes followed the man vacating it—a worker he had shared turns with a lifetime ago—and saw that the infirmary, which just recently had been the stage of an intense scuffle, was at full capacity. At first glance he hadn't seen anything he wasn't interested in noticing, but now he saw men and women waiting their turn to be seen by the doctor, lying in beds or sitting on the floor among upturned furniture and broken glasses. "What's the meaning of this?" he asked Randal.

"We've apprehended the Priestess," he answered. "We caught her trying to fly away."

Prince's fleeting interest in the Priestess's predicament died the moment he heard Linda swear. Pax was already asking questions, but he couldn't. Fear had paralyzed his tongue.

"What is it?" Pax's voice was small.

"The medicine cabinet has just been raided and I don't have any left." Linda was talking to herself.

"Any left of what?" Pax was trembling. "Linda?"

Prince took her hand in his, needing an anchor. "What do you need?"

"Antibiotics, disinfectants, vitamins. They're just lethargic now..." She waved her hands.

"Just lethargic?" Pax relaxed against him for all but a second. "Because of the surgery?"

Linda nodded.

"Where I can find medical supplies?" Prince asked.

"Ask your friends if they can give back some of what they have just stolen," Linda answered.

He faced Randal, who shook his head.

"The men you see here are the only left," Randal said. "They were wounded or too old to attempt crossing the desert." His head tilting toward the closest man sitting on the floor, he continued, "His leg is broken in two different places."

"But what about the medicine?" Pax leaned on the wall.

"The emergency cabinet was already vacant, thanks to the Priestess's orders, but anything left valuable and light has been taken." Linda offered Pax and then Prince a bottle of water. "And I wouldn't drink the tap water."

"Don't know about that for sure, but... I wouldn't either." Randal lowered his head, a brief touch of shame darkening his features. "And I believe the food pantry has been raided and the fridges smashed to pieces."

"Anything else?" Prince was mentally adding every detail to the overall conclusion that they were doomed.

"They haven't set the farm on fire yet." Linda had gone to retrieve a white elongated bottle from a cabinet setting askew on the wall and missing the glass. "This milk is still good. It's better if they drink it now. In a few hours, without proper refrigeration, it'll spoil." She opened the bottle, sniffed at the contents for good measure, and then attached a teat to its neck. "They'll have to share it. This is the only sterilized teat left." She hesitated a moment, then motioned for Pax to take the bottle from her hand.

"How long can we stay here?" Pax asked. The boy was already suckling, low satisfied noises coming from the small bundle.

"Depends…" Linda went to caress the crying baby girl. "We adults, probably a week or two, rationing food and water to the bare minimum required to survive. But I'm counting on Ginecea sending someone way before we have to start taking drastic measures."

"Them?" Pax's eyes didn't leave her kids. "What will happen to them?"

"Without medicines or proper food? No more than a few days. I'm sorry." Linda moved off the bed, the baby girl redoubling her cries when the calming hand left her.

"We can't go anywhere else." Pax gently detached the boy's lips from the bottle by stroking his cheeks and soon started feeding the girl.

"No, you can't. Even if they hadn't just gone through a medical procedure, they would be too small and frail to withstand the Desertica region's inclement weather, anyway. It's too dry and hot during the day, and too cold at night. Strong men had managed to escape Sundial only to find their end out there."

"So, what? We wait?" Pax turned toward Prince, seeking his thoughts on the topic.

"We wait," he answered. He didn't have to explain to her what they were waiting for. Their hands were tied. He took a sip from the water bottle and then replaced the lid tightly and laid it on the floor, slowly letting his body down along with it. Head absentmindedly thumping the wall behind, he hoped to fall into stupor before he had to talk again about his kids' destiny, eyes lost on some place beyond Sundial. Beyond Ginecea.

A single memory emerged and took shape before him as a vivid image of the ancient paintings on the tunnel's walls inside the Caves outside the City of Men. He saw, as if it were right there before his eyes, the mural depicting the family composed of a man, a woman, and their children. He had found Pax looking at it, her eyes lost in its beauty. His heart had ached for the longing of a life they weren't destined to have, but he had hugged her and said they were beautiful. Now that they were living minute by minute, he would have given anything just to feel, even only for a moment, that they had a chance. The image faded; he struggled to retain it, but when one of the babies cried, he was propelled to the present and felt broken inside.

"Is there more milk?"

He heard Pax asking, and he knew what Linda's answer was going to be, maybe not now, but soon. And when the answer was, "There's none left," what then? What was he going to do to keep his kids alive?

He took a decision then and walked the whole length of the emergency room to open a door he would have never considered opening before. "I'll let you free if you save them." Prince was standing before the Priestess, ready to sell his soul to save his kids.

CHAPTER 24

Prince heard someone gasp. He thought he recognized Pax's voice in the whispered sound, but stepped inside the room and paused at the end of the woman's bed, laying his hands on the metal frame of the footboard. He curled his fingers around the bars to ground his nervous energy.

"Get out of here. I don't make arrangements of any kind with a slave," the Priestess said, venom in her tone, moving on the mattress to put as much distance as she could muster between Prince and herself without leaving the bed.

"This *slave* can keep you alive and free."

"You can't promise anything like that—"Randal angrily strode inside the room, his steps muffled on the vinyl tiles, the rifle dangerously swinging from one hand to the other. He stood before Prince, his chest raising and falling heavily.

"Shoot me or let me be." Prince didn't look at Randal, but tightened his hold on the metal bars until he felt the skin on his fingers stretch to a painful level. His eyes were still fixed on the Priestess, who was smiling one of her irritating smiles. He fought the urge to slap the woman and his hands almost tore apart the footboard.

Another gasp resonated loud, just a few steps behind Prince.

"Prince?" Pax was soon by his side, followed by Lucas and Linda, equally alarmed by the turn the situation was taking.

"Prince, let's be reasonable…" Lucas raised his hands to touch both Prince and Randal in a vain attempt to defuse the spirits.

"Linda, remove yourself and those animals from my presence." The Priestess looked at the doctor with a disgusted stare, her nostrils flaring.

"She must pay for her crimes against men." Randal didn't budge. If anything, he moved out of his father's reach, stepped closer to the bed, and assumed the stance of someone who intended to stay. After a moment of heated discussion between Pax, Linda, and Lucas, all trying to make a point, he raised the rifle and effectively silenced everybody in the room. He swung his arm around, pausing for the briefest moment in the general direction of Prince's body, and then finally rested against the Priestess's temple. Several breaths were released.

The Priestess didn't flinch. She held her chin up, and although her eyes were glassy and slightly unfocused and her forehead was covered in droplets of sweat, she had enough energy to spit at Randal. "How dare you, filthy man, unworthy of breathing the same air I do, menace me."

By way of answering, Randal cleaned his face with the palm of his free hand and with the other pressed the rifle until the tip disappeared in the Priestess's skin.

"Release me at once," the Priestess said as if there wasn't a rifle poking her temple.

Prince looked as the woman insulted Randal repeatedly, seemingly uncaring she was making the person holding a gun against her angry. He wondered if she understood what was happening.

"You aren't going to escape this." Randal gave Prince a sideways glance. "I'm sorry, but you should know better than anybody else why it's important that she finally faces the consequences of her acts."

"I don't want to fight you, but I don't have time to explain my reasons." Prince was going to show Randal that he was armed too, but Lucas approached them.

"Randal—" Lucas walked closer to his son until he was standing between Prince and Randal again, and after a moment of hesitation, put one hand on his arm.

"What, Dad? Don't you dare tell me to set her free." The rifle didn't move one bit, but he gently pushed away his father's hand. "She's the reason why *he's* dead."

"Son… I know you're still grieving, but—"

"But nothing. She ordered the massacre in the desert." Randal's voice broke. "I lost everything there."

"She deserves to pay, but they also deserve to have a chance to live. Killing her will not bring him back. It will only kill two innocents," Lucas said, his voice soft but steady.

"I'm not a kid anymore, Dad. I've taken this woman in custody so that she can be judged for all her crimes. She can't have a free pass without…"

"My kids' survival is a good reason," Pax said, and as if on cue, the babies started crying. "They're still hungry," she whispered to herself, and then raising her voice, she added, "My kids' lives are the most important reason."

"I didn't mean that they aren't." Randal lowered his head, and Lucas came closer to him.

Prince was at the end of his patience. Every cry his kids made was a stabbing wound on his heart. He reached for the gun in his rear pocket, but Lucas saw it.

"Give me a moment," the man said to Prince before addressing his son. "Randal," he started, but then shrugged his head and proceeded to hug his son instead. "I know you. I know what lies in your heart. You'd never let vengeance govern your decisions. You'll do what's good."

"Dad, please."

"You're better than you think." Lucas released Randal from his tight embrace.

Prince saw the man was silently crying and didn't have the heart to raise his gun against Randal. "I'm not beyond begging if that's what you want," he said, sagging on his knees.

Randal's eyes widened at the sight of Prince kneeled before him, and at first, he didn't reply. Then he reached out his hand to help him up. At the same time, he lowered the rifle.

"Thanks." Prince took the proffered hand and saw that Randal was crying too, like his father.

"You have to understand… She should pay for the pain she has inflicted on millions of us."

"And she will," Lucas said. "But not today, and not at your hands."

* * *

338

Not even an hour later, Prince, Pax, and the kids, accompanied by Linda, designated to carry the Priestess in a wheelchair, were on the helicopter headed toward the Temple and its well-stocked nursery. Before leaving, they had looked for some more milk for the kids, but found nothing.

"Make them stop crying," the Priestess demanded for the tenth time.

Pax and Prince had answered the first time. Now they were more preoccupied in finding a way to soothe the babies.

"Is there anything we can use?" Pax asked Linda, who was sitting by the Priestess's side, more to control the woman's outburst than to help her.

"Try giving them some water." Linda opened a square box anchored to the wall by her seat and took a water bottle from it.

Pax filled the kids' bottle with it and gave it to the girl first.

Prince watched as his baby eagerly latched on the teat and drank the water, only to start crying again a second later when she realized it wasn't milk. He wasn't sure when he had eaten last. His stomach cramped agonizingly, and he wondered how painful it was for their tiny bodies to go without proper nourishment.

"It's your fault the Chosen is suffering." The Priestess's eyes were gleaming with satisfaction while looking at Pax.

"Don't say another word." Pax passed the bottle to Prince so he could give it to the boy in his arms.

"You know I'm telling the truth. You aren't fit to be a mother. Look what you've done to them."

Pax didn't answer back.

Prince put one hand on her knee and softly squeezed.

"It's okay," she said to him, but one single tear fell down and hit his hand.

"You could've saved your girl. Instead, you'll let them both die."

"There never was a choice." Pax caressed the girl, bringing her closer to her lips to give her a soft kiss on the fuzzy crown.

Prince would have liked nothing better than to throw the Priestess out of the helicopter and watch her fall to her death, but he had realized the love for his kids was stronger than his hate for her. So he stood silent, hoping she would faint by her own accord. The

339

boy drank the water without complaining and then burrowed his way toward the nook created by his father's elbow. Prince's anger was replaced by a sense of wonder at feeling his baby's soft movements. The little hands closed in two fists and lay by the boy's head, while his legs were curled up toward his belly.

"There's nothing in the world like this, is there?" Pax asked in a whisper, but the Priestess heard her.

"You won't enjoy them for long." The Priestess's cruel eyes changed focus and lingered on the girl for a long moment.

Prince's rage came back at full steam and he found himself towering over the woman, boy still clutched in his arms, which was the only reason why he didn't strike her with the back of his hand as he had envisioned so many times.

"Tell your dog to sit." The Priestess had to tilt her head to look at Pax behind the obstacle that was Prince. "You should've taught him how to behave in public."

He knew she was taking him to the edge of his own sanity to humiliate him. The boy startled, flaying his legs and arms in the opposite direction, probably in the middle of a scary dream, or maybe sensing his father's muscles tightening and tensing. "No, baby, don't be worried. Your dad is here," he cooed to him, leaving a trail of kisses on the boy's head.

"I pity you," Pax said, her voice calm.

"You... *you* pity me? You?" The Priestess moved all her torso and sat askew on her seat to face Pax.

"I do." Pax spoke in a singsong tone, and when Prince finally regained enough mental composure to realize he couldn't do anything but breathe on the Priestess, he walked back to sit by Pax. He saw that she was trying to calm the girl to sleep.

"You do. What does that even mean?"

To Prince's extreme satisfaction, he saw the Priestess angry.

"You'll never, ever in your miserable life, know what is it to love and be loved." Pax freed one of her hands to take Prince's and direct it over her heart.

Prince eyes locked his eyes on hers and felt dizzy under her direct and unwavering gaze.

"What you think you have won't last the day," the Priestess said, bringing Prince abruptly back to the helicopter. "You'll die for it."

"It will be worth it," Prince said, the words escaping his mouth while still looking at Pax. When he turned, he saw the havoc their private moment had created. The Priestess was furious, mouth open in a distorted silent scream, too disgusted he had dared to speak to her to even talk. Silent as well, Linda was staring back, eyes wide— an expression he couldn't decipher on her face, something akin to sadness and regret.

"We're flying over the Temple," the pilot announced.

Prince looked outside the window, thinking to take a glimpse of the burning reds and yellows reflected on the Temple's façade and share the sight with Pax. Instead, a sea of burnt blacks and browns lay before his eyes. For as far as he could see, the valley beneath them was a charred, still-smoking wasteland.

"Nobody is answering my call." The pilot could be heard frantically repeating the same words over and over again, waiting for someone to acknowledge their presence in the sky above the Temple. "Priestess?"

"Try until someone does. They can't be all dead."

"Maybe they are." Linda, after one last glance at the black fields, turned toward the Priestess. "Maybe there isn't anything else to do."

Prince thought about last time he had seen Aria just outside the Temple and shuddered. *Let her be alive.*

"Priestess?" the pilot asked again.

Prince kept looking alternately between the Priestess and out of the window, trying to gauge her thoughts as the woman's expression didn't betray any emotion.

"Priestess? I can't stay any longer here without wasting fuel. We could go somewhere else."

"Fly to my residence."

"But—" Pax and Prince said at the same moment. Prince's automatic reaction, before opening his mouth, had been to raise the gun and point it squarely at the Priestess.

The woman raised one finger to silence them at once and spoke before they could finish their sentences. "The infirmary in my residence equals the Temple's. I have doctors and nurses there specialized in ER procedures. They'll know how to keep those infants alive. They've seen worse."

Prince shuddered. He knew what she meant. The image of a ravaged mouth silently screaming gave body to her words.

The helicopter circled the Temple twice in a salute that didn't elicit any response from the Priestess, but that left everybody else, for different reasons, in tears.

* * *

They touched ground in a haze. After Prince had commanded the Priestess to call home and send her private guard on a goose chase far away from the house, the Priestess had reluctantly complied, and nobody had said a word during the remainder of the flight. Their spirits became more and more sedate as the magnitude of what they had seen at the Temple—of what had survived—sunk in. Even the Priestess's snarky comments had ended the moment she had been forced to give the order to redirect her loyal women away from her residence.

"You can come inside," the Priestess said to Pax, heavily leaning on the pilot for support—Prince had ordered to leave the wheelchair on the helicopter. She managed to look at Pax without making eye contact with Prince, who was standing next to her. The Priestess even overlooked the gun touching her elbow.

Prince was mentally exhausted and being back there awoke unpleasant memories. He pushed the gun slightly and raised his chin toward the big door dominating the façade. A dark spot on an otherwise immaculate light-blue wall. A white baluster marked the second story, giving the building levity foreign to the woman who owned it.

"No slaves are allowed in my home."

Prince didn't have the strength to argue or feel offended. He brought the gun at her right temple, took her by the elbow, and forced her to climb the remaining steps hopping on the same foot. Pax and Linda followed with the kids.

A woman wearing black and gold livery came out of the door to greet them. "Her Holiness, welcome back—" She gave the lot a better look and her expression changed from happy to horrified. "Priestess? What's the meaning of this?"

Prince thought the situation was self-explanatory and led the Priestess and the pilot past the threshold. The majordomo stayed behind, befuddled but not speechless. He ignored the shrilling protests and the indignation, then tilted his head toward the gun still aimed at the Priestess to make his intentions clear.

After the initial moment of shock, the majordomo followed them inside. "A man in the house," she kept repeating in disgust. "It can't be allowed. It just can't be."

"Where to?" Prince asked, nudging the gun closer to the Priestess.

"Priestess?" The majordomo was circling the trio, alternatively stepping closer and moving away as soon as the gun was pointed at her instead.

"Stop that." Prince felt the pressure building up behind his eyes, knowing a headache was soon following. His voice carried enough strain to freeze the woman a few steps behind. "My kids need food and medication."

"Prepare some baby formula and bring it back to the nursery," the Priestess ordered her majordomo.

"Two bottles." Prince made a flowery gesture with the gun.

The woman remained silent and rooted on the spot, as if she hadn't heard.

"Go." The Priestess nodded and the woman scattered away. "I need to rest," she said to Linda.

The doctor silently asked Prince for approval, but he shook his head.

"I'll take a look at you when I'm done with the kids." Linda spoke, but she didn't meet the Priestess's eyes, her head low as her voice.

A few minutes later, they reached a room decorated to accommodate a girl. The walls were a pale shade of lilac with cream vertical stripes running the whole length, and ivory furniture on spidery legs graced the room, which was dominated by a crib covered in layers of fine laces. Pax and Linda deposited the kids on the soft mattress, while Prince took a neat, folded blanket from a shelf and tucked them side by side.

"I'll go to the infirmary to take what I need." After Prince nodded his agreement, Linda left the room.

He bent over the crib to kiss his babies and lingered to caress them. "I love you," he whispered softly, bringing his lips closer to the small ears. He could have sworn they smiled back at the sound of his words, and he felt dirty at touching them with hands that had been handling weapons. He straightened to face Pax's liquid eyes fixed on him.

The majordomo came running into the room and woke the babies. Pax took both bottles from her shaking hands, gave one to Prince, and proceeded to feed the girl. Prince kept one eye on the Priestess and the pilot supporting her, showing them he needed just one free hand to shoot them while feeding his boy.

"She's fainting," the pilot said when the Priestess sagged against the wall.

Prince cursed, not wanting to leave the room and not sure if the woman was acting. One look at the bottle and he saw his baby had already finished his meal.

"She needs help." The pilot was doing a bad job at keeping the Priestess up. "I'll call for it—"

The gun was pointed at the pilot's chest before she could make the call.

"But you can't leave her like this," the pilot cried, trying to convince Pax.

Pax shrugged her shoulders and leaned on the crib to pick up the girl for the customary pat on the back. The Priestess hadn't spoken since they entered the home.

Linda came back followed by a nurse and a cart.

"Her Holiness needs to be seen now." The pilot looked at the doctor, and for the briefest moment, lost her hold on the Priestess, who fell on the floor in a heap of billowing clothes spread on the dark hardwood planks.

"Stay back, all of you. I'll check her." Prince kept the fainted woman under his aim and examined her to make sure it wasn't a ploy. When he was reassured the Priestess wasn't conscious, he made sign for the pilot to return. "You, help her," he called the nurse, who at first was too scared to obey his command. A second bark and she ran to help the pilot raise the Priestess from the floor. "Linda, I want you to stay with my kids."

The doctor seemed surprised by his request, but then something resembling gratitude showed on her tired face. "I won't let anything happen to them. I swear."

"Stay with her," he said to Pax. "I'll go with them and will be back soon."

"Prince…"

"Don't worry." He took a last look at her and at the crib where the babies were making happy noises. "Everything's going to be fine."

"Where to?" The pilot barely managed to keep the limp body from cleaning the floor like a mop, as the nurse was useless—her whole body trembled as she sobbed.

"The nearest room with a bed or a couch." Prince reluctantly steadied the nurse when she tripped on her shoe.

"Her Holiness's room is next to this," the majordomo answered.

"Take her place." Prince took the nurse by the elbow and jerked her away to a corner to make room for the majordomo to replace her at the other side of the pilot. "Okay, let's go there."

He left the room and his heart felt heavier with every step he took. His place was back there with his family. Closing the ranks of what looked like a small procession, his eyes on the back of the Priestess, his mind followed several trains of thought. *You should've left us alone. We weren't a threat to you. I only wanted to raise my kids in peace.*

Prince watched as the three women fussed around the monumental bed where the Priestess lay.

"She needs a doctor," the majordomo said again. She was the most vocal of the three.

"Linda has more important things to do." He went to open the curtain that covered a four-paned window. "What time is it?" Nobody answered, but he saw a wooden carved clock sitting alone on the mantelpiece by the corner. *Fifteen past seven. Is it still the same day? Is it possible this all happened in one day?* His stomach rumbled and his eyelids were refusing to cooperate. He sat on the padded chair facing the windows, and when he looked outside, he saw a familiar sight from an unfamiliar point of view. It took him a second or two to recognize it, but when he did, a pain akin to a stab wound made him shed a tear. Before him, several meters from where he sat, was the cage where he had spent one of the worst periods of his life. And right and left of it there were the other cages. He had to look away. "Give the order to free them." His voice came out too low for the women to hear him, but he couldn't articulate the words any better. His throat had closed and he felt like choking.

"What...?" The majordomo raised her eyes from the bed when the towering shadow cut the light out.

"Give the order to free the boys." Prince's anger had been woken by the sight outside and he was shaking, his hand barely holding the gun steady over the lying figure on the bed.

"I can't!" The majordomo, surprised by his request, acted boldly and stepped in front of the gun. "And I wouldn't give such an order even if it were in my ability to do so. Go back there and sit tight so we can take care of the Priestess." She gave Prince her back without a second thought.

"You think I won't shoot you?"

"You're just a man. Holding a gun doesn't make you anything more than what you are: worthless." The woman turned and slowly retraced her steps. Then she stood tall and pressed her chest against the gun to prove her point.

Prince lowered his hand, watched as the woman smirked in triumph, then waited a second to see if she would cotton on to his intentions and shot her in the knee. Once the screams and shouts waned to a low, frightened murmur, he said, "I gave my word to the Priestess I would let her live if she saved my kids. I don't remember doing the same with any of you. Did I?"

The pilot and the nurse hastily shook their heads. The majordomo was curled up on the floor, nursing her leg and whimpering.

"Give the order," Prince repeated for the third time, his voice carrying the slightest hint of having gone over the edge. *I'm so tired of you. I'm so tired of everything. I'm so tired of having to fight.* He pointed at the phone with the nose of the gun. "Bring it to her," he said to the nurse, who scrambled to please him.

Once the nurse placed the phone in the majordomo's hands, he only had to give a pointed look at her other knee to convince her to make the call. He listened while the woman requested the electricity to the Bestiarium be shut down, saw how pained she was at explaining what she had just asked, and how disgusted and shamed she was when she swore it was the Priestess's direct order. Nervousness and restlessness governing his actions, Prince strode to the window and opened the central pane to breathe some fresh air and clarify his thoughts. He heard the moment the low hum ceased in the Bestiarium. His heart beating fast, he waited for the men to come to the realization that they were free. Seconds become minutes. Nothing happened. The dark silhouettes moving slowly and silently inside the cages didn't attempt to open the gates. "What are you waiting for?" he yelled, and some of the men turned their heads his way. "There's no electricity! Get out!"

His shouting reverberated throughout the Bestiarium, and the quiet beginning of the evening was torn apart by a sudden commotion. The men, all of them, as far as Prince could see, came closer to the gates, hands grabbing the bars and shaking them to follow his suggestion. He could feel the anticipation in their taut expressions and held his breath waiting for the moment when the first of them opened his gate and walked out of his cage. And again, time stretched, but no one broke free. Then it hit Prince.

"Go outside and open the cages," he ordered the pilot.

"How?" The woman didn't try to argue with him.

"Find a way." He waived the gun in the air. "And I suggest you to keep this situation"—he gestured toward the bed and the Priestess—"to yourself if you don't want to see anyone else hurt."

* * *

Prince would have left the dark room and freed the men by himself, but he knew the power he held in his hands was ephemeral. At any moment, an overlooked detail could lead to his own demise. He was aware that having ordered the release of the men from the Bestiarium and letting one of the women out of his sight wasn't the smartest decision. But something had snapped when he saw the cages and he had to do something. He observed as the pilot, accompanied by another woman, approached the first cage. They turned to look toward the Priestess's window, saw him, and after a long moment of hesitation opened the gate. Although he was too far away to see the man's expression, he sensed in his heart the incredulity and exhilaration the man must have felt when the women stepped aside to let him go. With vision fogged by tears he tried to hold back, Prince's lips curved up in a smile.

"And when the last one is freed, what then? What are you going to give them? At best, tomorrow morning, they'll be back inside the cages." The Priestess, her eyes fixed outside the window as well, was sitting on the bed, her back and shoulders propped against a tall pillow the nurse must have brought for her.

Prince was startled by her words and mentally kicked himself for having lowered his guard in such a careless way. Completely engrossed in what was happening outside, he hadn't noticed the Priestess was awake. One brief look gave him the majordomo's whereabouts. The woman was lying on the floor, probably unconscious. He turned toward the bed to give the Priestess all the attention she deserved.

"It's all for nothing. What you did. Ginecea is still the women's city. There's nowhere they can go outside those walls without being shot on sight."

I'd rather die than spend another day here. Anything would be better than this.

"Your Holiness, the private line has been pulsating red the whole time. Would you like to listen to the messages?" The nurse was pointing at the phone on the nightstand.

The Priestess at first nodded, but then shook her head. "Cancel everything."

Prince snatched the phone before the nurse could follow through with her orders, her finger already pressing one of the buttons. Keeping the two women under his constant sight and aim, he raised the phone to his ear and followed the instructions a recorded voice gave him.

Your Holiness, we must inform you that the situation at the Temple is getting out of control.

The Temple is under siege. I'm ordering an evacuation immediately.

348

Tarin is lost.

Pale Harbor is not letting boats dock, and the rest of the Maritime District is without power.

Three sewage plants are under attack. The fathered women are revolting.

We have no communication from the Mountainous Region.

Nobody is answering at Sundial.

There are fires getting closer to the city.

Prince listened, eyes wide, at the different women's voices becoming increasingly more desperate, the messages spanning almost two days' worth of news, until the last and most recent message, dated a mere hour earlier, came broken and but a whisper.

Your Holiness, the fire is spreading throughout Ginecea City. There isn't any water left to douse the flames...

As if on cue, Prince's nose caught the distinctive scent of burnt material drifting in from outside, and for a moment, he was brought back to Sundial. His first reaction was to think about Pax and the kids and run away from there. Reason prevailed. He steadied his nerves and decided the Priestess's residence was still the safest place for them.

"Do you have any reserve of water anywhere?" he asked.

The nurse stared at him and remained silent, while the Priestess turned her head toward the wall to avoid having to look at him even by mistake.

"This place is going to be engulfed in flames. Soon." Prince didn't know how long they had, but if the burnt smell was any indication, they should have been making preparations already. "Maybe we have an hour." He was guessing, but if the wind blew one way rather than the other, it could have been less. At Sundial, the fire had spread in a matter of minutes. The phone rang in his hands, and without thinking, he brought it to his ear.

"I must talk to the Priestess at once," a familiar voice ordered.

"Anna?"

A long silence followed his question, and then, "Is this the Priestess's residence's number?"

"Yes, Anna—"

"Who's this?"

"Anna, it's Prince. Listen to me. Pax and the kids are here with me."

"Pax is there with you? Thanks the Goddess! And... the kids?"

"Yes, *kids*."

Anna seemed to think about the news for a moment, but then she asked, "What's going on there?"

"The Priestess is under my custody. Why were you calling?"

"Maurice is coming to talk to the Priestess."

"Now? Why now? And how? Last time I heard the president speak, the woman was barely coherent."

"She managed several days without medications—"

"She did?"

"I got rid of the nurse and helped her detox."

"What does she want with the Priestess?"

"Her mind finally clear, she's realized what the Priestess has done to her. She's coming to reclaim the baby girl for Pax."

"But the city is under attack..."

"Maurice doesn't want to wait. I must go."

"There's no need to come here," Prince said, but Anna had already hung up. "It seems that you have visitors."

"Madam President?" the Priestess asked.

"Yes, Maurice Layan—" From outside, the clashing sound of metal on metal interrupted Prince. He went to the window to take a look. "Stop!" he yelled at the closest circle of men intent in destroying the cages. The pilot and the other woman she had brought with her weren't in sight, until a sideways glance revealed two mangled bodies lying close to each other by the beginning of the paved trail that ended at the veranda attached to the Priestess's room. They had tried to run back inside.

"Chaos. It's the men's way." The Priestess's eyes were staring at the window.

Prince didn't know how much she could see from her bed, but chaos was a good description of what was happening outside.

"Do you think they'll make an exception for your lover?"

He shivered at the venom the Priestess put on the word "lover" and felt downright sick at the truth in what she had just said. "Come with me." He decided right there and then what needed to be done.

One hand firmly holding the Priestess's elbow he forced her to stand up.

"She can't walk," the nurse, lowered over the majordomo, cried at the sight of the Priestess gracelessly hopping on one foot. "Can't you see she's whiter than the linens?"

Prince didn't bother to answer the nurse. He went straight for the door opening onto the veranda and pulled the Priestess outside while keeping her half a step behind him. "Save yourselves! Don't waste any time here. Run."

"They are just beasts," the Priestess commented when her eyes paused on the women's bloodied bodies lying a few steps from where she was standing.

Prince ignored her, but the sight of the women elicited unwanted thoughts about Pax's safety. "Run away from here." *But where to?* His own voice lacked conviction as the sounds of the dying city of Ginecea wrapped the Bestiarium in its show of frightening, muffled screams and orange-red triumph. *There is nowhere they can run,* he thought. The irony of being the savior who had killed them wasn't lost on him. He looked at the transparent ceiling over the Bestiarium and had the unsettling feeling the air felt hotter already, although the flame hadn't reached the Priestess's property. *Let it be strong enough.*

The men, now approaching the veranda and regrouping in small circles—cage neighbors—were looking at him, eyes asking what their mouths couldn't.

"Go to the well with your buckets and fill them with water," he commanded, hoping that they would listen. "Then start digging a trench around the house." He wasn't sure it was even worth trying. Depending on the ferocity of the fire, if the glass dome didn't resist the high temperatures, it could be all for nothing.

Eyes darted from Prince to the woman behind him. A few eyebrows were raised. Nobody otherwise moved a single muscle to do what he had asked.

He moved the Priestess in front of him so he could keep an eye on both her and the men. "You'll have your justice, but now there isn't time. Look at the glass walls and what lies beyond." Prince pointed the gun at the orange sky peeking between the branches of the trees protecting the Bestiarium's privacy.

Finally, realization dawned on a few faces, and soon several more men looked first at Prince and then at the ceiling.

"Do as I say, please." Prince gave them one last look, saluted them with his right hand on his heart, and was going back inside the Priestess's bedroom when the glass ceiling opened and a helicopter descended in the garden, creating more confusion as the men scattered.

Anna exited the helicopter and looked only mildly surprised by the scene. Maurice, on the other hand, almost tripped as her eyes traveled from the Bestiarium's ex-captives outside their cages to Prince holding a gun against the Priestess's head.

He felt it was necessary to make clear his intentions and had raised the gun for maximum comprehension. Meanwhile, the men had reassessed the situation and thought it was safe to approach the two women. Soon, they were crowding them.

"Let them pass." Prince's voice carried loud enough in the surreal atmosphere permeating the place.

The men didn't attempt anything against the two women, but didn't move out of the way either.

Anna took the president under her protective wing and moved through the path, looking ahead of her. She couldn't help the casual contact while she guided the president through the sea of men who barely parted to let them walk, but managed not to flinch. "I think this has gone too far," she said to Prince when they reached the veranda.

"What's the meaning of this?" Maurice Layan asked, her eyes darting from the men to the Priestess, her expression changing from scared and repulsed to puzzled and finally worried.

"I'm a prisoner in my own home." The Priestess moved one step out of Prince's shield.

"What do you want to do?" Anna asked Prince.

Maurice gave her secretary a disbelieving look and then turned slightly to talk to Prince. "Release the Priestess and hand over the guns." She lowered her eyes, her mouth stretched to a thin line.

Prince had to remind himself the woman in front of him was Pax's mother. "Come inside. Pax is here."

The president seemed to be taken aback by the news. "Anna?"

"Let's go inside," Anna said.

"Did you know about this?"

"Yes—"

"And why didn't you tell me?"

"Because she's another man-lover. Your mother, your daughter, and your secretary. Maurice, you would've never been elected without me washing your dirty laundry." The Priestess jerked her arm free from Prince's grip, but the effort proved to be too much as she lost his support and fell backward. Her legs folded beneath her body at an askew angle and she let out a scream that resonated under the dome.

Anna and Maurice went to her side before Prince could do anything. "Help her inside," he said, gun aimed at the three women.

Anna raised an eyebrow but complied. "Do what he says," she gently suggested to Maurice.

Between the two, the Priestess was brought back to her bed. The nurse, who they had run to at the door, adjusted the woman's limbs and straightened her legs to inspect the injuries.

Prince observed from the corner of the room, one eye on the men outside, who were working on their task, and another on the Priestess, who was heavily shaking and whispering nonsenses under her breath. "Call the nursery and ask if Pax can come here," he asked the nurse when she stopped fussing over the older woman.

A few minutes later, Pax entered the room. "Mom?" She was genuinely surprised to see her mother and went to hug her.

Maurice's reaction to her daughter's display of affection was guarded at first. "What are you doing here?" she asked, her eyes lingering on Prince for a moment.

"I came here to save my kids' lives." Pax didn't wait for her mother to assimilate what she had just said and hugged her again. "I came so close to losing both of them. I don't care if we had differences anymore. I want to believe you had your reasons for doing what you did."

"Kids?" Maurice moved out of Pax's embrace enough to look into her daughter's eyes. "What kids?"

"I had twins. A boy and a girl. You didn't know anything about it?"

Prince saw the flicker of hope in Pax's eyes. Anna had told her already, but it was clear she hadn't truly believed the woman.

"Anna? What is she talking about?" Maurice's eyes widened.

"I've just been informed." Anna shrugged.

"*Your Holiness*? What is she talking about? Two kids?"

Prince couldn't help but turn and stare at the President of Ginecea using the Priestess's appellation with a tone that was everything but obsequious.

"Mom, you really didn't know?"

"You had a boy?"

"Yes, I did."

"Where are they?"

"They're sleeping in the nursery. Do you want to see them?"

"Is the girl okay?"

"Yes, she's doing great, thanks to her brother." Pax's voice was hurt.

"The Priestess needs to be seen by a doctor. There's something wrong with her." The nurse interrupted the conversation between mother and daughter, and a moment later, the Priestess's delirious rant stopped altogether.

"If Linda is done with the kids," Prince cautioned the woman who had already gone to the phone, "you call," he said to Pax.

She took the phone from the nurse's hands, spoke to Linda, and then nodded at him. "They're okay. She thinks they're safe now."

Prince's heart somersaulted in his chest at her words. He had been so preoccupied with them he had repressed the thought of them being anything but fine. "Tell her to wait for you before leaving the babies alone." He wanted to go as well.

Pax took a last, long look at her mother. Prince hated to see the pleading in her eyes first and the raw pain next, when she had to leave and her mother didn't follow.

"Prince, have you thought things through?" Anna had moved next to him. "You won't make it out of this alive."

Prince's senses were stretched thin. He was annoyed at the woman for being a distraction when he was tired, and he had to be vigilant. A low buzz, like an army of wasps, added a layer of noise to Anna's voice. *It's getting hotter.* He passed the back of his hand on his forehead to wipe the sweat.

"You know that you can't keep the Priestess hostage, right?" she insisted.

"And I don't want to, but what alternative do I have at this point?" His eyes felt dry and he blinked twice, but the feeling of sand didn't go away.

"I can arrange for your safe passage."

"*Our* safe passage?" He was listening to her, but there was lots of noise coming from outside. It had started slowly, and at first it was hidden by the overall ambient noise, but soft, crackling sounds were being followed by the thumps and bumps created by the men's activity just outside the open window.

"Yes, you, Pax, and the kids."

For the briefest of moments, Prince let his hopes soar. Anna's promise of a solution sounding sweet and so tempting, but then he came back to his senses and the bitter reality crashed the hopes and the weight of their situation hit him, once again. "We would've left already. Actually, we would've never come here if we weren't forced to by the circumstances—" Prince stopped in midsentence. The noise had become a full-fledged uproar of stomping feet and breaking glass. When he saw the first man entering the bedroom at full speed, he finally realized what was happening. "The dome's vault... Did you order to close it back?"

"No..."

Prince heard her, but he had known all along.

"Where are you going?" Anna asked him.

He didn't turn or slow down to answer her. "I'm going to the nursery." He didn't care what she did as long as she left him alone.

"What about the Priestess? And her majordomo?"

He didn't answer and was out and running in the hallway when Anna called him from the door, but he didn't catch what she was saying. When he finally slowed down before the entry to the nursery, his chest aching for the strain of breathing more air than his lungs could contain, he was surprised to hear other steps slowing down as well, but didn't have time to acknowledge Anna's presence.

Pax, Linda, who hadn't left for the Priestess's bedroom, and a young nurse were busy talking in hushed tones when he broke into the nursery.

"Prince…" Pax raised her head from the cribs, relief showing in her eyes at seeing him, then she looked at the person behind him. "Mom?"

Prince turned around to look at the woman.

"Mom…"

He hated to interrupt Pax and what could have been a mending moment between the two, but he could already hear the stampede of men escaping the flames and seeking safety inside the house. "Grab their medication."

"But, they should be kept here—" Linda gave Maurice Layan a double glance. "Madame President…"

"I can't defend them here." He grabbed the girl and prompted Pax to do the same with the boy. "Put all the medications they need in a bag… and also some milk and the bottles." He was mentally making a list of the items he saw on the shelves. "We need to reach the closest basin of water." Talking more to himself than anything else, he kept mumbling about the things they had to do, hoping to find a feasible plan among the thousands of ideas going in circles inside his already crowded mind. "You must trust me," he finally said to Pax.

"With our lives. Always." She looked at him and smiled. Pax smiled. In the midst of something horrific, she found the strength to give him the gift of a smile. They had nothing in the world, and they had everything at the same time.

Prince fought the urge to take her in his arms and kiss her until they had no breath left. "Pax…"

"Later," she answered, in her way of knowing his thoughts.

"Later." He leaned to brush her lips and then caressed the boy's head. *God and Goddess, please let there be an after for us.*

The floor rumbled with the power of hundreds of steps. Prince took Pax's hand and ran away from the nursery with the certainty that anywhere else was safer at the moment.

"The Priestess has a pool in the back garden," Maurice yelled from behind.

Prince turned, surprised by her presence again.

"That's true." Linda had reached them as well.

"Follow me," Maurice said, her eyes on him.

Prince was even more surprised the woman had spoken to him. Pax squeezed his hand and he saw the light in her eyes. He nodded at the President of Ginecea and let her pass to show the way.

The Priestess's house was built around a central courtyard. Maurice led them through one side to the other without having to walk the whole perimeter, as he would have done without knowing the house's layout.

"Here it is." Maurice led them to a glass wall, beyond which lay a luscious garden with a large free-form pool resembling a natural formation.

Prince went to push the glass panel, when a soft click resonated. The panel didn't move. "What...?"

Maurice looked at him and then at the panel before her eyes. She went to push as well.

"The Priestess had the same safety system installed that we have at Sundial. In case of fire, the house shuts down. Her pool garden contains some of the rarest orchids in the whole of Ginecea," Linda explained. Almost at the same moment she spoke, the hallway on their right was closed off by a metal wall, leaving them stranded between the stampede of men and a dead end.

Prince felt anger building up, and if hadn't been holding the girl, he would have broken his fists on the glass. The temperature was rising and the men were almost at their heels. *What now?* He looked at the serene, light-blue expanse of water and kicked the panel, obtaining nothing but a new ache. The blazing sunset, magnified by the fires destroying Ginecea City, loomed beyond the brick walls surrounding the garden. A hill with a narrow path, a safe passage to a higher ground, started only a few meters from the back wall. The means to escape certain death were so close. Only a glass wall detained them. An impenetrable glass wall, mocking them with its promises of a safe haven. They had nowhere to go. He wanted to tell Pax he was sorry, but he didn't have time. The men had finally caught up with them.

CHAPTER 25

Prince looked at the face staring back at him, hating himself because he couldn't command the hand still holding Pax's to stop shaking. "Don't hurt them. They've done nothing to you." He thought he recognized some of them, but his mind was in overdrive and he wasn't sure of anything anymore.

The men advanced, their muteness creating an eerie atmosphere that made their steps louder by contrast. They were a multitude, arranged in several rows filling the hallway.

"Please." He couldn't read their minds, but they looked as scared, starving, and disoriented as he was. "Please, let us go. This is my family, my kids. Please."

The girl woke up and stretched in his arms. He saw several eyes turning to look at her, at her tiny body, at her big eyes. He sensed Pax tensing by his side.

One of the men stepped out of the crowd. He was but a boy, his body scrawny and barely covered by a filthy, colorless rag.

"Prince?" Pax tightened her grip on his hand.

The boy heard her and paused, his eyes on Prince, a pained expression on his scarred face. He looked familiar.

Suddenly, a memory came back to him and Prince recognized the boy as the same one who had indicated the way out of the Bestiarium a lifetime ago. "It's okay," he murmured to Pax, gently released his hand from hers, and met the boy halfway. "This is my daughter."

The boy didn't do anything at first, but then the baby girl cooed and put her finger in her mouth, while she softly kicked her legs outside Prince's embrace, one small foot lazily dangling. The boy tentatively raised one long arm and he leaned closer to her, his eyes on Prince again, waiting.

Prince nodded.

The boy slowly reached out one finger and brushed the girl's foot. The baby's toes reacted to the touch by curling into a ball. The boy's mouth opened in surprise, and then the features in his face rearranged in what could have been a smile, and tears fell, but he didn't wipe them off.

"Help me break this glass." Prince tilted his head to indicate the wall behind him. "We can escape the fire."

Heads turned at his words, following his indication. Several men stepped closer to him and the baby.

"We must get outside." He turned to Pax. "Everything is going to be okay." He gave her the girl.

Two men laid their hands on the glass to test the solidity of the wall, and then several others joined. They started pummeling it, but it was soon apparent that it was sturdier than it looked. In a few seconds, the glass was shaking under the combined assault of more than twenty men. Still, it didn't budge.

The crashing sound of devouring fire reached them, with it its fumes and oppressing warmth.

Prince, who had been trying to break the wall along with the other men, paused for a moment to reorganize his scattered thoughts. *Think... think... think...* His eyes searched for anything they could use, when he finally remembered something he had seen while running away from the nursery. "You," he called to the closest men. "Come with me. I need help dislodging a pipe." He motioned toward the hallway, hoping that someone would follow. He didn't have time to explain his plan.

He ran back inside, toward the flames, sighing in relief when he heard steps echoing behind him. Ahead, the flames had already reached the nursery. Prince wondered why the sprinkler system hadn't activated. Then the presence of the men by his side answered his question. He had asked to have the electricity in the Bestiarium shut off; the two systems must have been connected. He cursed under his breath. *Was it too much to ask for the metal walls to be connected too?* He found the pipe by the nursery entrance, an alien sight so close to the lavender and lace of the girl's room. It had been painted in cream to make it lighter, but it was still an obstructing object jutting out of the wall. He went to pull it from the wall and the men immediately followed suit. They were back to the glass wall in no time, the flames following them closely.

Using the pipe as a ram, they hit the wall in waves. Prince, at the head, felt the shockwave biting all the way to his elbows, but just when he thought he couldn't command another wave, the glass cracked before his eyes. One last hit and the transparent wall crumbled in a shower of thousands of small pieces.

"Pax!" He looked for her, but she was safe, shielded by her mother's and Linda's bodies protecting her and the kids. He took the girl, grabbed her free hand, and led her outside and into the pool to soak them wet.

The water was cold and refreshing compared to the raising temperature in the air. It would have been nice to linger a moment more, but he pressed ahead to reach the back wall and their freedom. He couldn't see a gate, but the wall wasn't so high that he couldn't climb it or help Pax doing the same. A faint hope flickered in the recess of his mind, his heart racing now at the idea they had made it.

A single gunshot crashed his dream. He fell on his knees, holding the girl for dear life, a burning sensation radiating through his right leg before pain kicked in.

"Prince!" Pax cried, falling on the ground beside him, horrified eyes staring at him.

A second gunshot was fired.

His right arm flew backward without his consent. The baby girl fell on Pax's lap, her mouth open in a scream Prince didn't hear.

A third shot resonated in the air.

He was forcefully pushed out of the way by a body that clashed against his. He felt the boy land on him, then turned to see the child's eyes open in stupor one moment and close in peace the next. He screamed, anguished pain taking over, taking control of the physical pain. Rage possessed him when he realized the boy who, only a moment ago, had touched his baby with the reverence due to a goddess was now lying over him, still and breathless.

"No!" His voice sounded out of place. "No!" he repeated a million times over. When his eyes, fogged by tears and pure, undiluted murderous anger, finally found her, he wasn't surprised.

Staring at him, at the other side of the pool, was the Priestess. She wasn't alone. A frazzled-looking nurse was pushing her wheelchair through a path that led back to a different side of the building from where he had come. "You'll die, but first I'll kill your lover and your bastard so you can watch," the Priestess yelled, her eyes and the aim of her gun moving from Prince to Pax. "Give me the Chosen," she ordered Pax, her voice bordering on hysteria. "Release my Chosen."

"Run!" He pushed Pax away from him while reaching with his left hand for his gun. He didn't find anything inside his back pocket. His fingers frantically searched for it. The twins were crying, moving restlessly in Pax's arms and in danger of being shot at any moment. She was struggling to keep them both safe. "Help her, now," he said to Linda and Maurice and then stood up, held up by hatred, and moved toward the Priestess, hopping on his good leg. He was hoping to keep the woman busy long enough to give his family a chance to clear the wall. Ready to make peace with himself, he sent his love to Pax and sprinted forward. The Priestess looked up at him in disbelief and then cackled and raised the gun.

At the same time, a woman exited from the door the Priestess and the nurse had used. She ran to the wheelchair, screaming at the top of her lungs. It took a moment for Prince to recognize Anna. Her face was covered in blood and a wound opened on her right temple. Her intervention diverted a bullet that otherwise would have hit him square in the chest. He stumbled and fell on his knees when the bullet went in and out from somewhere in his body, but the sound of Pax's cries put him back on his feet. Anna was fighting both the Priestess and the nurse and gave him time to reach them before the Priestess could shoot again.

He single-mindedly propelled his body ahead, his only goal to reach the woman. Blind to anything else, he only saw her and ached to have his hands around her neck. When he finally stood a step from the trio, a guttural sound escaped his throat, and he launched himself against the Priestess, sending the wheelchair and the other two women reeling back. But he didn't lose his hold on the Priestess. His fingers pressed on her throat, while she tried to pry them open. He waited for her cold eyes to dull into oblivion, but felt his own strength vanishing. Just a few feet from them, Anna and the nurse were fighting and Anna was receiving the worst of it. The nurse punched her in the face, repeatedly hitting the gash on her temple, until she stumbled and fell. When she finally lay helpless on the ground, the nurse savagely kicked her and then went to retrieve something.

"Stop!" the nurse ordered.

He barely registered the woman was talking to him and directed all his energy on ignoring the spasms threatening to make him faint. The Priestess's face changed color, but she didn't stop fighting. He kept pressing on her throat, his own perception of reality foggier by the second, red spots dancing before his eyes.

"Stop! Or I'll shoot you!"

He raised his eyes at the nurse's cry, realizing the Priestess hadn't been holding her gun. She must have lost it when he had charged her or maybe earlier when she was fighting Anna. He lessened his hold on the Priestess for only a moment, but it was all she needed.

It all happened at once. The Priestess pushed him out of the way. The nurse shot him. He went sprawling on the ground. He didn't have time to feel the burning sensation spread through him. A mere blink of an eye later, the Priestess had the gun in her hands and was shooting in Pax's direction. Maurice's and Linda's shouts pierced his ears. He stopped breathing, strained his senses to hear Pax's voice and the kid's cries, but didn't dare turn. Rage beyond control possessed him and he stood one more time. He charged at the Priestess, aiming straight for the gun, pummeling against her with all the strength left in his mangled body.

A final gunshot was fired.

CHAPTER 26

"Did I tell you I love you today?" Prince went to open the window to let the moonlight in. It was a ritual he repeated once a month.

They had been living at the Village for three years, but every full moon he felt the spell all over again, as if it were the first night they spent together under the same roof without being afraid it was their last. At first, he had kept waking at the end of nightmares where he had lost Pax and the kids, thrashing and shouting, worrying her to no end. Then days, weeks, and months passed, and one night, full moon shining in the black sky, Prince finally realized their fight had ended the night he had killed the Priestess, and he had smiled in his sleep. Pax had told him so the morning after.

He still dreamed of what had happened that night at the Priestess's residence in excruciating, vivid detail. The worst nightmares were when he relived the events as they had occurred, down to the Priestess's death, only to wake thinking it had been just a dream. It normally took him several minutes to slow his heart and convince himself it had happened, that Pax was alive and well, and so were their kids. Sometimes, when the weather changed abruptly, the wounds on his body reminded him that if it weren't for Maurice Layan, he would be dead as well.

Pax's mother had saved his life by commanding the Priestess's private guard—they returned, fortunately, half an hour too late to help the Priestess—to rush him to the Goddess of Health, the private hospital in Ginecea that cured presidents and the like. Pax's voice still choked up when talking about what her mother had done to ensure he was seen by the best doctors. The President of Ginecea stayed in the OR the whole time along with Pax, who had refused to leave him, and Linda, who had been called to attest the women operating on him were doing their best to save him. Three years after, Pax still refused to tell him the extent of the damage his body had suffered; she couldn't talk about that. He only knew his surgery had lasted a whole day. He had been surprised to wake up two days later in an elegant room and being nursed back to health by women, who, although not necessarily willing, kept their distaste to themselves.

As soon as his body allowed, Prince asked Pax to travel back to the City of Men. He knew she wanted to see Rosie and Mauricio and she hadn't gone yet because she thought he couldn't make the trip. Maurice helped once again; she organized a relief mission to bring help to the fathered women who had suffered under the Priestess's regime. The City of Men and the Caves were added to her personal tour and Prince, Pax, and the twins hopped along for the ride.

Word was sent to Mauricio that they were coming, but the expressions on his and Rosie's faces when Pax entered their apartment were something Prince would never forget. She was carrying the twins in her arms and had never looked more beautiful.

"Grandma, Grandpa, I want you to meet my babies," she had said with a smile so bright it had illuminated the whole room.

Mauricio had wept, while Rosie had sobbed uncontrollably. Even Maurice, who had stayed a few steps behind, had looked taken by the moment. After the commotion died down, Prince and Pax told Maurice of their intention to stay in the City of Men for the time being. Maurice hugged Pax and then asked for a private moment with her mother before leaving for Ginecea.

"I'll let you talk to your mother," Mauricio had said, getting on his feet with the help of a cane.

"No, please, stay..." Maurice had left everybody speechless with her request.

Nobody ever knew what Maurice and her parents talked about, but she made them happy.

Prince and Pax helped Lucas with the rebuilding of the City of Men, carrying the Priest's vision further than he had ever thought possible. Six month after, Mauricio and Rosie died peacefully in each other's arms, locked in an eternal kiss. They were buried in the rock garden where hundreds of thousands of men and fathered women gathered to give them their last salutes. Mauricio was already a legend among the men all over Ginecea, but when their love story became known, Rosie ascended to a higher level in the collective imagery as well.

Even in their last days, busy spoiling their great-grandkids, Mauricio and Rosie committed whatever energies they had left to the betterment of Ginecea. They welcomed the young men from the Bestiarium—Prince had asked Lucas to help them, and in turn, Lucas had found them and brought them to the City of Men, where he knew they would have been accepted without reservation. Lucas was right. Mauricio and Rosie took them under their care, and those men—once brutalized and broken—flourished. They were the first to help rebuild the City of Men, loyal to the Priest and eager to do anything that could make him happy in his last days; they restlessly worked for months, enduring gruesome shifts without losing the smiles that had become one of their most recognizable features. That and their shaved heads, for which the nickname the Priest's Brothers had been coined.

Along with the Priest's Brothers, other men and women helped Prince, Pax, and Lucas rebuild the city. Soon after the Insurgence— the universal name for the series of events that eventually led to the current status quo in Ginecea—they started showing in throngs every day to that forsaken spot in the middle of the unforgiving desert, asking for a new start. Everybody was given a chance to earn a life. Mauricio reopened the City of Men to anyone who wanted to live in peace, and for the first time, families moved out of the Caves to take residence inside the city. Lucas and Cordelia were one of the first mixed couples, followed by a pregnant Celeste and Remy. Tai, Cara, Sonia, and Randal stayed in the Caves to help the families transitioning to the new life. After Mauricio's death, Randal shaved his head, made a vow of silence, and joined the Priest's Brothers.

Maurice was at the funeral, but she didn't reveal her presence to anybody but her daughter. Later she asked Prince and Pax if they wanted to assume an active role in the negotiations between women and men in the upcoming years. One single look at Pax cradling the boy in her arms and Prince decided for both of them.

"No, thank you," he answered.

"I understand." Maurice caressed her grandchild's crown and never asked them again.

Prince didn't care what was going to happen to Ginecea. Their part in the fight had been fulfilled, and he only wanted to take care of his family and leave everything else behind. A month after Mauricio's and Rosie's deaths, they left the City of Men and moved to the Village. News from the rest of the world reached them in their faraway haven, and sometimes it was painful to hear when familiar names came up for all the wrong reasons. But he was ready to build a new world for his kids, and the Village was the place to start.

Newlyweds Lexi and Aria arrived five months later with three adopted kids, two girls and a boy, respectively six, three, and two years old. Aria had suffered serious injuries while escaping the raging inferno the Temple had become during the uprising, but had survived the worst. Warned by Pax about Aria's last whereabouts, Lexi had left the safety of her mansion and went looking for her through the rubbles of the sanctuary. She found Aria a few days later, when she had lost any hope of ever seeing her again. After fighting for hours with the other fathered women, when Aria felt her strength deserting her, she hid inside a cellar deep beneath the ground. Lexi nursed her back to health, accepted her mothers' shunning over her decision to marry a servant, and never went back to Ginecea. They now lived across from Prince and Pax, all the kids growing up together.

Maurice Layan, helped by Anna, took the reins of what was left of the Ginecean society. Three years later, she was still fighting the conservative fringes, but she had the popular consent of the fathered women. Prince, Pax, and the rest of the Village had listened to the president announcing on unified channels that owning slaves had been banned. With the farms all around Ginecea firmly in the men's hands, she hadn't had any choice, but the purest of the pure breeds, while they had condemned the Priestess, weren't ready to release their power altogether. Eight months of social unrest and turmoil had followed. In the end, the president, a representative of the opposing party, and Lucas met to discuss the possibility of a truce. It was the first time a man had been accepted among pure breeds as an interlocutor. Later, the terms of the agreement were divulged.

Men on Ginecea were given the right to earn a living. So much was still to be done, but the first, important step had been taken.

* * *

"So, did I tell you how much I love you already?"

Pax was lying by his side, her legs wrapping his, her fingers lazily tracing the skin on his arms. "Yes, but I can't have enough of it." She kissed him, a long kiss that started chaste and progressed to burn them both.

"I love you," he repeated, voice broken and rough.

"More," she asked.

"Ego te amo."

"More."

And he said it again, ten times over, until there was no breath left for words.

Later, a pale moon shining over their entangled bodies, he said it one more time. He draped her in the white sheets and cradled her against his chest to inhale her scent. He knew her body by heart, but enjoyed discovering what would melt her in his arms. They dedicated to each other the wee hours of the night, when the kids were soundly asleep and they knew they weren't going to be interrupted by the twins' requests.

"Mommy!"

It didn't work every night.

"What is it, Bianca?" Prince asked, smiling at the ceiling. He had other plans for the rest of the night.

"Mommy, not Daddy!"

"Bianca, Mom's sleeping." It was his turn tonight.

"Not true."

"Daddy! Bianca doesn't let me sleep. She's mean."

"Lares, go back to sleep." Prince laughed softly.

Pax joined him in the laugh. "I guess we're done."

"It seems so."

"Later." She kissed him one more time.

"Later." He kissed her back, brushing the inside of her wrist and waiting for the suppressed moan he knew was coming.

"Hurry!" She sighed against the pillow and then added, stopping him at the door, "I love you. Always."

BACKSTORY AND ACKNOWLEDGMENTS

Mauricio, Rosie, Prince, and Pax have kept me company for so long that saying good-bye to them is bittersweet. Three books later, Ginecea has become a better place and kids like Lares and Bianca will grow knowing love can take many forms. *Amor Vincit Omnia.*

My heartfelt thanks to anybody who decided to give my stories a try. My life as an author would be way lonelier without the encouragement from my readers.

My gratitude to the wonderful people in my life who make it the most beautiful adventure. Thanks to my mom and dad for being my parents. Thanks to Alessandro Fiorini who has managed to create another breathtaking cover. Thanks to Claudia for being my beta reader from the very beginning. Thanks to Carmen for being my last beta reader—Anna is wearing a bracelet because of Carmen's fine eye for details. Thanks to Amy because, without her, The Ginecean Chronicles wouldn't be the same. Thanks to Gaia and Giuseppe. I couldn't have asked for better kids. And finally, thanks to Roberto for being the most wonderful man I've ever met.

Persons of Interest

A book is never a solitary endeavor, although the writer oftentimes thinks otherwise.

Amy Eye edited Prince at War.

Cassie McCown proofread it.

Roberto Ruggeri formatted the novel.

Alessandro Fiorini created the cover.

You, the reader, who liked The Priest and Pax in the Land of Women and came back for more Ginecean stories.

BIO

Monica La Porta is an Italian who landed in Seattle several years ago. Despite popular feelings about the Northwest weather, she finds the mist and the rain the perfect conditions to write. Being a strong advocate of universal acceptance and against violence in any form and shape, she is also glad to have landed precisely in Washington State. She is the author of The Ginecean Chronicles, a dystopian/science fiction series set on the planet Ginecea where women rule over a race of enslaved men and heterosexual love is considered a sin. She has published *The Priest, Pax in the Land of Women*, and *Prince at War*. She is currently editing the fourth in the Ginecean series. She also wrote and illustrated a children's book about the power of imagination, *The Prince's Day Out*. Her latest published short, *Linda of the Night*, is a fairytale love story celebrating inner beauty. Stop by her blog to read about her miniatures, sculptures, paintings, and her beloved beagle, Nero. Sometimes, she also posts about her writing.

Monica La Porta's blog: www.monicalaporta.com

The Ginecean Chronicles Facebook page:
https://www.facebook.com/ginecea

The Prince's Day Out Facebook page:
https://www.facebook.com/ThePrincesDayOut

Goodreads Author page:
http://www.goodreads.com/author/show/5757332.Monica_La_Porta

Twitter: https://twitter.com/momilp

OTHER BOOKS BY MONICA LA PORTA

To keep up to date with Monica's new releases and promotions scan the QR code with your smartphone or mobile device.

The Priest – Book One of the Ginecean Chronicles
Mauricio is a slave. Like any man born on Ginecea, he is but a number to the pure breed women who rule over him with cruel hands. Imprisoned inside the Temple since birth, Mauricio has never been outside, never felt the warmth of the sun on his skin. He lives a life devoid of hopes and desires. Then one day, he hears Rosie sing. He risks everything for one look at her and his life is changed forever. An impossible friendship blossoms into affection deemed sinful and perverted in a society where the only rightful union is between women. Love is born where only hate has roots and leads Mauricio to uncover a truth that could destroy Ginecea.

Pax in the Land of Women – Book Two of the Ginecean Chronicles
Love doesn't obey preordained rules. Sometimes, social status and gender mean nothing. The purest of affections can be born between two people living in different worlds. In a society where women rule over an enslaved race of men and love between a woman and man is considered a perversion, Pax's and Prince's union is destined for a tragic end. Coming from an existence of privilege, Pax has

never endured harshness. She has never had any reason to doubt the rules Ginecea was built on. Everything changes when she is sent to spend her summer on a desolate farm and is exposed to the ongoing brutalities against defenseless men. A wrong turn leads her to witness Prince's thrashing at the hands of the guards. One look from him and Pax's perfect life is shattered, the memory of his dark eyes haunting her night and day. As a pure breed, born to one of the most prestigious family in Ginecea, she would have never thought it possible to fall in love with a man. Marked as a sinner, Pax abjures her ancestry to save Prince's life. She hopes they can disappear into the desert, but social prejudice and political schemes give them no respite. The Priestess, the ruler of all Ginecea, has other plans for Pax Layan and her family. Second in The Ginecean Chronicles, Pax in the Land of Women is a dystopian tale set on the planet Ginecea.

The Prince's Day Out

Once upon a time, in a faraway land, there was a young prince who lived confined to his bedroom. Accompanied by his sister, he traveled to the most incredible places thanks to his imagination. Follow the Prince and the Princess's fantastic journey through a magic kingdom where seagulls transport cities and ships sail on pearl necklaces instead of waves. Twelve whimsical drawings illustrate the story.

Linda of the Night

Linda was born with hair the color of the mature grain and eyes of the lightest shade of blue. Tall and willowy, she's the ugliest girl alive. Kept inside her house by her parents for fear of being ridiculed for her hideous appearance, Linda dreams of being like the dark-haired, curvaceous girls who live just outside her walls. One night, she dares the inconceivable and leaves the safety of her home. For the first time alone, Linda walks for hours until she is lost—only to find her destiny in the arms of a mysterious stranger.